THE CHOKER

To [name scribbled out] with good wishes—

THE CHOKER

BY
LEE CARL

northern liberties press

Philadelphia, Paris, London

Published by
Northern Liberties Press
Old City Publishing Inc.
628 North 2nd Street
Philadelphia, PA 19123, USA

Visit our web site at: oldcitypublishing.com

This book is a work of fiction. Names, characters, places and incidents either are products of the author's imagination or are used fictitiously. Any resemblance to actual events or locales or persons, living or dead, is entirely coincidental.

ISBN 978-1-933153-35-3 (paperback)

Library of Congress Cataloging-in-Publication Data

Carl, Lee, 1929-
 The Choker / by Lee Carl.
 p. cm.
 ISBN 978-1-933153-35-3

Previous books by Lee Carl published by Northern Liberties Press:

The White Squirrel

Under The Burdock Weed

The Cherry Tree

The Floor of T.P.'s Office

Arnold's Revenge

Leo's Legacy

Packet of Seeds

Bones Don't Lie

The Key

Project Implant

Dedication

To the author's dear friend,
Charles Geltz, for an idea
that gave birth to this novel.

Chapter One

Birds lay eggs, not diamonds, or rubies, or emeralds. They gather twigs, weeds and grasses for nesting, not expensive jewelry. So, what extraordinary and glittering thing happened along the creek that separates East Bitterlick and West Bitterlick Townships?

The pair of bald eagles returned to the same location high above the rocky Bitterlick Creek for the third year in a row and rebuilt their nest. The female laid three eggs again, just as she had done the two previous seasons. Piece by piece she pulled nesting material close about her eggs as she settled down and sat upon them. But her slightly smaller and attentive mate wasted no time in sharing the home-care duties. When it was time for her to fly, he would spread his wings slightly and gently lower himself on the nest.

Large locust trees sucked water from the creek far below the nest and twisted their roots like tentacles around the rocks that formed the bank along the east side of the rapids. They reached high up the rocky cliff and lay gnarled limbs on a broad ledge of smooth rock that protruded from the precipice. It was upon this flat projection and amidst the locust branches and leaves that the eagles nested. And it was there that the eggs hatched.

Again, mama bird and papa bird shared all duties, each tucking the chicks—little white balls of fluffy fuzz with heads and beaks—under their broad wings and drawing nesting material close around them, particularly when the winds blew hard and whistled among the locust trees. When one parent was supplying warmth to the chicks, the other was winging his or her way above wooded land and open water in a search for food.

Charley and Claudia Silvester had no need to climb rocks or trees to watch the eagles go about their daily activities. Actually, they couldn't have managed the hunt and the climb if they had wanted a real-life, close-up view. All they needed to do was activate their computer, click on the right link, and the birds would pop up on the screen. They became so enthralled by the nesting activities that they placed their laptop on the kitchen table for frequent looks each day. The middle-aged couple lived in a ranch-style house about three miles from the eagles' nest. And they were well acquainted with Dr. James T. Barnes, retired Cornell ornithologist, who had set up the visual and sound monitoring devices that allowed millions of viewers around the world to gawk and smile at the heart-warming images of the bald eagles and their young.

Since retirement, Barnes had been director of the local chapter of the Audubon Society and actively championed the protection of wildlife. Charley and Claudia knew him as Jimmy the Birdman, having been his "neighbor" for many years—"neighbor" meaning a couple miles north where wealthy rural homes occupied large lots just south of the suburbs of Cloverton City, the county seat. The Silvesters socialized with Jimmy and his wife, Laura, an assertive and go-getting woman who loved animals and volunteered at the local SPCA. Lanky and agile, she seemed in constant motion and was a perfect sidekick for a birding naturalist. She underplayed her Cornell Ph.D. degree in animal husbandry.

"Look at that!" exclaimed Charley as he stood and leaned across the table, stretching close to the computer. "Claudia, come here! Look! Daddy bird brought home a fish!"

As the male eagle began to pull apart the fish, making small pieces for the chicks to swallow, Claudia hurried to Charley's side and watched as the big bird moved to get a better grip on the remainder of the fish. Red, white and green sparkles suddenly gleamed from between a wad of nesting material and the baby birds, whose mouths were wide open as they squawked for food. Claudia put on her glasses and edged closer to the screen. She was a slender woman with fair skin and blonde hair twisted into a French braid. Next to her husband, she appeared slight, indeed, for he was a tall, muscular, broad-shouldered soul who immediately put his arm around her.

"My God!" she exclaimed. "That's a bracelet or necklace, or something."

"It's jewelry, all right," Charley said. "Look at it! It's a brilliant, wide band of gems. I guess the eagles thought it would brighten up their nest."

"I know that piece!" Claudia's head popped up. She broke away from her husband and jumped backward. "I can't believe it! Charley! Oh, Charley! You've seen that choker around her neck! Holy shoot!"

"Whose neck?"

"Cousin Ruth's neck! That damn thing is Cousin Ruth's precious choker from some mysterious friend she won't talk about. You've seen her wear it, Charley. Each time we dared venture to her place in recent years she was wearing it, showing it off to us. But she refused to wear it anywhere outside her house." Claudia walked nervously in circles several times around the kitchen and then returned to Charley. Seconds later, she turned her back to him and anxiously adjusted the window curtains—white café curtains below yellow valences and olive-colored ball fringe, fabric colors that went well with the kitchen's dark green appliances and white, yellow-dotted wallpaper.

Claudia had a first-rate sense of color and used her talent to smartly decorate the one-story, three-bedroom house designed by an architect noted for picturesque ranch-style dwellings—rustic houses that fit well in heavily wooded areas. And the Silvesters' home lay far back from a two-lane county road and rested on grassy acres before a dense stand of pine, maple and oak. Far to the rear snaked the Bitterlick Creek at a more gentle flow than at its white-water rapids below the eagle's nest some three miles upstream. No high cliff or low drop impeded Charley when he wanted to sit on his favorite tree-stump and fish. He had a fervent fondness for pieces and parts of the woods, often digging up ferns, jack-in-the-pulpits, May apples and other shade-loving plants and setting them in fertile earth near the house.

"Oh, yeah!" Charley exclaimed as his wife turned toward him. "I had almost forgotten about that last encounter. She was acting so theatrical, briefly putting on a show for us." He rolled his eyes. "Hah! How could I forget her sudden glow? Fake or real, those gems lifted Ruth's chin and brightened her eyes, if only for a moment. Strange. Where does a recluse like Ruth Nettlebaum get such a treasure—obviously a precious gift that turns her on?" Charley spun towards his wife and gazed into her eyes. "She's your cousin, Claud. Batty as hell."

"Reclusive, I know. Poor thing. Partly her mother's fault. Aunt Fanny kept her sheltered." A slight but plaintive smile turned Claudia's lips. "She loves her cat."

"What brought that on?"

"Just thinking. I'm glad she has Pinwheel to love."

Charley put his hand on Claudia's shoulder, felt her twitch, and began to sense trouble. He squeezed her in a comforting way. The protective type, he was a former school teacher, a warmhearted mentor with a real human touch. Early retirement had turned him to gardening, fishing, woodcarving and beekeeping, among other things. Handy about the house with just about any tool, he was also a good listener and always had time for his beloved wife.

Claudia lowered her head again and took a close look at the eagles' nest. "Cousin Ruth swore that that choker was the only one of its kind, never copied. Look at how each precious stone gleams. I know costume jewelry when I see it. And that's not paste. Besides, I remember exactly the shape and placement of the stones. Ruth let me hold it. Remember? You had trouble with the clasp when you put it back on her neck."

"Well, if the bald eagles' choker is not a fake, it could be the genuine thing, but a duplicate."

"Didn't you hear me? Ruth made a big deal about it being one of a kind."

Charley pondered the thought. He rubbed his forehead, muttered to himself, and said, "That eagle, or its spouse, didn't fly miles from St. Louis or Memphis or some other far-off place with valuable jewelry hanging from its beak. Nursing birds stay in the area so they can feed their young. That choker had to be picked up in this township or across the creek, or at least within the county." Charley sat on a chair and leaned his elbows on the table. "Oh, my God! Remember what Cousin Ruth said about it? No one was ever to know. Now thousands, maybe millions, of people have seen it."

"Seen it, maybe. But they don't know. They don't know her or anything about her secret."

"Neither do we, really."

"Call the police! It may have been stolen before the eagles found it. She might be hurt, or in trouble."

"Now, wait a moment." Charley pushed back his chair and walked to the refrigerator and leaned against it. "Your oddball cousin hinted that a scandal would explode if anyone found out she had that choker. I didn't believe her and brushed off her prattle as fantasy or make-believe. Face it, Claud, little that came from her mouth ever made much sense. So, it was easy to erase it from my mind. But now?"

"But now what?"

"Well, I wonder. Since she was always talking nonsense, maybe I didn't give her enough credit." Charley chuckled. "Maybe, just maybe ..." He grinned. "Just maybe your cousin's got herself a secret paramour who's wealthy as hell."

"Charley! Stop it! You're making fun. Ruth with a secret lover? It couldn't happen. My God, she never leaves that tiny house of hers."

"Some rich dude might have come knocking on her door. She's not bad to look at in an enigmatic sort of way."

"Now you're being silly. Both of us should shut up and do something. Ruth may have been robbed or raped, or even killed by thieves, for God's sake."

"Now who's exaggerating? Call her! Go on! Grab the phone."

Claudia hurried from the table and grabbed the wall telephone near the dishwasher. "While I call her, you call Jimmy on your cell."

"Jimmy?"

"He can get to the nest, can't he? He can retrieve the choker. Well, can't he?"

"I thought you were worried about Ruth's plea for secrecy. You sure you want me to draw Jimmy into our shrouded web?" After seconds of thought, he added, "The truth is, millions of people have seen that damn choker. Right now, I'm sure the Internet is flooded with pictures of it."

"Call him. You don't have to tell him everything."

"I wish I knew everything. Or maybe just a little something. It's fun but ludicrous to imagine that some handsome prince came calling and placed that broad band of jewels around the neck of such a shrinking enigma."

Claudia glared at her husband and shook her head.

"I'll hold off calling Jimmy until you talk to Ruth," Charley said.

"If she answers."

Charley walked up behind Claudia as she dialed, put his arms around her waist, and whispered into her ear: "I think we've both gotten carried away."

"Maybe. You certainly have." Claudia held the phone to her ear. "She's not answering."

"Give her time." He kissed her on the neck.

"She doesn't have voice mail. She's way behind the times."

"No kidding!" Charley bellowed. He laughed sardonically, then put his hand over his mouth. "Let it ring," he said softly. "She could be in the bathroom. I'll call the Birdman." Charley returned to the table, sat, and pulled his cellphone from his pocket.

"Be careful what you say. After all, Ruth is family. Keep her secret, if you can."

"What secret? Most of that is locked away in her freakish head."

Jimmy's wife answered Charley's call cheerfully in a singsong manner: "Hello, hello, whoever you are."

"Hi Laura! Charley Silvester here. Is your hubby available?"

"He's glued to his computer, watching the bald eagles. He's been swamped with phone calls and e-mails about a hunk of jewelry in the nest. Believe me, it's been a circus around here. He's been up since five. Hold on. I'll get him."

"Cousin Ruth is not going to pick up," Claudia whispered in frustration. Raising her voice, she continued, "The phone just keeps ringing and ringing. Now I'm really worried." She breathed heavily for a few moments. "Oh, Charley, something's wrong." After returning the phone to the wall, she hurried to her husband.

"We'll drive over there. Grab your jacket. I'll only be a minute with Jimmy."

Charley winced when Jimmy's deep, booming voice vibrated the cellphone: "Goddamn! You, too! I should be keeping a list. Y'don't have to tell me why you're calling, Charley. Everyone I know is buzzing me. Yes, yes, yes, I've seen the gleaming gemstones in the nest."

"I should've guessed."

"It's been a crazy morning."

"Is anybody claiming that thing?"

"Not yet, but they will be. The calls and texts are mostly from friends who know about my cam setup. But when the news spreads, watch out! The crazies will come out in force."

"Can you get that choker out of the nest before others go hunting?"

"I'd have to enter the creek bed a couple miles upstream, hike to the right spot and then pull myself up the cliff. It wouldn't be simple. I don't have easy access like people think. I can more easily reach my cam equipment. It's quite far from the nest. I have the zoom set to its fullest. Anyway, we can't disturb the nest until the chicks are big enough to fly away. Bald eagles are protected. Even if they weren't, no way would I dare disturb them. Wish I knew if that trinket is really worth anything."

"Oh, it is!" The words popped from Charley's lips without thought. He stammered: "Claudia thinks ... Well, we both think it's a ... well, it looks like a high-priced choker we've seen somewhere before."

Claudia punched her husband in the side as her eyes flared.

"You're kidding!" Jimmy exclaimed.

Charley didn't respond.

"You there, Charley?"

"I'll get back to you, Jimmy."

"Don't you dare hang up on me. What the hell were you trying to say?" Jimmy's voice vibrated with emotion and disbelief.

"Gotta go. We've got an emergency to deal with here. Don't worry. I'll fill you in. Just don't let anyone else get their hands on that choker."

"Damn it! Don't you ..."

Charley disengaged his cellphone. "Oh, boy," he muttered as he looked into Claudia's eyes. "I hung up on him. And I know he didn't like it."

* * *

Charley had driven their white minivan a few miles along the twisting two-lane road when Claudia tugged on his shoulder and said, "Do you realize we never finished breakfast. We left your second piece of French toast in the frying pan and the coffeepot half filled."

"I guess I lost my appetite"

"I'm surprised you're not complaining of a headache." Claudia kissed his cheek. "Thanks for doing this."

Southbound, the county road twisted and turned as the Bitterlick Creek veered east and west while flowing south. For the most part, it separated heavily wooded areas where trees were getting their bright green leaves of spring and budding in soft shades of yellow and pink. Now and then, small open fields of grasses and weeds separated the extensive stretches of hardwoods and evergreens, allowing sunlight to stream into the van as it bounced along on the uneven macadam damaged by a severe winter. After passing a small pond where migrating geese were watering, Charley asked, "When did we last see Cousin Ruth?'

"It's been awhile."

"How long?"

"Maybe eight or ten months ago. She wasn't happy to see us."

Although they lived only 12 miles north of Cousin Ruth, the Silvesters seldom visited her, primarily because they were never invited. A twinge of guilt plagued Claudia now and then because her aunt, Ruth's mother, had pled on her death, "Promise me you'll always watch out for poor Ruth. You're the only family left." So, at least once a year Claudia would make an effort by calling her cousin and suggesting a need to get together. Last time she had beseeched: "I've got to see you. I have something for you. Pecans. I found them on sale and thought of you and remembered Aunt Fanny raving about your pecan pies. So, I bought you several pounds of them. Charley and I will drop them off. Don't fret, now. We're on our way."

That visit was awkward and short.

Today, after Claudia complained about the odor of skunk, the van hit a pothole with a loud clank, and Charley cursed. He stopped the car, got out for a quick look, and returned fuming. "Notice how the county keeps the road north to Cloverton City in better shape than this southern stretch. They know where the moneyed and privileged folks live, and where Senator Rimespecker hangs his hat." The Silvesters often drove north for shopping, dining out, entertainment, or a visit to Jimmy the Birdman and his wife. They had little reason to drive south toward Cousin Ruth's.

"Any damage?" Claudia asked.

Charley shook his head, grunted, and revved up the engine.

Claudia kissed him on the neck. "Thanks again for doing this. You're a good hubby."

Charley smiled. "I really don't dislike Ruth. It's just that ... Well, she's such an anomaly or deviation from the norm."

Several miles later, they drove across a small bridge above a narrow tributary to the Bitterlick Creek, a trickle of a stream edged with reeds and bright green arrowhead plants. Above, puffy white clouds moved gently across the blue sky, now and then dimming the sunlight.

"We're almost there," Charley commented. "Just a couple miles more."

"I'll know it when I see her pink plastic flamingo."

"This is the first time you haven't brought her a gift. Remember the nuts? She fed them to the squirrels."

"No she didn't. They were pecans for pies. Why would you say such a thing?"

"You know I'm right."

"Charley! Don't start something, now. Frankly, I wish we did have a gift or some groceries for her. She gets all her food delivered. That's why I like to bring her something."

"But nuts?"

"As far as I know, baking pies was her major hobby." Claudia reflected for a moment. "No. I'm wrong. She loved to paint pictures. You've seen her landscapes and still-lifes. They're beautiful. She started drawing pictures at age four and never stopped. Pies and paintings have kept her alive."

"Befitting things for a withdrawn introvert."

"Withdrawn introvert? That's redundant."

"No, my dear. Not every introvert is totally withdrawn."

"She was a shy teenager. The delivery boy from the Supergrand

Market used to carry her pecan pies to Calvary Methodist Church for their spring bake sale."

"How do you know that?"

"Aunt Fanny told me."

"Might not be true today. Fanny's been dead for years."

Cousin Ruth's home was a small, square, two-story, redbrick house with white trim. It was of no particular style. Built by the former owner, it set back only about fifty feet from the county road. To its rear stretched an undersized concrete patio shaded by feathery hemlocks and tall tulip poplars. The nearest neighbor was a small-time chicken farmer about a quarter mile south.

Charley drove the van onto a short, pebbled driveway that curved in front of the steps and small portico. He beeped the horn.

"Don't do that!"

"Sorry."

"I see the flamingo's gone," Claudia said as she exited the van. "Thank goodness."

"Looks like fresh paint on the door," Charley remarked as he followed his wife. "And the railing's been fixed. And ... Ah-huh! Not a dandelion on the lawn. Someone's been taking care of the place."

Claudia expected a clean and neat interior, for Ruth was a fastidious housekeeper. So excessive was her need for tidiness that she vacuumed the rugs and furniture at least twice a day. Cat hairs never rested long on the living-room couch.

"Well, here goes," Claudia said as she tapped on the door. No one answered, so she knocked harder.

"Ring the bell."

Claudia pushed the bell button, waited, then pounded on the door. Seconds later, she grabbed the handle and the door moved slightly. She looked up into Charley's eyes.

"It's open. Go ahead. Push."

Claudia pushed the door open slowly as she whispered, "She always locks her door."

Inside, the Silvesters found a clean and orderly living room. Tan-colored upholstered chairs and a couch, hand-me-downs from Aunt Fanny, were unsoiled and located where expected—in the same spots they occupied during previous visits. End tables were well polished. Tables and chairs formed a small dining area toward the kitchen, for the house had no dining room.

"Cousin Ruth!" Claudia called. "Yo! Ruth! Are you here?"

"Hello! Anyone home? Ruth! Can you hear us, Ruth?"

"Ruth! Ruth!" Claudia tugged on Charley's arm. "She's not here. Nobody's here. Why was the door unlocked? My cousin would never leave the door unlocked."

"That's new," Charley remarked while pointing to an oil painting on the wall above the couch—a stately portrait of a beautiful woman dressed in flowing, blue-gray eveningwear and adorned with a gleaming ornament of diamonds, rubies and emeralds around her neck.

Claudia raised her fingers to her lips as she whispered with quivering emotion: "My God! That's the choker. Ruth's choker. The one in the nest. But who's the woman?"

"Well, it definitely isn't Ruth." Charley shook his head. "Holy smackeroos, I can't believe this. Is this day for real? I feel like we're moving through a crazy dream that started this morning and is not going to end." He examined the portrait closely. "I've seen this woman somewhere. I swear I have. But damn if I can place her. Of course, with an oil painting, you're never sure the artist got the likeness perfect." He glanced down toward the lower left corner. "Look at that!"

"What?"

"Down there in the corner. The signature. See it? 'R. Nettlebaum'. Holy hell! Ruth painted this! I didn't know she was a *portrait* artist. Well, I'll be."

"It's beautiful."

"More than that. It's extraordinary."

Charley turned and glanced up the staircase. "Ruth! You up there, Ruth? Can you hear us?"

"Ruth!" Claudia yelled. "Ruth! Are you here?" She hurried toward the rear of the house.

Charley was half way to the second floor before he called out, "I'll check upstairs. You check the kitchen." He rushed from bedroom to bedroom, then stepped into the bathroom. Breathing deeply, he slowly opened the shower curtain, then paused and caught his breath.

After a quick glance and spin about the small kitchen, Claudia opened the backdoor and stepped out onto the patio—a concrete slab that held two lawn chairs and a picnic table. She immediately screamed. It was a blood-curdling scream followed by choking and guttural sounds.

"What is it?" Charley yelled as he raced down the stairs, nearly tripping and falling, but catching himself and grasping the railing. "I'm coming!" He hurried to the backdoor and wrapped his arms around his wife before looking down at her feet and seeing Pinwheel, the cat, lying dead in a pool of blood, his black fur streaked with gore. Kneeling, Charley examined the cat closely. "He's cut open around the neck and ears. Looks like his eyes were poked out."

"Aaah, poor Pinwheel." Tears streaked Claudia's quivering cheeks. "Who would do such a thing? This is terrible. And where is Ruth. Oh, dear God. Hold me close, Charley." Shivers ran up and down her body. "What's that beside Pinwheel, in the blood near his back leg."

"A feather. Maybe an eagle's feather."

Chapter Two

White-haired Senator Joseph J. Rimespecker stepped into his office, not the one in Washington, D.C., but the specially designed one in his home—a spacious room with gold fleur-de-lis wallcoverings and heavy drapes of green velvet on tall windows. He was readjusting the belt over his bulging belly as he looked up at his secretary, Exton, and said, "Well, what's on the docket?"

"Karl Ludwig called from Geneva," Clarence said as he stood behind the senator's desk shuffling papers. The secretary was a bald, lanky, slightly stooped man who had worked for Rimespecker for decades, starting back in the days when the senator was a slim, dark-haired governor, not the over-weight, red-faced, full-cheeked man of today.

"Oh, God, he probably wants to sell me a diamond-studded watch. Why didn't you shake him loose?"

"He was anxious as hell. Asked whether you lost track of the Ermengarde Choker. I think you'd better talk to him."

"What the hell? That's crazy!" Rimespecker pointed to an artist's rendering of his grandmother on the south wall above a carved mahogany stand topped with a globe of the world. The portrait hid his safe. "It's been in that safe since I gave it to my wife. I've never touched it."

"I believe Mrs. Rimespecker wore it to the inauguration ball."

"Yes, she did. And she found it uncomfortable as hell. Said she felt shackled in irons. Lillian is so ungrateful at times." The senator shook his head. "I'm not one to *invest* in jewels. But that's how I look on the choker now, strictly as an investment."

The secretary began to move out from behind the senator's desk, a heavy, handsomely carved square of polished cherry wood that stood between floor-to-ceiling bookshelves at left and right. A family portrait of the senator, his wife, and his 14-year old son, Jordan, hung on the wall between the massive bookshelves. Clarence stopped suddenly when the telephone rang. He looked up at Rimespecker with a question in his eyes.

"Go ahead. You get it. If it's that German-Swiss merchant again, I suppose I should talk to him if he's fretting about the fate of the Ermengarde."

Clarence lifted the phone to his ear. "Senator Rimespecker's office. Clarence Exton speaking. May I direct your call?"

The senator silently mouthed the words, "Do your thing, Exton. Take care of it."

"Please hold." Clarence focused his eyes on his boss. "Sir, it's not Mr. Ludwig. It's Maurice LaMont, your broker in Monaco? Same subject. The choker."

"Ah, the only other person in the entire world, outside of this family—and that includes you, Clarence—who knows I own the Ermengarde Choker. Dear, dear Maury, my head-strong and annoying middleman. No, no, no, not right now." Rimespecker waved his hands in the air, stepped close to his desk, and whispered, "Tell him I'm in touch with Ludwig. Then hang up and call Geneva."

Clarence was well aware that the only times the senator called him by his first name was when things were about to get close and personal, when the senator decided to include him in the family's inner circle, or tell him secrets or dirty stories. He had yet to hang up the phone. "Mr. LaMont, would you please repeat that. I didn't understand what you said. We have a poor connection." Clarence was aware of the senator's impatience and lifted a finger indicating the need for one moment more. "An eagle's nest? Thank you, Mr. LaMont. I'll tell him." The secretary hung up, smiled weakly, scratched his bald head and said, "This is kinda nuts, Senator. It seems that something that looks like the Ermengarde Choker is popping up on computer screens, I-pads and all kind of hand-held gizmos. Don't laugh, now. A couple bald eagles are trying to hatch it. It's in their nest."

"Well, it's not our choker, for chrissake. It can't be. Tell you what, Clarence." The senator started to push himself up from his chair, but sank back into it. He smirked as he stared at his secretary. "Go move grand-mother out of the way, open the safe and bring the Ermengarde to me."

"I don't have the combination, sir."

"Are you sure? I thought I gave it to you when we cut the ribbon and opened this room." A teasing smile played about Rimespacker's lips. His eyes twinkled. "Think hard."

"You're testing me, aren't you, sir? I'm certain, senator, that you never gave me the combination to your safe. And I think you know that. If you're wondering if Mrs. Rimespecker gave it to me ..." Clarence stepped directly in front of the senator's desk, and with emphasis, pronounced, "She did not."

"Where is my wife, anyway? Have you seen her?" With effort, Rimespecker rose from his chair, stepped away from his desk, and started toward the portrait of his grandmother. "I expected Lillian to join me for coffee when I got home, but couldn't find her anywhere. Even Hilda, our malcontent cook, hadn't seen her."

"You were late last night?"

"Oh, yes. I slept in the Blue Room. Didn't want to disturb Madam when I rose. I played a short round of golf with Peter Lutz this morning. We grabbed brunch at the club."

"Up early, eh, sir?"

"With the birds, Exton. With the birds."

The senator slid the portrait of his maternal grandmother, the late Victoria Montgomery, out of the way to expose his safe. He put his fingers to work, and after a few turns of the knob, the safe opened, and he reached for a steel box. He held the box high as he faced Clarence, grinned, and then tried to imitate the trumpeting of a horn. Lowering the container to waist high, he reflected for a moment before lifting the lid.

The scream that echoed from the senator was like none Clarence had ever heard. It screeched high like that of a terrified woman, then swooped low, only to rise again until it choked off into a series of coughs. Unable to speak, Rimespecker struggled to catch his breath, stamped his feet on the floor and shook the metal box.

"Are you okay, sir?" Clarence asked with true alarm as he stepped toward the senator, who began to gag and retch. It was clear to the secretary that the Ermengarde Choker was missing. It was also clear to him that Rimespecker's behavior was far from that appropriate for a U.S. senator.

When able to talk, Rimespecker spoke in raspy utterances: "It's gone. This is impossible." He struggled to catch his breath. "No one could come into this house and open my safe." He sucked in a deep breath. "No one! You hear me? No one."

"Perhaps Mrs. Rimespecker had reason to remove it, sir. After all, it is hers—a magnificent gift from you."

"No way, Exton! She would not do such a thing without telling me."

"Perhaps to show someone its beauty?"

"Shut up, Exton! That's nonsense!" The senator strode with anger to his desk and slammed the metal box on the well-polished cherry desk, causing Clarence to wince. The secretary had often been told to safeguard the imposing desk from even the slightest scratches.

"I'm sure there's a simple explanation," Clarence suggested softly. Actually, he was not sure at all, but was at a loss for appropriate words. He wanted to point out that a gift is a gift and the recipient should be able to do whatever he or she pleases with it. Yet, while believing that, he didn't really think that Lillian Rimespecker availed herself of the Ermengarde Choker.

"Where the hell is my wife?" The senator hurried to the entryway that opened into an impressive central hall, flung open the heavy doors and yelled, "Lillian! Lillian! Where the devil are you?"

"Shall I contact Mr. Ludwig or Mr. LaMont?"

"What the fuck for? To confirm that we've been robbed? Make sense, Exton!" The senator spun around with a confused look on his face. "Those brokers are in Europe, for God's sake!" With fire in his eyes, he glared at Clarence. "Don't fret. I'll call them when I feel like it. Now, make yourself useful, damn it! Go find my wife! Go on! Get out of here!"

As Senator Rimespecker was ordering his secretary out of his office, a bright yellow school bus was pulling to a stop in front of the house—a grand residence that looked as though it could have been transplanted north from the antebellum South. Most striking from the road were the portico's eight Doric columns. Jordan Rimespecker headed for that impressive entranceway after leaping from the bus. He ambled up a winding flagstone pathway that divided sloping, well-manicured sections of lawn edged with boxwood. Thin and fair-skinned, Jordan owned a wild crop of unruly blond hair that blew freely in the breeze. He carried a backpack of books that hunched his shoulders. With effort, he was slow to reach the portico. After climbing the steps, he opened the weighty twin doors where he bumped shoulders with Clarence, who was pushing his way out.

"Hi, Uncle Clarry!" As usual, the boy showed delight in seeing the secretary, a man known to him since birth. In some ways, he was closer to Clarence than to his own father. And his mother encouraged the relationship from early childhood, urging Jordan to call the secretary "Uncle Clarence." It was the youngster himself, however, who shortened the name to Clarry, and that moniker, preceded by uncle, seemed to make the relationship even more intimate.

"Hey, Jordy!" Clarence rubbed the boy's head, tossing his hair. "How'd school go today?"

"Okay." Jordan held the door for the secretary.

"Just okay?"

"Well, actually *great* in biology class. Mrs. McDonald showed us these bald eagles and their babies in their nest. You should have seen them."

"Outside? On a field trip?"

"No, no, no. At our computer stations. But it was live action. It was all happening as we watched." Jordan let go of the door as Clarence started down the steps. "I can't wait to tell Mom and Dad."

"Your mother isn't home, and you father is in a bad mood. Do you have a little time for me?"

"Sure." Jordan tossed his backpack on the steps and followed Clarence. "I thought Dad was heading to Washington."

"Not 'til Monday when the highway bill comes up for a vote in the full chamber. It's his committee. He'll probably leave Sunday night because he wants an early morning talk with Senator Nelson before the vote. He'll be here for most of the weekend." Clarence tugged on the boy's arm. "Come on. Let's take a walk. Have you seen your mother?"

"This morning. She made breakfast for me. I've never seen her in such a happy mood. She was laughing, cracking jokes, and actually dancing around the kitchen with a box of cornflakes. 'It feels so good to pull a sad snail from its shell,' she said. Wouldn't tell me what she meant." The teenager looked up and focused his sharp blue eyes on Clarence. "She's been dressing up and acting kinda crazy."

Clarence led the boy around the side of the stately house toward the rear. They trod by dark green Japanese spreading yews that alternated with gray green upright junipers—well-tended and flawlessly shaped evergreens that edged the house and contrasted sharply with the stark whiteness of the imposing residence.

"So, tell me about your biology class," Clarence asked as he patted the teenager on the back.

"Mrs. McDonald is an awesome teacher. We even talk about male and female stuff. You know."

"Sex?"

"She uses the word 'reproduction'." Jordan giggled. "She corrects us.

'Reproduction' she'll say again and again." He ran ahead of Clarence and entered the formal gardens that spread far to the rear of the house.

Clarence was quick to catch up with the boy, joining him between rows of boxwood hedge and pathways that separated rose gardens into evenly divided squares and rectangles. An ornate fountain marked the center of the English-style garden, which had perfect symmetry, but no blooms as yet. The buds were awaiting the warmth of June.

"Did you know that the tassel atop a cornstalk is the male part and the ears are female parts. When pollen from the tassel falls on an ear, well, that's self-pollination. Cross-pollination gives us better corn. That's when two different cornstalks get together." Jordan giggled. "With the help of the wind, of course." He turned and looked up at Clarence with a self-satisfied look on his face.

"Don't be smug, now." Clarence ruffled the boy's hair again. "I'm glad you're learning these things."

"Some technical stuff is boring. All this freakin' DNA and RNA and amino acid crap isn't easy to learn."

"I guess not."

Jordan leaned over, picked up a pebble and tossed it. "Mrs. McDonald brings in great speakers. We had one guy from the zoo. He came in with a snake around his neck. Some of the girls screamed. It was awesome."

Clarence shielded his eyes as he gazed up at the sun, a deepening orange fireball that was sinking toward the horizon. "It's getting late." He tugged on the teenager's arm as he thought of the senator's vindictive mood. "We better get back to the house." As they started to retrace their steps, he said, "Tell me again about the bald eagles."

"Cool, man. Really cool. We saw the little peeps being fed by the big eagles."

"Do you know where the pictures were coming from?"

"What do y'mean?"

"The nest, was it nearby? Or was it in Colorado or New Mexico or some far-off place?"

"I don't know. Y'couldn't tell by looking at it. Mrs. McDonald didn't say. She did say she wanted to invite some Audubon guy to come talk about the eagles."

"Audubon guy? Did she give his name?"

"I don't think so. Jeez, Unk, what's with the quiz?"

"I'll explain later. Tell me about the nest. What was it made of?"

"Sticks and stuff. I saw some corn husk. The big eagle took up a lot of space in the nest. When it moved, the screen suddenly went blank. We lost the picture. The kids all groaned. Mrs. McDonald said someone pulled the plug and we missed seeing the bling. Then the bell rang and the kids got noisy. I couldn't hear what she was saying as we left."

Clarence was flabbergasted. In his mind he immediately translated 'bling' as a slang word for jewels. He uttered "bling" under his breath, almost unconsciously.

Jordan asked, "What's bling?"

A shiver ran up the secretary's spine at the very idea that Mrs. McDonald had seen jewelry in the eagles' nest. His thoughts spun, and he struggled for words. "Holy shit," he mumbled to himself. Gathering his wits, he repeated the word, "Bling. She used *that* word? How old is Mrs. McDonald? I picture a gray-haired schoolmarm like my biology teacher. Maybe I'm wrong, but I thought 'bling' was today's street talk for gems."

Jordan laughed loudly and spun around in a circle. "Uncle Clarry, Mrs. McDonald is not only cool, she's totally with it. She's a good-looking blonde. Mr. Gordon, our gym teacher, calls her volup ... voluptis."

"Voluptuous?"

"Yeah. That. And the kid next to me in her class says he'd do her, anytime."

"Do her? Hey, Jordy, I don't like that kind of talk. You know better." Clarence put his hand on the boy's shoulder and squeezed.

"They're not my words! That's what Rufus Duffy said. He's brainless. We call him Rufus-the-Dufus."

Jordan had a peculiar look on his face as he and the secretary neared the front of the house. His expression seemed to question Clarence's behavior even more deeply. He was an intuitive youngster for his age, and he had grown to recognize almost every move, mood and manner of his beloved 'uncle'. After all, it was Uncle Clarry, not his father, who helped him with his homework, tended to his cuts and bruises, took him to the zoo and baseball games, and drove him to school when he missed the bus. Their togetherness offered an abundance of time for scores of meaningful discussions and, therefore, the secretary had as much to do with the teenager's character building as did his parents.

"Let's go talk to your father," Clarence suggested as they approached the front portico.

Chapter Three

Laura Barnes lifted two bags of groceries from a supermarket cart, placed them on the back seat of her silver-blue sedan and slammed the door closed. She had not intended to shop until next week, but needed an escape from the frantic goings-on at home. Although her pantry was well stocked, she used shopping as an excuse to get away from the incessant phone calls and her overwrought husband. She mumbled something about "those damn eagles," opened the driver-side door, slid behind the steering wheel, fastened her seatbelt, breathed deeply and sighed twice before starting the engine.

The drive home was short, but replete with turns through the Oakwood neighborhood where Jimmy and Laura lived in a four-bedroom Dutch Colonial house. They had chosen the property more for its grounds than for the two-story dwelling of white stucco and clapboard. Jimmy, a slight, agile man with short salt-and-pepper hair, needed sufficient land for his trees, birdhouses, feeding stations, birdbaths, and special plants. Youthful for a man of 66 years, he had recently planted a patch of milkweed to help attract and feed the red knot, a migrating bird suffering from the scarcity of its choice food.

Minutes later and about a half-mile from home, Laura turned onto Maple Lane and immediately slammed on the breaks as a minivan backed out of a driveway, zigzagged in front of her car, brushed against an animal and sped away. Laura yelled out the window, "Damn you, stop! You just hit one of God's creatures!" It was second nature for her to leap from her car and run to the opossum lying in the gutter. "Oh hell, another road-kill," she muttered to herself as she stooped over the animal, which was either dead, injured or playing dead. Athletic and lithe, she dashed back to her car, opened the trunk and seized a large, blue towel, spun around quickly and raced back to the gutter. She carefully wrapped the opossum in the towel and gently laid it on the grass between the curb and sidewalk. Because opossums play possum, she left the scene not knowing if it were dead or alive.

Upon arriving home, Laura parked the car in the driveway at the rear of the house, near the garage, and stepped briskly to the backdoor and entered the kitchen. "Jimmy!" she shouted. "Please carry in the groceries for me. Only two bags." She immediately realized that her husband probably couldn't hear her, for he was talking loudly and excitedly to someone while the landline telephone continued to ring.

Jimmy entered the kitchen holding his cellphone to his ear. Although a short and slender man remindful of the birds he loved, he owned a booming voice that often startled people and caused them to step back. It exploded from a small mouth below a sharp beak-like nose. "No! No! You don't understand! It's against the law to even own a feather from a bald eagle." He nodded to his wife as she grimaced. "They're a protected species. Even their parts are off limits." He sat on a stool at the kitchen table. "Damn it! Listen to me. Can you imagine what would happen if you messed with one of those baby chicks? And frankly, speaking as an ornithologist, and as a lover of birds and nature, I wouldn't mess with those eagles even if they were not the symbol of this country and protected by the government."

The landline telephone stopped ringing, only to start again within seconds. Reluctantly, Laura said, "I'll get it." She reached for the amber-colored phone on the pine kitchen cabinet just as Jimmy disengaged his cell, shook his head, and eyed his wife.

"That might be Chief Morris," he said as he paced back and forth.

"Hello?" Laura grimaced again. "Hold on. He's right here." She whispered to her husband: "Yeah, it's the police chief."

Jimmy seized the phone as Laura hurried off to get the groceries. Nimble and quick as ever, she allowed the door to slam as she hurried to the car. Within seconds she was carrying both bags into the kitchen. Bouncing about like a busy chipmunk, she unloaded the ice cream and other perishables and quickly left the house again.

Possessed by the thought of the opossum, Laura drove back to Maple Lane, only to discover her blue towel strewn across the sidewalk. The animal was gone, giving her a surge of good feeling. She was certain now that it had been playing possum. Such impulsive actions regarding animals were characteristic of her ways since she mended a cardinal's wing as a child. Today, her love of animals meant periodic trips to the

Nagelstone Veterinary Center for Large Animals where she volunteered and often sat up all night with newly born horses. Years ago she started protesting against painful methods too often used for castration and dehorning of animals. Recently, outside the fencing at a pig farm, she carried a sign blasting the use of gestation crates for pregnant sows. Inadequate housing for any farm animals—from chickens to bulls—raised her ire.

While Laura usually ate only a small amount of meat with her vegetables, she often argued with herself for chewing and swallowing it, usually placating her self-reproach somewhat by insisting that she needed the protein. Her intellect kept telling her that the herding and killing of animals on a big industrial scale, just for the eating, was wrong. She often unloaded on Jimmy her belief that tomorrow's kids would look back on today's Homo sapiens and find it hard to believe they were so heartless and unfeeling.

Laura's fervor for animals and her husband's passion for birds built an unbelievable intensity to their daily living, their lengthy discussions, their heated debates and their occasional arguments. But after 40 years of marriage, they still loved each other with gusto.

Jimmy had just hung up the phone when Laura come bouncing into the kitchen to find the non-perishables still in the grocery bags on the floor near the refrigerator.

"Thanks a lot," she said in a deliberately grouchy tone as she began to pick up and shelve the remaining groceries.

"Sorry, I couldn't get to it. I just got off the phone with Chief Morris. Y'know, I've been his friend for years, but he treats me like crap when I need his help. No way, he says, can he supply manpower to keep sneaky creeps, lustful people and the curious away from that nest. I asked him to put a man in or near the creek bed and a patrol car on the high ground this side of the creek. That would cover things from east and west. You should have heard the blubbering idiot. You might think I asked for a fleet of army tanks to guard Fort Knox." Jimmy sighed in frustration and began to pace in circles. "What the hell am I going to do?"

Laura finished shelving the store-goods, frowned and stared at her husband, then asked, "How long before the little birds leave the nest?"

"Ten to twelve weeks. And I'm not going near them until they fledge."

"Fledge?"

"Acquire enough feathers to fly from the nest. To fledge." Jimmy tightened his fists. "Damn it, Laura, I need help. What the hell am I gonna do without help?" He raised his already-loud voice. "I'd tie my body to the newel post before I'd let myself go near that nest. And, I'll be goddamned if I'll let anyone else near it. No matter what I have to do, I'll keep them out. So help me. Maybe I should dust off Papa's old shotgun."

"Jimmy!"

"Kidding. Just kidding."

"You can't protect the baby birds for ten to twelve weeks. That's a long time. Somebody's bound to find that nest within that time and snatch that glittering ornament whether its costume jewelry or a million dollar bracelet."

"I could sure use James."

"Now, don't involve our son in this. Jamey is three hundred miles away. I know he'd do anything for you. But ... Please, Jimmy. Don't stir things up."

"He loves birds."

"Don't go there!" Laura raised her hand as if she were a school pupil. "I'll help you." She squeezed her fist and made a hefty biceps muscle. "But face the facts. There's no way you're keeping the total citizenry— hoods, thugs and the lustful included—away from that crown jewel, or whatever it is, for three-to-four months." Laura placed a can of beans in a cabinet near the sink, then stepped quickly to her husband and hugged him. "You're killing yourself over this." She stepped away from him, but looked kindly into his eyes. "Just think. Perhaps that thing in the eagles' nest is a piece of tin studded with colored glass. And all this uproar is for nothing."

"Maybe so." Jimmy reached for Laura's hand and pulled her to him for a quick kiss. "But it looks so precious. My viewers are going to believe what they're going to believe." He pulled away from his wife. "By the way, I used the remote to shut down the system while you were at the store. Around four o'clock, I think. Nobody can see the eagles now. That won't change things much, I realize. But it might slow things down. I'll switch the cam on early in the morning when I get up. I can watch from five to seven and then pull the plug again."

Laura was well aware that 5 a.m. was not too early for her husband to rise. He was used to it. During his teaching and research days at Cornell University, he would get up before dawn, as did the other ornithologists, and greet the birds as they chirped their morning songs. Jimmy would often hike on the pathways through Cornell's Sapsucker Woods just when the morning sunlight was beginning to break through the dense canopy of trees. Once he dragged his reluctant teenage son, James Jr., along for the hike in hopes of deepening the boy's interest in birds. That approach didn't work, but Jamey did become an eager birdwatcher later in life, after his father stopped trying so hard. Anyway, Jimmy, the elder, enjoyed solitary walks where he could silently speak to the trees, the ferns, the May apples, the skunk cabbage, the frogs, the toads and the birds. He would then settle in the ornithological laboratory, pick up a pair of binoculars and look out over the adjoining pond as the waterfowl swooped in for a splash and a swim.

Habits are hard to break. Even today, years after leaving the Finger Lakes region of New York State, Jimmy did not need an alarm clock. And soon after he stirred each morning, Laura would have coffee perking and bacon and eggs sizzling in the frying pan. On many a morning, it was barely light out, and often still dark, when they gazed across the kitchen table at each other and began chatting incessantly about what the day might bring.

"I asked the chief about putting up barriers, and he just laughed. 'Where?' he said. 'In the creek? On the cliff?' I got so pissed off, I screamed at him."

"Well, screaming is nothing new for you. You do it well." Laura sat at the kitchen table—a small Formica table covered with a pale blue cloth that matched the window curtains. The room was heavily decked with knotty pine cabinets giving it a woodsy flavor that the Barnes liked. "Come join me. The phones haven't been ringing."

"That's because I unplugged the landline and turned off my cell." Jimmy sat on a stool opposite his wife and folded his arms on the table. "I need a break. But not a long one. I'll give myself a few more minutes. I'm still waiting to hear back from Charley Silvester. Can you believe that he hung up on me? Charley! He hung up on me!" Jimmy unlocked his arms and pounded the table three times with his fists. "I can't get him back. I keep getting voice mail and it's driving me up the wall. He either fell off the edge of the earth or he's refusing to answer. I must have left him a dozen messages. Bastard!"

"Jimmy, he's one of your closest friends."

"That makes him even more of a bastard. Friends don't hang up on friends."

"Come on, now. He did say goodbye, didn't he?"

"I'm not sure. But I know he cut me off abruptly."

"Tell me again exactly what he said." Laura rose from the table. "I'll put on some coffee."

"I can't. Not exactly. But, I swear to God, he did indicate that he knew someone who owned—or might own—that damn piece of jewelry. I wasn't dreaming. I heard him say it. Can you believe?"

"Charley and Claudia?" Laura shook her head. "Of all people. Why or how would they know something like that?"

"Oh yeah!" Jimmy pounded the table again. "So help me, he did say it was worth big bucks or a fortune or something like that. I'm not insane! Honest t'God, I did hear that. I wasn't hallucinating."

Minutes later, Jimmy turned on his cellphone and got up from the table. As Laura poured coffee into oversized mugs, he ambled to the landline phone and fed its wire to an outlet. "Here we go again."

Laura carried the mugs—each bearing a colorful imprint of a smiling clown—to the table, seated herself, and took a sip of the hot brew. "Dinner will be late. As if you didn't guess. So come on, drink some java."

Jimmy's next conversation on the house-phone amused Laura because he kept repeating and spelling Arabic names. When he hung up, he stared incredulously at her and said, "A total fake! Pretended he was some Saudi dude. The jerk had a North Jersey accent, for chrissake. He didn't even know Mecca was located in Arabia."

Laura laughed. "Come get your coffee while it's hot. I used the clown mugs to help improve your mood."

The phones rang at the same time that someone knocked on the front door.

"I'll get the door," Laura said. She took another sip of coffee, sprang from her chair and hurried to the living room while the knocking continued. "I'm coming! I'm coming!" Opening the door, she found Charley and Claudia Silvester standing there bearing grim expressions.

"Sorry to barge in without calling," Charley said. "We tried to reach you, but couldn't get through."

"Busy! Busy! Busy! The phone calls have been driving us crazy. Please come in. Jimmy will be glad to see you, even though he might not show it." Laura hugged Claudia and pecked a kiss on Charley's cheek.

"I know he's pissed." Charley called out loud enough to be heard in the kitchen, as intended.

"Really pissed!"

"Sit down. I'll get him." Laura pointed to a grouping of living room chairs as she started toward the kitchen. The sofa and wingchairs, all slipcovered in colorful early American prints, were arranged into a semicircle facing a Colonial-style fireplace framed by a handsomely carved mantel. Within the half-circle lay a knotty-pine cocktail table holding a brass pitcher and a green-glass candy dish. The living-room walls were painted off-white and displayed landscape and still-life oil paintings, as well as a water-color portrait of a boy and his dog above the fireplace. Claudia and Charley were well acquainted with the teenager and the fox terrier portrayed in the gold frame, because James, Jr., and his beloved dog, Buster, had played a major role in bringing the two families together years ago. Buster and the Silvester's greyhound, Bingo, each died of food poisoning on the same day at the old, now-defunct Cloverton City Veterinary Hospital as the news of contaminated dog food from China made headlines throughout the country. Red-eyed and shaken, Jamey, his parents and the Silvesters met at the hospital, cried together and became solid friends.

Charley and Claudia seated themselves on the sofa to await what they expected to be a loud-barking and disagreeable greeting from their spare but heavy-throated friend, Jimmy the Birdman.

Minutes later, when Jimmy followed Laura into the living room, the phones were silent thanks to his intervention. The house was as quiet as a funeral parlor, and the Birdman's silence puzzled his wife and the Silvesters. He stared at his visiting friends, but said nothing. Claudia was nonplussed, but Charley soon recognized Jimmy's theatrics. A beastly stare and down-turned mouth presented the message Jimmy intended.

"You're right!" Charley declared. "You're absolutely right. No words are necessary. We get the message. Now quit the act and hear us out. We're in a hell of a nasty and confusing pickle."

"Whatever your pickle, you shouldn't hang up on a good buddy and refuse to call back."

"I didn't hang up on you. But I did close out fast." Charley raised both hands, palms out, as if to say hold tight and listen. "If you had a reclusive cousin you seldom saw, a peculiar child-like creature who never left the house, a quiet little thing who dressed up in feathers, ribbons, spangles and bows, a wisp of a woman who wore a glittering choker around her neck and did little but fantasize, fantasize, fantasize ... " Charley stopped to catch his breath. "... would you think her choker was worth millions, or would you see it as an piece of the fantasy, part of a cheap custom in a dream world?"

"I suppose it might depend on how much it sparkled," Jimmy said.

"Well, I don't know real diamonds from pressed-glass imitations," Charley proclaimed with emphasis.

"Before you all get deep into conversation," Laura asked, "may I get you something to drink? Some of Jimmy's homemade root beer, maybe?"

"No thanks, Laura," Claudia said as her husband looked up, shook his head and forced a brief smile.

Jimmy was dumbfounded, and it showed in his expression. "So you're telling us you have a strange cousin who you saw wearing this thing," he uttered in a doubtful tone. "Is that what I'm hearing?"

"So help me God!" Charley raised his right hand like a Boy Scout. "Cousin Ruth."

"I didn't know you had a Cousin Ruth. We've known you for all these many years, and you've never mentioned a Cousin Ruth."

Claudia joined the conversation: "She's my cousin. And what Charley says is true. We saw her wearing the choker on three separate occasions, but paid little attention until we viewed the eagles' nest. The fact that she swore us to secrecy finally drew our attention and made us wonder. Now we've broken our promise to her, but we realize we have no other choice. She's missing. We've been trying to find her. Cops in three townships brushed us off. They say it's too soon to report someone missing."

"We seldom saw her," Charley explained. "She really wasn't part of our lives. But, God as my witness, she wore that thing around her neck during our visits to her place—three quick visits."

"Hard to fathom." Jimmy shook his head slowly. "Well, then, maybe it is only paste." He rubbed his chin. "Could be the way the light hits the glass, y'know ... It could be playing tricks on us."

Laura said, "Excuse me," as she cut in front of the guests and sank into a wingchair next to Claudia.

"After three years, I've come to think there might be more to it," Charley said. "The way Ruth looks when she touches it. The way she fingers it. The expression on her face. I paid no attention to any of these things until today when I saw this portrait of a strikingly distinguished-looking woman wearing it. The strangest thoughts came into my mind. I started thinking back to ..."

Jimmy interrupted with a shout: "Three years! Did I hear you say three years?"

"We think the first time we saw her wear it was about three years ago," Claudia said. "Maybe, two and a half."

Jimmy finally sat in one of the wingback chairs and shook his head again.

Laura's expression showed she was anxious about something. Her eyes wide, she held up a finger for attention. "A portrait of a woman? What were you saying about a portrait?"

The Silvesters went on for the next 40 minutes explaining their visit to Cousin Ruth's house, including such details as the portrait's signature, the dead cat's bloody condition, the location of a feather, and the unlocked front door. Then the conversation switched to efforts to retrieve the choker. Suddenly something Charley suggested sparked an idea in Jimmy's head.

"What did you just say?"

"Get volunteers! If the cops won't help protect the chicks, round up some volunteers."

Jimmy leaped out of his chair and danced a jig. "Why didn't I think of that? Birdwatchers! I know hundreds of birdwatchers. They'd love to help. They'd swarm here if I gave the call. Wow!" Jimmy pulled Charley out of his chair and punched him playfully in the ribs. "Thank you, Mr. Silvester!"

"We can set up camp on my property," Charley suggested eagerly. "In fact, we can also use the wooded land that extends from my line all the way to Bitterlick Creek. We can pitch tents."

"Why not?" Jimmy asked. "We'll put together a real bivouac. And assign different teams to different duties at different times."

"And Claudia and Laura can organize the daily cookouts," Charley remarked half jokingly.

"Hey! Hey! Watch what you're saying, mister!" Laura pronounced firmly. "And speaking of food. It's way past dinner hour. What say the four of us hit the Black Bear Inn. Okay?"

"Sounds good!" declared Jimmy. "We can celebrate the swarming of the birdwatchers."

"Let me hook up the kitchen phone before we leave and lockup," Laura said, "so we don't forget later. I'll be right with you." She sped to kitchen in an upbeat mood. No sooner had she plugged in the wire than the phone rang. Briefly hesitating, she picked up the headset and answered, "Hello?"

"This is Senator Joe Rimespecker, may I speak to Mr. James Barnes, please?"

"Hold on." Laura stepped toward the living room and called, "Jimmy! Senator Rimespecker? He's on the phone? Do you want to talk?"

"Who?"

"Senator Joe Rimespecker."

"You're kidding. What's he want? He doesn't know me from Adam."

"Everybody knows the Birdman."

"I've never met the senator, and I don't care to. I don't read his op-ed piece in the *Beacon*. And he's not getting my vote."

Chapter Four

As the Barneses and the Silvesters ate cheeseburgers and french fries at the Black Bear Inn on Old County Road 33, Ruth Nettlebaun and Lillian Rimespecker dined outdoors on Lobster a la Monte Cristo at the French Gateway Café in New York City. Ruth and Lillian had spent the entire day in Manhattan visiting museums, shopping at expensive boutiques, enjoying a concert, trying to get tickets for a Broadway show, and walking in Central Park where they occasionally hugged and kissed when no one was looking. Now, they smiled and giggled at each other as they sipped Apricot Coolers with their savory lobster, au gratin potatoes and maple-glazed carrots. The sidewalk was crowded with diners because the evening was warm for a day in May. Luckily for them, their table-for-two was located at the far end of a long strip of tables. They had an overwhelming desire to separate themselves as much as possible from the other patrons.

Ruth's blithe spirit was lifted to new heights by her trappings. She was well aware that her pageboy haircut, smartly styled white blouse with flared collar and rhinestone necklace enhanced her appearance, because Lillian had told her so nearly a dozen times. An almost, but not quite pretty woman by nature, Ruth had learned to embellish her looks through Lillian's direction many months ago. As for Lillian, she knew how to dress since childhood days, having been born and reared by a sophisticated mother, a true blue-blood of Newport society. She had chosen, for this trip to New York, an expensive suit of lavender linen, adorned by a pearl necklace and matching earrings. Whether dressed for day or evening, she generally displayed a regal bearing with her upright stance, solid chin, high cheekbones, fair skin and soft brown hair, traits that had been captured in the portrait by Ruth. Men's eyes were often drawn to hers, but her hazel eyes never answered the messages.

"Do you realize that you wouldn't have come here with me ten or twelve months ago?" Lillian's words were spoken with softness and care. "We've made great progress during the past year."

"I know." Ruth's eyes sparkled as she gazed on Lillian. "How can I ever thank you? You tried so hard during those first two years. I don't really know how you put up with me. But you never forced me out the door, so to speak."

"We needed those early years to slowly grow a sturdy sprout from a reluctant seed, then cultivate strong stems, then encourage one bud after another to swell. Otherwise there would have been no bursting and blooming of the blossoms this year. And, oh, what a magnificent bouquet we have now."

"You have a crazy way with words. Do I remind you of any special flowers?"

"Oh, many, indeed. Beautiful white lilies. Gorgeous blue morning glories. Brilliant lavender orchids. I could go on and on."

Ruth giggled. "Ah, you mean I'm no longer a poor little petunia struggling to grow in a pot of clay." She purposely grunted as she tried to pull a succulent piece of lobster from its tail with the proper fork. "It's so delicious. I refuse to lose this battle."

"Here, let me help. I was trained to eat lobster." Lillian stood and stepped to the other side of the table, leaned over Ruth's shoulder, rubbed cheeks with her and seized the tiny lobster fork. With skill and deftness, she removed the lobster meat and fed it to her beloved companion.

Minutes later, back in her own chair, Lillian dramatically lifted her drink high as if toasting her majesty the queen. "To you, because you tried so hard. I want you to know that I actually enjoyed those first difficult times because I was certain of what was coming. I felt it deep in my heart. I knew you'd eventually break loose and come out of your shell. Besides, think of what we had during my visits inside that little house of yours. We gave ourselves completely to each other. You blossomed in a passionate way before you were able to expand your world outside."

"I'll never forget that first time. Those feelings ... They were completely new to me. Oh, Lillian, I didn't know. I had never felt like that. Never had I realized certain things about myself. Never had I felt those tingles racing through my body."

"I knew, the first time I looked into your eyes. Neither of us spoke at first. Remember? There was no need." Lillian reached across the table and took Ruth's hand. "Thank God those church leaders got together and tried to save that food program. The Reverend Harold Pitts embarrassed every wealthy woman in the county into partaking in that effort. It was the first and only time I've ever knocked on doors. What was it the sexton at Calvary Methodist called us?" Lillian's eyes twinkled as she deliberately paused for affect. "Oh, yes. The gathering of the rich bitches." Her quiet laugh turned into a titter. "As they say, pardon my French." She cleared her throat and touched her lips with the corner of her napkin.

"I almost didn't answer when you knocked that day."

"Thank God you did." Lillian's eyes watered slightly. "There you were." She smiled warmly. "Standing there holding a pecan pie."

Ruth and Lillian sat quietly in deep thought for several minutes. Each offered an affectionate gaze to the other as many of the diners began to stroll away from their tables. Twilight brought with it a chilly breeze.

Ruth's expression grew serious. "Since we couldn't get show tickets for tonight, what say we just walk a bit and return early to the hotel."

"Well, there's this little place I had hoped to show you. It's a club called the Black Cat. I think you'd like it. It's for gals like us. Nice, friendly crowd."

"Oh, my God!" Ruth showed alarm as she rose from her chair. "Black Cat! Oh my God! I left the Ermengarde choker on Pinwheel."

"What?"

"Oh, I can't believe I was so foolish."

"Sit down! Don't make a scene. Now, what are you talking about?"

"The choker! I'm talking about the choker! What an idiot I am!"

"Please sit down, Ruth, people are looking."

Ruth slid slowly into her chair. "I was just fooling around. The choker looked so beautiful against Pinwheel's black fur. It was much too loose around his neck, so I laid it across his back and fastened it under his belly. I enjoyed watching it glistening and sparkling as he walked around, slithering here and there."

"Ruth! That thing's worth millions!"

"I know I was foolish. I just love to look at it and think of you. I often hang it on lamp shades and lean it against window glass. I kiss it before I go to bed. It's a piece of you that I can touch when you're not with me."

"Ruth, sometimes I think I haven't been able to take the child completely out of you." Lillian bit her lower lip. "Remember our discussion about childish behavior? Do you?" Lillian gazed steadily into Ruth's eyes. Her expression was grim. "Your cat, he can't get out of the house, can he?"

"There's one of those little flapping doors for pets that leads in and out of the patio, but Pinwheel seldom uses it. He's a good boy. Likes to follow me around the house, in and out of this place and that, up and down the stairs. He always uses his litterbox. And I have a special food dispenser for him now that I leave the house."

"Oh, dear God," Lillian muttered under her breath. She kept shaking her head. "I wanted you to be comfortable for the rest of your life. From the very beginning, I've worried that I might not always be here for you. The Ermengarde was your security."

Their waiter—a young blond wearing a red bowtie and a black blazer with red trim—approached their table and asked, "Is there anything else I can get you, ladies? Perhaps some dessert? Tonight's feature is our walnut rum cake, a specialty of Chef Antoine."

"I'm quite satisfied," Lillian said. "Ruth?"

"No, no, no. I couldn't eat another thing."

"May I take your plates?" the waiter asked politely. He didn't wait for an answer and scooped up the dishes gracefully. "Thank you, ladies. I'll have your check in a moment."

The young man was barely out of earshot when Lillian leaned toward Ruth and quietly questioned, "I've been meaning to ask you why you included the choker in the portrait you painted of me? Why did you put that heavy thing around my neck? I wasn't wearing it when I sat for you?"

"It's so beautiful. And it shows off your graceful neck lines."

"Don't get me wrong, I adore the painting. It's exceptional, as I've told you often. Never, never, never could I have dreamed of such a magnificent portrait of myself. But I still don't understand ..."

"Like I said, the choker represents you. To me, it means you, it is you. It's the most beautiful gift in the world. Sometimes I fall asleep with it between my breasts. That you could give me such a thing ... Well, it was overwhelming. And still is."

Lillian said nothing. She simply stared at Ruth, first with incredulity, then with pathos as Ruth's expression saddened. As compassion grew, so did her sensual feelings. "About the Black Cat," she whispered.

"You're a senator's wife. People know you. They've seen your face in the newspapers. Remember what you used to say about exposure?"

"I've been to the Black Cat only twice, but even at that, I've seen prominent people there. They stay mum, and so do I."

"You know better. I might not be worldly, but I read the papers and watch the news."

"I've become more careless, I know. It's like part of me wants to shout the truth to the world, proclaim who I am and what I am from the mountain tops. It eats at me, claws at me. Yet the other side of me knows this can't be. I worry about Jordan more than I do Joe. I can't tolerate the thought of hurting him. He's a wonderful son with a good heart, and I love him so much it hurts."

The waiter returned with the check. Lillian searched in her bag for a credit card, then changed her mind. She quickly placed cash on the table, a means of paying for things that was uncommon to her. "Let's go." She rose from the table and waited a moment while Ruth drew a small mirror from her vanity bag, examined her face and applied lipstick.

As they walked northward on the avenue, Ruth tugged on Lillian's arm and, with a slight quiver in her soft voice, asked, "Why did you marry the senator?"

Lillian ignored the question as they maneuvered along the busy sidewalk where window shoppers strolled and gazed at mannequins clothed in silks, satins, wools and cottons of all colors. "Look at those red leather boots." She pulled Ruth toward a store window. "I'd like to buy those for you."

"Sorry I asked about your marriage," Ruth said more to herself than to her companion. Her under-the-breath whisper was easily heard by Lillian.

"I'm the one who's sorry," Lillian said sharply. She sighed twice. "The answer to your question is mighty complex, and frankly I don't think I've put it all together in my own mind. Mother said Joe was a good catch. Dad seemed to favor him over others. I was comfortable with him in the early days when most men turned me off." She put her arm around Ruth's waist and pulled her close, only to let go right away. "I wanted no part of an array of men who were pushed on me after my debutante coming out party. I was expected to marry."

"How did you meet?"

"At a boat-house party. He was a rower for Columbia. My roommate at Vassar dated a rower from Brown. After that first time, we kept being invited to the same parties by the same crowd."

"Was it habit more than ... Well, you know?"

Lillian ignored the question. "Oh, God, I wish I had been born later and just coming of age today. The world's changing. Some are calling it a revolution. When I heard that the Irish voted for gay marriage, I choked on a lamb chop at a luncheon of the Daughters of the American Revolution. My blood pressure must have soared. Governor Tadwell's wife slapped me on the back while other DAR members gathered around me fussing and fuming. That bunch of old fuddy-duddies didn't know how to help me. But I survived after coughing up a sliver of lamb bone."

Lillian led the way as the twosome walked past an array of shops to the next intersection, where Ruth tugged on her companion's elbow and said, "Please. Let's go back to our beautiful room at the hotel."

Not a word came from Lillian's mouth for a lengthy moment. But her slight smile broadened. Finally, she lifted a bit of Ruth's page-boy hair and whispered into hear ear: "Yes. That's a good idea." She grasped Ruth's hand. "Let's do that."

Chapter Five

Jordan stood in the doorway of his father's office as the senator spoke to him from behind his desk: "I want you to do two things. First, grab Exton before he leaves. I need him for an important errand. Second, tell Hilda to serve my dinner in the library. We will not be using the dining room this evening. *You* can eat with her in the kitchen."

"Dad, it's a weekend, a Friday night. Clarence might have plans. Besides, he may have left already."

"Then run. See if you can stop him. Oh, and tell Hilda I want light fare. I'm not hungry. Just a taste of this or that on a tray will be fine." He smirked. "I plan to gobble my food. I'm hoping to entertain the local chief of that Audubon outfit in the library."

Jordan looked puzzled, but didn't ask. He pulled his cellphone from his pocket and showed annoyance as he tapped the numbers. "Uncle Clarry, it's Jordy. Dad wants to see you before you take off." The teenager fidgeted while he listened to remarks he would not repeat to his father. "Gotcha. Yes, I'll tell him."

"I want to see him as soon as possible," the senator said. "If he doesn't understand that, call him back."

"No need. He said he'll be right with you."

Jordan's father bristled, then cracked a dubious smile. "Don't lecture me, now, about modern-day communications. Old habits die hard. Or maybe I just like to look in a person's eyes when I give orders."

Within seconds, Jordan was rattling off instructions to the cook. When finished, he waved his cellphone in the air—his way of again reminding his father that a cellphone can be used for communicating within the house in the same way it's used to reach contacts in Washington or Europe. The teenager began to back away, but was stopped by another request from the senator, one that, to his ears, sounded like a demand.

"Tell me about your mother."

"What do y'mean?"

"I'm well aware that you know her comings and goings better than I do." The senator rose from his chair and steadied himself by putting both hands on his desk. He leaned forward and kept his eyes focused on his son. "You're a bright young man. Give me your insight."

"Dad, it's your fault if you and Mom don't hang out together. You're in Washington much of the time, and when you're here, you're busy. Yeah, she dresses up sometimes and goes off here and there. Can you blame her?"

"She used to like the Washington crowd. Hell, if it weren't for my needs, I'd unload our property down there. As for you ..." The senator grimaced as he gave an up-and-down look at his 16-year-old son. "You'll be off to college soon."

Jordan suddenly became cocky in his stance, facial expression and words. "If you're asking whether Mom is cheating on you, damn if I know. I haven't seen anything lustful in the Rimespecker boudoirs of late. Mom hasn't dragged any dudes home. And I don't have to be here to know what's goin' on. Clarence polices the joint all day long."

The senator's face reddened. His jowls quivered. "Don't be so self-assertive with me, boy. I won't tolerate that kind of arrogance."

"Only your kind is acceptable, is that it, Dad?"

The senator picked up a paperweight and was about to slam it down on the desk, but gained control and held back. He tossed the donut-shaped piece of purple glass from hand to hand, wet his lips with his tongue, and said, "My father once told me that if I continued to be flippant he would tie a rope around my balls using a stevedore's knot. I would never do that to you, son." He smiled sardonically, put down the paperweight, motioned with both hands for the boy to step forward, reached across his desk, patted him on the shoulder, and made an effort to turn his smile into an amiable laugh.

Jordan opened his mouth as if to speak, but held back. After an awkward moment, he asked, "Do you need me?"

His father stood quietly in thought, breathed deeply, then muttered, "Maybe later. Stick around."

Jordan turned to leave and immediately faced an out-of-breath Clarence in the richly adorned hallway. The secretary was quick to smile and ruffle the teenager's hair. After turning his eyes on the senator, now seated at his desk, the secretary looked back at the boy and winked before stepping into the office.

Jordan sang loudly and out-of-tune as he hurried away: "I'll be dining in the kitchen with Hilda, dining in the kitchen I know, know, know, dining in the kitchen with Hilda, strumming on the old banjo, la, la, la."

"What can I do for you, Senator?" Clarence asked as he approached the desk.

"I want you to take the limousine, drive to the home of James Barnes, and bring this so-called Birdman back to me. I'll be downstairs in the library." Named for the senator's grandfather, the Karl J. Rimespecker Library was located just below the second-floor office. Its doors opened onto the front entrance hall, a spacious, semi-circular area highlighted by flooring of inlaid tile depicting Egyptian art.

The senator's chauffeur immediately came to Clarence's mind. "Is Tony not on duty, sir?" the secretary asked meekly.

"I need *you* for this particular mission." Rimespecker pushed himself up from his chair. "You're familiar with the facts. Tony is not. I'd rather keep it that way. Understand?"

"Yes, sir. Any particular instructions?"

"No. Just see that he gets here." The senator tapped his desk again and again with his fingertips. "Well, wait a minute. Yes, there is something else. While you have him trapped in the limousine, pump him for what he knows. Subtly, of course. I'll do the rest."

Clarence started to leave, then turned back. "Am I to bring him and *only* him. He's a married man."

"What do you know about his family?"

"The Internet tells me he's got a son. Little else about family. College professor. Retired. Active with the local chapter of the Audubon Society, but then you know that. It seems he's a very popular fellow. He knows his birds! Speaks on ornithology throughout the area at various organizations and schools." Clarence cleared his throat and broke eye contact with his boss. "You've invited him here at a specific time?"

"No. In fact, I haven't invited him. He won't talk with me. You're simply to get him and bring him here. I think I've made that clear."

"But Senator ..."

"What do you know about her?"

"Who?"

"His wife."

"Nothing, really."

"Well, you can bring her, too, if it facilitates things. Come to think of it, her presence might open up the conversation. Sometimes with two, you can play one against the another. However, I don't think this occasion will call for that." Rimespecker leaned back in his swivel chair and began to move it to and fro. He smiled at the ceiling. "Remember Irene Pittman?'

"The horse woman?"

"Yes. She convinced her husband, right downstairs in our library, that their horses' excrement was suitable for growing mushrooms, and that the odor would not be carried by the wind to the Liverton housing development." The senator increased the speed of his swiveling. "Yes, indeed, sometimes it's good to have the wife along."

* * *

Laura had chosen herself as the designated driver for the trip home from the Black Bear Inn because she believed that her husband had imbibed in too much beer. Charley and Claudia occupied the back seats of the silver-blue sedan. Darkness was closing in on Route 33 when Laura reduced the car's speed after a "Deer Crossing" sign on a curving stretch of macadam through a heavily wooded stretch.

"The news hounds love little human interest stories," Charley remarked. "You take a picture of a puppy dog stranded on a piece of ice, flowing down the river. It'll be on every paper's front page, and it'll cap the six o'clock news on television. So, you can bet your bottom dollar that our bald-eagle story will hit the mainstream media if it hasn't already.'

"I shut down my eagle cam," Jimmy said to remind the others. "You know that, don't you?"

"Yeah, Jimmy, but you can't bring back what's already out there," Charley said. "Who knows how far this thing has gone. None of us saw tonight's six o'clock news."

"I enjoyed my cheese burger without the news," Laura said. "Peace. Peace at last."

"You may have started things, Jimmy, but you know damn well that the Twitter, Facebook and Instagram folks have already flooded the social media with it," Charley said. "Next up? Take a guess. Any reporter who chases after a cat-in-the-tree rescue would eagerly go after a tale of diamonds in an eagle's nest."

"Cat in a tree!" Laura exclaimed. "That reminds me." She tapped on Charley's shoulder. "Excuse me for interrupting, but what did you do with your cousin's cat?"

"I wanted to bury the cat right there in Cousin Ruth's backyard, near the patio," Claudia said quickly, before her husband had a chance to reply. "But Charley was insistent that Pinwheel might be evidence."

"Evidence of what?" Laura asked.

"We didn't know if Ruth's house had been burglarized," Charley explained. "We didn't even know what happened to Ruth. And we still don't. She might have been kidnapped or something. I just figured the cops wouldn't want us to touch anything. I covered the cat with one of those bulbous lids from a large roasting pan."

"Bugs will get at it," Laura said. "Flies will plant maggots."

"Let's hope we can push the cops into action by tomorrow," Jimmy said. "I'll follow up on your visits to the cop shops as well as my chat with Chief Morris. Another urgent call or two or three might light a fire. What's the reporting time for missing persons? Twenty-four or forty-eight hours?"

"Don't know for sure," Charley said. "I'm hoping it's just twenty-four."

"Maybe you should have talked to Senator Rimespecker when he called," Laura said while poking her husband in the side. "Senators get action."

"We don't know what the hell he wanted. Besides, at that point, I had had enough of the freakin' phone calls and was hungry for a cheese burger. I sure didn't need a lot of ballyhoo from Senator Rimespecker about the upcoming primary."

"Holy hell!" Charley exclaimed. "I'll be damned! Rimespecker! Oh, Jesus! I'll be a purple-spotted loony bird! It can't be, can it?"

"My God, what is it?" Claudia asked in a frenzied tone, shaped that way by her husband's outcry.

"Have you ever seen his wife?" Charley asked excitedly. "Her picture in the newspapers, on television. Oh, my God, I can't believe this. I could be wrong, of course. But I don't see how. I'm sure I'm right. Oh, jeez."

"What is it, Charley?" Jimmy barked. "Out with it, damn it!"

"Cousin Ruth's oil painting of that woman. That beautiful picture in her living room. It's a portrait of Senator Rimespecker's wife. I'm sure of it. Claudia! You saw it! Am I right?"

"I guess it could be her. But why would ..."

"Watch it!" Jimmy yelled when a car with flashing high beams came toward them, around a bend, causing Laura to swerve her sedan and nearly drive it into a tangle of Osage orange trees that leaned into the roadway. The twisted and knotted branches of the trees picked up flickering light from the moon, as did the surrounding brush, road surface, tulip poplars and other stately trees in the distance—all because a stream of small, fleecy clouds were racing across the sky breaking the moonlight into pieces. Laura maneuvered the car well, lining it up with the lane markings. It flickered with moonlight as it moved forward.

"Let's all calm down now," Claudia suggested. "It's been a long, long day for all of us. We're tired and yet worked up at the same time. I can actually feel my heart beating." She sucked in a deep breath. "Okay, yes, I do think that Ruth's oil painting could be a portrait of the senator's wife. The more I think of it, the more it seems so. It's not just the facial features. It's the way she's portrayed proudly holding herself in a certain way."

"This has really got me shaking in my boots" Charley said. "The choker! It's around her neck in the portrait. Why would Ruth paint that thing around her neck?"

"Calm down, folks," Jimmy said. "Man oh man, it does look like we have a mystery on our hands."

Attempts at calmness, didn't stop the chattering about the strange circumstances as Laura steered the sedan out of the darkness and onto a stretch of highway lighted by commercial establishments, including a motel, a car dealer, fast-food restaurants, office buildings and a plant nursery. Driving more slowly, she turned the car onto suburban streets that led to the Oakford neighborhood. There, she turned it onto Maple Lane from where the foursome traveled a circuitous route to the Barnes home. As they approached the house, they each exclaimed surprise in seeing a large, shiny, black limousine parked along the curb, partially blocking the driveway.

"What in the world have we here?" Laura asked in an intense whisper. She tapped the horn twice, prompting the limo driver to move his vehicle slightly, allowing the sedan room to enter the driveway. Laura made a quick decision to stop, rather than drive to the rear. She braked the car only a few feet from the limousine, choking off the engine abruptly.

"What the hell?" Jimmy muttered. "Perhaps we have some rich visitors. Anybody have a guess?"

"There's only one guy aboard," Charley commented. "The driver."

"Well, let's greet him," Jimmy suggested.

Without another word, Jimmy and Charley, followed by their wives, exited the sedan and stepped toward the limo, where Clarence had already slipped out of the driver's seat and stood against the door of the large, luxurious automobile.

Rimespecker's secretary believed it was his duty to speak first: "Please excuse my intrusion, ladies, gentlemen." He tipped his head. "My name is Clarence Exton. I'm Senator Joseph Rimespecker's personal secretary. I'm here to cordially invite Mr. James Barnes to a tête-à-tête with the senator." Clarence glanced from Charley to Jimmy and back again.

"I'm Jimmy Barnes." Stepping forward, Jimmy offered his hand tentatively.

After greeting Jimmy with a polite smile and a handshake, Clarence turned to the women and tipped his head again. "I'm assuming one of you gracious ladies is Mrs. Barnes.

Laura nodded. Her eyes revealed apprehension.

"Please, Mrs. Barnes, feel free to accompany your husband if you so wish. The senator would be most pleased to welcome you."

Jimmy grimaced. "And when is this meeting ... or, excuse me, this tête-à-tête ... When is it supposed to take place?"

"Right away, sir. As soon as we arrive at the Senator's residence."

"Sorry, but I'm not accustomed to being picked up and rushed off to a meeting on demand. Or tête-à-tête. What's this all about?" Jimmy looked up and to his left. "Let's go over there." He pointed. "Under the lamplight. I want to see your face." He moved and the others followed.

"The Ermengarde Choker," Clarence answered as he backed up against the lamppost.

The others formed a semicircle near him, each staring questions into his eyes. The light cast a shadow of the group on the sidewalk and the arborvitae shrubs that marked the corner of the Barnes property. The Oakford neighborhood was heavy with evergreens, pink and white dogwoods, azaleas and ornamental Japanese maples. Soon to offer deep shade, Norway maples lined the curving avenues of the community—an area with diverse styles of homes—some, new ranch-type houses and split-levels; others, older residencies like the Barnes' Dutch Colonial.

Before anyone had a chance to speak, a blue-and-white police cruiser pulled up to the lamppost. "Everything all right here?" asked the muscular, bull-faced sergeant who projected his head through the car's open widow. He was accompanied by a youthful blond patrolman in the passenger seat.

"Yes, officer," Jimmy responded. "Thanks for checking."

The sergeant took a lengthy moment to examine the group with intense up-and-down stares. "Have a good night." The sergeant gunned his engine, the cruiser moved away and the policemen continued to inspect the community.

"Perhaps you didn't catch my words," Clarence said to the group of four. "The senator wishes to speak with you about the Ermengarde Choker."

The women stared blankly at first. Charley and Jimmy looked confused. But all four were awakened quickly from their daze by the word choker. Claudia was the first to ask, "Do you mean the choker in the eagles' nest?"

Clarence nodded and smiled. "Yes, of course."

"What connection does Senator Rimespecker have with that piece of jewelry?" Claudia asked as thoughts about Ruth, the choker, the portrait and the dead cat raced around and around in her head.

"He owns it."

The Silvesters and Barneses were stunned. They glanced at each other with dumbfounded looks. Charley kept shaking his head. Jimmy frowned in puzzlement and bit his lower lip. Claudia muttered, "No, no, no," and lifted fingers to her mouth.

Charley pulled himself together and said, "We know the owner of that choker, Mr.... . What did you say your name was?"

"Exton. Clarence Exton."

"Yes, Mr. Exton. Our cousin ... That is, my wife's cousin, Ruth Nettlebaum ... She owns that choker. We're quite sure of that. Believe me, we're very familiar with that piece of jewelry. We first saw it three years ago."

"I'm sure that the senator will clarify things when we get together." Clarence directed his next words directly to the Silvesters: "May I ask your names?"

"Charley Silvester. And this is my wife, Claudia."

The secretary continued to focus on the Silvesters: "Since you folks seem to have an interest in the matter, I'm certain that Senator Rimespecker would insist that you join us." Clarence wondered briefly if he were taking a chance by inviting the entire group, but thought better of it within seconds. Surely his boss, he figured, would demand an explanation from anyone claiming to know the choker's owner. "So, why don't we all step into the limousine."

* * *

The trip to Senator Rimespecker's residence began in silence, in a large part because the Barnes and the Silvesters were still numbed by Clarence's disclosure and its implications. The secretary, too, was quiet, having no desire whatsoever to pump his passengers as requested by his boss. He offered a few pleasantries now and again.

It was Claudia who opened up discussion, one that was far afield from the subject plaguing the group: "Every time I see that beautiful painting of Jamey and his dog, Buster, I get weak in the knees and twitchy in the stomach. Not just because of what happened years ago, which still disturbs me, but from gnawing heartstrings, a yearning for another dog. Maybe we should rescue another greyhound, one just like Bingo."

Charley felt that his wife's effort to change the subject was deliberate. He stayed on topic. "Claudia, you're the one who resisted getting another greyhound. All these years you've fought the idea because you didn't want the trauma of losing a dog again. If you've changed your mind, hell, I'm all for it."

"I guess I'm pushed and pulled," Claudia whispered.

"Jimmy and I didn't get another dog because of the birds," Laura explained. "Buster wouldn't stop chasing them. And, as you know only too well, Jimmy's in the bird business. We have more birdhouses than cats have whiskers."

The escape into dog talk was brief. Silence reigned again until Clarence announced, "We're almost there," as he turned the limo onto a broad drive that curved among costly homes. "Just a few minutes more." Those words descended on his four passengers like the blade of a guillotine—not because of an upcoming tête-à-tête with a senator, but because of the incredulous circumstances and a dread of revelations. A queer feeling ran through Claudia's body as the image of Ruth's dead cat repeated itself in her mind, stirring up ugly thoughts of abhorrent things that might yet happen or be revealed.

* * *

Hilda appeared in the doorway of Senator Rimespecker's library ready to retrieve his dinner tray. A round and squatty woman with leathery skin, she cleared her throat twice to get the senator's attention before he looked up from the far end of a long, well-polished, mahogany table that occupied the center of the spacious room.

"Oh. You can come in, Hilda."

"Was it adequate, sir?" She waddled awkwardly along the table.

"It was just enough, Hilda. Thank you." Rimespecker found his cook to be an unpleasant woman who, it seemed, never smiled. But he relished her cooking. "I was particularly taken by the peppermill that accompanied my plate. Something new?"

Hilda nodded as she lifted the tray from the table where the senator had pushed it to one side. "It's not just black pepper, sir. It's a blend. I think they call it a medley."

"I'm well aware that it's a spicy medley—now." Rimespecker rattled off the ingredients without taking a breath: "Black peppercorns, pink peppercorns, coriander, white peppercorns, allspice and green peppercorns."

"You memorized that, sir?"

"Yes, I wanted to know exactly what was attacking my throat."

"Sorry, senator, if it was too ..."

Rimespecker interrupted: "Fear not, Hilda. I discovered it was fine in moderation. When I tempered my grinding, I found the acorn squash to be seasoned just right. A little warning was all I needed."

"My regrets, sir."

Clarence appeared in the doorway prompting the senator to immediately dismiss Hilda with a brisk thrust of the hand.

"Your guests are here, sir," Clarence announced as Hilda waddled away.

The senator was taken aback when four people followed his secretary into the library. The visitors were unaware of his jolt, however, because the ambience grabbed their attention. They were surrounded by a magnificent structure of wood panels between shelves of books on all four walls. The luster of the soft reddish-brown wood, accentuated by lighted sconces on the walls, gave a warm glow to the library and its large collection of richly, leather-bound books. Each wall held a ladder that reached from floor to ceiling and moved on rails, enabling easy removal of books from the upper shelves. Comfortable black leather chairs were arranged around the periphery of the room.

Senator Rimespecker rose slowly from his seat at the far end of the massive table as Clarence attempted to introduce all four individuals. He presented the Birdman with a flourish of details and explained why it was important that Laura accompany him. As he began to describe the Silvesters' place in the choker dilemma, he lost his usual smooth and unruffled manner, floundered slightly, and was interrupted by his boss, who displayed impatience.

"Exton, what are you trying to say? We're not holding a convention here in my library. I asked for one person, perhaps two. It was my intent to see Mr. Barnes."

"Please, sir. Let me finish. Mr. and Mrs. Silvester insist they know the current owner of the Ermengarde Choker."

"I own the Ermengarde Choker!" the senator proclaimed sharply.

Claudia's ire was piqued and she chimed in boldly: "I've seen that choker around the neck of my cousin several times. It meant the world to her, because it was a gift she cherished, apparently given to her a few years ago by someone she cared for deeply."

"You must be mistaken."

"No, Senator, I'm not mistaken." Claudia was forceful, emotional and red-faced. "And since there's a portrait of your wife in my cousin's living room, I'd say there's a good chance they know each other."

Charley stepped close to his wife and took her hand. He squeezed gently.

Senator Rimespecker was totally flabbergasted. His jowls quaked. Everyone in the room recognized his quandary. He shook his head and then spit out the words, "My wife's portrait?"

"At first, we were about ninety percent sure the painting depicted Mrs. Rimespecker," Charley explained. "Now we're one hundred percent certain. Put the puzzle together. The choker is on her neck in the portrait. Our cousin painted the portrait. The choker had been in your family, but was now our cousin's cherished belonging."

"Had been in my family! Hogwash!" The senator moved from behind the table and stepped toward the visitors. "I have the Geneva papers to prove ownership."

As the conversation grew tense, Jordan slipped quietly into the library. No one paid attention to him as he advanced toward one of the ladders, moving slowly with his back against the bookshelves. When he began to climb the ladder, he was noticed by his father and the others, but given little regard as the uneasy discourse continued.

Clarence waved his hand. "May I speak?"

"What is it, Exton?" The senator's tone was sharp.

"Sir, we do not have the Geneva papers. When you gave the Ermengarde to Mrs. Rimespecker, you signed the papers over to her, granting her full ownership. I signed as a witness to the transaction, notarized the papers and actually placed them in her hands." Clarence did not like the angry look on his boss's face, so he added, "She was overwhelmed by your magnificent gift, sir."

"But we still have the papers, don't we? In this state, what is owned by the wife is owned by the husband, and vice versa."

The room fell silent. Clarence hesitated to respond.

"Go on, Exton, say what's on your mind," the senator uttered gruffly.

"I looked for the papers, sir. I don't believe they're in this house. Keep in mind that Mrs. Rimespecker most likely would have signed the papers over to the new owner if she gave the choker away. It's even possible that the new owner would have already listed a beneficiary as recommended in the preface."

"No way would Lillian have done that!" The senator stepped close to the visitors, who could feel his rage and stepped back. He looked directly at Claudia. "This cousin. Who is she?"

Claudia hesitated. She wet her lips. Her mouth was dry. "We're talking about my cousin, Ruth. Ruth Nettlebaum. On my mother's side of the family. We've not been close, but have kept in touch over the years."

"This is insane! My wife doesn't know any such woman. I've never heard of anyone named Ruth Nettlebaum."

"She's missing now," Claudia added. "We can't locate her."

Senator Rimespecker stepped back as his chin dropped and his neck muscles quaked. He was suddenly so shaken that he was stymied for words. Clarence and the visitors sensed an outburst on the way, but nothing was said for a lengthy moment of tension. Finally, the senator said, "So is my wife. She's missing, too."

"They're both missing?" Jimmy questioned in a near whisper.

"That bitch!" the senator yelled. "That fuckin' bitch! What the hell are you up to, Lillian? Goddamn you. You can rot in hell if you did anything with that choker. Your portrait in some freakin' woman's house? What the hell? After all I've given you, how could you be so deceitful?"

From the top of the ladder came the heartbroken voice of a 16-year-old boy: "Stop it!" Jordan screamed. "Stop it! Stop it! Stop it! She's my mother," he cried as tears trickled down his cheeks. "Don't say things like that about my mother!" He drew his fists, reached out with his arms, lost his balance and came crashing down the ladder, hitting the floor with a heavy thud.

Several in the gathering shouted, "Call nine, one, one!" Others pulled forth their cellphones, and all six ran to the teenager and hovered over him. Clarence knelt and felt the boy's pulse. Jordan was conscious, breathing hard, and whimpering. His left arm was obviously broken, for it was twisted into an odd angle. Blood dripped from his mouth where his tongue had been ripped open by his teeth.

Chapter Six

Clarence Exton lived with his 87-year-old mother in a brownstone row-house in Cloverton City. Gertrude Exton was not in good health, and Clarence did his best to care for her. She had been a hypochondriac for most of her life, so tending to her needs was nothing new for him. A next-door neighbor, a jovial woman named Terry Smythe, looked in on her daily. Clarence had known Terry for a host of years. They were more than good friends, and many in the neighborhood wondered why they hadn't married years ago.

Senator Rimespecker's private secretary had struggled through a strenuous day, capped by a trip to the hospital with young Jordan. So, clocks were pointing to midnight by the time he arrived at his mother's bedside.

"Where have you been?" Gertrude whined as her only son stood looking down on her as she lay curled on her side in a four-poster bed, a blanket pulled up and wrapped tightly around her neck. The handsomely decorated bedroom was adorned with organdy curtains and prints of oil paintings by Matisse and Monet. Clarence had bedecked the room with care and even nursed a struggling fern attempting to grow in a pot on a window sill. His mother turned from her side and lay flat on her back as she looked up at her son from a heavily lined face and asked, "Did you pick up my Depends and Metamucil?"

"Mom, I didn't have time to stop at the drugstore." Clarence leaned down and kissed her on the cheek. "I'll get your things tomorrow, Saturday. I'm home for the weekend."

Gertrude turned her head and glanced at the clock on the bedtable, which was but inches from her pillow. She kept her blanket above her breasts, covering her thin, undernourished body. "Oh, my goodness. It's after midnight."

"I came directly home from Bitterlick Memorial Hospital. Jordy Rimespecker may have a concussion. We don't know yet. He fell off a library ladder and broke his arm. He's pretty banged up. The senator was still with him when I left the emergency room."

"Oh, the poor boy. I hope he'll be all right."

"I'll tell you more tomorrow. Okay? I'm exhausted. Gotta hit the sack before I collapse."

"Terry called for you three times."

"I'll see her in the morning for our usual Saturday coffee klatch." Clarence quickly added, "That is, after you and I have breakfast and time together." He kissed her again.

* * *

Clarence tapped on the door of the adjoining brownstone to the north side of the Exton property at mid-morning—a three story house nearly identical to the other brownstones in the city-block of 12 dwellings dating back to the days of carriage houses. Only items such as window boxes, shudders and other add-ons distinguished the row-houses from each other. Saturday morning was bright with sunshine, and, in the brilliance of the morning, Clarence looked like a different species of hominid than the one who walked the halls of the senator's residence attired in a suit and necktie. He wore a red sweatshirt that pictured a cartoonish, smiling raccoon on front and the words "Save Wildlife" on the back. Even his manners differed. He seemed to swing his arms more freely, perhaps like someone freed from a straightjacket.

Terry Smythe wore a broad grin when she opened the door and welcomed her friend and neighbor with a bear hug. "Where have you been? You slept late this morning. And what happened last night? I waited up." She broke loose, kissed his nose and backed up. "Come in! Come in!" She grabbed his hand and tugged. "How's your mother?" Terry was a boundlessly happy person, a truly cheerful soul, but one who could cry easily over the misfortunes of others. Compassionate to the nth degree, she was the kind of friend that Clarence needed. Pleasant looking and middle-aged, she was slightly rounded, but not fat, and owned a thick head of died amber-colored curls.

"Mom's okay, but I had a bitch of a Friday night."

"Come on. The coffee pot's on." Terry led the way. "You can tell me about all your troubles." She hurried through the house to the kitchen and beyond into a sunroom affixed to the rear of her home only a year

49

ago. The glass-enclosed room offered a full view of her small garden outside. "Sit down. Guess what? I got you those glazed doughnuts you're so crazy about."

"You know how to please a guy," Clarence said as he took a seat at a white table against the back wall of glass—a table already arranged for company with placemats, dishes, cups and a pot of coffee at center. All the furniture in the sunroom was white, including the wicker chairs, as Terry had long envisioned it. The addition was a dream she had long fancied, something she wanted to create for herself and her guests. Having it built was a huge step for Terry, for she didn't own much and lived on inherited income. After placing a dish of doughnuts on the table, she poured the coffee.

As soon as Terry sat, Clarence began pouring out the traumatic events of the previous night. He didn't forget much, but avoided a major one with broad aspects. He laid out most details from when he picked up the Silvesters and Barneses until Jordan's fall from the ladder. But he held back when it came to innuendos regarding a serious relationship between the senator's wife and the woman known as Ruth. At this stage of the conversation, he was protective of Lillian Rimespecker. Why? He wasn't sure. Loyalty, perhaps. He had known her and admired her for so many years.

Terry punctuated the discourse with an abundance of outcries and a few expletives.

"As I drove everyone home from the hospital, I listened to the Birdman and this guy Charley talking about using Boy Scouts to help move rocks in Bitterlick Creek. Apparently they want to damn part of the creek to force the rapids to one side so they can pool some of the water and build an open, flat area to stand on under the eagles' nest. It seems the scoutmaster at Troop 24 is open to the idea—if, in return, the Birdman teaches the scouts about eagles. I guess the kids'll earn some merit badges."

"Are you saying someone's gonna climb up to the nest from this open spot in the creek?"

"I don't know. Nobody's allowed to get near the nest until the eagles leave it. Even the cops won't touch it."

"This is all so crazy." Terry mused for a moment, studied Clarence's face, and then showed a knowing expression as if awakening from a thought. "You're worried about the senator's son, aren't you?"

"Oh, yeah. And not just because of his crash-landing in the library.

He'll heal physically. I'm more worried about his mental well-being. There are things going on inside that kid that scare me. For years, he never acted up. Was never smart-alecky. Never talked back to his old man, even when the going got rough. But now-a-days I see signs of rebellion. Don't get me wrong. He's still a good kid, but I'd like to help keep him that way."

"How old is he?"

"Sixteen. Two years ago they hung a painting of the happy family in the senator's office. Jordy hugged his father that day. It was a real hug of pride and happiness. I don't think I've seen such a hug since. These days, I see a slow burn in his eyes too often. I want so damn much to heal his wounds, but I don't know how."

"Kids that age often rebel, often get angry with their parents."

"In this case, it's the senator's fault. He's become more and more difficult in recent years. It wasn't that way back in the governor's mansion. And things at home poured like gravy during his first years in the Senate. I'll admit that Rimespecker was always somewhat aloof, but Jordy seemed proud of him back then." Clarence sipped coffee and bit into a doughnut. He cleared his throat. "I'm well aware that my feelings for the boy are a sticky element in all of this. I'm not stupid. I know I'm too closely bound to Jordy. I can't help it. I feel like his father. It's not something I can squeeze or cut out of my body or brain."

"How does he feel about you?"

"Oh, we're tight. I know he cares. And that's part of the problem, too. Say you have a daughter, Terry. And she becomes emotionally attached to your secretary and alienated by you. How would you feel? How would you react? What would that do to your relationship with your daughter? With your secretary? The steam in your pressure cooker could blow."

"Maybe you're overreacting."

"No, no. Listen to me. When Jordy was a little tot, he'd get so excited when I'd stay over on a rare occasion. He'd get all wiggly and crawl into my bed in the middle of the night." Clarence stared at Terry with beseeching eyes that asked for understanding. "I'm trying to say, the bond was built long ago and tightened through more than a decade."

"How did you meet Mr. Rimespecker in the first place?"

"At the golf club."

When a young man, Clarence had become involved with the Rimespeckers when he was a caddy at the West Bitterlick Golf Club. He had caddied for an elderly gentleman named Peter Moorley, a retired dentist, who failed to show up one day. That same day, Governor Rimespecker's caddy tripped in the rough, broke his leg, and was whisked away in an ambulance. Clarence eagerly filled in and caddied for the young governor, who was experiencing only his second year in office. Dinner with the Rimespeckers followed. And the relationship was born. Lillian quickly grew to like Clarence and started to call on him for other duties. She was impressed by his easy rapport with her only child, and grew even fonder of him when Clarence introduced the boy to books. The first story he read to the youngster was Toby Tyler, the tale of the boy who ran away from home to join the circus and suffered a broken heart when tragedy struck his beloved monkey, Mr. Stubbs. During those early days, Clarence was quick to point out to Lillian the many lessons a child learns from a book such as Toby Tyler.

"You love him?" Terry asked, already knowing the answer.

"I could never stand by and see him hurt. I'd have to throw some sort of a lasso. But what? How?"

"Maybe we should change the subject." Terry couldn't miss seeing the moisture in Clarence's eyes. "You're getting worked up, and you're still on your first doughnut. I brought a dozen, especially for you."

"I'm sorry." Clarence sipped coffee and bit into his doughnut. "They're good. Really good."

"You haven't looked out at my garden. We all have such tiny backyards in this block. And I made mine smaller by adding this sunroom. But look what I've done with my puny space."

"I see. I see. What are those clusters of white flowers? They're beautiful. And I like the way you've arranged them. They contrast with the greenery."

"They're called stars-of-Bethlehem. Each plant has thick clusters of star-shaped flowers. They're a perennial, so they'll come up every year. I'm told they're aggressive. They spread and take over. But I don't care. Let the yard fill up with them. Picture what a deluge of them will look like each spring." Terry laughed heartily.

"Well that solves springtime planting for the future, doesn't it?" Clarence's eyes told Terry that he needed to get back to the subject haunting him: Jordan Rimespecker's plight.

"I know where your mind is."

"Sorry."

"Go on. Get back to the boy." Terry presented her compassionate smile and tipped her head to the side. "You never mention his mother."

"Oh, but I was about to! That's the icing on the cake. Or, I should say, the putrid icing on the rotten cake. That festering mess exploded last night." Clarence's coffee had cooled somewhat, permitting him to gulp it, and he did, sputtering with his last swallow. "Sorry."

Terry tossed him an extra napkin. "You're excited. Calm down."

"Jordy always had his mother to run to if he were hurt. Their love was boundless. And I'm sure that love is still there, but it's being shrouded by her obsession with something or someone outside the family. She's pulling away into some sort of fanciful delight. She's floating in a happy bubble. I always admired her levelheadedness. Now? Well, her head is somewhere else."

"Sounds to me like she's passionately in love with some guy. And if the Senator is growing horns, maybe she has reason. It's easy to fall out of love with a bastard."

"That crossed my mind. But it's not that. I know that now. But only since last night." Clarence rose from his chair and stood.

"Where are you going?"

"Nowhere." Clarence walked around in a circle. "The senator's been oblivious to it all! Has been for months, maybe years. Her euphoria isn't new. It's been building over time. But recently it's blossomed. It's really speeded up. Like I said, he's been blind to it." Clarence returned to the table and sat. "Until last night's explosion." With his elbows on the table, he hung his head between his hands.

"You're avoiding something, aren't you?"

"What do y'mean?"

"Well, let me get this straight. A piece of jewelry worth big bucks is transferred somehow from a senator's wife to a woman named Ruth and then to some bald eagles. And little old Ruthy hangs a portrait of the senator's wife on her living-room wall. And, by coincidence, both women are missing today." Terry crossed her eyes and made a silly face. "Come on, now! Maybe you're the one who's missing something."

"We don't know how these things are linked together."

"Clarence! For God's sake! I know how you were brought up. I know how you find certain subjects distasteful. And I know how protective you can be. On top of all that, you care deeply for the senator's wife." Terry shook her head. She rose and looked down on Clarence. "The first thing any other person with your knowledge would have said on coming into my house today is: 'Guess what, Terry! Senator Rimespecker's wife is having a lesbian affair with a woman name Ruth!'"

"No! Because we don't know if that's true."

"Are you that naïve, Clarence? You just don't want to believe, do you?"

"No one has used the words lesbian or gay yet. Having known her ..." He struggled for words. "It's almost impossible for me to ... It could be a close relationship that's not sexual. Do-gooders can get mighty close to someone they're helping. Mrs. Rimespecker might be getting a high from helping a poor soul named Ruth find her way out of a miserable life. "

"And I'm a cockeyed polecat." Terry rolled her eyes. "Have another doughnut."

Chapter Seven

"It's for you," Claudia said as she reached out with the kitchen phone, holding it toward the table where Charley was drinking his third mug of coffee. "It's Jimmy the Birdman." Charley grabbed the phone and Claudia returned to the sink to rinse more breakfast dishes before placing them in the dishwasher. She had guessed it was Jimmy when the phone rang, because early morning calls on Sunday were infrequent and Jimmy had called at least a half-dozen times on Saturday. Claudia suspected the high frequency was the new normal.

"We might have a serious problem," Jimmy said.

"Why? What's up?" Charley pushed aside his coffee mug.

"One of those ... Damn, what are they called? My mind just went blank."

"Baby eagles?"

"No! No! Those new toys that men like to play with. They buzz around, snoop on people, hover overhead, blow things up in the Middle East."

"Drones!"

"Yeah, drones!" Jimmy screamed. "Drones, drones, drones. Why do I forget that word?"

"Lower your voice," Charley suggested. "I've got drones in my backyard. Live ones."

Jimmy didn't respond.

"My male honeybees, Jimmy! Actually, I've got only a few of them left this spring. The gals tossed out most of the guys during the winter cold."

"This is serious, Charley. We got a man-made drone flying overhead along Bitterlick Creek. Chief Morris called. Said it was first spotted about seven o'clock this morning. He figured it might be hunting for the nest. I figure so, too. It went away at seven-forty and came back, then took off again about twenty minutes ago."

"Oh, boy! And I keep worrying about guys on the ground. Climbers. Every scenario that twists around in my head is a bottom-up job. Never thought of anybody looking down from above."

"Something else. A reporter from the *Beacon* named Carney Cox called me late last night. Got me out of bed. He asked me questions about Senator Rimespecker's wife. I told him what I knew, which wasn't much. Apparently, Chief Morris gave him my name."

"Surprised he didn't call me."

"Cox was on deadline and really rushed. He picked up something about Lillian Rimespecker last night on the police radio and followed up with Morris. Apparently the senator's wife is officially missing now. I guess the hunt's on."

Claudia reached over her husband's shoulder to retrieve his coffee mug, but he grabbed her hand and held onto the mug. She pecked a kiss on the back of his neck, then stepped to the window and pushed back the curtains to allow more sunlight to stream across the table. The morning was bright and cloudless. After glancing at her husband with a questioning stare, she seized a notepad from the cabinet, scribbled words, and placed the note before him: "Don't forget you promised to plant marigold seeds today."

"Getting back to the drone," Jimmy said. "We're lucky in one regard. Our eagles didn't build at the very top of a tree. Some nests are way out there in the open. In our case, the outcropping of rock from the cliff, coupled with those tangled branches, gives some cover."

Charley held Claudia's note in the air, nodded to his wife and smiled briefly while speaking to Jimmy: "I know we're gonna surround the area with watchdogs, but, let's face it, we can't hang anyone up in the air."

"Which reminds me, I completed your list of birdwatchers. I'll drop it off today. I've talked to a few from my list, and they're eager to help. The older, retired guys actually get excited about camping out together. We're adding a little adventure to their lives."

"What about the maps?"

"They're finished. I'm about to draw vertical and horizontal lines through them. That'll create squares of land, each to be assigned to a captain and his team." Jimmy cleared his throat. "Listen, Charley, I'm aware there'll be leaks in our effort. But I figure our overall scheme will keep people away if we make a big enough splash. The media will eat it up. Now, we have to synchronize things."

"I've been toying with that. I know we have computers to link us together, but I think we'd do a far better job if we worked at the same location. Get the wives to join us, and we could have four phones going at the same time. That way, we can help each other when we have questions. Hell, you know birdwatchers better than I do. I can hear myself asking, 'Will this guy make a good captain?'"

"Well, you wanna come here?"

Claudia left the kitchen and hurried through the house, remembering that neither she nor Charley had fetched the morning newspaper. Outside, she looked skyward and breathed in the fresh air twice before picking up the newspaper and returning to the house. As she entered the kitchen, she heard Charley say:

"No, Jimmy. You and Laura come here. I'll clear the dining-room table, and we can lay out the maps, lists, and whatever. I'll even lower our Tiffany lamp so it floods the table with light like in a factory."

"Okay," Jimmy responded. "I'll buy that."

Claudia hit Charley on the head with the newspaper before tossing it on the table.

"Ouch!" he yelled. "What the hell?"

"You okay, Charley?" the birdman asked.

With her hands on her hips, Claudia glowered at her husband. "Turn our dining room into a factory? Lower the Tiffany lamp?"

"I gotta go, Jimmy. See you when you deliver the stuff."

Claudia grabbed the phone, lifted it high, and pretended she was going to strike his head with it. Instead, she returned it with a thud to the cabinet.

"Stop it!" Charley grinned, grabbed his wife and hugged tightly.

"I just wanted to be consulted." She kissed him.

"I know." Charley unfurled the newspaper and laid it out on the table. "Wow!" he exclaimed as he gazed down on the front page. "Quite a headline. But I'm really not surprised."

"Oh, my! They did play it big." Claudia quickly sat in the chair next to her husband, and together they read:

Senator's Wife Missing, Police Initiate Search

Rimespecker Alleges Spouse Kidnapped By Jewel Thief

By Carney Cox
Staff Writer, The Cloverton Beacon

The wife of U.S. Senator Joseph Rimespecker has been missing for two days and police from East and West Bitterlick Townships have joined with Cloverton City police in a joint effort to locate her.

The search will be expanded nationally by Tuesday if the local effort fails to find Lillian Rimespecker and a woman named Ruth Nettlebaum of Old South County Road. Both women have been unaccounted for since Friday morning and are believed to be together, according to Police Chief Harry Morris of East Bitterlick.

Senator Rimespecker, in an interview with *The Beacon*, claims that Nettlebaum is a jewel thief who kidnapped his wife. The Ermengarde Choker, a gift from the senator to his wife worth millions of dollars, was reported missing Friday and is believed to be the jewelry sighted in a bald eagles' nest high above Bitterlick Creek.

No authority has confirmed a kidnapping, according to Chief Morris, and the FBI is not involved in the search at this time.

Professor Emeritus James Barnes, well known locally as the Birdman, told this reporter that relatives of Nettlebaum insist that she is the owner of the Ermengarde Choker. "Somehow that choker was lifted from her house and landed in that eagles' nest," said Barnes, a retired Cornell ornithologist and president of the local chapter of the Audubon Society. "Nettlebaum's cat was found dead on her property, apparently attacked by a large bird of prey," he said.

Barnes is organizing an effort to protect the baby eagles and secure the choker until it can be retrieved after the young birds leave the nest. Bald eagles are a protected species.

Legend has it that the Ermengarde Choker once belonged to the princely family Hapsburg and has been passed down since the 11th Century. Despite investigative research by many, this lineage has never been proven. The choker ended up in Swiss hands before its transfer to this country.

The Beacon was unable to reach Clarence Exton, the senator's private secretary, for comment on this story. Jordan Rimespecker, the senator's 16-year-old son, refused comment.

* * *

As the Silvesters read the *Beacon* news story, a New York City taxicab driver was on his last lap of a long drive from Manhattan, carrying two women he eyed again and again in his rear-view mirror. He had just turned onto Old South County Road when he took another look and saw Ruth's head on Lillian's shoulder. Although riding down from the north, the women had insisted he approach Ruth's house from the south, which meant a circuitous route around Cloverton City and two townships before making his approach.

It was Lillian's decision to travel by taxi rather than take the train in an effort to avoid crowds. An incident in the hotel lobby had made her a bit paranoid—something she couldn't shake off no matter how many times she scolded herself for being silly. Ruth had admired and picked up a silver sugar bowl from an elegant tea service on display in the gift shop, held it in an obscure manner, and carried it a considerable distance to show Lillian. A male security employee quickly seized her by the elbow believing she was stealing it. The incident created a brief scene that ended quickly thanks to adroit handling by Lillian, who was unnerved by the episode, especially because she was forced to show identification.

Lillian's mind was in hectic mode during much of the trip home. Ordinarily unruffled, she fretted over their next moves, feared confrontations she wanted to avoid, and worried about her son, Jordan. She spent considerable time listening to incoming calls on her cellphone—recorded calls she had not answered, yet she had not erased. Responding to any cell calls had been ruled out, by her command, before the start of the trip. But tearing at her heartstrings were the many recorded pleas she heard from Jordan. His were the most frequent calls and the most painful.

Ruth's house was suddenly in view in a clearing ahead.

"Stop!" Lillian yelled as she pushed Ruth aside. "Driver! Stop immediately!" Her heartbeat raced and her hand trembled as she knocked on the glass divider between her and the driver. "Can you hear me, driver? Stop the car!"

The cabbie, an elderly man of Mediterranean descent, jammed on the brakes and pulled the yellow cab into thick brush. The county road had little shoulder. "What is it?" he asked in a startled voice.

Lillian poked Ruth. "Look! Look ahead! On your lawn!"

It took Ruth but an instant to focus on two blue-and-white police cruisers in front of her house. "What are they doing at my place?"

"Turn around!" Lillian ordered the cabbie. "Quick! Get us out of here! You hear me? Turn completely around and take us back to New York. Understand?"

The driver was stunned. "But Miss, we just came about two hundred miles, and you took me way out of the way to get ..."

"Don't talk! Just go, damn it! Go!"

The cabbie, a short but stocky man with olive skin, gunned the engine and attempted a difficult U-turn, having to pull the car out of dense growth to make a tight turn on a narrow, two-lane road. Twice he had to back up the taxicab before going forward.

"What about Pinwheel?" Ruth yelled. "We can't go without him!"

"Ruth, listen to me. We have to get out of here. Understand? Right away!"

"I left him only enough food for a couple days. I love that cat! What will happen to him? Please! Turn around and get my cat. I love Pinwheel! I love him so much!"

"What do you want me to do?" the driver asked angrily.

"Keep going! Get us off this road," Lillian bellowed. "There's an intersection about a half mile ahead. Make a left there onto Pine Hollow Road. It'll get us back to Route 9, which leads to the Throughway Bypass."

"No!" Ruth screamed. She began to pull on Lillian's sleeve. "Pinwheel's been my companion for more than a decade. He's all I had for a long time. I love him so much! Please!" She pulled so hard on Lillian's blouse that it tore at the neck.

"Stop it Ruth!" Lillian barked. "You're hurting me! You're ripping my clothes!"

"Please! Please! Those cops? What will they do to my cat?"

"They'll probably take him to the SPCA. They're not going to hurt someone's pet."

Minutes later, the cab driver turned the taxicab onto Pine Hollow Road, an extremely narrow roadway composed of pebbles and tar spread on uneven earth. The narrow lane was remindful of a rural driveway through the woods to, perhaps, a farmhouse or a camper's cabin. The taxi rocked and bumped its way forward under low hanging branches of pines, hickories, pin oaks and silver maples that eventually gave way to scrub pines, sassafras and low-growing woody shrubs and thick underbrush. The change reduced the canopy, opening up the sky at stretches.

"Y'sure y'know watcha talkin' about, lady! I don't think this road's gonna ..."

"Yes it will!" Lillian barked. "I know this country. I know these roads. Just keep going. When I was a young Governor's wife I traveled with the state surveyor to every piece and parcel of land governed by my husband." She raised her voice. "On his orders! He didn't want a wife, speaking at women's clubs and elsewhere, who didn't know our constituents' territory."

The driver was dumbfounded by the fact that one of his passengers claimed to be a former governor's wife, yet he was taking her and a too-cozy companion on a backroad escape route. He was troubled by his speculation that the women were fleeing police. All kinds of bizarre thoughts raced through his head.

The sassafras and brush soon gave way to cultivated land. A field of dark green alfalfa seemed to stretch endlessly on one side of the road. Recently plowed earth awaited spring planting on the other side. Also, the road became less difficult to travel. Now, the constant bright sunlight turned the taxicab into a steady glow of yellow as it picked up speed. At the ramp to Route 9, Lillian directed the driver to turn left on the highway and stop at an upcoming strip mall.

"Please pull up to the drugstore at the far end of the strip," Lillian said.

The mall was small and relatively new—one of those redbrick and white-trimmed strips of Early American design with display windows divided into many small panes of glass. The cabbie did as directed, parking the car under a lamppost in front of the pharmacy. But even a move as simple as that caused apprehension within him, simply because he was so distressed and distrustful. Surely they weren't going to rob the store? The thought was there, though he tried to shake it off as ridiculous.

"Stay here, Ruth." Lillian instructed. "I won't be long."

"What are you looking for?"

"A newspaper. I want to see if the press is on top of things." Lillian didn't wait for the driver to help her out of the cab. He was on his way when she pushed right by him and strode quickly to the double doors of the drugstore. Inside, she looked for a newspaper or magazine rack.

"May I help you?" asked a young, freckled, redheaded clerk who was busy sorting and arranging packages of cough drops on a nearby counter. He glanced up and did a double take.

"I'm looking for today's *Beacon*," Lillian said in rushed words.

"Over against the wall." The young man pointed while feeling a tingle race up his spine. "Near the cosmetics."

Lillian hurried, found the *Beacon*, and stood there in front of cosmetics reading the front-page story about her disappearance, the choker, and her husband's claim of kidnapping—a claim that caused her to laugh out loud. Her roar was cynical and contemptuous. After reading the last few words, she folded the newspaper, hurried to the clerk, tossed a few coins and immediately threw the paper in a trash receptacle at the front exit.

The salesclerk watched her leave and took note of the taxicab.

Ruth had remained quiet but slightly weepy since her outburst over Pinwheel, but was eager for Lillian's return to the taxi with the newspaper and immediately asked for it when her companion slipped into the back seat next to her—this time with the help of the cabbie, who politely held the door.

"Where's the paper."

"They were sold out," Lillian responded. "Let's move, Cabbie. Continue north, the way we were going."

Inside the pharmacy, the young redhead hurried to the trash receptacle and retrieved the newspaper. He scanned the Rimespecker story, reading only parts of it, before sliding behind the cough-drop counter, pulling forth his cellphone and punching numbers.

"Ma, it's me. Hey, look, remember that pink rally for breast cancer you forced me to drive you to last fall?"

"At the school grounds," his mother responded. "Yes, I remember. I wore that pink hat that Sally gave me."

"That lady speaker with the pink scarf that kept blowing in the wind? Remember? Senator's wife? She was the speaker at the rally before the march."

"Senator Rimespecker's wife. She's missing. Her husband says she was kidnapped. I know all about the choker in the eagles nest."

"She was just here! Honest t'God. I'm sure it was her."

"In the drugstore?"

"Yeah! That's what I'm saying. Right here. Bought a copy of today's *Beacon* and tossed it away. She took off in a taxicab. New York cab, I think."

"Call nine-one-one."

"You think?"

"Yes. Call nine-one-one. Did Harvey see her?"

"No. He was in the back of the store. This happened only minutes ago. She just took off."

"Call nine-one-one."

Lillian was unsettled because of the lack of sympathy she had shown when Ruth displayed anguish over the possible loss of, or separation from, her beloved cat. Highly empathetic as a rule, she was well aware that apprehension was messing with her psyche. Now, with knowledge of the cat's death, she was truly fearful of how Ruth might respond if told. But lying about the newspaper had only deepened her discomfort.

As the taxicab approached the throughway ramp, her thoughts of Jordan and his pleas, added more distress on top of her anguish. Ruth could feel Lillian's agony. She sensed that this was not the resolute and unfaltering woman she knew—a woman who seemed so sure of her every move.

Lillian was quiet for the next several miles of travel on the throughway, where traffic was heavy. Then, all of a sudden, she blurted: "I've got to see my son! Somehow, I have to see Jordan."

"Do you want to turn back?" Ruth asked as she slipped her arm under Lillian's arm and squeezed.

"I want to go on a cruise with you. I want us to cruise the Caribbean or the Mediterranean. That's what I want. But I want to see Jordan first. I have to talk with him. He'll never understand completely. But I have to try to ..."

Ruth interrupted: "Then let's go back."

"No. We'll go to New York, stay tonight, and then make arrangements for a cruise. But before we sail, I will somehow see my son." Lillian pecked a quick kiss on Ruth's cheek, and then confessed, "I lied to you about the newspaper. I read the story about us in the *Beacon*, then tossed it away because I didn't want you to know."

"Know what?"

"This is going to hurt."

"What is it?" Ruth tensed.

"Pinwheel's dead, honey. I'm so, so sorry." Lillian wrapped her arm around Ruth.

"What are you saying?" Ruth's words quivered. She pushed herself away from Lillian. "What do you mean he's dead?"

"Oh, sweetheart, I didn't want to tell you. He was found dead in your house."

"No!" Ruth screamed. "No! No! No!" Tears began to run down Ruth's cheeks. Within seconds she was weeping heavily and struggling to breathe. Her crying turned into heavy sobbing. Loud guttural bawling followed as her body shook uncontrollably.

"Hold onto me!" Lillian demanded as Ruth's blubbers slowed to sniffles.

"Why my Pinwheel? How could this happen?"

"I don't know. The paper said maybe a big bird attacked him."

Suddenly Ruth cried out again, "Oh, my God, no! I love you, Pinwheel! Oh, Pinwheel, I wanna hold you, sleep with you. You never hurt anyone, Pinwheel. Why would ..."

"I know it hurts, honey." Lillian said. "But you have me now. You have me to love. I'll take care of you." She started to say something about the choker, but held back. Seconds later, it blurted from her lips: "Aren't you worried about the choker? You fret over your unfortunate cat, but what about those diamonds, emeralds and rubies worth millions?"

Lillian's words didn't rest well, turning Ruth's whimpers into wails. She cried out with imperceptible words. Her screams, bellows and shrieks so unnerved the cabbie that he pulled the car to the shoulder of the highway, applied the brake and removed his trembling hands from the steering wheel.

"What's the matter, driver? Please keep going."

The cabbie said nothing. Within minutes his foot fed fuel and the taxi proceeded north again.

Speaking softly, Lillian said, "Ruth, I'm going to settle you down in a beautiful hotel room for the night. I want to see my son. I have to. I'll be back for you in the morning."

"No!" Ruth screamed.

Chapter Eight

Senator Rimespecker sat at his office desk, at home, not in Washington as intended. His expression showed embitterment and ire. His eyes did not focus on anything in the room, but stared distantly. He was jolted when Clarence stepped into the office, even though he had summoned him from his brownstone home several miles away in Cloverton.

"You missed your plane?" the secretary asked.

"I cancelled." The senator shook his head as if trying to stir himself from deep reflection. "I rescheduled for an early morning flight, but I'm coming back right after the vote on the highway bill." He rose from his swivel chair and motioned to Clarence, telling him to approach. "Thanks for coming in on a Sunday night."

"You saved me from tomorrow morning's traffic." Actually, Clarence was not as pleased as he pretended, since his weekend was ending quickly without completion of his goals. His mother's coughing spells and shortness of breath had kept him home for a good part of Sunday afternoon. Chores had eaten away much of the day. He had been forced to scratch his plan to visit Jordan at the hospital.

"I want to work out a strategy with you and Jordan."

Clarence stepped close to the desk. "What kind of strategy, sir?" He was immediately apprehensive.

"Fetch Jordan. I don't intend to explain things twice. Oh, and be sure to use your cellphone. That, apparently, is the only way he wants to be summoned."

Clarence was dumfounded. "He's in the hospital, isn't he?"

"No. I had Tony pick him up a couple hours ago."

"You're kidding? How is he?"

"He's fine."

"I intended to visit him ..."

Rimespecker interrupted: "He doesn't need to be pampered. He's fine." The senator sat again, opened a bottom drawer, grabbed his electric shaver and began to trim above his upper lip. "Two days growth," he muttered.

While the secretary used his cellphone to call Jordan, the boy's father continued to shave and talk at the same time: "Jordan won't like it, but I'm going to keep him home from school tomorrow and everyday thereafter until the trap has sprung. And you will be his jail keeper, Clarence. Understand? I know he's been trying to contact his mother. And that's been okay until now. I'm sure it's stirred the juices. But it's time to close that portal and let the juices boil."

Even though Clarence was on his phone, he heard his boss use his first name, and he recognized a particular tone of voice—both indicators that he was about to be dragged into a family matter of great concern. "Jordy is on his way, sir."

The senator said nothing as he continued to shave. But as soon as his son limped into the room wearing blue-and-white striped pajamas, he returned his shaver to the bottom drawer. "Why don't you sit over there, Clarence?" He pointed to his left where a couple ladder-back chairs hugged the wall. "And you sit over there, my boy." He pointed to his right, the opposite wall, where more ladder-backs awaited visitors. All chairs in the Senator's office were strategically placed—some for separation, others to encourage contact, most to put the senator in a dominate position.

Clarence was slow to take his assigned seat, for he was eying Jordan, examining him from head to foot. The boy's left arm was in a plaster cast and held in a sling. He was patched with bandages around his mouth and chin. Cuts, scratches and discoloration marked his flesh here and there, and Clarence suspected the boy's pajamas covered body bruises. The secretary took his seat only after watching Jordan limp to his chair.

Jordan made no effort to improve his mood. He displayed the same seething expression that had marked his countenance on the night he fell from the library ladder. Breathing hard, he leaned his arms on his legs just above the knees, gripped his hands and entwined his fingers, hung his head and stared at the floor.

"This is the way things are going to work around here for an extended period," the senator said. "Except for a few hours tomorrow, I'll be here in this house indefinitely, but will appear to be in Washington. No one is to know I'm returning here tomorrow. Understand?"

Remindful of statues by Rodin, Clarence and Jordan didn't even nod their heads or move a muscle.

"Jordan, you will remain here, in this house, incommunicado, until my plan has succeeded. Clarence will make sure you do, in the event I can't keep track. Hilda will be temporarily dismissed. You will prepare meals, Exton. Sandwiches will do."

Rimespecker's sudden return to calling Clarence by his surname made the secretary feel he had been demoted from a member of the family to a slave of the workforce. Actually, he preferred it that way, because it created a sense of distance. Finally, he had the guts to question: "What's this all about, senator? Why the deceit?"

"Don't call it deceit, Exton. It's just a little subterfuge, the kind used to catch cheaters." The senator's laugh turned into a cackle like that of the wicked witch from Oz. "I want you to prepare press releases on United States Senate stationery that give the impression I'm in Washington and that my only son, Jordan, is in serious medical condition here at home." He looked at the boy for several seconds before saying, "I suspect that little or none of this subterfuge is necessary, Jordan, because your mother is probably already aching to see you. But I was taught years ago to always prepare backup. Didn't Exton teach you such things? I'm sure he did."

Clarence fixed his eyes on Jordan, as steady and warmly as possible, in an attempt to silently say, "I'm here for you, kid." He had no way of telling if the teenager understood, for he saw not a glimmer of response.

"Oh, and each of you will relinquish your cellphones before you leave this room tonight. Fear not. You'll have them back in no time. I suspect our little game will be over within a day or two. By the way, the landline is down." The senator rubbed his chin and cheeks to check the closeness of his shave. He looked at Jordan. "Cheer up, son. You'll see your mother very soon."

In truth, Jordan was bitterly angry with his mother, so inflamed that his stomach was churning with pain. But he would never admit to his father that his mother begot his mental anguish or physical pain. In fact, he would defend his mother, all the time not understanding why she turned to this woman, Ruth, and hurt him to such a degree. His love for her only swelled his agony.

"I know what you're thinking, Exton." The senator played with his purple paperweight, rolling his fingers around it again and again as he stared hard at his secretary. "It's not the first time you've felt like calling me a bastard, resigning on the spot, and walking out of here. Go ahead if you wish. Leave. I can't stop you."

Clarence couldn't have agreed more. That was exactly the way he felt. But he would not leave because of Jordan. Even if he tried, he realized, without doubt, that he'd be pulled back by love and the need to protect. Beyond that, he was well acquainted with the games the senator played and suspected he was being tested again.

"Now, we will deal with another matter, a related one." The senator pushed his paperweight aside, leaned back in his chair and began to swivel. His expression was disquieting. "Exton, please summon Tony."

"Tony, sir?"

"I believe I spoke clearly." The senator glanced from Clarence to Jordan and back again. "Yes, Tony Paluto, our enterprising chauffeur. Did you know he can climb trees like a monkey? He once worked for the Cloverton Electric Company, climbing poles. Have him come here, now. You may stay or go, Exton. And you also, Jordan. Whatever you wish."

Clarence kept his eyes on Jordan, but was quick to use his cellphone. While waiting for Tony to answer, he winked at Jordan when the senator was briefly distracted by a buzzing housefly. The boy showed no response, limped to his father's desk and placed his cellphone on the blotter near the senator's right hand. Avoiding his father's eyes, he said nothing, turned and limped as quickly as he could toward the door.

"Hello, Tony. Exton here." Clarence's eyes followed Jordan. "The senator wants to see you." Concern for the boy pushed his voice up an octave. "Now. In his office."

Clarence had no desire to make conversation with the senator. He sat quietly after his call to Tony, aware of the chauffeur's lengthy walk to the senator's office from the flat above the garages. But, despite the discomfort of silence, he had no intention of leaving the office, knowing that another chapter in the senator's "strategy" was about to unfold.

The awkward period passed briefly when Tony, smiling broadly, bounced into the office and cheerfully called out, "Hey, yous guys! How y'doing?" His broad smile was genuine. But a steady stare from the senator cooled his enthusiasm. "Yes, sir, Senator, what can I do for you?" He removed his chauffeur's cap.

"What do you know about birds, Tony?"

"Birds, sir?" Tony was a small man, remindful of those ageless jockeys, the kind who look young in stature, particularly from a distance, but when viewed close up show their years in craggy facial features.

"Yes, birds. Especially, big birds." The senator's voice was not in the least bit jocular. It dipped deeply and seriously on the words, "big birds."

"Well, they fly. They lay eggs." Suddenly, Tony showed a touch of nervousness, both in quickness of speech and body movement. He shifted from foot to foot.

"And they make nests," the senator added. "How would you like to be a spy, Tony? Not an evil spy who does something illegal. As a U.S. senator, I would never involve you in anything like that." He glanced at Clarence, then turned a steady stare on the chauffeur. "You would just be someone who joins a cause, and reports to me."

Clarence's eyes lit up. He was catching on. Was the senator making a clandestine move toward the choker?

"You're familiar with the bald eagle, of course?" The senator's voice was deliberately probing, like that of a school teacher.

"Yep! Symbol of our country."

"You'd be helping to protect baby bald eagles until they can fly from their nest," the senator explained. "I want you to go see a gentleman named James Barnes. He's a bird scientist who's organizing a haven and rescue team."

"I don't think it's my kind of thing, Senator."

"Oh, now, Tony, I think we can make it your kind of thing. I'll instruct you as we go along. How about horses? You into horses, Tony?"

"They're okay. But I'm not ..."

"Not a horseman," the senator interrupted. "I get it." He pushed himself to his feet, leaned on his desk with both hands, and squinted at Tony. "Are you familiar with the Nagelstone Veterinary Center for Large Animals?"

"Not really. No, sir." Tony grew more uncomfortable.

"How about a jockey named Vinny Esposito?

Tony shook his head.

"Do you remember a colt named Big Red, expected to be put down, but nursed back to health there by a volunteer? A woman?"

"Big Red! That I remember! He went down at Belmont. Never raced again."

"Okay. But I see we have some work to do. First, I want you to become closely engaged with the inner circle."

"Inner circle?"

"Mr. Barnes and his associate, Mr. Silvester, and their wives. The operation revolves around those four individuals. So, I want you to be especially accommodating when it comes to them. Fear not, Tony. It will all fall into place in time."

* * *

Slightly after midnight, Clarence slipped out of his bedroom—the one he always used when required to stay overnight at the Rimespecker's—and moved stealthfully down the hallway, passed a lighted sconce that cast a dull pink glow on the wall, to the closed door of Jordan's room. He placed his hand on the knob and turned it slowly.

"Yo, Jordy," he whispered as he stepped into the dark room. "You awake?"

"Yeah."

"Don't turn on the light." Clarence knew the bedroom well and could feel his way to the teenager's bed in the dark. Actually, he had helped decorate the room, pleasing Jordan by purchasing and mounting the pennants of four universities on the walls—Syracuse, Temple, Missouri and Northwestern, the schools on the 16-year-old's list of possible choices for studying journalism. Uncle Clarry had also given the boy a desk and a set of bookshelves for his study alcove—a niche now stacked with SAT educational material that Jordan hadn't touched in days.

Clarence sat on the edge of Jordan's bed, gave him a friendly pat on the leg, and asked, "How y'holdin' up?"

"I could kill him."

"No, no, no, y'couldn't. Believe it or not, your father thinks he's teaching you to buckle up and be strong. But I do think he's brought too much of Washington home with him. He thinks he's playing cat-and-mouse with his senate adversaries when he baits us."

"You're much too kind, Uncle Clarry." Jordan turned from his side to back, a difficult move because of the plaster cast on his arm. "I don't wanna talk about it."

"It'll do you good. Come on. You've always been comfortable with me."

"I can't put the right words together." Tremors marred Jordan's voice.

"Don't be afraid to unload your feelings."

"I don't like my feelings. Especially those for my father. Any other dad would give his kid a hug when things turned rotten. He hasn't even talked to me about Mom."

"He can't. Don't expect it." Clarence was pleased that the teenager had strung together several sentences.

Jordan sniffled and blew his nose.

"You crying, kid?"

"I'm okay."

"No. You're far from okay."

"I've tried to reach out to him so many times."

"Well, even during the good years, when you were just a pipsqueak, he had trouble with closeness. Some people do. I bet his childhood would reveal a few things, but he never talks about it. As for your mother's situation, that's eating him up alive. Right now, I think he could kill her."

"Why is she pulling away from us?" Jordan's voice quaked and quivered. "And who the hell is this Ruth person, for God's sake?"

"If your mother took off with a guy, would you feel any different?"

"She would still be breaking up the family, still be leaving her husband. It would hurt just as much. But you know damn well that the media and Dad's enemies in D.C. will feed on this lesbian stuff. I'm not anti-gay." Jordan became almost too worked-up. "This kid in my homeroom, Jerry Cadwell, he's an all right guy. He's gay." Agitation sped up his words. "Most kids today, they don't care. It's the old dudes who try to kill rights for gays."

"Calm down, and listen to me." Clarence took a deep breath. "I suspect your mother was living a lie most of her life, and got to the point where she couldn't stand it anymore, and had to break away and be herself."

"Now, you're assuming she is really ..." Jordan couldn't finish his sentence. "Uncle Clarry, you told me never to make assumptions."

"I'm sorry. You're right. It's still possible that we're looking at an innocent weekend escapade of some sort."

"But you don't really believe that, do you? Like me, you look back over the years and begin to see other tell-tale signs. Lots of little things. They come together." The boy's words had become sharp and clear. "It's not just the choker and the oil painting. Although anybody that would give away that choker has gotta be hooked on somebody mighty hard."

"You're a smart kid for a 16-year-old."

"I've had a wise mentor."

"Do you realize that each of us wants to think one way, but is pulled toward another?"

"Hell, you taught me the word ambivalent. What a shitty place to be."

"It's never comfortable to remain between two opposing choices."

"Hey, what about Tony? What the hell's going on there?"

"I think your old man is gonna sic 'im on Mrs. Barnes while her hubby's building his tent city."

"You're kidding?"

"If he sets him up as a jewel thief, I'll blow the whole thing open. I'll stay on top of it, and I'll fill you in." Clarence shifted closer to Jordan's upper body and lowered his voice to a near whisper. "I came to your room tonight to tell you something I've wanted to say for years." Clarence cleared his throat. "Y'know, Jordy, it's often hard for men to express love for one another. Straight men, that is." Clarence patted Jordan on the leg again. "I love you like a father loves his son. I have all along, since the early years. And I've never told you until this moment."

"You didn't have to tell me." Jordan wiped his eyes. "I've always felt your closeness. I think you were afraid to say it."

"Yes, I guess I was. Because you have a father. And it wasn't my place to ..." Clarence couldn't find the words to finish his thought.

Chapter Nine

Monday brought a bright and sunny day with mild temperatures, pleasing Tony, who had no stomach for traveling to unfamiliar locations in the rain. Tony drove Rimespecker's red pickup truck, not the limousine, to the Birdman's house, following directions laid out by Clarence. He parked it on the street in front of the Barnes' property, remained in the cab, and continued to practice new words, directions, names and numbers. He was not comfortable with his assignment and sucked in a deep breath before stepping from the truck. Troubling him in particular was the senator's instructions not to unveil his fraudulent connection until he extended his introductory remarks. With emphasis, the senator had directed, "Don't jump when the door opens and ask, 'Hey, remember me? We knew each other at Nagelstone!' That won't work."

Tony wasn't sure he understood. But he was determined to try, although certain his effort would be imperfect.

He tapped lightly on the front door at first, but knocked harder after lack of response. Laura Barnes was out of breath when she answered, having dashed into the house from the backyard only seconds earlier. She had been filling the birdfeeders in Jimmy's absence.

"Hello. May I help you?"

"Yes, hello, my name is Vinny Esposito. Are you Mrs. Barnes?"

"Yes, I'm Laura Barnes?"

"Your husband's the Birdman?"

Laura chuckled. "Some people call him that."

Tony shifted from foot to foot. "I know yous people been lookin' for volunteers to protect some bald eagles. I'd like to join, if that's okay?"

"Are you saying you'd like to volunteer?"

"Yes, ma'm. May I come in?"

"My husband isn't here. But ... Yes, I guess it's all right. Come in." Laura did exactly what Jimmy told her not to do. She ushered her visitor to the semicircle of chairs in her living room—her Early American slipcovered chairs facing the colonial fireplace and the portrait of James, Jr., and his dog Buster.

"Nice place y'got here," Tony said as he took a seat.

Laura remained standing. "Mr.... . Sorry, I didn't get your name."

"Esposito. Vinny Esposito."

"Mr. Esposito, I'm afraid I don't make decisions for this effort to protect the eaglets. You'll have to talk to my husband and his partner, Mr. Silvester. Right now they're busy working on the project several miles from here. I could draw you a map. It's an easy drive."

"Could you call Mr. Barnes for me?"

"Yes, but I don't think that would do you any good. Dr. Barnes would want to see you, talk to you, and even check your background. We've had a number of questionable people approach us. Anyway, we've turned the Silvester home into headquarters, and volunteers are gathering there. Who gave you this address?"

"It's *Doctor* Barnes, is it?"

"Professor Barnes holds a Ph.D. degree." Laura found herself being stiff, formal and snobbish, and she didn't like it one bit. It was far from her usual bouncy, free-floating, lighthearted way.

"Lady, please, would it be too much trouble to make a call? I want to talk to them guys before I head over there. How about it?"

Laura pulled her cellphone from her jeans' pocket and pushed numbers. "He's probably busy with something. I know they're going to receive Boy Scout pup tents today. And they have to move Charley's ... Mr. Silvester's honeybee hives so the bees won't be in the middle of the bivouac."

"I can help put up tents," Tony said with a crooked grin. "What's a bivouac?"

"It's a military-style encampment, usually with lots of tents." Laura disengaged her cellphone and returned it to her pocket.

"Gotcha!" Tony pulled on his left ear. "If yous guys need a climber, I'm your man. Don't let my size fool you. Ever see a monkey climb? I almost made number one on Ripley's list. Missed the top of the tallest tree by a couple feet. Got beat by a Montana logger." Tony rose from his chair, stared directly at Laura and said, "Yous guys could really use me." Then, as suddenly as a trap snaps, his high nasal voice cracked and dropped to a hushed tone, "You don't remember me do you? At the Nagelstone Center? Big Red? You saved that's colt's life."

Laura was momentarily stunned. For seconds, she searched his face and bit her lip. "Oh, my God! Let me look at you. You're *that* Vinny! You came every night with Mr. Hathaway, the owner, and George what's-his-name, the trainer. Oh, my goodness. I can't believe it."

"I loved that horse. I didn't care if I never road him again. I just wanted him to live, to be put out to pasture, enjoy mounting the mares. You made that possible."

"Holy smackeroos! Remember what we went through? From tears to smiles. I'll never forget those days."

Laura seized her cell again and quickly pushed numbers she knew by heart. The wait was long, but she chatted cheerfully with Tony.

"Birdman here," Jimmy answered.

"Yeah, hello, hon, it's me. Gotta guy here who wants to talk with you. A potential volunteer. I tried to send him over, but ..."

"Watch out for sneaky infiltrators," Jimmy said.

"I'm sure he's okay. I met him before. Years ago, back when Big Red went down. He was Mr. Hathaway's jockey. Anyway, he wants to help." Laura smiled broadly at Tony. "He can climb. Almost made Ripley's list."

"Are you joining us for lunch?"

"I'm thinking about it. Is Claudia prepared?"

"Hell, yeah. Tell y'what. Drive over with ... What's his name?"

"Vinny Esposito."

"Drive over with Mr. Esposito, and you can ride back with me. That way I won't need to come getcha. We'll be getting home late tonight, 'cause we can't move the honeybees until it gets dark, after they settle down. Charley says we have to screen them in and move them just a little each night, then take the screens off each morning so the scout bees and workers can go do their thing. It'll take us three or four nights."

"Gotcha. Look, we'll get there before lunch. Is Claudia there?"

"Not near me. I'm outside in the township's underbrush. She's in the house."

"If you can, tell her to call me if she needs anything for lunch or dinner."

"Will do."

After hanging up, Laura offered to perk coffee for Tony. She ushered him to the kitchen where they sat at the table and chatted about their experiences at Nagelstone—experiences Tony never had. He was nervous, fearing he knew too little about the large animal center. With every comment, he was scared of being tripped up. His right knee bounced incessantly.

After Laura poured coffee, Tony tried to steady his hand, but had trouble drinking without dribbling. As time passed, he grew to like Laura a bit too much. It frightened him.

The morning sun was high in the sky and lunchtime was beckoning by the time they climbed into the cab of the pickup truck. Laura carried a bag for the SPCA. Tony was already captured by her fun-loving nature, her athletic vigor, her charm, her spirit, her love of animals. Now, he hated himself, could barely tolerate his lies, wanted to ditch the assignment, yet feared the senator. He felt trapped.

On the road, Laura tried to teach Tony words to a song her mother used to sing: "Mares eat oats and does eat oats and little lambs eat ivy ..." He even started to laugh, just before Laura urged him to make a stop at the SPCA where she dropped off some supplies no longer needed by a neighbor, an old man whose dog died.

Things got worse for Tony at the Silvesters' where he was graciously accepted by Jimmy, Charley and Claudia, warm and pleasant do-gooders, ready to protect baby eagles and rescue the choker. They were joined in the kitchen by Randy Houck, scoutmaster of Troop 24, and by an unexpected visitor—Chief Harry Morris of the East Bitterlick police. The chubby, round-faced, bald chief popped in to deliver a permit from the Township Board of Supervisors, granting use of land from the Silvesters' rear boundary to the creek bed. Claudia served chicken-salad sandwiches and tea-and-lemonade coolers to the convivial gathering as Tony's mood deepened.

After downing cheesecake dessert, Jimmy took time to explain the afternoon chores. He gave Tony several assignments, including cutting back underbrush on township land—a stretch of earth heavy with huckleberries, wild grape vines and woody shrubs. He announced the upcoming arrival of a busload of birdwatchers from Cape May, N.J., and another group coming by a caravan of cars from the Chesapeake Bay area. "Both groups'll bring bigger tents than the scouts two-man pups," Jimmy explained. "The Chesapeake guys are loading a trailer with outdoor cooking stuff. So, after we finish helping the scouts lay out their camping site, we'll help the birdwatchers unload."

"We probably don't need your help," said the scoutmaster, a full-bellied, jovial soul whose uniform fit too tightly, nearly popping his buttons. "The boys can finish up on their own early this afternoon."

Tony excused himself after lunch and found his way to the bathroom even though he had little urge to go. After forcing a short dribble, he remained in the bathroom for several minutes, simply to gather his wits and focus on the hours ahead. His thoughts were spinning.

He joined Jimmy in the kitchen, told himself he was ready, and followed the Birdman out of the house.

Outside, near the backyard's north boundary, a circle of 15 Boy Scouts sat cross-legged on the grass, around a smoky fire, munching on hotdogs. Scoutmaster Houck was quick to join them and warn them again to stay away from the bee hives—five trim white boxes buzzing on the south side.

Carrying sickles and shears, Jimmy and Tony trudged to the far end of the Silvesters' property where the heavily wooded area began. Little instruction was needed before Tony was swinging his sickle with force at the underbrush. Angry energy propelled him. He needed to slash out at something, and it seemed that every swing lowered his ire. Time moved quickly, and at one point the two men rested, sat on a log, and picked and ate huckleberries. "They're like little blueberries," Tony commented. He grew to appreciate the Birdman's warmth and comradery long before they stopped clearing the area and joined the crowd to help unload tents and other equipment.

Tony revved up the pickup's engine before dinnertime and started for home feeling more guilt than ever before in his lifetime.

* * *

Clouds had gathered and the early evening was gray when Tony approached the Rimespecker home. As he drove the pickup truck up the driveway, heading for the spread of garages that rested beyond the back gardens, he saw two women step out of a taxicab and make their way toward the front door of the house. Suddenly he recognized one as Lillian Rimespecker and felt a shock race up his spine. For an instant he had been unsure, but then he knew, without question, it was definitely the lady-of-the-house. He was so startled that he did not get a discerning look at the other woman, except to realize she trailed Madam by inches only, and grabbed for her arm.

Clarence had made it clear to Tony that any delay in reporting to the senator might be unwise. So, shortly after he settled into his flat above the garages, he washed his face and hands, gulped water, and began trudging to the house with full knowledge that the senator would be in his home office and not in Washington as propagated. Inside the house, he stopped abruptly when he saw the library doors closed, for it was the senator's custom to keep them open when the room was not in use. Puzzled, he proceeded to the stairway that so handsomely rounded a portion of the elegant entrance hall. The two women were on his mind with every step, and he suspected that Lillian Rimespecker had hastily and surreptitiously fled with her consort to the third floor of bedrooms and sitting rooms.

Quietness reigned in the house. Tony had often found the big residence heavy with stillness, but for some reason the silence spooked him this time. He was daunted again when he discovered the doors to the second-floor office closed. He counted to 10 before knocking softly. To maintain silence, the senator answered in person, rather than by voice. He opened the door inches at a time, saw Tony and motioned him into the office without a word. A chair had been placed in front of the desk, and it was to that seat that Tony was directed. Rimespecker quickly rounded his desk and slid into his swivel chair.

The shaken limo driver was almost in tears when he blurted, "I can't do it, sir. I can't lie like I did today. No, senator, I can't. I'm sorry." He continued to rattle off words: "These people, they're so nice. And they're so dedicated to what they're doing. No, no, Senator, I can't, I won't, please."

"Stop sniveling, and be a man, Tony."

"Sorry, sir, but every time I called myself Vinny Esposito I felt sick in the stomach. These people treated me so well. I could never do anything to hurt them."

"But you didn't hurt them in any way, did you? You helped them, right?'

"I lied!" Tony raised his voice. "I lied, again and again! It was a terrible feeling."

"Shut up, damn it!" The senator rose to his feet, leaned on his desk, and glared at Tony. "Be quiet! Understand? Now, report to me in a proper manner."

"What do y'wanna know? We cut down a lot of weeds and stuff, unloaded tents from South Jersey and Maryland, dug barbeque pits, sang a camping song with the Boy Scouts. A bunch of birdwatchers took up positions upstream, near the eagles' nest. Is that enough? Is that what you wanna hear?"

"Get out of here! You're fired!"

"What?"

"You heard me!"

"Hey, wait a minute, senator. So, I got excited, that's all. I'm upset!"

"You're fired! I said, get out of here! Exton will see that you get your final pay check. Now, go on! I don't want to see you again."

Little Tony didn't move. He simply stared daggers at the big man. Finally, the senator came out from behind his desk and gave Tony a shove with both hands, grabbed him by the collar and pushed him toward the exit. Tony resisted briefly, then turned and deliberately walked slowly toward the door. Before leaving, he turned back prepared to shout curses and tell the senator, in extremely nasty terms, that his lesbian wife was in the house. But he held his tongue. Actually, he liked Lillian Rimespecker. Always pleasant toward him, she often slipped him a 20-dollar bill after an excursion in the limousine. Now, with his heartbeat racing, he sought Clarence Exton for several reasons, not the least of which was simply to unload his bitterness. He didn't know the interior layout of the house as well as Clarence or Hilda, but believed the West Wing would take him to the secretary's room. Although he had worked for Rimespecker for years, he had been to Clarence's room only twice. Then again, the closed library made him wonder. Perhaps Clarence was hiding behind those doors. He decided to go down before going up.

In the Green Room in the East Wing, Ruth Nettlebaum was in her merry mood, prancing about as she hummed a tune, touching just about everything in the silk-and-organdy-trimmed room. Now and again she flopped on the queen-sized, four-poster bed, under the fancy green canopy of ruffles and tassels. Lillian sat in a green slipper chair and watched her lover with delight, despite her underlying worries. The room, one of her favorites, was decked out in French provincial furniture and gold-framed prints of oil paintings by Degas. It was her choice of boudoir when not compelled to sleep with her husband in the master bedroom.

"It's time," she said, halting Ruth's playfulness. "I've got to see him. I want you to stay here. Please, don't go anywhere else. Stay right here. In this room."

Ruth giggled, threw a kiss, and flopped on the bed.

Minutes later, Lillian found her way to the West Wing. She hurried past Clarence's room and beyond the pink-glowing sconce to the door of her son's bedroom. She waited a moment, then lifted her fist to knock, only to hesitate again. After a few deep breaths, she forced herself to strike a pose similar to that in the oil painting by Ruth—a pose of strength, dominance and surety. She knocked.

Jordan tossed a manual of sample SAT questions on his desk, slid his chair back, and lifted himself from his study alcove. He was certain that the knocking came from Clarence. "Just a second, Uncle Clarry. I'm coming."

Jordan opened the door to find his mother standing there. The emotion that engulfed him was so strong that he teetered between inability to move and the need to crush her in his arms. His fervor gave rise to heat that brought bubbles of sweat to his forehead. Amidst his fullness of heart were upsetting agitations that messed with his head and body functions. He grabbed his mother, and despite his plaster cast, hugged her tightly, cried, and then pushed her away and backed up.

Lillian stepped into the room. She closed the door behind her as her son continued to back away. "I'm sorry, Jordy." Aware of his cast and injuries, she began to ask about them, but was cut off.

"Sorry!" he yelled. "You're sorry? How could you do what you did? How could you go away with that woman?"

"I don't want to talk about her right now. I want to talk about us."

"Us? If 'us' existed you wouldn't have gone to her." Tears streamed down Jordan's cheeks.

"She gave me a kind of happiness I never had. And I want you to meet her and maybe appreciate her. But I didn't what to get into that now. You're not ready."

"Not ready? Oh, I'm ready for anything you have to say. Come on! Lay it on me!"

"Jordan, I love you with all my heart and soul. And I will always love you, no matter what. Hate me if you will. But I'll always love you."

"Yeah? And how do I fit into your new life. And what about Dad? I know he's difficult. But you are a married woman, you do know that don't you?"

"Frankly, I don't know how things will work out. It's gotten complicated."

"So, now you're saying you didn't think it out. Is that it?" Jordan grabbed a heavy book from a shelf in his alcove and tossed it to the floor with a thud. "Three years ago? Is that when this started? That's what I hear through the whispers. My God! Yeah! I can see it in your eyes. You've been finger-fucking this woman for three years."

"Jordan! How dare you!" Lillian turned as tears streamed down her face. She sobbed heavily as she hurried to the door and left.

"Wait! I'm sorry, Mom! I shouldn't have said that." Jordan rushed to the doorway and looked down the hall. "Mom, I love you! I love you so much." Lillian was gone. "Please," he whispered, "come back."

* * *

Tony Paluto had found the library doors locked and for the last 20 minutes was looking elsewhere for Clarence, but had no luck. The secretary was in the kitchen preparing a tray of food for his boss. Two tuna-salad sandwiches made up the main course. Chicken broth and fruit, straight from the cans, rounded out the light supper.

The senator assumed it was Clarence when someone knocked on his office door, but as before, he opened the door quietly, a little at a time. Standing there was a man or woman covered with a bedsheet, looking much like a Halloween ghost. Holes were cut in the sheet for eyes.

"What the hell!" the senator exclaimed in a hushed voice. "Is that you, Jordan?"

Gunshots rang out—close-up shots from under the bedsheet aimed directly at Senator Rimespecker. The sheet-covered figure pumped shot after shot into the senator. Blood spurted from entry wounds in the chest, neck, forehead and gut. U.S. Senator Joseph Rimespecker sputtered, gagged, choked and produced gruesome guttural noises as he fell to the floor where a pool of blood grew bigger and bigger.

Chapter Ten

Clarence moved slowly as he approached the senator's office carrying the tray of food, mainly because the chicken broth wouldn't behave. From the kitchen, up the steps and down the hallway it tested the secretary's skill at balancing. With every step, the broth flowed back and forth in the cup, spilling drops at a time.

When Clarence suddenly came upon the senator's body in a pool of blood, electricity ripped through him, sputtering his scream into a series of strange-sounding squawks and squeaks. The tray flew out of his hands and landed with a crash. His next scream was an attempted yell for help, but it choked off into a pathetic squeal. Now, the pool of blood on the highly polished parquet flooring was dotted with lumps of tuna, pieces of bread and hunks of fruit.

The secretary's body was shaking uncontrollably as he dug into his pockets, hunting for his cellphone. Gathering his wits somewhat, he leaped over the dead senator and raced to Rimespecker's desk where he found his confiscated phone lying next to Jordan's. His hand was shaking as his index finger managed with difficulty to tap nine-one-one.

"This is your emergency operator," a female voice spoke. "Please give your location and the nature of your emergency?"

"Senator Rimespecker's been shot!" Clarence spit out nervously. "He's been murdered!"

"Who is this please? And give me your location."

"My name's Clarence Exton. I'm the senator's personal secretary. He's dead! Right here in his library."

"Your location, sir?"

"One-fifty Dorian Boulevard, in the Oxhaven section of East Bitterlick." Clarence was gaining control of himself. He breathed deeply. "Just west of Cloverton, off Route 77. Believe me lady, the cops know the senator's house."

"Are you alone, sir?"

"I think a few other people are in the house. I'm alone with the body." Clarence's arm twitched. He dropped the cellphone, but caught it with his other hand, juggled it, and held it to his ear just in time to hear the emergency operator.

"Have you checked his pulse?"

"No need! He's got about six bullet holes in him, including one in the center of the forehead. He's dead. Very much dead."

"Two patrol cars from East Bitterlick Police are on their way. And I've notified the coroner's office. Please stay where you are until the officers arrive, and remain on the line."

Clarence jumped and electricity lifted his hair when he heard a voice yell, "Oh my God!" He turned to see Tony standing over the body.

"Damn, you scared me! What are you doing here?"

Tony's words were fast and hysterical: "He's dead! The senator's dead! They'll blame me! Oh my God! He fired me! We had an argument, and he fired me. They'll think I killed him." Tony maneuvered around the body and hurried toward Clarence. "I didn't do it, Mr. Exton. Honest to God, I didn't do it."

"I didn't do it either, Tony." Clarence tried to focus in on the chauffeur's frenzied words. "Did you say he fired you?"

"I laid into him about them eagles'-nest people and how I didn't want to be his spy on them. Right then and there he canned me."

"Well, now it doesn't really matter much that he fired you, does it? Now that he's dead, that is."

"Except it gives me a good reason to want 'im dead."

The chauffeur kept looking back at the body and then at Clarence. His neck muscles bulged as he repeatedly turned his head back and forth. Finally, he steadied his stare on Clarence and said, "Mrs. Rimespecker's in the house."

"What?" Clarence was stunned.

"She's here. With her lady-friend."

"Y'gotta be kidding."

"Nope. Seen them both."

"When?"

"Just as I was pullin' in from the eagles'-nest job. They was entering the house. I did a double take. It was her, all right."

"My God! The senator's trap actually worked. Can you believe that?

He caught 'em! But, in turn, got himself killed."

"You think she killed him?"

"His wife? I don't know. Don't really wanna say. Lots of people hated him. Where's Mrs. Rimespecker now?"

Tony shook his head. "Upstairs, I guess." He squeezed his upper arm to quell a muscle spasm. "I think she did it. Shot him dead. Killed him. But them cops'll blame me. That I know. You wait and see."

"I can hear the sirens already. Tony, go down and let the cops in. Please. I gotta stay on the line for a minute."

Tony leaped over the body of the late senator and sped to the stairs where he descended two steps at a time. He raced through the entrance hall and pushed his way outside into the night air. Two patrol cars were already on the front lawn, their sirens winding down, but their red, white and blue lights casting blazing flashes on the house and grounds. The coroner's wagon—the cops' name for a hearse—pulled up behind one of the cruisers. Six men exited hastily, two from each vehicle, and followed Tony as he waved them into the house.

Chief Morris was out-of-breath by the time the group of seven reached the top of the stairs, but he managed to stay with the others until they stopped suddenly right before toppling into the senator's body. Grunts, groans and expletives echoed through the corridor.

"Holy hell!" the chief exclaimed. "Bag everything you can. Even the dust. Tiny particles can teach us big lessons. Look at this mess. Those entry wounds tell me this was definitely a crime of passion. The shooter was right on top of him, blazing away."

"Sorry about the food, Chief," Clarence said. "I was bringing him supper when I dumped the tray."

"Spread apart, boys, and let the coroner have a close look." The chief glanced about. "Let's grab a full picture of the scene before the evidence gets cold. Lieutenant, you and Smitty work here with the coroner and his man, Sam. Sergeant Pendexter, you and your partner search the house from top to bottom for anything suspicious. Like a gun, maybe. And if you run into any human beings—family members or others—bring them here." The chief glanced about for Clarence and made quick eye contact. "Who's in the house, Mr. Exton, as far as you know?"

"Well, there's Tony, here, the family chauffeur. And me, of course. Then there's Jordan, the senator's 16-year-old son. And we believe Mrs. Rimespecker is in the house."

Chief Morris showed sudden surprise, as did others. "She's here?

She's in this house? I have people looking for her all over the place. Just yesterday I sent a cruiser to a drugstore where a young clerk spotted her. And New York is trying to pin down a yellow cab for us, and we couldn't even give the NYPD its medallion number. Jesus! And now you tell me she's here?"

Tony chimed in: "And that woman is with her."

Chief Morris stared at Tony. "Who? Y'mean, Ruth Nettlebaum?"

The chauffeur nodded.

"Holy hell! Well, let's gather everybody together." The chief looked down at the coroner, who was kneeling over the body. "When will you clear the way, Fred?"

"We'll have the body out of here in no time," replied Fred Carter, the tall, lanky coroner who was examining chest wounds with his assistant, Sam Block, a chubby middle-aged forensic expert. "We won't need an inquest in this case," Carter said. "The cause of death is obvious."

"Don't forget the gun-shot residue."

"We're on top of it, Captain," said Carter, who glanced up at the chief with annoyance. "We know our business. We'll check everyone in the house. Just get 'em here before they change clothes or wash."

"Okay then," the chief said. "Round up the suspects and gather them here in the senator's office. We'll want to interrogate each of them separately at the station tomorrow morning. But tonight I'd like to play them against each other."

The chief's words made Clarence and Tony extremely uncomfortable. After all, they were suspects, weren't they? To them, his words and tone suggested he forgot they were standing right there with him.

"Not all your suspects are here in the house, Chief," Lieutenant Goldstein said. "There are plenty of dudes in Washington who hate this guy. And don't forget the Ermengarde Choker hunters who'd like to see both the senator and Ruth Nettlebaum rubbed out, killing any legal battle over ownership of the choker."

"What?" the chief exclaimed. "Where the hell y'been picking up that stuff, Benny?"

"Talk radio. Ever listen to Rudy Reubin on WJPY late at night?"

"Hell no. Talk radio'll give y'plenty of twisted ideas."

"One of Rudy's scenarios has Nettlebaum's relatives plotting a million-dollar grab after her demise. He's got them inheriting the choker if anything wipes her out."

"That's crap!" the chief said with force.

* * *

Jordan was still in his room on the third floor of the West Wing when the police chief ordered the house searched. Sergeant Pendexter and Patrolman Martini were checking out the East Wing while Jordan was cursing the world and God. He pulled a pillow from his bed and actually tried to bite a hole in it with his teeth. When that didn't work, he ripped the pillow open with a letter opener powered by a forceful thrust that strained his biceps. He threw the torn pillow against the wall and watched the feathers fly.

He thought back to when Billy Ortlieb, a student in his chemistry class, called him a "lucky bastard" to be the son of a "rich dude loaded with money and power."

"I'd rather be poor as shit than live in this house!" Suddenly realizing that he had shouted aloud, Jordan put his hand over his mouth and whimpered. A moment later he went to a window and scratched the glass with his fingernails. Next he attacked a Pay-Day candy bar that he yanked from his desk. After one bite, he began pulling the peanuts off the bar and flipping them around the room using his thumb and forefinger. Up in the air he flipped some. Over to his bed he flipped others. Up against his closet door he flipped more.

With a sudden impulse, he left his room in a tear, intending to go to the Green Room in the East Wing where he felt certain he'd find his mother. He stopped at Clarence's door, knocked, became impatient, kicked the door, and quickly moved on. Ahead of him, where the West and East Wings met the staircase and a broad landing provided access to a linen closet and utility room, he was alerted by two anomalies that slowed him down: an open closet door and a noisy washing machine.

He glanced into the closet and saw that a folded bedsheet had fallen to the floor, probably pulled out of a stack of sheets when someone had hastily yanked one off the shelf. He slammed the closet door, then walked into the utility room and looked into the rumbling washing machine that was off-balance and bouncing slightly during its spin-cycle. He opened the round, glass door and grabbed the still-wet, rolled-up and knotted bedlinen. He saw what looked like gunshot holes in the sheet even before shaking it. With a quick, jerking move, he flipped the sheet open and saw more holes just as Sergeant Neil Pendexter stepped into the utility room and grabbed him from the rear, circling his upper torso with his strong arms.

"Whatcha got there, Kid?" the sergeant asked through clenched teeth as he tightened his hold. "Y'trying to wash away evidence?"

"What the hell!" Jordan yelled.

Sam Martini stepped right up behind his partner, spun around him, and took hold of Jordan while Pendexter grabbed the teenager's wrists and snapped on handcuffs.

"Hey, dudes!" Jordan exclaimed. "What's going on?"

"Maybe you should tell us why you killed your old man?" the sergeant questioned.

"My father's dead?"

"Shot a half-dozen times through this bedsheet," Martini said.

"Hey, dudes! I didn't shoot anybody." Jordan suddenly realized that if he didn't kill his father, his mother may have. In fact the more he thought about it, he figured it most likely had been her. So, his protective instinct—long felt for his mother—told him to shut up and not proclaim his innocence.

"See this!" Sergeant Pendexter pushed his fingers through the eye holes in the sheet. "Your peep holes while wearing this sheet."

Jordan's lack of response prompted the sergeant to say, "Cat got your tongue, huh? You're guilty as hell, boy. Let's move!" The officers led Jordan down the broad stairway to the second floor and along the hallway to the crime scene. Little was said on the way, except for the sergeant's repeated words: "Keep moving!"

The body of Senator Rimespecker was gone. Clarence, Tony, the police chief and the rest of his men were gathered just inside the office. The sergeant yelled as he and his partner approached with Jordan: "The women are gone! They had been in the Green Room, without question. There were plenty of telltale signs, from the smell of perfume, to a wrinkled bedspread, to spilled cosmetics, to lightbulbs burning in the bathroom. But we caught you a big fish—a young shark named Jordan who was trying to wash the signs of murder from his ghost custom. He doesn't know hairs stick like hell. So does lint. Can't always remove the little bits with soap and water."

"Take the cuffs off him," Chief Morris said. "He's not gonna run."

"Y'sure?"

"Yeah. Did you find the gun?"

"No," Pendexter said as he removed the handcuffs from Jordan's wrists.

"Well, I'm concerned that the women escaped. That means you and I, Smitty, are gonna take a ride down along Bitterlick Creek to a little house on Old South County Road. In the meantime, Lieutenant, you take charge here and at headquarters. See that all the hotels and motels in the area, including those in Cloverton City, are checked for Lillian Rimespecker and her sweetheart. As for the boy, here. We'll consider him prisoner number one. Take him in."

* * *

"She kept a neat house," Chief Morris explained as he and Patrolman Lee Smith, a broad-shouldered mesomorph, entered Ruth Nettlebaum's tidy, little home. "She had a cat, but you won't find cat hairs on the sofa. Even her cans of soup in the kitchen cabinet are lined up in alphabetical order, with the labels all facing forward."

"I think they call that obsessive-compulsive behavior," Smitty said.

"Well, I think she simply didn't have that much to do except paint pictures and bake pecan pies. That is, before the senator's wife came along. So, she formed neat habits. Probably waxed the kitchen floor twice a day. You should check out the filing cabinet in the kitchen alcove. You might learn something and start keeping a neater desk."

"So, that's the painting I keep hearing about." Smitty eyed the portrait of Lillian Rimespecker. "Wow!"

"It's a beauty." Chief Morris glanced about. "Anybody home!" he yelled. "I'll go upstairs, Smitty. You check around down here. I don't think they're here, unless they're hiding in a closet or something." He started up the steps. "Be sure to open all doors."

Smitty took his time, opening and closing far more things than he had to. He certainly knew Lillian and Ruth weren't hiding in the breadbox or the oven, but he pushed and pulled on just about everything. He was amazed when he opened the filing cabinet. All files were color-coded, numbered and in alphabetical order. And he was particularly intrigued when he spotted the file labeled Ermengarde Choker. In quick order, he pulled it from the file drawer and began to scan it. Seconds later, he sat in the living room and studied it more closely.

When Smitty heard his boss descending the stairs, he called out, "This document definitely shows the transfer of the choker from Lillian Rimespecker to Ruth Nettlebaum. It also lists Claudia and Charles Silvester as heir to it. Chief, did you hear me? It's bequeaths the choker to the Silvesters if Ruth Nettlebaum expires! And it's all properly signed, sealed and stamped!"

"I know, Smitty. I know. I've read it more than once. In fact, I have a copy of it back at headquarters in my bottom desk drawer."

"Holy shit! You really are on top of things, Chief." Smitty grinned. "I'll be damned. Even though you don't let us know. You keep things all wrapped up inside that bald head of yours."

Chapter Eleven

Terry Smythe was truly surprised when she opened the door to her brownstone and found Clarence standing there with a box of her favorite cookies in his right hand—oatmeal, raisin, walnut cookies from a local bakery. It wasn't the cookies that surprised her. It was seeing Clarence standing on her stoop on a weekday morning. She smiled broadly as she gave him her usual bear hug, then pulled back and pecked a kiss on his cheek.

"What the hell are you doing here?" she asked with obvious delight. The rapture faded quickly, however, when she recalled the recent headlines. "You're in trouble," she uttered. "I've been keeping up with the news."

"Yes, I'm not quite a suspect. I'm what they call, 'a person-of-interest.' But I'm in good company. I believe there are five of us so categorized."

"Not all five are in good shape, from what I hear." She grabbed his hand. "Come on in! Come! Come! You're in luck, there's still coffee in the pot." She pulled him through the house to her sunroom. "Sit!" she demanded as she grabbed the cookie box. "My favorites! Thanks." She opened the box, placed some cookies on a plate, and slid them under Clarence's nose.

"I know what you like," Clarence said. "And I'd like to give you more than cookies."

"And what's that supposed to mean?" Terry poured coffee.

"I don't know if I have a job. I don't know the future. All kinds of crazy ideas are flying around in my head. I'm worried sick about Jordan. I keep dreaming about jails and court trials and all sorts of things. And I think of you. And Mom. And tomorrow. What will it bring? I have no straight answers. I have a feeling I might have a lot more free time. And ..."

Terry interrupted: "Stop it! Stop it! Stop it!" She put her hand over his mouth for a few seconds, then sat across the table from him. "You're wound up tight. Calm down. Take a deep breath."

"Sorry."

"How's your mother?"

"Good, today. I left her sitting in her favorite chair, that two-hundred year old Boston rocker that squeaks. She's watching TV, some soap opera, I guess. Anyway, she was laughing and poking fun at something when I left."

"I played checkers with her yesterday afternoon."

"I know. She told me. Thanks." Clarence sipped coffee. "Let's get off Mom. Listen to me. My life is gonna change in a big way. And I'm not sure how. My future could be going up, down, or around in circles." He sipped more coffee. "Are you paying attention?"

"Sure." Terry focused on his eyes.

"Right now, I guess I don't have a job. Or I'm working for a dead man. Or for a woman on the run. Or for a rich teenager who's the closest of the five to be considered a suspect because of a holey bedsheet. My guess is, I'll be building a new life. I'll be starting all over again at my age. And I want you to be part of that life. Let's cut a hole though the wall."

"What?"

"Let's turn our brownstones into one house."

"Clarence! You're not making any sense! Are you on something?"

"I'm serious. We could open up our common wall on all three levels. It could become one big house. Ours!"

"You're nuts! Have you become too feeble to leap from stoop to stoop? Too frail to go out one door and come in another?"

"Terry, I'm asking you to marry me."

"Oh, dear God, here we go again."

"It's different this time. The future could be a whole new world for me. We love each other. We have for years. Okay, it didn't begin as a hot-pants thing. Those hot-pants things often don't last. Once the fire is out, she looks at him, and he looks at her, and they say, 'Who the hell are you?' They have nothing in common. We've built a friendship into a warm and wonderful relationship, the kind of love that builds and builds and lasts and lasts."

"Oh, Clarence, you're grasping to hold onto something because of what's happening to you. You're afraid."

"Not grasping in that way. No. Maybe grasping to build onto the one big part of my life that's still standing."

"It's not a good thing to make major decisions when your life is in turmoil."

"That's not true in my case. For my own sanity, I have to know there's something there to build on. Otherwise I won't succeed. You're the only thing I have that's grounded. You're my anchor in a swirling ocean of debris. Why not marry me? What do you have to lose?"

"Take a cookie. And munch quietly for a moment."

"No. I'm not hungry." Clarence began tapping on the table with all ten fingers. He stared hard, directly into her eyes. "Answer me. Please."

"First of all, you may not have a job. And I'm not in great financial shape."

"So what! We have our brownstones, and we have us. I'll get a job, maybe one in which I won't be a prisoner anymore. I've been playing the role of a rich man's secretary just about my entire life. I've really been the senator's houseboy." Clarence shook his head and waved goodbye, his way of saying, "No more!"

"But you can't be hasty about ..."

Clarence interrupted: "Freedom! Maybe I need freedom. Maybe I wanna be who I am, what I am, not a yes-boy. Not anymore. Oh, I played the game well. For years I've been this calm, cool, collected robot. Now, I want to be with you, no matter what the future."

"Wow! The last time I suggested marriage you ran right down a rabbit hole."

"We've been ambivalent assholes for years. Forget who said this or that in the past. Here's another scenario: We sell the brownstones. They'll bring big bucks. We buy a cottage on a hilltop or in a valley or along a creek or wherever. You can grow all the flowers you want. You won't have to squeeze them into a small, square plot surrounded by concrete. You can have your cockscombs, your zinnias, your morning glories."

"You're not going to like what I say next. But here goes, anyway." Terry breathed deeply, got up from the table, walked aimlessly around the sunroom, and sat down again. "You sure you don't want this marriage just to create a stable-looking environment so you can adopt a rich teenager?"

"Jesus no! That's an insane thought! People don't adopt millionaires. They adopt kids in need."

"He's in need, don't you think? Emotional need?"

"Oh, yeah. He needs to feel passionate, soul-stirring, heart-warming emotions. But he's laden with what I call black emotions—wrought up anger, hysterical eruptions, and dangerous urges." Clarence pondered his words, turning them into internal fears that caused him to bite his lip. Now it was his turn to rise from the table. He walked toward the kitchen and leaned against the doorjamb with his back to Terry. Suddenly he spun around. "Do I want a relationship with Jordan? You can bet your ass I do! In that regard, I'll take what I can get. You've met him a couple times. You like him, don't you?"

"I met him with you at the zoo, and again at Six Flags. He seems like a good kid."

"I can't control the part of our future that might involve him. That's pretty much in the hands of Jordy and his circumstances. But you and I can put together a beautiful, comfortable, warm and loving tomorrow for ourselves. And just maybe, somehow, we can give him a taste of it."

"And your mother?"

Clarence simply stared at Terry. Finally, he said, "You tell me. But before you say a thing, let's get out of here. Let's drive down to the river and walk along the towpath. I feel antsy. I want to move and smell the water and the grass."

"You're nervous as hell." Terry gulped coffee, took the last bite of a cookie, and said, "Okay. Let's see what the fresh air will do. I think I need it, too."

* * *

Clarence parked his little, blue Chevy along a low, fieldstone, retaining wall that separated Riverside Park's off-street parking from the towpath that followed the twists and turns of the Babette River. Hopping the wall and following the river upstream or downstream was nothing new for Clarence or Terry. In fact, it had been a much more frequent exercise years ago when they were considerably more limber. And Terry suspected Clarence's choice for this venture was a throwback aimed at influencing her. Not that she had any doubt that he needed to breathe, move and vent in the open air.

He helped her over the wall and their eyes were drawn to the flowing water—a mesmerizing flow that could calm the nerves of a frantic sole at the brink of a major shakeup. The river water, often a shade of green, was a splendid azure, a reflection of the pure blue sky that marked this first day of June. Terry and Clarence were in deep thought, but said nothing as they began to tread northward, or upstream, on the pathway—a trail that long ago followed a canal where mule-drawn barges carried logs to mills downriver. Though the canal was long gone, residents of the area still referred to the mules' track of years past as "The Towpath." Sections of it were refurbished by the city time and again.

Clarence and Terry remained thoughtful but voiceless as the towpath took them between stretches of rich green grass well nurtured by spring rains and dotted by yellow dandelions and butter cups. They walked a quarter mile past outcroppings of rocks and clumps of pink-blooming wild phlox tangled with bindweed. The near banks of the river were heavy with the thorny stems of wild roses—tiny white roses that burst from their buds each June. They fought for sustenance with blackberry brambles, bur reeds and honeysuckle, building an entanglement that protected the muskrats and mallards from encroachment.

A small elongated island in the river displayed all shades of green— from the deep dark greens of many conifers to the brilliant green of the locust trees, to the yellow-green of the willows, to the ashen green of the sycamore trees. What a resplendent mosaic of greens the sunny day presented to the hikers, rowers, walker and runners. Rowing south from both sides of the island were collegiate sculls making v-shaped ripples in the water that glistened in the sunlight. Clarence took Terry's hand as he stopped to watch.

"I have a strong and warm relationship with your mother," Terry said. "I would want her to be part of anything we built together. I enjoy her company. She's different with me than she is with you. She can carp and complain with you, because you're her son. With me, no, no. Frankly, she and I have a ball when we get together and try to solve the world's problems. Her mind is strong. She's quick, and sometimes blunt, almost too blunt. There would come a time, of course, when you and I might not be able to care for her, and we'd have to face the same choices other families face. She knows that, and talks about it. Believe it or not, she's not afraid of ..."

Clarence interrupted: "Are you telling me you'll marry me? Boy oh boy, that's probably the worst marriage acceptance speech ever conveyed."

Terry couldn't help but laugh. "Well, it's no worse than your proposal." She pulled on his ear and ducked for fear of a return poke or pinch. "If we're gonna do it, I've got to lose some weight before the wedding."

"It'll be a small, quiet wedding."

"Of course. I know that." She took his hand. "Let's sit down." Terry pulled him toward a park bench that rested under a crabapple tree on the opposite side of the towpath from the Babette River. It faced the path and was a good spot for people-watching, yet still gave an overview of the river, its banks, and the small island.

"You needn't lose weight, Terry. I can't get rid of my bald head, gray sideburns and bent back. That's the package you're gonna get." Clarence made a funny face, sat next to Terry, and tickled her under the arm.

She pushed away his hand. "Let's get serious. Is there any chance of your getting charged with Senator Rimespecker's murder?"

"I doubt it. If they think I'm the guilty one, they must think I'm a great actor—a combination of John Wilkes Booth, the assassin, and his brother, Edwin Booth, the brilliant thespian. But I haven't had any compliments about my performance. There was no curtain call, believe me. I never shook so much in all my life. I guarantee you it was not an act."

"I know that." Terry squeezed his hand. "Because I know you. It's not in you to kill, or even hurt an earthly creature, for that matter. I remember when Tommy Johnson killed that butterfly. I thought you were about to have a stroke."

"I'm sure Chief Morris and his investigators listened to my frantic nine-one-one call over and over again. And they got a good look at the food I spilled. If I had killed Rimespecker, I'd have escaped the scene. Anyway, I think I have fewer reasons to see the senator dead than the other four."

"So, I don't have to worry about your being jailed on our wedding night or anything like that," Terry said in a light-hearted manner.

"Heaven forbid!" He kissed her on the cheek, then leaned down and picked a sprig of yellow wood sorrel from a cluster of it growing amidst grass and clover at the side end of the bench. "We used to call this sour grass when we were kids. Ever taste it?"

"No."

Clarence put a couple of the small clover-like leaves in his mouth. "Here, taste it."

"No."

"Come on! It's sour, but it's a pleasant sour. Please, just take a leaf. As a toast to this special day. We can always remember the day of our engagement as the day we tasted sorrel, not the day I gave you a ring." Clarence held the sorrel in his left hand and raised his right hand as if about to take an oath. "Now wait! Here goes: We gather here together, Terry and Clarence, to pledge, in the name of the sorrel we taste, to give to each other comfort, warmth and love."

"You're crazy, y'know it!" She grabbed a couple leaves from his hand, tossed them into her mouth and chewed. "Wow! It is sour. But kinda tasty."

"Lots of weeds are edible. They tell me lamb's quarter tastes like spinach." Clarence stood, bowed to Terry in the comical way of a jester, took her hand and helped her from the bench. "Let's walk."

"My, you're being courtly!"

"Frankly, my dear, I'm trying to be a mixture of different sorts of humankind—far, far from that of a wealthy man's private secretary."

"Don't go too far astray. I've always liked your many good traits." She ran her finger up and down his backbone. "Especially, your kindness. Why do you think Jordan worships you?" Running ahead of him, she stopped, turned and threw him a kiss. "Tell me about him. How's he holding up?"

"Not well at all." Clarence quickstepped toward Terry and took her hand. "His father's dead, murdered. His mother's on the run, possibly the slayer of his father. And she's fixated on a strange woman. He's angry. He's hurting. Mad at the world. And why wouldn't he be?"

"He wouldn't hurt himself, would he? Or do anything else foolish?"

"I worry all the time. It's eating at me."

"I wish I could help."

"You are. By being with me. You give me strength. If I'm going to help him, I need that strength."

Clarence and Terry walked quietly in deep thought for another quarter mile or so. At an outcropping of rock where the towpath took a turn, they turned back. He picked an early blooming toadflax from a budding cluster and tickled her under her nose with it before slipping it into a buttonhole on her blouse.

"So, have you made up your mind?" Clarence asked. "Do we remodel the brownstones or build a cottage on a hillside of blue lupines?"

"Can I plant hollyhocks?"

"You can plant anything you want."

"Then I think I'll take the cottage. As long as you'll be there to keep me safe."

"Safe?"

"You like the words warm and comfortable for our relationship. I prefer safe. I've always felt safe with you."

* * *

The sun was high in the sky when Clarence drove his Chevy to a stop in front of the Exton brownstone. He and Terry were more than surprised to see his mother, her steel gray hair tied into a knot atop her head, sitting outside on the stoop talking with a man.

"Who's the guy?" Terry asked.

"Oh, my God! What's he doing here? That's Rimespecker's chauffeur, Tony Paluto. You've met him a few times."

"Years ago. I didn't recognize him."

"The guy's a total wreck. I hope he's not upsetting Mom." Clarence opened the car door and stepped out. "Come on."

Tony saw them coming and waved. He pushed himself up from the steps and called out, "I hope yous don't mind." He fidgeted and shifted from foot to foot. "I need your help." As Clarence and Terry approached, he continued, "I need to clear my name with them bird people."

"Hello, Tony," Clarence greeted. "Perhaps you remember Terry Smythe. Terry, I believe you met Tony Paluto some time ago."

Terry smiled and took Tony's hand. "Nice to see you again. It's been awhile."

Tony turned and looked at Clarence. "Your mother and I have been enjoying the sunshine. She's been telling me a lot of crazy tales about you."

"Oh, no. Mothers aren't supposed to give away secrets."

"He's been keeping me company," Clarence's mother said in a rough and broken voice. "And telling me his problems. He's a nice young man."

"Not so young, I'm afraid." Tony turned toward Clarence. "I'm living with my parents these days. I couldn't sleep last night, kept frettin' over that spying stuff. So, I took off in my old man's car for the Silvesters' place to confess and explain why I lied, why I played the role of Vinny Esposito. I kept practicing, and my words and excuses sounded awful in my head. But I gotta do it somehow, or I can't live with myself." His words were fast, broken, almost frantic. "So, I pulled to the side of the road and thought of you." He looked pleadingly at Clarence. "I turned around, couldn't find you at the Rimespecker house, so I headed here. I need your help. You're the only one who can help me."

"You'll probably never see those people again, Tony. Why not just let it go?"

"No, Mr. Exton. I can't do that. I want to make amends. Besides, my name's been in the news with yours and the others. Oh, jeez, they're gonna find out that Vinny is really Tony. I gotta tell 'em first. Come with me. You can explain it to them. Together, we can make them understand."

"I don't know, Tony."

"Please, Mr. Exton. You gotta make them nice people understand. Besides I wanna help them. I want to be the dude who climbs that tree and rescues that choker. I can do it. I know I can do it. And I wanna show them nice people that I can. Show 'em that I'm the champ. And I wanna help them baby eagles, too."

Terry poked Clarence in the ribs. "Do it! Or I'll take back our sour-grass oath."

Clarence smiled. "Okay." He looked at his mother. She nodded. "I guess I'm outnumbered. To tell you the truth, Tony, I'm delighted to help you. We'll take my car. But first, Terry and I have something very special to tell you." He smiled and looked warmly into his mother's eyes as he pulled Terry close to his side.

Silence reigned for nearly a minute. All Clarence did was stand there and grin until Terry nudged him. Then he whispered, "Okay. Okay." But he continued to grin, until she kicked his shoe.

"Well, out with it!" his mother barked in her craggy voice.

"Terry and I are getting married!" Clarence finally proclaimed.

"Well, it's about time!" his mother bellowed. "How many decades did it take you to decide? Seriously, that's the best news a mother can hear. Come here, Terry." She gave her future daughter-in-law a big hug and a kiss. Then, she suddenly sat upright as if startled. "I hope I heard right."

"You heard right," Terry said. "It's true. As true as a sorrel leaf is sour."

"Well, I'll be damned. Thought it would never happen." Within a second her smile faded and she looked puzzled. "What's sour?"

"That's a special secret, Mom. May I call you Mom?"

"You better!"

"If Tony and I are heading for the Silvesters, we better get moving," Clarence said. "We can celebrate later. You wanna join us, Terry?"

"No. I'll stay here and make lunch for your mother. I'll fix up something special to mark the occasion."

Mrs. Exton smiled broadly. "You're a sweetheart, Terry."

Tony, who was wandering nearby, finally joined in. "Congratulations to yous guys. Hope yis always be happy." He forced a smile. "Mr. Exton, we'd better go, now, don't you think?"

* * *

A patrol car sped past Clarence and Tony as they neared the Silvester residence. Clarence honked his Chevy's horn and waved as he recognized Chief Morris and one of his men. The chief answered with a beep, beep, beep.

"I wonder what's up," Clarence said. "I'm guessing they were at the Silvesters."

Tony shivered. "I don't like seein' them."

"The chief's not a bad guy. He plays it fair and square."

After a quarter mile more, Clarence and Tony were waved to a stop by two men who swung red flags rapidly to and fro. Clarence rolled down the Chevy's window as his car smashed clumps of sumac at the side of the road.

"What's up?" he asked.

"You're entering the Bald Eagle Zone," called out one of the birdwatchers, a lanky 30-year-old blond wearing U.S. Army fatigues. "May we ask where you're headed?"

"To your encampment. We have business with the Silvesters and Barneses."

"Okay, but our guys'll stick with you. Randall, here, will lead you to the next blockade." The rangy blond pointed to his partner, an elderly gentleman with white hair, whose orange headband held a purple feather above his ear. "You can drive slow as he walks, or he can jump aboard. At the next juncture, a woman named Thelma will escort you to our bivouac. Have a good day."

* * *

The bivouac was fully formed. Row after row of tents filled the rear acres of the Silvesters' property. Beyond that, encampment tents were mingled among the trees in the township land that led to Bitterlick Creek—land cleared of underbrush by the volunteers, with the careful eyes of the Boy Scouts who saved many of the jack-in-the-pulpits, the May apples, wild geraniums, Dutchman's breeches, wood anemones and other tender woods-loving plants. Every third tent in the open area was provided with a barbeque pit replete with cooking tools. The four corners of the Silvester land had been set aside for special needs. The Boy Scouts camped in one, near the house. The honeybees buzzed in another, at the far northern corner. And, not typical for such encampments, Johnny-on-the-Spot toilets stood tall in the two remaining corners. Why the commercial toilets? Because the usual part of an Army

---

or Boy Scout bivouac was eliminated for practical reasons—the digging and preparation of military-like latrines.

Open areas for powwows were situated here and there. Locations were kept clear of trees and brush because nighttime powwows gave rise to fires that sent sparks into the night's darkness. The volunteers circled about these fires, often sitting cross-legged on the ground. The Boy Scouts would break out into camping songs learned at troop meetings. While the birdwatchers were more reticent, they usually joined the scouts after the second or third song.

Foot and vehicle traffic between the encampment and the area mapped out around the eagles' nest was at times fairly heavy on the road and along several pathways as the volunteers moved to and from their assigned positions. That became clear to Clarence and Tony as they reached the Silvesters' property.

"Have a good day, Thelma!" Clarence called out as he and Tony walked up the pathway to the house, nodding to others who were coming and going. They were amazed at the number of cars parked on the front lawn and in adjacent fields of tall grass and mustard weed.

Wearing farmer's jeans, Thelma, the stocky female escort, waved as she turned away and began trudging back to her post, carrying her red flag on a long stick.

Inside the house, Clarence and Tony found the Barneses and Silvesters busy at the dining-room table, under the lowered Tiffany lamp. Qualms aplenty, Tony hung back behind Clarence and was tortured by the warm greeting from the foursome.

"Hello!" exclaimed Laura in her usual upbeat manner. "Good t'see you! Come! Come! Come! Both of you!"

The others chimed in with cheerful greetings. All rose from the table and offered salutes and handshakes. Smiles radiated, except from Tony, who spilled out words quickly: "I'm not Vinny Esposito. I'm Tony Paluto. I was told to use a fake name, infiltrate your ranks, and spy on yous."

Laura and Claudia giggled. Charley and Jimmy kept smiling.

Tony was dumbfounded. His body shook when he uttered, "What's wrong wit yous people? Din't y'hear me? Y'nuts or somethin'?"

"What he means is, he was performing a task for the late Senator Rimespecker when he last saw you," Clarence explained. "And he's very upset. He didn't want to do it. He's so, so sorry."

"We know all about it," Claudia said with warmth. She smiled broadly. "At first, when you didn't come back, we were disappointed. But then ...

Charley interrupted: "Chief Morris told us everything. We understand. Really."

"Now, we want you back," Jimmy said. "We know you're not Mr. Esposito. You're Mr. Paluto."

"But how did the chief know?" Tony looked from one to the other, then stared at Clarence.

"Don't look at me, Tony," Clarence said.

"The chief knew because the senator told him," Charley explained. "He laid out the whole plan over the phone for Captain Morris right after he gave you the assignment. He wanted to make sure he wasn't doing something that might get him in trouble. As Morris put it, 'The senator might be gruff, even mean-spirited, but he skirts the law.' By telling the police, he made you a police operative, if they went along with his plan."

"And the chief is often open to the wishes of elected officials, anyway," Jimmy added, "until he figures out what cards they're holding. In this case, by saying nothing, he acquiesced. He never agreed or disagreed. He just hung up and stayed quiet. He's slick that way. He gets what he wants in all sorts of ways by being coy."

"Chief Morris told you this?" Clarence questioned with wide-open eyes of surprise.

"Right here," Jimmy said. "Right here in this room. We've had three visits from him in three days. Mostly he comes to see Claudia and Charley. He takes them off into a tent for a private go-round." Moving his hand in a sweeping motion, he suggested, "Let's all sit down. Please."

"He pumps us about Cousin Ruth," Charley said while taking his seat. "Over and over again the same questions. I don't say much. Claud, here, she holds her own."

Others sat around the table after Tony grabbed two additional chairs from the kitchen. "I don't know how to say this," he said, "but thanks for ... for ... for, whatever. I mean ..."

"You needn't say anything, Tony." Laura said. "Come on. Sit with us."

Tony was the last to sit. He was still nonplussed and it showed.

Clarence stared wide-eyed at Claudia. "What did Morris ask you?"

"Oh, let's see," Claudia began. "How often did we see Cousin Ruth? *Seldom.* Did Ruth like jewelry? *She wore it sometimes.* What was her childhood like? *Strange.* How did she learn to paint? *Self-taught, I think.* When did she meet Lillian Rimespecker? *Don't know.* Did she ever talk about the Ermengarde Choker before it came into her possession? *No.*

Why were pecans so important to her? *Don't know*. Was she fascinated by diamonds and rubies? *Not that I'm aware of*. Emeralds? *Don't know*. How did she feel about her cat? *I guess she loved him*. Did she ever talk about Senator Rimespecker and his family? *Not to us*. Did you and she have secrets from your husband. *No!*" Claudia threw up her hands. "That's a sample for you. The questions went on and on."

"God almighty," Clarence muttered.

Tony was paying scant attention. In fact, he was close to daydreaming. Suddenly, seemingly out of nowhere, he proclaimed, "I want to climb that tree and get that choker. I can do it. I know I can do it. I can feel it deep inside me. I'm your man."

Chapter Twelve

Jordan sat on the edge of the canopied bed in the Green Room. His clothes were soiled. Blond stubble marked his youthful chin. Piles of small pieces of papers covered much of the comforter, and a black leather pocketbook lay on his lap along with a long pad of yellow paper. Purses, wallets, handbags, clutches, shoulder bags and satchels were scattered on the floor. Closet doors, a vanity, a chest of drawers, cabinets, bureaus and even jewelry boxes remained open.

He tossed the pocketbook and the pad of paper to the floor and reached for the ornate, French-style telephone on the French-Provincial bedtable. After hesitating, he started to dial, only to stop, hang up, and try again.

"Hello, Mrs. Paluto. This is Jordan Rimespecker. May I speak to Tony?"

Jordan felt more like punching a wall with his bare fists than talking with anyone. He felt more like hitting someone than seeking help or asking favors. Schools in the area were closing for the summer, and he had not seen his fellow students or teachers for days, missing a number of important classes that would have ended his junior year. Whether this broke his bridge to his senior year and college preparation seemed of no matter to him. Despite this lack of regard, he realized that he needed help to move forward, whether up a worthy pathway or down an undesirable road. He wasn't totally blind to his need for the right guide. But he couldn't turn to Uncle Clarry for fear of disappointing him. Too many ugly things tempted him, any one of which he knew would deeply sadden the man he loved and respected.

"Hello," Tony answered. "That you, Rimes?"

"Yeah, it's me."

"How y'holden up?"

"Not well. That's why I'm calling."

"What do y'need?"

"This might surprise you, my friend, but I think I need you. How about a ride to New York City in the limo?"

"Y'gotta be kidding! I'm no longer employed by the Rimespeckers, remember? I was fired by your father."

"So, I'm hiring you back for a day or two. I got the cash. You wanna do it?"

"You could drive to New York on your own. Better yet, take the train. Y'don't need me or the limo."

"I'm making up a list of hotels, restaurants and other places where my old lady might be hanging out." Jordan rattled off his words almost too fast for Tony to grasp them. "Right now I'm sitting in a pile of receipts from scads of places she frequented. She kept every receipt for years, I swear." His voice trembled, and he choked from a dry mouth. "I'm out t'find her. But I confess that I don't have what it takes to do it alone, and there's nobody else I dare ask, no one who knows or understands the situation."

"Ain't you forgetting Mr. Exton?"

"No! No way can I ask Uncle Clarry. He'd forbid me from doing certain things. Actually, he'd be shocked by some of my thoughts."

"You're not out to kill anybody, are you?"

"Don't worry. If you join me, I'll keep you outta trouble." Jordan paused to catch his breath. "The truth is, I'd like to have you with me right now, here at the house, to help me prepare this damn list from hundreds of receipts." He grabbed a fistful of papers and tossed them into the air. "I'm frustrated. I've ripped up a couple lists already. I feel this constant unease and agitation. A moment ago I felt like setting a match to the whole pile of receipts."

"Hey! None of that shit, Rimes! Don't set any fires, man!" Tony sucked in air and exhaled loudly. "I'm on my way. See you as soon as I get there."

"You still have a key?"

"Yeah. Guess I'm not supposed to."

"I'm in the Green Room. Third floor, West Wing."

"I'll find you."

Jordan continued to scan receipts and other papers while awaiting Tony, who lived about 20 minutes away on the southern rim of Cloverton City. He came upon a matchbook cover advertising the Black Cat. It displayed a cat-like woman on both exterior sides. Inside, in what looked like his mother's handwriting, was a telephone number and the words, "Ask for Jenny." After some troubling thoughts, he telephoned and waited.

"Meow! Welcome to the Black Cat," said a woman with an extremely sexy inflection. "How may I help you?" She continued to purr.

"Sorry, wrong number." Jordan hung up. But a few minutes later he dialed again. This time, after a long purr that gave him shivers, he asked for "Jenny."

"Who?"

"I only know her first name. Jenny."

"You must mean Jenny Nikolavich. She no longer works here. Sorry."

"Thank you." Jordan slammed the fancy-phone's headset down and pushed the unit off the bed and onto the floor where it crashed, separated, tinkled and buzzed with dial-tone. He was certain that he would have hung up anyway if Ms. Nikolavich had taken his call. "What would I have asked?" he questioned aloud, surprised to hear himself. "Did you romp and tongue-it with Lillian Rimespecker?" His own words turned his face red and sped up his heartbeat. He jumped angrily from the bed and kicked the French phone. After a few deep breaths and with considerable effort, he dug into the tight pocket of his jeans to make certain his cellphone was available.

Jordan circled the room several times and threw himself back onto the bed. He twisted his body this way and that, sat up again on the edge of the fancy comforter-covered mattress, and hung his head and stared at the floor for several minutes before shuffling through more paper. For the third time, he came across a receipt from the French Gateway Café and placed it on a pile marked, "Restaurants (frequently used)." After a long sigh that sounded more like a cry for help, he stretched out until his head fell upon the pillow, not seeming to care how much paper he crimpled. Minutes passed before he suddenly sprang from the bed and hurried from the room.

The distraught teenager was aware that the police had confiscated two of his father's guns—one from the bottom drawer of his office desk, the other from the top shelf of the late senator's private closet in the master bedroom. But he also knew that the house had contained four guns, having seen them often displayed by his boastful father, who had warned against their improper use in lecture after lecture. One of the four was given to his mother by his father for protection after riotous protests for equal rights in Washington some years ago.

Jordan ran as fast as he could through the hallways and down the stairs, and was able to reach the first-floor library before Tony's arrival. Hoping to return to the Green Room just as quickly, he hurriedly pushed the movable ladder past the section of shelves marked DEF to the books listed under GHI. He climbed halfway up to the ceiling, and reached for what appeared to be a heavy book. It was actually a hollow box designed to look like a red, leather-bound book with gold lettering that read *The Guns of Navarone.* He knew the .22 automatic pistol would not fit inside a pocket of his tight jeans, so he tucked the faux book under his arm and marched directly out of the library just as Tony was entering the house through the front doorway.

"Hey, Rimes, I'm here!" Tony called out as he saw Jordan rush toward the stairs.

"So you are," Jordan said as he slowed his pace and tightened his hold on the gun-box. "Thanks a hell of a lot for coming, Dude. Follow me. Now, you won't have to hunt for the Green Room."

"I'm pretty sure I know the way. After your mother's shopping sprees, I often carried her packages from the limo to her room. Yous was just a freakin' tot when I showed up. Your father stole me away from a sleazy politico named Harvey Hatfield. Now, I'm back home with my parents, and I ain't no happy camper. I love 'em, don't get me wrong. But living with 'em is somethin' else. To top all, my divorced sister has come home to roost. And she's still a freakin' pissy pot."

Tony kept pace with the teenager, following him by a couple steps.

"As you can see, the cops didn't keep me locked away in the hoosegow," Jordan said. "But I think I'm still high on their list."

"They ain't talked to me lately. I don't know where the hell I stand."

"Fret not. You're in good shape. They liked your honesty."

"Honesty?"

"About the Vinny Esposito caper."

"Mama taught me not to lie." Tony snickered. "What's that big book you're carrying?"

"The Guns of Navarone."

"It made a good movie. I saw it on late night television. Gregory Peck, David Niven and ... Who was it?"

"Quinn. Anthony Quinn."

"Yeah. He fit the part. They always stick 'im in that kinda role."

"It's called type-casting."

When Jordan attempted to open the door to the Green Room, the "book" slipped easily from under his arm. He grabbed for it, but it fell to the floor. Tony was quick, seized it, and knew at once by its feel that it wasn't a book.

"What the hell y'got here?" Tony unsnapped the clasp and opened the box. "Holy shit! What the fuck y'doing with a freakin'gun? And you lied to me! A book, my ass! Y'know I hate liars!"

Jordan grabbed for the pistol, but pint-sized Tony was too fast. He raised the weapon as high as his stature would allow and let the box fall to the floor. Keeping the gun pointed toward the ceiling, he raced into the bedroom to escape the distraught teenager who quickly followed.

"What did you intend to do with this?" Tony waved the gun at the ceiling.

"Take it to New York."

"Why? To shoot your mother?"

"Hell, no!"

"Oh, I see. You planned to shoot her lover."

"I just wanted to scare her. Understand? I wanted to feel strong and face her with anger and a gun. God almighty, how I wanted to show rage. That's what I wanted. Rage! You can't imagine how much I wanted to shove something into that bitch's face."

Tony interrupted: "You're out of control, man." He lowered the gun, but kept his distance from Jordan. "So, tell me what you been doin' wit that mess on that bed."

Jordan pushed some papers aside, sat on the bed, and relaxed his posture. "Every time I make an alphabetical list, I find another hotel to squeeze in. And I'm only listing places that she's been three or more times. When there's no squeeze-room left, I rip up the page and start all over again."

"Are you checking dates? How far y'goin' back?"

"All the way! Decades!"

"That's your problem."

"What do you mean?"

"Just go back two or three years. Jesus, Rimes, you don't need decades of hotel visits. All you need to know is where she's been hanging out in recent times. If she hasn't gone back to the Black Hole-in-the-Wall Hotel in ten years, I figure she ain't headin' there again."

"You're right. I've been making a helluva lot of extra work for myself."

Tony began to unwind because of the teenager's gradually relaxed demeanor. He sat on a frilly boudoir chair and placed the gun between his legs. Minutes later, he offered his help. "Let's see what y'got goin' over there on the bed." He pushed himself up, leaving the gun to slide to one side where it positioned itself between the cushion and arm. Jordan was aware of what happened, and immediately stepped toward the chair to retrieve the weapon with no intention of using it to frighten or kill. Seeing movement and unaware of the 16-year old's intent, Tony spun about and charged for the chair where all four hands met on the gun at the same time and pulled, twisted, scratched, dug, jerked and grabbed. As for words, neither man nor boy offered more than grunts and groans as they struggled to hold on, moving their skirmish inch by inch across the floor from chair to bed.

Suddenly, with the barrel of the gun aimed downward toward the comforter-covered mattress, the .22 automatic discharged with a startling bang that so jarred Tony and Jordan that they were shocked speechless. Both dropped the weapon immediately. They simply stared at each other as their bodies quaked. Shaken from head to foot, each one pled with eyes that seemed to tell the other that he didn't mean to cause the discharge. Their eyes kept repeating their regret until finally words were able to do the same.

"My God!" Jordan howled. "I didn't know it was loaded! I'm so, so, so sorry." He knelt and looked under the bed. "Jeez, man. We shot right through the mattress and into the floor boards."

"Holy shit!" Tony exclaimed. "What've we done? Saying we're sorry doesn't do justice. Lucky we didn't kill each other."

Still shaken to the core, they embraced each other, holding so tightly they felt each other's twitches and rapid heartbeats. Tony broke away and aimed for the bed. Jordan followed. They sat next to each other, with their chins resting on their fists and their elbows on their upper legs.

In time, the ex-chauffeur slapped the teenager on the back and said, "Still wanna find your old lady?" He picked up a handful of receipts and began shuffling through them.

Jordan nodded. He reached down for the gun without alarming Tony, picked it up and slipped it under the pillow. "Yeah, but I don't know how to handle it. Thought I did. Now I wonder what I'd do after confronting her."

"What do the cops tell you about their hunt?" Tony continued to read receipts.

"Not a damn thing. But I'm not bitchin' about Chief Morris, because I know how he works. He stays quiet, but taps into all sorts of networks." In a sarcastic tone, Jordan added, "That, I did learn from my hellish father, the irascible United States Senator Joseph Rimespecker."

"Hey, Rimes, look at this." Tony handed a receipt to Jordan. "It's for a cruise. Check the date. Up there at the top."

"Holy crap! That's around the time Dad was killed. It's the same weekend."

"That's the date of the transaction. Not the date of the cruise." He moved his forefinger down the slip of paper that Jordan held on his knee. "Look! Here! Damn, it hasn't happened yet."

"The eleventh of June. That's next week. Holy macaroni! A Caribbean cruise for two aboard a Carnival flagship. With several ports of call, including Jamaica and Belize."

"Where's Belize?'

"In Central America, just south of Mexico, on the Caribbean coast. Used to be called British Honduras. I've been there."

"Ah, you're reminding me that you're a rich kid. I guess you've traveled a lot."

"Sometimes they dragged me along. I'd have been happier with ordinary parents. Maybe like yours, Tony. So, count your blessings."

Tony could almost read Jordan's change in expression—his increased alertness, his darting but thoughtful eyes, his active facial muscles, his tongue movement across the lips and teeth. Surely a storm was brewing.

"Spill it, kid. Or do you want me to guess?"

"They'll board in New York. Which means they'll probably stay overnight in the same hotel from which Mom usually ships out."

"Now you're full of ideas, right? And maybe not such good ones."

Chapter Thirteen

Jordan sat in his study alcove staring into his computer having just Googled for a list of New York City hotels. His room remained a mess, for he had yet to pick up feathers, peanuts and other scattered results of his angry outbursts. Cleaning up would have to wait, he decided, until he gained information that would rest his mind. When a computer window listed more than 800 hotels, Jordan felt frustration again and immediately clicked the message off the screen. He remembered what Tony had said about "fewer being better," and wondered if that would apply here.

A brief period of rumination led to a spark. "Yes!" he exclaimed. He would narrow his hunt and Google for a list of hotels near the port facilities that catered to cruise-line travelers. "Bravo!" he exclaimed to himself when a list including Doubletree, Ritz-Carlton, Cosmopolitan, Soho Grand, Conrad, Hilton and a few others popped up on the screen. It was, indeed, a short list, and his heartbeat raced as he read the names again and again. He had been certain that a name would stand out. When one did not, he muttered "Fuggit" under his breath and bit his lip. "Ouch! Damn it!"

After more thought, Jordan decided that the number of hotels was so small that he could call each one, closer to the sailing date, to see if his mother or Nettlebaum had registered. But, he reasoned, no such inquiries would pay off for him if the women used false names, something he found likely since they were on the run from the police. Encountering the women near the ship at boarding time was a possibility, but that would give him little time for the kind of robust confrontation he wanted.

Again Jordan's active brain pondered the ups and downs. It's not possible, he thought, for those women to be carrying the amount of cash needed to pay expensive hotel, restaurant and cruise-line charges. A mental picture of his mother buying anything with cash made him smirk. Even if she and her wench started out with pockets full of cash, which he doubted, "It would be gone by now," he muttered. "They gotta use plastic." Surely Chief Morris has that figured out and is checking ATM machines from here to wherever, Jordan thought as he jumped up and punched the air with his fists. His muscles tightened and he pressed his fists against the wall.

Maybe it was the shot of pain that ran up his right arm. Maybe not. But something awoke a part of his brain that must have been sleeping. "Holy hell! You stupid jerk! What are private secretaries for, if they don't arrange travel plans?" Jordan seized his cellphone from his pocket and quickly hammered out a series of numbers he knew by heart.

"Hello!" Clarence answered while glancing at the caller ID. "About time I heard from you! I've been trying to reach you for days, but you don't pick up." He wiped his lips and pushed away his dish of tapioca pudding. Smiling broadly, he looked up at Terry who sat across the table from him in her stark-white sunroom. Mouthing the name, "Jordan," he pointed at his cellphone and winked at Terry.

"Sorry about that," Jordan muttered

"Guess what, Jordy! I asked Terry Smythe to marry me. And I want you to be my best man."

Breaking into Jordan's train of thought with this news was disruptive. It threw him a wild pitch. Ordinarily such tidings would have brought a profuse amount of joyful words and congratulations from the teenager. He struggled, stammered and spewed out, "Hey, that's good news." His words were flat. "I mean, that's great."

"Can you believe it? Me, finally getting married. You'll be my best man, won't you? I'll smack you in the butt if you say no." Clarence was well aware of Jordan's anger and depressed mood, so he decided to tread softly and curb his exuberance. An unexpected and revealing phone call from Tony Paluto had also made him aware of the boy's erratic behavior. Although about to say that he was with Terry in her house, he held back, fearful that it might hamper open dialogue.

"Uncle Clarry, I wanna ask you something."

"Yeah, Kiddo, what is it?"

"You arranged Dad's trips, didn't you? And Mom's?"

"Sure. What the hell's a good secretary for? I arranged all their travels. Business and pleasure. His and hers together and separately. His with political partners. Hers with her lady friends. Long elaborate cruises or quick flights abroad. But if you're asking about anything current, sorry, I'm all out of gas."

"But their typical itinerary must be implanted in your head. When do they generally leave? Where do they stay? When do they board? And so on and on. Where did they usually stay in New York before shipping out?"

"Your mother and father stayed at the Ritz-Carlton for years, but in recent times it was the Conrad for your mother. She liked its location, the view of the water, its sleek ultra-modern look, its contemporary appointments and dining facilities. And, the fact that it offered "*suites only*" really turned her on. Expensive suites with all the amenities, no less. Yes, that might be where she'd depart from these days. That's what you wanted to know, right? Why didn't you come right out and ask?"

Jordan said nothing.

"You there, Jordy?"

"Yeah, I'm here."

"Y'gotta understand. Cruises on those big ships are often planned far in advance. If she left the country or is leaving soon, she could have set things up a year ago. In fact, she had me arrange to have some cruise registrations automatically repeated. Are you in your bedroom?"

"Yes."

"Look up. Above your book rack. Next to your Temple pennant. What do you see?"

"That Mayan mask she brought back from Central America."

"From Belize."

"Belize?"

"Don't you remember her telling you about the masks and costumes used at celebrations, fiestas, rituals and dances?"

"Oh, yeah, yeah, yeah! It's coming back. She talked about the two groups of Mayas returning after being pushed out centuries earlier—one group by the British, the other by German coffee growers. That stuck in my mind. The name of the exact country didn't. Those Mayas were all over the place down there. Weren't they?"

"That's right. The Mopan Mayas migrated back to southern Belize in the Nineteenth Century, and the Kekchi Mayas migrated to Belize from Guatemala around the same time after losing their land to the coffee growers."

"Do you think she'd take this Ruth woman to Belize?"

"She loved it there. Loved everything about it. Said the temperature was the most perfect on earth."

"Jeez! Maybe they planned to disembark there. Maybe they planned to stay there, hide out there."

"Now you're really guessing. Don't let your imagination carry you off to la-la land. Maybe they're simply taking a little cruise around the Caribbean. And maybe they're not going anywhere. Chief Morris knows the possibilities. I filled him in about Belize and other reasonable hypotheticals."

"I've been wondering about the cops. I guess I tread water where Chief Morris has already scuba-dived."

"Nice going, Jordy. I like your metaphors. You're sounding more like yourself." Jordan's tone encouraged Clarence, who sensed it was time for him to make his move. "Look, I wanna see you. It's important that we get together. I'll come over. When's a good time?"

"Not right now, Uncle Clarry. I got things on my mind, things I gotta do."

Terry reached across the table with the coffee pot and filled Clarence's mug to the brim even though he had tried to wave her off. He was deeply intent with his phone conversation.

"I can help you. We can think things out together. Like we used to do. If it hadn't been for both our minds we'd never have hung that swing in the old pear tree."

"Dealing with a crooked limb can't compare with ..."

"Don't say it! I know a bit about your scheming mind and it frightens me. We have to get together. I'm coming over, whether you like it or not."

"Scheming mind? Where'd you get that?"

"I wasn't going to tell you, but Tony Paluto called me and pled for help. He's scared to death you're heading for serious trouble. He's been having nasty dreams since he last saw you."

"Paluto called you? Bastard! I didn't think he'd break a confidence. What did he tell you?"

"Just enough to let me know you need help. He was doing you a favor, man. Told me I was the medicine you needed. He begged me to arrange a face-to-face with you. Don't put him down, Jordy. He really cares."

"Why?"

"Ah, come on, Jordy. Don't be that way. Tony's an unusual person when it comes to things or people who touch him. Just like with this eagles'-nest stuff. He gets passionately involved. I know he doesn't seem like the type, and he's not very polished, but he has deep feelings.

He wants desperately to help the Silvesters and Barneses, folks he barely knows. Even wants me and Terry to get involved with the eagles and the choker."

Terry's eyes widened and her chin fell in surprise.

"When Tony spoke with me about you, he truly struggled," Clarence continued, "because he didn't want to say too much or reveal certain things. But he knew he had to do something to help you. And he saw only one way to go. Through me."

"It's not that I don't want to see you, Uncle Clarry. Honest to God, there's nothing I want more. Just give me time. Something's eating at me. It's damn fierce, and I gotta tame it or beat it t'hell."

"Like it or not, I'm knocking on your door tomorrow morning. Although I've lost my job because of the senator's death, I'd like to stick my nose into your affairs, if you don't mind, and if I can help."

"Uncle Clarry, please ..."

"Now, don't say anything. Just listen. There's something else y'gotta deal with. No funeral arrangements have been made for your father. I'm assuming his body is still at the morgue under the coroner's care, since his murder is police business. With your mother missing, we've got an odd situation on our hands. Ordinarily, she would make arrangements, and maybe she still will. Have you talked to anyone at Dewitt, Boyton and Dexter?"

"The law firm?"

"Yeah. Have you heard from Peter Dexter, your old man's attorney? You know him, don't you?"

"The landline's been ringing like crazy. But I don't answer. And I'm sure enough not calling anybody. Except for you, now."

"But you do know Dexter, right?"

"I've met him often enough. But I don't really know him."

"I'll tell you what, I'll get in touch with Dexter while I'm with you tomorrow. You do realize, don't you, that your father's last will and testament has to go to probate. And probate might drag out in this case because of your mother's absence. Actually, I don't have the answers. I'm no lawyer. But I'm guessing things could get messy."

"What is probate exactly?" The boy's tone of voice and inflections denoted a touch of panic. "I mean, I've heard of it."

"It's a legal step in handling the estate of a dead person. It has to do with the distribution of property and things like that, stuff spelled out in the will of the deceased."

Jordan felt sick. He didn't want to think about funerals, lawyers and wills. Such details crowded his mind and interfered with his present train of thought, which was tormenting enough.

Clarence was fighting himself for the right words. For a brief moment he couldn't find any. He deliberately coughed and cleared his throat. "Please, Jordy," he said in an elevated voice. "You gotta straighten up. You have no choice. Be a man."

Jordan's voice quivered as he asked, "Why are you laying all this on me now?"

Clarence knew that quiver only too well, from a day when Jordan dropped his ice-cream cone at age 4, from a day when he fell off the pear-tree swing at age 6, from a day when his father scolded him for a bad report card at age 7, and from a myriad of boyhood disappointments. He knew it meant tears, and he pictured them rolling down the boy's checks. He felt immediate remorse and chastised himself for pushing too far before seeing Jordan face-to-face. As he made an effort to speak, he heard a click and feared that Jordan had hung up. "Jordy? You there, Jordy?" He sucked in air and blew it out. "Shit!"

"Did he hang up?" Terry asked.

"Yeah."

"You should stay away from disquieting stuff when on the horn. Seriously, the telephone doesn't give complete communications. You don't see the person's eyes or read his expression. But don't worry, I think you and the boy have ties that are too tight to break. Euripides said 'Life has no blessing like the prudent friend.' So, be prudent with your words."

"My oh my, I hadn't realized you'd become a philosopher of sorts. Come here, you little devil."

"Not so little, I'm afraid."

"I like you just the way you are." Clarence pulled Terry close and kissed her.

"What's this about the eagles and the choker?" Terry whispered into his ear. She pulled back and presented a dizzy smile as she stared into his eyes. "I've never climbed a tree in my life!"

"I think Tony wants to display his tree-climbing talent in front of us. Or, he's hoping we'll get caught up in the whole Bitterlick Creek adventure that's got everyone talking. To tell you the truth, Terry, I'm kind of interested in seeing this so-called bivouac or encampment. Did you see the picture in yesterday's paper?"

"A bunch of dudes pushing rocks to divert the white water?"

"Yeah. Crazy, isn't it? They're actually building a huge patio of rocks on the east side of the creek. It blows my mind." Clarence sprang from his chair. "Let's go check in on Mom, and then we'll shove off."

"Shove off?"

"Oh, here we go a wassailing among the volunteers," Clarence sang out resoundingly as he attempted to swing Terry into a dance.

Backing away after two spins, Terry called out, "You're trying too hard to be happy, Uncle Clarry. With an old English drinking song, no less. Save it for Christmas. You're not going to blow off thoughts of Jordan that way. Calm down. I'll go bivouacking with you."

"You mean you'll stay overnight in a tent?" He licked his lips. "With me!" He scrunched his nose. "In a two-man pup tent. I'd like that."

"No! No! No! We'll just go take a look, and then you can buy me dinner at the Clam Tavern on the way home."

Chapter Fourteen

Clarence and Terry passed inspection, clearing through the checkpoints as they approached the Silvesters' home where they found activity in high gear. Volunteers were dashing this way and that as the couple entered the house where they found only Charley working at the dining-room table.

"Hi! What a surprise!" Charley greeted them warmly. "For some reason, I never expected to see you here, Mr. Exton." He stood and offered his hand.

"Please call me Clarence."

"Okay, Clarence. Nice to see you again. And please call me Charley."

"This is Terry Smythe, my fiancée," Clarence introduced. "We've been reading and hearing so much about your project that we figured we'd come take a look."

Charley smiled broadly and took Terry's hand. "Welcome to our bivouac. We'll be glad to find some work for you to do," he said with a jocular expression, followed by a sigh of exhaustion. He turned to Clarence. "There's one thing forbidden. You can't claim the Ermengarde Choker in the name of your late employer." He winked at Clarence.

"Fear not!" Clarence exclaimed. "Although, it might look good around your neck, Terry." He squeezed his own neck, made a funny face and stuck out his tongue. "Seriously, we'd just like to look around. Maybe we'll find something we can do." He stretched in an effort to look out a window. "Is Tony Paluto here today?"

"Oh, yes. He's become a regular. Right now he's showing off his tree-climbing gear to a group of fascinated onlookers—actually, bird watchers who would often like to climb trees for close-up looks, but don't dare. They stay quietly positioned in the bushes, peering through their binoculars." Charley held his slightly open fists to his eyes and scanned the room. "Claudia and Laura left a few minutes ago to carry sandwiches and drinks down to the creek where a bunch of our guys are working. The gals hinted that they might take the long trek upstream for a first-time look at the actual eagles' tree. It's a tall, beautiful black locust that you won't forget once you've seen it. As for Jimmy, the Birdman? He's holding class with the Boy Scouts."

"Holding class?" Terry questioned.

"All about bald eagles. You should hear the kids' questions. How fast can they fly? Why are their eyes yellow? What do they feed their young? On and on they go. Jimmy has the answers. He's good. Really good. He lectures all over the place."

"We've heard," Clarence said.

"Why don't you go out back and join him. He loves an audience. Step outside, turn left, and you can't miss him. He might be a scrawny guy, but he's got a big voice. He usually stands on a box and swings his arms in the air. And no matter how noisy the crowd, his piercing voice cuts through it. I think you'll enjoy the interaction."

Outside, Terry was immediately in awe of the rows and rows of tents that filled so much of the open space leading to the woods. "Holy smackeronies!" she exclaimed. "Can you believe this?" She took a lengthy gaze over the encampment before grabbing Clarence's hand and pulling him toward the left where a circle of Boy Scouts sat cross-legged around an animated man of slight stature who stood atop an old rabbit hutch.

"Do bald eagles stick with one mate for life?" asked a slightly built scout with a mop of curly amber hair and protruding ears.

"Almost always," Jimmy answered. "But if one dies, the other will seek a new mate. Occasionally, an adult bird, usually a female, will intrude and battle for territory, win, and take over a nest. But this is rare. Very rare."

"Can a bald eagle swim?" asked a freckle-faced scout sporting a military-style crewcut hair.

"Oh, yes! And very well," Jimmy responded. "They eat fish, and when they swoop down to the water to grab fish, they'll sometimes swim before they fly off. I've even seen them swim all the way to shore with a heavy load. Usually, however, an eagle on the hunt will skim the water, and then take off into the air with the fish dangling from its beak. Back at the nest, mama bird or papa bird will break the fish into little pieces for their young."

"I heard they nest very high," commented a lanky scout with ebony-colored bangs that nearly reached his eyebrows.

"The higher the tree the better," Jimmy said. "Bald eagles like to build their nests way up near the tree's peak. Because of that, the nest can sometimes be seen for miles. No thick coverage of greenery for these birds. The situation with our eagles here at Bitterlick is unique, however, since we have a rocky cliff on one side of the tree, allowing us access only from the creek side. The tree, a black locust, is extremely tall, its upper branches extending high above the cliff, but it can be climbed only from the creek where we are diverting the rapids. As soon as we've finished with the work on the creek bed, we'll all take a hike along the waterway and each of you will be able to see this tall, rangy locust tree that holds the eagles' nest and, hopefully, the Ermengarde Choker."

Clarence and Terry moved closer to the gathering of Boy Scouts and were noticed by Randy Houck, the scoutmaster, who immediately tried to push his well-rounded body up off the ground where he sat between two Eagle Scouts. When his effort paid off, Jimmy noticed, turned toward him and saw the visitors.

"Greetings!" called out the scoutmaster. "Please join us."

"Hello, Mr. Exton!" Jimmy stepped down from the rabbit hutch. "Welcome to our discussion of the bald eagle."

"Please don't let us interrupt you," Clarence said.

"Scouts, please welcome Mr. Exton and his lady-friend," Jimmy instructed

*　*　*

Later, Clarence and Terry mingled with a gathering of birdwatchers who had returned from their security posts and were comparing notes.

"This crazy dude tried to slip by me," said one of South Jersey's most prominent birdwatchers, a lanky, pale-faced resident of Cape May, who was the leader of a group called Save the Red Knot. "Stupid jerk was wearing camouflage fatigues and actually tried to climb the cliff. He couldn't get around a gigantic bolder surrounded by a tangle of vines and burdock. Alex Garber and I scrambled up and grabbed him by the seat of his pants, which were covered with burrs from a left-over patch of last season's dried-up burdock weeds."

"Mr. Exton!" The shout came from a distance. "Yo! Mr. Exton!"

Clarence recognized Tony's voice and spun around to see the former chauffeur waving at him from a half-dozen tents away. "Hey, my man, I was told you were here." He started walking toward Tony. "Terry, come on!"

"Thanks for showin' up," Tony yelled. As he neared the couple, he smiled broadly and danced a silly little jig. "Mr. Barnes said you was here, so I've been huntin' y'down. "

The three met near a barbeque pit and shared greetings.

"This place obviously puts you in a good mood," Terry said as the two men embraced. "Y'gotta nice wiggle to your hip movement."

"It's the greatest," Tony replied. "I've been showing off my gear. Come on. I'll show you." He led them to a powwow circle where the circumference of the grassy turf was edged with colorful rope that tied together woodcarvings that Charley had fashioned over many years of whittling. Inside the circle, Tony had arranged row after row of tree-climbing gear that he had collected, much of it awarded to him at climbing contests. In neat rows he had positioned climber straps, saddle bags, pulleys, climbing spikes, ascenders, snaphooks, rope runners, harnesses, swivels and dozens of other pieces of equipment needed for safe and successful tree-climbing.

The immediate look on Clarence's face was one of questioning Tony's need to display his tools. To prove something, maybe? An ego trip, maybe? He quickly caught himself, smiled and said, "Wow! This all belongs to you?"

Tony was astute enough to catch Clarence's first expression and retorted, "I'm still trying to prove that I can do it. I've got to be their first choice to climb that tree. I know I can do it."

"Look at the little animals," Terry said, pointing to the circle of woodcarvings. "There's a squirrel and a rabbit. Even a skunk."

"They're not mine," Tony explained. "Mr. Silvester carved them things out of odd-shaped hunks of tree branches he found in the woods." Tony sounded defensive when he said, "I guess he likes to show off his stuff, too."

"Your collection of gear is amazing, Tony," Clarence said to placate the assertive "climber."

"Yous guys wanna go down to the creek?" Tony asked. "If yis don't mind walkin' a couple miles along the bank, I'll take you to the tree that holds the eagles' nest. You gotta wear boots, 'cause the path is broken up here and there. You can't avoid stepping in water. That's why we're not allowing the scouts to make the trek yet. We're working hard to patch and clear the rocky and root-tangled bank and path."

Tony's tone and his use of the words, "We're working hard," revealed that he considered himself among the leaders of the pack. This project had become just as much his endeavor as it was the venture of the Birdman and his friends. Clarence couldn't help but smile.

"You're really into this, aren't you, Tony?" Clarence said with a chuckle of amusement.

"Ah, man! You said it! There ain't nothin' better than an undertaking like this. Think of it. Saving the birdies from the mean monsters of the world and recovering the Crown Prince of Hapsburg's jewels or whatever the hell they are. Hell, I ain't gotta real job yet, but, yeah, I'm sittin' on top of the freakin' world." He giggled, then chuckled, then roared with laughter. "Now, do you want a beautiful, but wet and rocky walk to see the tall locust tree that brings us all together. It's a dazzling sight on a gorgeous day like today."

Clarence looked at Terry. "Let's do it." He pulled her close. "What do y'say, Hon?"

"Well, I said I wanted to lose weight. I suppose I could launch my effort with a long walk along Bitterlick Creek. Where do we get our boots?"

"We have a supply hut at the water's edge," Tony explained. "Follow me."

Tony led the couple amidst the tents and other bivouac paraphernalia until they reached the woods. "We're now on East Bitterlick Township land," he explained. "We've got a permit for use, thanks to the efforts of Police Chief Morris. From this point on the land slopes toward the creek. It's heavy with maple, oak, beech, locust and ash trees."

The long wooded slope to the creek offered a touch of magic on this perfect day because the bright sunlight streamed into the woods here and there where the thick canopy permitted and where the gentle breezes parted the branches. The effect was a splattering of brilliant patches among the deep, dark shadows on the forest floor. The constantly moving patchwork of dark and light created an almost mesmerizing impact on the human intruders. Here and there a streak of light would strike the flowers and the delicate leaves of wild geranium clusters, bringing to a glow the light purple color of the blooms and their pinkish tinge. Mushrooms, tree fungus, toadstools, puff balls, and other fungi of all shapes and colors grouped themselves in fascinating arrangements near rotted wood, decaying vegetation and damp, dark niches. Vines of the wild grape and bittersweet draped some trees and woody shrubs, creating waterfall effects when streaked by splashes of sunlight.

"Look who's heading our way!" Tony cried out when he saw Claudia and Laura coming toward them through an opening in the woods.

Laura ducked and pushed some hanging bittersweet vines out of her way—vines that still held a small cluster of orange-red berries from the previous autumn, a surprising fact since the berries were a hungry pheasant's favorite fall-and-winter food. "Howdy folks!" she called out. "If you're considering the entire trek, do it! It's fantastic! But be prepared. Carry a big stick." She rolled her eyes. "I'm beat! But it's worth it. Believe me, you'll see it in your dreams for a long time to come." She hurried to Clarence and took his hand. "What a surprise! Nice to see you again. This guy next to you is a dynamo." She tapped Tony on the head. "He's become the number one motivator around here."

"So we're beginning to find out," Clarence remarked.

"Are you joining the team?" Laura asked.

"Maybe."

Laura turned to Terry and introduced herself. When she learned that Clarence's lady-friend was his fiancée, her eyes sparkled and she took it on herself to introduce Claudia to Terry before Clarence and Tony had a chance.

"Good to see you again, Mr. Exton!" Claudia greeted. "We finally got to see the eagles' tree. It's a beauty. If I were an eagle, it would definitely be my choice for nesting. I won't dare describe it, not if you're heading that far upstream and can see it for yourself."

Small talk among the five was cut short when Tony insisted, "Enough chitchat!" and demanded, "We gotta march on!" As they neared Bitterlick Creek, Tony pointed to a heart carved into the trunk of a beech tree. Inside the heart read the words, "Charley loves Claudia."

"Ah-hah! It appears Charley Silvester harbors a romantic side," Clarence remarked.

Terry stepped to the tree and placed her hand on the heart. "Mutual love, the crown of all our bliss," she said with poetic flare. When Clarence gazed at her with astonishment, she said, "No, no. Not my words, I'm afraid. We must thank John Milton for such a thought. But I willingly adopt it."

The creek water glistened but ran smoothly, giving off a greenish glint as it reflected the trees and thick vegetation that grew abundantly on both sides of the stream. Although the sky was blue, it played only a minor role in the creek's mix of colors because of the tall trees that leaned inward over the water. Rocks at the brook's edge added to the overall greenish look, for they were heavily coated with verdant moss and pale gray-green lichens.

Clarence and Terry were surprised when they saw the supply shelter. It was actually a handsome toolshed that Charley had ordered from the American Handyman's Catalogue. Resting at the water's edge, it was supported on the creek side by large rocks partially submerged in the stream. It was designed to look like a small house, with an attractive doorway and shuttered windows, obviously created for the backyard of an affluent family's suburban home. Jimmy and Charley had experienced a difficult time moving it from where the delivery man had unloaded it in front of the Silvesters' house. At first they could barely budge it, until they found Laura hiding inside its clapboard walls. After minutes of successful silence, she had lost control and given herself away with a burst of laughter. She was chased into the heart of the bivouac by both men.

Moving it through the woods had not been easy, even without Laura's weight. Charley and the Birdman were forced to cut a broad zigzagging pathway among the tall tree trunks. Pushing and pulling rather than lifting, they scraped the forest floor and sometimes uprooted plants they had hoped to save. "Oh, God! There goes those huckleberries," Charley grumbled at one point.

Now, on this adventurous day for Clarence and his fiancée, the couple gaped at the supply shelter until Tony said, "Not what you expected, I see."

"What a beautiful playhouse for kids," Terry remarked.

"Go in one at a time," Tony directed. "The boots are lined up against the left wall. Don't try to put them on without sitting down. You'll find a stool just inside the door. Take a black pair, Mr. Exton And you, Miss Terry, pick from the olive-green ones."

"Go ahead, Terry," Clarence urged. As she entered the shack, he gazed at Tony pathetically. "I know it's been years of 'Mister' but you can drop it now. Try hard, Tony, and you can call me Clarence. Work on it."

* * *

The first quarter mile of the hike upstream was uneventful for the threesome who appreciated the creek's smooth currents and occasional languid pools where small fish could be seen swimming in circles. The pathway had been patched with clay and solid earth where years of runoff had washed away the soil and created large gaps. The birdwatchers had also moved rocks to fill pits and sinkholes along the bank where the depth of some underwater cave-ins had proved dangerous for slipping and sliding trailblazers.

The beauty of the hardwood trees that reached high above the stream and almost closed out the sky was doubled by their reflections in the stream, sometimes a perfect mirror image, while at other times a shimmering or diffused semblance. Occasionally a reflection was split by a smooth rock that held itself above the water, the broken image creating a rainbow of colors and streaks of white light in the separated currents around the boulder.

The threesome heard the buzz of a chainsaw and the clink-clank of workers' tools as they rounded a curve at the one-mile marker. Soon they heard voices. And, as the stream straightened, improving their view, they saw a group of male and female birdwatchers in the water and on shore sawing and hacking at a huge fallen limb that blocked the pathway. The bank of rocks, tree roots and earth had caved in under the weight of the silver maple bough that stretched across the water causing a partial dam where branches, clusters of brush, twisted and rotting logs, stones, muck and other debris had gathered.

"Welcome to your first benchmark," called out a female volunteer worker who laid down her shovel. "I need an excuse to rest. And you're it."

Clarence, Terry and Tony were soon surrounded by eight birdwatchers. Fast and furious conversation ensued. The threesome quickly learned that difficulties lay ahead, that they had traveled the easy pathway—a trail and waterway patched, cleared and repaired by crews of volunteers working their way upstream. Also, they were told that within the next mile they would begin to face the rapids. The gathering got lighthearted, however, with tales of a feisty family of muskrats who claimed territory along the bank beneath the fallen tree limb. Several nasty encounters had led to a final lecture by wet-and-wiggly mama muskrat. She stood upright on her little hind legs atop the maple limb and in shrill squeals chastised the human intruders before leading her family away.

Impatient Tony was the first to cross the bough and begin the next leg of the trek upstream. He did so in shallow water since the thickest part of the tree trunk and its giant root ball rested on the collapsed pathway. He urged Clarence and Terry to follow. The only mishap occurred when

Terry slipped, despite the helping hands of others. She roughed up her buttock on the bark, and got water in her boots, but brushed off the discomfort like a good teammate.

Deep gullies, caused by years of runoffs after storms, posed the most serious threats to foot travel for Tony-and-company over the next quarter mile. A slip could slide a hiker right into swirling water, a languid pool, or onto a bed of underwater rocks. After passing a waterfall, Tony noted that the water was calm and shallow and the creek floor sandy and pebbly.

"Jump down!" he said after lowering himself into the water. "This is great for walking." After a few steps, he shouted, "Wait! Miss Laura knew what she was talking about when she said 'Carry a big stick.' See if you can find three straight and sturdy branches in the woods. They'll help pull us along this sandy bottom."

After a speedy but successful hunt, they put their new-found but primitive canes to work. The sticks helped, and the threesome picked up speed in the water until they felt pressure on their legs indicating the approach of rapids.

"Couldn't Jimmy the Birdman find a shorter route to the eagles nest?" Clarence asked.

"He tried, but the freakin' forest thickens south of the Silvesters' property and becomes impossible to penetrate. One time, our wise ol' Birdman goes and gets himself totally lost. Another time, he hadda back out after trying to cut through a bitch of a tangle. On top of all, he tells me, he came down with a fierce case of poison ivy. Bitterlick Creek is the only open pathway this side of the cliff, which, they tell me, is really a small mountain split by thousands of years of rushing water."

"How the hell did he find the eagle's nest?" Clarence asked.

"That's not hard to figure. Take a guess."

Terry answered first: "Birdwatching, of course!"

"You said it. Where's a better place to birdwatch in these parts than Bitterlick Creek. Look over there! Across the creek! Thems not yellow leaves in them trees."

"Oh, my God, they're moving."

"Goldfinches!" Clarence explained. "The females are light yellow. The males are brighter yellow with black wings. Am I right, Tony?"

"If you say so. I don't know my birds, I'm afraid. But I'm learning. Y'can't hang with these bird-lovin' dudes and not learn."

"I learned about goldfinches from my Pennsyvania Dutch grand-mother," Clarence said. "She called them salad birds. I don't know why."

Tony led Clarence and Terry to an inlet where beavers had built a dam out of an assortment of branches. Next to the inlet, they rested on a gigantic rock where Terry studied an assortment of strange-looking lichens growing atop it.

Later, as they hiked, Tony grabbed a frog from a small pool of water and handed it to Terry, who screamed and dropped it. "Don't do that!" She hurried ahead on pockmarked soil, suddenly stopping when she saw two deer—a doe and her fawn—drinking creek water. "Shhhush," she whispered. "Look!"

The last half-mile of the hike presented the most difficulties, for the rapids kept the threesome on land heavily loaded with obstacles. At two locations they joined birdwatchers working to remove fallen limbs and fill sinkholes. "We're the last crew you'll meet up with before reaching the daytime camp beneath the nest," explained a chubby, red-face birdwatcher dressed in bulging overalls and holding a spade over his shoulder.

White water slapped the banks and tumbled over rocks of all shapes and sizes across the width of the stream, roaring as it splashed over rocks worn smooth by years of burnishing and splattering high over jagged rocks of recent descent from the banks and upstream elevations.

The trek was coming to an end. Clarence and Terry stood in awe as Tony pointed ahead to the finish line—a row of rocks that edged the north end of a giant work patio constructed to divert the rapids to the west side of the stream, to create a hard, flat surface for the volunteers toiling under the tree, and to establish a base for the climbers. Jimmy the Birdman's original hope was to station the East Bitterlick Fire Company's hook-and-ladder truck on the stone platform he had designed. But the fire chief rejected the idea. The firetruck's only entry point to the creek bed would have been miles south of Ruth Nettlebaum's distant neighbor's small chicken farm, near the township's dump, about 23 miles from the Silvesters' property line, and about 20 miles from the bald eagle's nesting tree. "Too far to travel in that rocky water," Chief Bobby McKenna had insisted again and again. "The only time I'd put a truck in that creek would be in desperation to suck up needed water to put out a fire."

The sight of the water-gap—the area between and including the east and west sides of Bitterlick Creek—was spectacular. A riveting sight, indeed, was the rushing water, the broken and crumbling rocky incline in West Bitterlick, the high monument of colorful rock called the cliff in East Bitterlick, and the swaying of the feather-like branches of the locust trees that sucked water from the creek and like giant dancers dressed up their rocky backgrounds with reflections of their undulating arms. Frond-like leaves on spreading branches gave the crown the look of a plume. Huge boulders displaying exposed strata in colorful strips marked the west side, while a spectacular, sheer and multicolored rock formation that reached 70 feet high stood on the east side, protecting the bald eagles' tree from easterly winds. That tree, the most striking of all, formed a fanciful pattern against the high-reaching cliff. Its limbs could go nowhere to the east, but reached out freely elsewhere, its shadows breaking up the colorful solid-rock background into mosaic patterns.

Tony urged Clarence and Terry to look skyward where the top 10 feet of the black locust tree stood above the cliff and blazed in the sunlight like a torch. There at the highest reaches was the big nest of the bald eagles, in the brightness of the day, among thinned out branches and exposed to the elements.

"That's it!" Tony exclaimed. "That's our nest! That's where our babies are hanging out. If we stay here long enough you'll see mama or daddy bird swoop in with a fish."

"What I want to know," Clarence said, "is how the Birdman got his pix."

"Pictures?" Tony smiled. "Look up!"

The threesome stared directly up into a tree that shaded them, a tree almost identical to the eagles' black locust. It stood perhaps 100 feet from its "twin" and held a black box in its upper branches.

"See that thing up there?" Tony asked. "It contains the latest in sophisticated equipment. They make stuff small these days. Tiny lenses can see things miles away. Did y'see them pictures of Pluto sent to earth by NASA? Jim Barnes' stuff up there is aimed right at the eagle's next. And it all operates by remote control from his house."

"But how did Barnes get it up there?" Terry asked.

"Those guys shot them big hooks high in the air—hooks that was attached to ropes that looped around branches. Then they lowered them and attached whatever."

"What guys?"

"The Birdman's buddies from Cornell. Professors of engineering. Theys got an article comin' out in some mechanical engineering journal about the whole operation. And theys been invited to some symposium in California to demonstrate their use of all sorts of big and little pulleys."

* * *

Early that evening, back at the encampment, Clarence and Terry felt like sloths forced to run the decathlon several times over. They were so exhausted that they turned down a cookout of hot dogs, baked beans and coleslaw. After well-meant thankyous and goodbyes, they splashed water on their faces, hurried to their car, waved, tooted the horn and began a tedious drive home. The first rest stop came none too soon.

Smoke and the smell of roasted hot dogs hung heavily over the bivouac area well into the darkness of the night.

The night's last song from the youthful voices of Boy Scout Troop #24 was a rewritten version of an old camp tune. Scoutmaster Randy Houck had remembered his boyhood days at Camp Pahaquarra on the Delaware River in northwestern New Jersey. The camp's number-one fireside song had never left his mind. He wrote it down, scratched out words, and filled in the blanks with new words that fit today's bivouac. He began by changing *Delaware* to *Bitterlick*. Tonight's rendition followed a few days of practice.

Charley and Claudia opened the window of their bedroom, peered out, and listened as the scouts sang:

There's a camp along the Bitterlick, Eagle-Nesting is its name;
Among the buzzing bees and the leafy trees, there's lots of fun and cheer;
In the water deep, we move some rocks and guard some flocks ...

Verse flowed into verse until sleep called. The scouts crawled into their pup tents. Claudia and Charley yawned, smiled, kissed and squirmed their way into their four-poster bed. Yet they could not calm their active brains. They talked, tried to sleep, and talked some more.

"I'm glad I finally saw the nesting tree," Claudia said. "But that hike is a bit much. You'd think I'd fall right off to sleep."

"Jimmy says the choker's barely visible on the computer screen."

"Why's that?"

"Shifting leaves and twigs and stuff. And the young birds are getting bigger, and the winds keep blowing."

"What if it's not there when we finally go up to get it? What if it falls? What if a fierce storm carries it off? What if a thief's drone manages to snatch it?"

"Are you afraid you won't inherit it?"

"Are you kidding? No way!" Claudia popped up and sat with her back against the pillow and headboard. "I don't want the damn thing. Why do you ask? You think something's going to happen to Cousin Ruth?"

"No! She's the kind of crazy nut who'll live forever."

"I'm serious, Charley. I don't want that choker. It would change our lives. Think of the publicity we'd get? The notoriety? We'd have to change our names and move away. And you know damn well I'd never wear it."

"They say it's worth millions."

Claudia slipped back under the covers. "We don't need the grief that'd come with it. We'd only sell it and give the money away."

"And that would be fun."

"Forget it, Charley!"

"Well, I suspect that Ruth is going to live a long life in some far off place. And hopefully disappear from our lives. Unless, of course, they find her and charge her with murder."

"You don't think ...? No. She's not the murdering type."

"I don't know. Actually, Claudia, I pretty much agree with you about the notoriety. I don't want it either. Look at the publicity we're getting now. When someone goes up that tree, we'll be swamped by the media. Yet again ..."

Chapter Fifteen

Clarence held his umbrella in his left hand while knocking on the Rimespecker's door with his right. He kicked a few newspapers out of his way. He had seen the headlines and read the stories day after day and didn't blame Jordan for ignoring them, although he suspected the boy wouldn't have picked up the papers anyway, even if his family's story failed to generate news. Today's lead story in the *Beacon* reported that the U.S. Senate was about to authorize a memorial service for the late senator, despite his missing wife, the scandal and the lack of funeral preparations. After knocking again and again, Clarence finally closed his umbrella and set it aside by leaning it against the door frame, realizing that he was sheltered from the rain by the portico. He rang the bell. Still, no response. He pulled on the heavy brass knocker and slammed it down. No answer.

The rain beat hard on the portico roof.

Reluctantly, he fished for his packet of keys, pulled the wad from his pants-pocket, shook and jingled it until he spotted a key marked with a red R. He unlocked the door and pushed it open slowly. No longer was he the late senator's personal secretary, so, he figured, that made him a trespasser. Was he "breaking and entering?" Maybe. Surely, Jordan wouldn't care.

"Jordy!" he whispered loudly. "Jordy!" He increased the volume. "Jordy!" he yelled.

He stepped quietly at first, practically tiptoeing across the broad foyer. He headed toward the library because of its closeness and frequent use by Jordan. It was homework haven for the boy. Slowly, he opened the door to the ornate repository of books that he had grown to know so well over many years. He faced nothing but darkness. Regardless, he called out softly, "Jordy!"

After a considerable amount of stealthy exploration, he gained conviction and began a more vigorous search of the house, calling out the teenager's name around every corner and in every room. The gloominess of the rainy day didn't help his spirits, yet he did not turn on lights as he prowled through the living room where the bulky stuffed furniture—large sofas and wingback chairs—rose like giant mushrooms in the darkness. He tripped over a hassock.

He gained more nerve in the music room, enough to pluck the harp. But when he ran his fingers down the keyboard of the grand piano, the loudness made him shudder. He said, "Shush," to himself and hurried off.

The long, formal table in the dining room was a straight-arrow guide to the kitchen. So, despite darkness, Clarence had little concern, with the table on his right, of hurrying safely past the vast collection of silver tea and coffee services and other dining accoutrements that lined the wall on his left. He had often thought it peculiar that such a small family needed such an extensive table. As for the kitchen, he knew it well. He could not begin to count the times that he and Hilda had drunk their morning coffee together at a table surrounded by as much stainless steel equipment as that of a small restaurant.

Clarence took the back stairs to the second floor—circular stairs built primarily for the use of servants.

It was Senator Rimespecker's office that gave him haunting feelings because it had been so much a part of his life for so many years. As he stood in the doorway, he could actually hear the senator calling out those frequent demands. Backing away, he struggled to subdue a brief shudder.

Later, Clarence could not quell his anxiety as he searched the upper floors in the East and West Wings. He felt panic every time he opened a door to a bedroom, sitting room, or bath. He was fairly certain by now that Jordan was not home, but went on looking for fear the teenager was in distress or worse. He scolded himself again and again for his feelings of foreboding, yet he could not conquer them.

Opening bathroom doors caused particular unease. Clarence blamed that on late night movies and their projected images of bathtubs and showers in murder and suicide scenes. How many times had he watched Janet Leigh slide down that wet tile in Hitchcock's *Psycho*? Probably too many, he thought. "Stop being such an idiot!" he said aloud.

Was he being deliberate in opening so many other bedroom doors before reaching Jordan's? "Shake it off," he whispered to himself. "You goddamn wimp."

Clarence paused before opening the door to Jordan's bedroom. "Jordy, you in there? It's your Uncle Clarry." He raised his voice. "If you're in there, open the door." A moment later, he grabbed the knob and pushed. The door opened easily and Clarence simply stared without moving. He saw no one, and stepped into the room. Neither the bed nor the floor held a dead body. Clarence struggled to catch his breath. And, again, he scolded himself for being so foolish. "You silly, ridiculous nut!"

A quick look told Clarence that something was awry. Neckties were strewn on the teenager's bed along with two white shirts, well starched with stiff collars. Clarence questioned why Jordan would have been choosing from among dress shirts and ties. T-shirts and jeans he'd understand. At first he couldn't remember the last time he saw the boy wearing a suit, blazer, dress shirt, vest or necktie. Then the pieces slowly came into focus: His navy blue suit. Billy Bradshaw's funeral. Two years ago. After the teenager's drowning in Messenoming Quarry.

Thoughts of all sorts raced through Clarence's head, but nothing plausible came together. He opened Jordan's closet and saw a tan suit and a gray one. The navy one was missing.

His cellphone played a jingle, startling him. He pulled it from his pocket, and noted that Terry was calling.

"Hello, Ter!"

"How's it going?"

"He's not here. I've gone through the entire house."

"Well, at least he hasn't harmed himself."

"That we know of. Actually, it looks like he took off somewhere, dressed up in a suit and necktie."

"You're kidding? Do you think he's searching for his mother?"

"Don't know. Maybe. Could be something I said pushed him into it. I hope he's not on his way to Belize."

"Don't you go sailing off to Belize."

"Fear not! Look, I better get moving. I'll be home soon."

"Love you."

Clarence suddenly told himself he was in serious need of coffee. That thought pushed him quickly from Jordan's bedroom all the way back down to the kitchen. He knew where Hilda kept the big electric pot and the ground coffee beans from Columbia. He fetched water and united the three. His intent was to sit in that familiar seat where for years he had joined her morning after morning before facing the senator. Today, he would drink a couple stiff mugs of brew, and allow fleeting reflections to grow to deep pondering and serious contemplation.

* * *

Jordan was glad that the rain had stopped before stepping off the train in New York City. He discarded the cheap plastic poncho that protected his suit, the kind purchased at football games, soon after tipping the taxicab driver in front of the Conrad Hotel. He tossed it into a trash receptacle before hurrying into the contemporary structure where he could not help but be somewhat in awe of the smooth and sleek lines of this ultra-modern hotel, a look he had not encountered in many trips with his parents. Such trips, however, did give him poise.

Holding himself erect, he moved quickly with practiced assurance from area to area within the hotel in an effort to show he belonged. His navy blue suit, white shirt and red necktie fashioned him into a handsome young man. His smooth, youthful skin was devoid of the whiskers that had marked his chin. And his usual mop of blond hair was severely combed, slicked back and parted on the left.

He was certain, before he inquired, that no one would be registered under the names Lillian Rimespecker or Ruth Nettlebaum, but he asked a clerk at the main desk to check anyway and got the answer he expected. "Sorry, sir. We have no one registered under either of those names."

His awe of the hotel's contemporary use of color, texture and sleek lines was not overwhelming, however, because he had done his homework via his computer and the Internet. To a large degree he knew what to expect at the Conrad. He stood in an area where blue lounging chairs formed circles around puffy blue cushions and white globs of light, where large triangular pillars rose to the ceiling, and where walls glowed from indirect lighting. His mind raced with thoughts as he pictured the hotel's entire layout and attempted to tie locations and times to his mother's normal schedule of doing things at home.

Surely his mother would eat lunch in the Atrio, a sleek wine-bar and restaurant poised in the center of the hotel's 15-story lobby. The Atrio, which specialized in Mediterranean dishes, would not attract her at noon, but at her usual 1:30 p.m. time. If she followed tradition, she would drink a late afternoon cocktail, so he would scan the Loopy Doopy Rooftop Bar beginning at 4 p.m. Typical times for his mother to relax would follow lunch and dinner, so he planned to check out the well-publicized atrium and the lounging areas following each period of dining. He hoped to find adequate locations to sit or stand at distant but clear views of the elevators. His mother loved art, and the hotel boasted about its "2,000 pieces of stunning artwork." So, he told himself to check out the displays, fearing, however, that they were too far spread around the rooms and corridors to serve his purpose.

Jordan's biggest fear was that Ruth Nettlebaum would throw off all timing. Lunch at 1:30? Maybe not. Dinner at the Atrio? Perhaps room service instead.

At 1:15 p.m. he focused on the Atrio, checking out all diners that entered and left the restaurant. He moved a chair slightly, hoping no one noticed, into a shadowed corner some distance away and sat hunched, lifting his eyes every time he saw the movement of legs and feet. He was certain he observed everyone who came and went. Disappointment distressed him severely when he hadn't spotted his mother by 2:30. Lunch at the Atrio had been at the top of his list, his number one hope of finding her.

Letdown after letdown plagued him throughout the afternoon, so his disappointment kept growing until it generated stomach-churning agony. Not eating since morning didn't help. Nor did his nervous traversing from atrium to art display to elevator to river view to cocktail lounge to corridor to sitting room. But, despite not finding his mother, he still had no doubt that she was in the Conrad. "She's here, damn it!" he muttered to himself. "I just can't find her. But she's here. She's gotta be. Sonofabitch!" It couldn't be otherwise in his way of thinking. This was the right date. The Carnival cruise-liner was set to leave port tomorrow morning. That liner was scheduled to stop at Belize. This was her choice of hotel. No way dared she wait for another ship. She was wanted by the police. This was her only choice. Around and around in Jordan's mind went these elements that gave him assurance of her whereabouts.

He descended from the rooftop Loopy-Doopy with tears welling it his eyes. Why wasn't she there? Why wasn't she having her late afternoon cocktail?

Jordan carried his credit cards and a wad of bills, but he feared eating in the hotel where his mother and Ruth Nettlebaum might dine. Perhaps they would come upon him first. He had no plan nor gumption for such an encounter. So, before dinner time he hurried to the doorman at the hotel entrance and sought directions to eateries in the area. He walked to a pizzeria.

After a room-service dinner in their suite, Lillian and Ruth giggled and toyed with each other as they waited for the elevator and descended to the lobby. They whispered secrets to each other as they ambled toward the doors, intending to stroll through the TriBeCa and SoHo neighborhoods.

"Oh, my God!" Lillian exclaimed. "No way! It can't be!"

"What is it?" asked a startled Ruth.

"That young man in the navy blue suit. Did you see him? He looked just like Jordan! I swear it was Jordan!"

"Where?"

"Over that way. Near the Atrio. He's gone now. I don't see him. He was coming from the hotel entrance and headed toward the restaurant. He didn't see us, I'm sure. Oh my God, Ruth, what'll I do?" A terrified expression marred her face.

"Calm down. I'm sure it wasn't him."

"I don't know."

"What would he be doing in New York? There are lots of young men in dark blue suits, for gosh sakes. Lots of look-a-likes."

"I've got to find out." Lillian quivered. She had difficulty catching her breath.

"Lillian! Please! Shake it off. You look like you're about to have a stroke."

"I swear it was Jordan. A mother knows her son. Oh, Ruth, what if it was? What'll we do?"

"Come on. Let's get out of here."

"No, I can't."

"Lillian, people are looking at you. Come on. Snap out of it."

"Ruth, listen to me." Lillian breathed deeply several times. "We're not going anywhere if that was Jordan. Not today or tomorrow. You think I could settle down on a cruise? I love that boy."

"But I thought ..."

"Yes, I love you, too," Lillian whispered. "But he's my flesh and blood. He's my baby." She turned toward the Atrio and pushed among a crowd waiting to enter the restaurant when she suddenly came face to face with Jordan. She muffled her scream, but it was loud enough to draw the attention of the many patrons around her.

"Mom!" Jordan exclaimed. It was not the angry, explosive greeting he had planned. He tried to put together the volcanic charge, but he spit only juice. Tears ran down his cheeks when he finally managed to shout parts of his rehearsed lines—vindictive squawks not only meant to hurt, but to show his turmoil and return her to the nest: "You're not going anywhere with that freakin' woman! You hear me, Mom? I'm not letting you go." He began to sob. "You don't have the right to destroy what's left of our family. Do you hate me?"

"No, no, no. Of course I don't hate you."

"Then come home and we'll fight the good fight together. We'll talk to Peter Dexter, Dad's lawyer, and we'll win the battle, whatever it is. Rehire Uncle Clarry, Hilda and Tony. We can build on what we have."

"I love you."

"What the fuck kind of love do you call this? What are y'gonna do, hang out with the freakin' natives in Belize? Did you ...?" He had no heart to use the words *kill* or *murder*. He struggled, then asked, "Did you do it? You know. Dad."

Lillian parted her lips, but before she could speak a word, Ruth leaped at Jordan and with all her strength, caught him off guard, and shoved him hard into the crowd where he grabbed an elderly gentleman around the neck while kicking a small, bespectacled woman in the shins. From the large gathering of onlookers, many voices grunted, oohed, groaned and called out for hotel security. A hotel clerk at the registration desk also notified security in addition to calling 911. Jordan quickly brushed himself off and apologized to the white-haired gentleman and the petite woman. He picked up her glasses from the floor, examined them, and politely handed them to her. When he turned toward his mother, she was in the hands of two security officers and was sobbing hysterically. Seconds later, he was being questioned by two officers of the New York City Police Department while a tall, uniformed NYPD detective handcuffed his mother. "We have a warrant for her arrest," the detective informed his approaching lieutenant, a heavy-set, bull-faced officer in plainclothes. "She's the wife of that senator who was murdered."

Hotel security and New York police tried to disperse the crowd.

Jordan looked for Ruth Nettlebaum in anger. She was nowhere to be seen. He stretched his neck and tried to circle about, but was still held by an officer, a tall, blond uniformed policeman.

Ruth had disappeared.

"Where's that woman?" Jordan asked hysterically.

"Who are you?" the officer asked.

"I'm Jordan J. Rimespecker, son of the late senator. I came here to find my mother. I see your men have apprehended her."

"What woman were you asking about?" the officer questioned. He stared at Jordan, looked him up and down, and asked again, "Who? What woman?"

"My mother's companion," he uttered. "The squirrelly woman in the red dress. Didn't you see her? Oh, what the hell!" he screamed. "My mother's lover, damn it! She's on your wanted list for chrissake!"

* * *

Several days after Lillian Rimespecker was extradited from New York, District Attorney Matthew Biddle joined Captain Harry Morris and Lieutenant Marvin Goldstein in the chief's office to examine the extent of their investigation into the senator's murder. In particular, the D.A. wanted a clear look at evidence gathered against the deceased's wife.

"What we have is pretty much circumstantial evidence," said Biddle, who sat directly in front of the chief's desk. "Am I right?"

Seated, Morris leaned on his desk blotter, focused on the D.A. and answered, "It's all circumstantial at this point. What we need is *the* smoking gun. And I mean the real weapon. The actual twenty-two caliber automatic pistol. Rimespecker is registered as owning four guns. We have all but one, and we're pretty damn sure the missing one killed him."

"It was most likely a gift to his wife," added Goldstein, who sat to one side of the chief in the crowded office. "Forensics clearly showed the bullets came from such a weapon."

"Marv, you've won plenty of cases with only circumstantial evidence," the chief said.

"But this is pretty light stuff, and not a lot of it," Biddle said.

"We know she was in the house at the time of the murder," Goldstein said. "We have a witness."

"And she knew where the linen closet was," Chief Morris said. "Grabbing a bedsheet was no problem for her. And she knew where and how to wash that sheet." He pulled a cigarette from a package on his desk. "Do you mind, guys? I limit myself to a couple a day." He shoved the package toward Biddle. "Take one." He knew Goldstein would refuse.

"No thanks," the D.A. said. "But go ahead."

"We've timed the distance to and from the Green Room to the senator's office using front and rear stairs," Captain Morris said. "The fastest and smartest way to accomplish the deed was by using those back stairs. And she had quick and easy access from the Green Room. She not only knew the way, she knew the quickest way." He lit his cigarette, puffed on it a few times, and quickly put it out when he saw smoke circle around the district attorney's head.

"What about motive?" Biddle asked.

"I think she had a stronger motive than any of the others," Goldstein said. "Not only did she slip the Ermengarde Choker out from under his roof, she gave herself away to a woman. In his eyes, two of his possessions were stolen. I'm surprised *he* didn't kill *her*. But knowing his temperament, she must have been scared shitless. She knew she had to get rid of him."

Chapter Sixteen

Clarence and Terry sat in the sunroom, in the brightness of a perfect morning, for there was not a cloud in the azure sky. The sunlight streamed across the white table that held their coffee mugs and cherry-cheese Danish. At center stood a small arrangement of sweetbrier roses in a gold-and-white Chinese vase, their stems reaching out and arching over gracefully, their pink flowers giving off the fragrance of apples.

"They have a fresh and penetrating scent," Clarence said as he leaned forward for a sniff. "I remember them from before."

"Yes, aren't they a nice touch? You're right. You've seen and smelled them more than once before. Margaret Mountford grows them. You know, the white-haired dentist's wife from up at the corner house. She gives everyone on the block a small bouquet each summer. They're perfect for the sunroom, don't you think?"

Clarence smiled as he nodded. But his smile faded quickly. And within seconds, Terry said, "Something's troubling you. What are you thinking?"

"You can probably guess."

"It's Jordan, isn't it?"

"I don't know what's up with him. The *Beacon* says his mother is back from New York, in the hands of authorities, awaiting a preliminary hearing. But not a word about Jordan's return, only his fracas with the cops at the Conrad Hotel. I can't imagine that they held him in Manhattan. My educated guess? He's home and deeply depressed."

"What'll happen to Lillian Rimespecker?"

"Judge Nutley'll hear arguments and decide whether or not to indict her. If she's indicted, he'll decide if she gets bail, or is released on her own recognizance, or is held over for trial." Clarence gulped coffee and held up his mug for more. "In the meantime, I gotta get to Jordan. But I can't go empty handed."

Terry stood, reached across the table, and filled his mug, then sat and refilled hers. "Empty handed? What do you mean?"

"I need a plan. I want to go armed with ideas that will pay off."

"Like what?"

"I've been giving it a lot of thought. It would be great if I could put together an entire package of ideas. We've seen how Tony Poluto has leaped from misery and fear into joy by getting deeply involved in the bivouac's protection of the birds and the pursuit of the choker. That might not be Jordy's thing. I don't know. But I can put it in the mix along with Charley Silvester's beekeeping and Laura Barnes' nurturing of animals."

"Are you kidding?"

"No! I'm damn serious. Let's say we can get him to stay up all night with Laura at the Nagelstone Veterinary Center for Large Animals. If he helped save a newly born foal, that might completely change his life."

"And if a horse drops dead, what then? That might send him into deeper depression." Terry chewed on a piece of Danish. After clearing her throat, she said, "And as far as beekeeping goes, I'd guess that many of today's teenagers would stay far away from that. Bees and kids? Jeez, Clarence, I don't see it."

"Charley could teach him so many fascinating things about bees. Did you know that if a queen bee dies, the worker bees know how to create a new queen by nurturing one of their own and feeding her royal jelly? Jordy's a bright kid. He likes fascinating stuff like that. Who knows, he might jump in all the way."

"And get stung! Why not get him a dog? Teenage boys love dogs. Hell, I'd put that on your list. Maybe at the top."

"Hey, why not? He never had a dog. Years ago he begged and begged for one. But the mean old senator said, 'No way!' what with the family traveling back and forth to Washington so much in those days."

"I know you have good intentions, Clarence, but he's gotta cut his own path in life. Give him time."

"Time doesn't necessarily cure depression."

"You're not a psychiatrist or psychologist, Clarence. Your diagnosis of what ails the boy might be wrong because you're so involved."

"You don't get it. I fear that we don't have time with this kid. And there's nobody else around him that's doing anything. He's alone. Believe me, no depressed person should live alone in a big house full of all sorts of memories. I'm not going to watch him sink or swim on his own. No way! I will say he's smart and gutsy. He had the guts to go to New York City and find his mother. But, at the same time, that kinda action worries me. He'll try something else. Something big that might get him in the worst kind of trouble. Remember. He's only sixteen. But I suspect he thinks he's far above that age in being able to cut his way through trouble. We gotta catch him and divert him before his next move, maybe a fatal move."

"What about us?"

"What do you mean?"

"Jordy, Jordy, Jordy. It's always Jordy. I mean, come on! You don't say one thing about our plans for the days ahead. Or don't we have any? I hear were gonna get married. Oh, is that right? That's what I hear. When?"

"Uh-oh! You're angry." Clarence grimaced and pushed away his coffee mug. After a moment of frowning, he said, "Jordan's getting in the way of our relationship, something you said wouldn't happen. You told me you understood."

"I understand you want a close relationship with the kid. Fine. I get it. You raised him. You love him like a son. But I think you have to learn to multitask, even when your tools are just your thoughts. At least when it comes to dealing with personal relationships. What about us? Where are we headed."

"Okay. You've made your point. Let's set a date for the wedding. It's just going to be a quick and simple thing. Isn't that what we decided?"

Terry looked aghast. Her mouth hung open. "Wow! Quick and simple, eh? Don't underplay it too much."

"I'm sorry. That sounded bad. I didn't mean ..."

Terry interrupted: "I know we're not young sweethearts. But our wedding should be an important milestone in our relationship. I want it to be a celebration of our life together." Terry rose from the table, turned her back to her fiancé, stood silently for a lengthy moment, and finally walked from the room.

"Hey, come back! I'm really sorry."

"Apparently, our wedding isn't as important to you as I thought."

"Oh, it is! It is!"

"I want it to commemorate what are relationship has been up unto now, what it is today, and what it will be in our future together."

"And it will," Clarence shouted loud enough to make sure Terry heard his words in the adjoining kitchen. "We'll make it that. Sorry. I got carried away. I want our wedding to be special. Small and special are not opposites. They can work together."

"Yeah, you got carried in the wrong direction." Terry stepped back into the sunroom. "Because of Jordan. That's what I mean. Damn it."

"Please, Terry. I get it. I see where you're coming from. But try to grasp this. I'm having nightmares about the kid. I'm losing sleep. I wake up scared. One night I dreamt he was being sucked down a deep, dark whirlpool. My sleepless nights are affecting my days. I actually fell asleep and hit my head on my computer the other day."

Terry stepped close to Clarence. She leaned over and kissed him on the back of his neck. "Hey, at least we know how to talk things out." She kissed him on the cheek, but returned to pacing about the room.

"Let's talk to the Reverend Inglesby soon about a wedding date. Okay? Maybe as soon as tomorrow. How's that? And we can call the caterer you mentioned. Why don't you start working up a guest list? A small one." He giggled. "Pretty small. At least, not too big."

"And I guess it's my place now to encourage you to call Laura Barnes, the animal lady. I will admit she's a spirited gal who really does love animals, and I suppose that can rub off and help others. That day at the Silvesters, she told me about the time she went back to check on a possum she thought got hit by a car."

"Let me confess right now, hon, that you're absolutely right about my one-track mind. I gotta tell my brain to spread itself and not concentrate on one segment of my life at a time. In your words, I've gotta multitask, even when it comes to just thinking. Even when under pressure. You and I can play life's games with each other or against each other and still come out on top together. Maybe. At least, sometimes. Right? Do I have it straight? Is that it?"

"That's a complicated way of putting it, but I think the right idea is buried in there somewhere." Terry laughed as she continued to pace about the sunroom. "My problem? I'm not sure whether you're being serious with me or being facetious. But I do think it's my turn to give you the go-ahead. Call Laura Barnes."

"Only after you stop moving, sit down, and enjoy your coffee and Danish. Do we have the Barnes' number?"

"She's probably at the Silvesters. Unless she's hanging out with some elephants or hippos somewhere. Try Claudia's cellphone." Terry returned to the table, sat opposite Clarence and forced a silly grim.

Clarence pulled his phone from his pocket and fiddled with it for a moment before sending warm signals with his eyes and saying, "We'll start wedding planning tomorrow. It's a promise." He bit his lower lip and punched numbers.

After a lengthy wait, Claudia answered, "Hello." She was out of breath but managed to say "Greetings from Eagleland."

"It's Clarence Exton, Claudia. How are things at the bivouac?"

"Hi, Clarence. Things were fine here a few minutes ago. But we've spotted a couple drones flying low over the encampment. We don't know what they're up to. One of them looked like it carried a claw-like devise under its belly. That's a little scary. They headed upstream, and that worries us. Jimmy just took off for home. He wants to check out his cam system and see if the drones are hovering anywhere near the nest. We alerted the police."

"Damn. Don't like the sound of that. Hope all goes well." Clarence paused and sucked in air. "Sorry I'm bothering you with this." He paused again. "Look, the reason I'm calling. Is Laura Barnes at your place?"

"She's outside. Near the beehives. Last time I saw her she was scanning the sky like the rest of us. I'll get her for you. I'm heading over that way anyway."

"You sure? I don't want to put you out."

"Hold on."

Clarence turned toward Terry and whispered, "I think I called at a bad time. Sounds like they've got spies in the skies."

"Spies?"

"A couple drones encroaching on the bivouac. Dipping down for a look-see, and then flying upstream toward the nest. Don't like the sound of that."

While Clarence waited, Terry gathered the empty plates and mugs from the table and carried them to the sink in the kitchen. "Someone's bound to try to steal that choker. Why wouldn't they?" She rinsed the dishes and placed them in the dishwasher. "There are plenty of thieves in this world. I'm surprised scads of them haven't tried. It's a tribute to Mr. Birdman and the others that they've been kept at bay." She returned to the sunroom, and, with her hands on her hips, stared at Clarence and asked, "You talking or waiting?"

"Shush! She's coming, I think. I can hear her chit-chatting with others. She has such a cheerful way about her."

Next, he heard Claudia's voice: "It's Clarence Exton for you, Laura."

"Hi Clarence!" Laura mouthed in her usual enthusiastic tone. "What's cooking?"

"Sorry to bother you while drones are spying from above."

"Think nothing of it. It's not the first time they've buzzed us. It's part of the new world we live in today. Soon, the skies will overflow with them. Can you imagine? Soooo, what can little old me do for a dude like you on this beautiful morning?"

"I've called you for two reasons. You radiate joy. And you love animals. And I'm hoping you can dish out some loving help for a teenage boy who means the world to me."

"Jordan Rimespecker."

"You're a mind-reader, too?"

"I do read the newspapers. And I bet you forgot that I was with you that night when he fell from that ladder and crashed on the library floor."

"Holy cow! I did forget that. Then you have met him?"

"Hardly. I was not introduced. We never spoke. All I remember is a slender, blond kid in pain. I'm assuming he's still in some sort of pain."

"You said it. Father murdered. Mother runs off with a lover and will likely be charged with the old man's murder. What kind of a storm does that kick up inside of a teenager with his own growing pains? Another year of high school, and then he was supposed to enter college. Talk about turmoil and depression and, I fear, desperate acts."

"Well, I guess I know why you called. The love of and for an animal will heal some of the worst afflictions. To me, it's an absolutely beautiful thing to see."

"I was thinking that maybe you could take him to that large-animal clinic where you've gotten involved with horses."

"I have a much better idea. The local SPCA. It's a top-notch place for attaching a boy to a dog. They know me well there and like what I do. And you've called at just the right time. They've got a labradoodle there that would capture any boy's heart. How old is Jordan?"

"Sixteen going on seventeen."

"Perfect! Boy, have you got me excited. But we'd have to work fast. This dog won't stay there long, once the public hears about him. Or sees him. Look into his beseeching eyes and you'll melt. And he's got this thick curly hair that invites you to sink your fingers into it. He's a little standoffish with strangers at first, which makes me think he might have been abused. But once you gain his trust, he's all over you. Do you know much about labradoodles?"

"They're a mix breed, aren't they?"

"Yes. Labrador retriever and poodle. But they're deliberately bred together, not like the usual mixed strays that end up at the pound. Don't get me wrong. I love 'em all. Some of my favorites of all times were cute little mutts. Anyway, there's a good chance that labradoodles will be declared a breed in the near future. They're really gaining in popularity. They're just so lovable. Perfect for a boy Jordan's age. It's rare that we have one at our SPCA. He was found eating garbage behind a supermarket. No one's claimed him, so the time for adoption is coming up. In fact, it's just about now. Thank God you called. I'm gonna reach out to my friends there and ask them to put a hold on any outreach until I meet with Jordan."

"They'll do that?"

"For me? You betcha!"

"Does this dog have a name?"

"George."

"George?"

"Yeah. And somehow it fits. He's just a sweet, curly haired George with pleading eyes. Boy-oh-boy, you've got me excited. I can't wait to bring Jordan and George together."

Terry interrupted: "Excuse me."

"Hold on, Laura." Clarence looked up at Terry. "Yeah?"

"I'm heading next door to check on your mother."

"Good thinking. I'll join you in a few minutes." Speaking into the phone, he said, "Laura, I thought maybe we'd drive over to the Rimespecker's place one day this week."

Terry tossed a kiss and headed for the front door.

"Hold on now!" Laura asserted. "And don't be hurt. But I want one-on-one with Jordan. That's the way I work. And, believe me, I'm good at it. It's my thing. Let me tell you about seven-year-old Karl Peters who tried to commit suicide over in the Eastmount Section of Cloverton. I convinced the kid that he could rescue Puffy from being put down. God, almighty, the love that blossomed. They not only saved each other, they've become a team that helps bring other kids and dogs together."

"It won't be easy with Jordan."

"Let me at him! Please! I promise you I'll put them into a blender and screw the lid on tight. Just let me at 'im."

"Okay. He's yours."

"Oh, my God!" Laura exclaimed.

"What is it?"

"I see smoke. Oh, no! Flames! I see flames!"

"Where?"

"I think we've got a fire in one of the tents. Holy hell! It's more than one tent. That blaze is spreading. Sparks are flying high and landing on other tents. Move! Everyone run. Get out of here. Scouts! Get into the woods and keep going down to the creek. Yo! Charley! Get the fire company. I'll call nine-one-one."

"Hello, Laura!" Clarence yelled. "Hello! Hello!" The phone went dead. Seconds later it went to dial-tone. "Uh-oh!" He dialed his mother's landline. "Mom, it's me. Put Terry on."

"Hello?"

"Terry, they've got a fire at the bivouac. Sounds bad. I'm worried."

* * *

All tents at the bivouac were made of fire-resistant canvas that slowed the fire and kept it mostly confined to the southern boundary of the Silvesters' property. A gasoline-like smell made it obvious to everyone in the area that an accelerant had been used to start the blaze, and, therefore, that the fire had been deliberately set. Many wondered if there was any connection between the drone flyovers and the arson.

The Boy Scouts were herded together and chased toward the creek by several of the adult volunteers.

A dozen tents made up the southern boundary, and each blazed and sent thick black smoke and a shower of sparks skyward. Since the highest flames were aligned in an unbending streak from tent one to tent twelve, it appeared that the arsonist had poured the flammable liquid as he or she ran a straight line along the southern periphery. Bedding material and clothes within the tents caught fire easily and continued to burn and smolder after the roaring flames from the accelerant on the outside canvas began to subside. Flying embers troubled the volunteers. Stiff breezes carried them far and sent the birdwatchers running here and there to smother them and prevent spread of the fire. Charley turned his garden hose on, not only to fight the tent fires, but to wet down the south side of his house. In addition to worrying about his house, he was concerned about his honey bees, even though they were located on the far north corner of his property. He was aware that smoke might affect their functioning, perhaps causing them to swarm, bringing about division in the hives and causing the bees to emigrate or fly off into the trees where they'd regather in new swarms.

"Smoke can cause the bees to gorge themselves with honey and take flight," Charley yelled to Claudia as she raced toward him.

"Not much smoke is headed that way," she responded excitedly as she grabbed the hose from Charley. "Probably less than your bee-smoker gives off when you're calming them. I think we have a southeast wind. Go take a look at the hives."

"No!" he shouted as he took the hose back. "Go grab Laura and get the hell out of here."

"I want to help."

"Did you hear me?"

Claudia and Laura were ordered by Charley to flee the area. They finally complied and moved toward the creek with the scoutmaster. Laura called Jimmy every now and then, learning that the baby eagles were safe, but that one of the drones was caught in a tangled web of locust-tree branches, a few feet below the nest. Jimmy had actually seen the mother eagle, on his computer screen, attack the drone and dive-bomb on it, sending it well below the nest before it crashed.

Fire-engine and police sirens roared in the distance as Charley and a group of birdwatchers continued to fight the blaze while other volunteers left their distant security posts and ran to the bivouac to join in. Brooms and shovels were put to use as the crowd pounded and stomped on the burning and smoldering materials.

Their sirens still blaring, three fire engines, including a ladder truck, pulled up along the south side of the Silversters' property. A team of fireman leaped into action as the sirens quieted and two police cars roared to a stop alongside the engines. Police Chief Morris was quickly at Charley's side as the heavy firehoses were uncurled and aimed at the burning and smoldering lineup of tents and their contents. Police were vehement in the efforts to push back all citizens not in uniform.

"Get back!" Lieutenant Goldstein yelled. "Clear the area for the firefighters."

Chapter Seventeen

Laura felt comfortable as she walked up the pathway to the main entrance of the Rimespecker house. A reticent teenager didn't faze her. She had dealt with scores of reticent dogs and horses. As for melancholia, she had siphoned black bile from the saddest of animals. Anger presented a more difficult challenge, but she had won those battles, too. And she didn't expect Jordan to be a raging pit bull.

When she reached the shade of the portico, she looked back down the pathway toward her car and was thankful for the sunshine that cast sharp shadows of the boxwood that edged the flagstones. A gloomy day would not have served her purpose.

Her first tapping on the door was gentle and did not bring a response. She waited, carefully counting off the seconds. She was aware that even the way a person knocked or rang a bell carried a message and set a mood. How well she remembered the German shepherd that charged at her on Halloween after she pounded on a neighbor's door. She was but 12. It was then that she learned to gently reach under the chin when first greeting a dog, and never to frighten the animal with a fast overhead reach.

Laura rang the bell, but briefly. Still no response.

She waited patiently as her thoughts played with ideas and approaches. Finally, she knocked a bit harder, but only twice with the intention of waiting a full minute and then leaving. Well studied in behavior, she had high hopes that Jordan's eyes would follow her down the pathway, perhaps from an upper-story window. Now was the time for her composed and serene nature to show itself as she ambled in a non-threatening and feminine way toward her car. She was trying to set him up for her return in case he didn't call her back.

She heard tapping and turned to see Jordan peering down on her from a window just above the portico. Without hesitance, she put on a gleeful show, waving and smiling warmly. Now it was time for a spritely but non-menacing gait as she aimed for the front door. Jordan opened the door slightly just as Laura mounted the steps. She tossed out a greeting: "Hi, there! I hope I'm not disturbing you."

"What do you want?" Jordan asked in a subdued tone. His blond hair was mussed and pointing in all directions. He wore a soiled T-shirt and faded jeans sporting holes in the knees.

Laura thought it best to unload the crux of the message quickly. "Your Uncle Clarry wants me to talk to you about a dog in desperate need of help from a boy such as you."

Jordan simply stared blankly at Laura. He showed no emotion whatsoever.

Laura's eyes sparkled as she grinned and, in a teasing and comical way, said, "We met before on a night when you went boom, bang, boom down the ladder in your library and lived to tell about it." She wasn't certain that a lighthearted manner would work with such a serious subject as that dreadful fall. But she gave it a try, following quickly with, "My name is Laura Barnes. You may know my husband as The Birdman. I know you're aware of our bivouac at the Silvesters since it involves the Ermengarde Choker, once owned by your father."

"You just had a fire," Jordan said, showing his first wee bit of emotion.

"Yes, someone's trying to do us in. We think the fire was a diversionary tactic. The real target was the choker. But nothing's going to stop us. Already we're cleaning up the mess and bringing in new tents. We have a dedicated crew that includes people you know well— Tony Paluto and your Uncle Clarry and his fiancée. We'd love you to join us, but first we need your help in the rescue of a magnificent dog, a beautiful labradoodle who's begging for a master such as you. Please, may I come in."

Jordan stepped back and allowed Laura to enter the house. He looked a bit bewildered before deciding to lead her into the library where he pointed to a cluster of chairs. She took a seat. A moment later he joined her, sitting stiffly a few yards away.

"Don't you dare climb any ladders," she said playfully. She searched for a smile on his face, but saw none. Quickly, she aimed the conversation toward canines. "Have you seen the new wing at the local SPCA?"

Jordan shook his head.

Laura waited for more, but it was slow coming.

"I've never been to the SPCA," he finally offered.

"No! Oh, wow! We gotta fix that!" Her tone and manner was so upbeat that he winced. "You are really exciting me!" she went on. "I love to introduce animals and their surroundings to guys like you. I can't wait to get going and ..."

For the first time, Jordan projected his voice as he interrupted Laura and said, "I know what you're trying to do. I'm not stupid. Whatever you and Uncle Clarry are cooking up, I'm not going for it. I can't. I have other things on my mind."

"What do you know about labradoodles?"

"What?"

"Labradoodles?"

"They're a cross between a Labrador retriever and a poodle. They're kinda curly or wooly looking."

"Some guy in Australia first crossed the two breeds. He ended up with a sociable and intelligent dog that is affectionate and growing more popular by the day. The labradoodle is friendly with kids, other dogs and even strangers, and is very easy to train. Listen to me. Please. George is waiting for you. Come with me. We'll go see him. What do you have to lose?"

"George?"

"That's his name. And he's a beauty. But he won't be available for long."

"I don't know. I'm not sure I could handle it."

Laura felt hope. She sensed his wavering. This was not the time to give up, she told herself. "I understand that your Uncle Clarry did a lot for you during your growing-up years. He wants you to have this dog. Don't you think you owe it to him to give it a try? Believe it or not, it would be a way of thanking him for the love he's always heaped on you." Laura hoped and prayed she wasn't intruding too deeply into Jordan's youthful evolution. She did not want to collapse her intent by treading too far. Whatever the case, she pressed on. "You know, he hurts when you hurt, and he's been hurting. So this would be a three-way fix. What joy he would feel to see you romping with George."

"Uncle Clarry wants me to be best man at his wedding."

Bringing Clarence's wedding into the mix could not have pleased Laura more. She could feel a tingle race up her spine, and, without saying a word, she thanked Jordan again and again. She deliberately waited to allow the teenager's own words to echo in his head. Then she quietly and plaintively said, "I never thought about the affect George would have on the upcoming wedding."

* * *

Wearing a clean golfer's shirt and chinos, Jordan stood next to Laura at the main desk inside the waiting room at the SPCA. They faced two women who busied themselves behind that desk: Fanny Mason, a gray-haired, stocky black woman, and Patty Parnell, a middle-aged, bespectacled string-bean with died ebony hair.

"You know why we're here, my dear ladies," Laura said cheerfully. She was well acquainted with Fanny and Patty, having known them for many years. Dogs, of course, had brought them together. But it had been their interaction that had tightened their friendship. Many an animal owed its life to their mutual dealings and the emergency engagements they found necessary. If one of the women called with an urgent need, the other two would come running without hesitance. Another member of the crew, freckled-faced, sandy-haired, 28-year-old Zane Cooper, was deeply in the mix, for he carried out many of the assignments, suggestions and emergency demands of the women.

"Zane's cleaning the cages right now," Fanny said. "He'll be finished in minutes. Then you can go in." She looked Jordan up and down. "So, this is the young Mr. Rimespecker, is it?"

"Oh, yes, excuse me. I should have introduced you. Jordan, may I present Fanny Mason and Patty Parnell, two of my lifelines."

"Hi," Jordan said softly.

Zane suddenly popped into the waiting room from a steel door to the right of the desk. "Hi, Miss Laura!" he greeted. "George is ready for you." He smiled at Jordan and nodded.

Laura led the teenager into a lengthy wing of the building that contained up-to-date, roomy, shiny steel cages at left and right. The barred enclosures ran the full length of the bright, new, whitewashed addition to the building. Dogs of all shapes and sizes began to bark and push their noses between the bars. Some leaped for attention and wagged their tails as Laura and Jordan walked down the middle of the wide passageway.

After hurrying past a yipping terrier mix, they reached the last enclosure on their left, where George was huddled in a far corner. He raised his head slightly. His eyes revealed mistrust. But even from the rear of his cage, his resplendent honey-colored curls stood out strikingly against the white walls and steel bars.

"I told you he'd be standoffish at first," Laura said in hushed tones. "Give him a little time. Talk to him. Go on. I'm gonna sneak out of here, sign some papers, and leave you and George alone."

"Maybe he really doesn't like me," Jordan whispered.

"No, no, no. That's not so. He's timid or shy at first with strangers. Talk to him."

Laura moved swiftly, hoping for a happy coalescence in her absence. She hurried back the full length of the kennel and pushed open the heavy steel door. After catching her breath in the waiting room, she turned to Fanny and Patty and asked for the paperwork. Zane was busy helping a UPS delivery man unload packages from his truck, parked out front. One by one they carried the boxes into the building and stacked them near the door to the medical wing, opposite the main desk.

"Is Dr. Kennoski in?" Laura asked as she handed the signed papers to Patty.

"Not yet," Patty said. "Give him another half-hour."

"Is the big Examination Room available? The Blue Room?"

"Yeah. Right now it is. But when and if we get heavy traffic ..."

"Zane!" Laura called out. "Would you unlock George's gate and move him into the Blue Exam Room as soon as I give the word, after I check out what's cooking at his cage?"

"It's okay, Zane," Fanny said as she watched Laura cross her fingers and hold them high above her head while stepping toward the steel door.

"No problem, Miss Laura." Zane lowered a package from his shoulder to the floor. "We're just about done unloading."

"Peek through that high window, Laura, before you go in there and disturb George and the boy," Fanny suggested.

"Gotcha!" Laura responded.

Four small panes of glass comprised the only window in the door. Laura stood on her toes and peered through it and down the long passageway between the cages—a walkway brightened by overhead lighting designed to reflect illumination off the stark white walls. She almost split her windpipe with a "Yowl!" of joy and a squealing "Yeeeek!" when she saw Jordan kneeling on the floor nose to nose with George. She opened the door and hurried down the lane to get a better look. The dog's tail was wagging wildly and he kept pouncing toward the teenager. When his front legs were not pawing at the bars, they were flopping flat, with each pounce, on the cage floor. And while he was prone, his hind legs were spread wide, his tail wagging between them. His frisky frolicking slowed when Laura reach his cage, but never completely stopped. He tipped his curly head one way then the other as he looked pleadingly from Jordan to Laura and back to Jordan again.

Zane opened the steel door and called, "You ready for me, Miss Laura?"

"Yes, I guess so," Laura said. "George is eager to trot. In fact, I think he's asking for a wrestling match with Kiddo, here." She reached between the bars and ran her fingers amidst his curls. "Can you get me a hard rubber ball."

"Already done, Miss Laura," Zane said as he made his way past all the barking dogs. "I put a couple balls, a chew toy, a tug-of-war rope and some other playthings in the Blue Room." He unlocked George's gate and gave the labradoodle a good head-scratching before snapping on his leash. Outside the cage, the dog immediately stood on his hind legs and pawed at Jordan above the teenager's belt.

As Zane led George and Jordan across the waiting room, Laura stopped at the desk, now manned solely by Fanny, and asked, "Could you make a phone call for me while we're working with George and the kid? You may have to hold for quite some time while they locate this dude."

"Yeah, I'll do it."

Laura wrote numbers on a slip of paper and passed the note to Fanny. "I'm giving you two phone numbers. Try the top one first. Ask for Clarence Exton. When he gets on the line, tell him that Jordy's in the dog house and singing a perfect tune."

"Will do."

"Eureka!" Laura exclaimed as she danced in a circle before following Zane, Jordan and George down a corridor toward the Blue Examination Room—a wide-open expanse where equipment was kept near the walls so that a broad central area could be employed for testing and training. It was in this room that loud noises and sudden movements were used to check an animal's reaction. Abruptly opening an umbrella in a dog's face, crashing a tin bowl to the floor, taking away a hungry dog's food with a fake hand on a stick—these and other stunts were used to determine a dog's aggression or lack of it.

George had passed all tests and had received glowing reports when examined by the SPCA staff the day after Township Animal Control found him dirty and disheveled in an alley behind the Fair Deal Supermarket.

Laura and Zane took positions at a distance from Jordan and the labradoodle so as not to interfere with the interaction between the boy and the dog. Laura sat atop a sack of kibble in a corner, while Zane stood nearby, leaning against a huge, padded, cat-climbing pole. Jordan immediately dug into the collection of toys Zane had gathered and put in a basket near a chair placed in the open area for the teenager. He tossed the ball and George leaped and ran after it, seizing it in his mouth and returning it.

"Good boy!" Jordan cheered as George dropped the ball at his feet.

"Bravo!" Laura called out.

Jordan glanced at Laura and smiled broadly. His smile filled Laura with so much joy and hope that a tingle ran through her body as her eyes sparkled. Her delight grew each time the teenager threw the ball and the excited, playful, high-spirited dog raced after it and returned it. Jordan slid from his chair and squatted on the floor so he could more easily tussle with George after each fetch. He soon learned that George wasn't going to give up chasing and retrieving.

"Try something else," Laura suggested.

Still sitting on the floor, Jordan hid the ball between his legs and drew a braided rope from the basket. Within seconds George grabbed an end of the thick braid and was pulling one way as the teenager was struggling to hold onto the other end. For a moment it appeared that the dog was going to win the tug-of-war. But Jordan suddenly yanked, the rope gave way, Jordan fell backward, and the ball slipped out from between his legs to the pleasure of George, who grabbed it, ran around the room, then stood before the youth as if to challenge. Gleefully, Jordan attacked, and within seconds they were engaged in a playful wrestling match. Jordan's laughter was abundant to the delight of Laura.

A smoky smell entered the room when the door opened. It came from Clarence, who had been shoveling ashes into containers at the site of the bivouac fire. He was quite a sight standing in the doorway in work-clothes splotched heavily with black and gray soot streaks and smears. As the door closed behind him, he said, "Forgive my appearance."

"Wow!" Laura exclaimed. "You stink!"

"The tent fire," Clarence muttered. "It's nasty clean-up work."

Jordan, who was used to the ex-secretary's meticulous dress and fastidious ways, was at first stunned by Uncle Clarry's appearance, then burst into laughter as he ran to him and hugged him despite his look and the odor of fire-and-ash. The labradoodle, inspired by the boy's excitement and joy, ran and leaped at the hugging pair.

"I can't believe that George is my dog," Jordan uttered in a broken voice. "He's unbelievable!"

Smiles spread the lips of Laura and Clarence. Even Zane, who was unaware of the full circumstances, got caught up in the moment and grinned in pleasure.

"How are things at the Silvesters?" Laura asked.

"Messy, but we're getting it cleaned up. The new tents have arrived, but they're not yet in place. A lot of the volunteers lost valuables. It's a shame. The grass and shrubs on that side are all burnt. Chief Morris suspects that a partner in crime may have planted himself inside the encampment early on and waited for the right time. The drone flyover was most likely operated from the outside by the other half of the team, be it one thief or more."

"Well, those of us here at dog haven have nothing but good news to report," Laura said. She thrust her fist in the air. "Never have I ever enjoyed such a complete and heartwarming breakthrough." The boy and dog raced to the toy basket as she stepped close to Clarence and whispered, "Did you take care of the financial obligations."

"Yep. Everything is signed, sealed and delivered."

The door opened again. This time it was Fanny with a message. "Mr. Exton. There's a Miss Smythe on the phone for you. Says she's been trying to reach you on your cellphone."

Clarence felt his pants pockets. "Oh, damn it. Must have left it in the car." He glanced at Laura. "I hope Mom's okay." After one more gratified look at gleeful Jordan and frisky George, he hurried into the waiting room, followed by Fanny, who grabbed the desk phone and handed it to him.

"Hello?"

"It's me, hon. You okay?"

"Yeah, Terry. What's up?"

"Lieutenant Goldstein called. He said that Chief Morris wants you at his office, if possible, this afternoon."

"Why me?"

"It's not just you. He's gathering a small group together for a pow-wow. I guess he thinks you're smart enough to solve high-flying puzzles."

"No. He thinks I know more than I've already dumped on him." Clarence looked at his dirty hands and soiled clothes. "I'm filthy. I can't go there like this. What time's this meeting?"

"Two o'clock. You have time to get home, shower and change clothes, eat lunch and fill me in on Jordan and the dog before you head for the cop shop."

* * *

Clarence gave up the smell of soot for that of a fresh bar of soap. He was scrubbed clean and wearing a crisp white shirt and tan slacks when he arrived at East Bitterlick Township Police Headquarters. He hurried directly to Captain Morris' office, suspecting that he was the last one of the group to arrive.

The surprise was a giant barrel-shaped cactus filling a corner of the small office and crowding the room more than usual. It had never been an attractive office, and Chief Morris never thought it needed to be. Filing cabinets lined three walls, all painted dark metallic green-gray, and old radio equipment was heaped upon two of them. The only interesting accent in the room, other than the new cactus, was a small globe of the world on a Greek-like pedestal. Chief Morris had been pestered for years to enliven his office with plants.

Clarence exclaimed, "Yike!" on seeing the enormous cactus. And the entire group of five laughed loudly.

"We all reacted the same way," Lieutenant Goldstein said with a silly smirk on his face. "Come join us."

Clarence took the last chair in the circle of six, joining the chief, the lieutenant, Jimmy Barnes, Charley Silvester and Tony Paluto. It was Tony's presence that surprised Clarence, leading him to think that the get-together must have something to do with tree-climbing. Tony, the ex-chauffeur, grinned at the former Rimespecker secretary as he saw some sort of irony in the fact that they were both chosen to join this select group. His once deflated ego was at an all-time high, and it even showed in his erect posture and expression of self-esteem.

"For years people have been yappin' that I needed plants to dress up my office," Chief Morris said. "So, I tried to please my constantly carping visitors and went to the trouble of ordering this thing through a catalogue. And now everybody laughs."

"We expected maybe a couple little ferns or a rubber plant, not a prickly monster," Goldstein said as he winked at Clarence before looking up at the ceiling where the top of the cactus pressed its prickly flesh upon a florescent light. "Some of your favorite officers sent you that catalogue, Chief," Goldstein said with a twinkle in his eye.

"I suspected." The chief frowned and gave everyone a serious stare. "Let's get started," he said in a commanding way. "Our investigating team needs that smashed drone that's trapped in that locust tree. Also, the claw hanging beneath it. If we learn the manufacture, we might learn the buyer. It's crucial that we bring down that damn buzzing bug and its appendage."

Jimmy raised his hand.

"Wait!" the chief demanded. "Excuse me, Barnes." He looked at

Goldstein. "Take minutes, Marv. I know you hate the task, but try to bear with it and be at least half-way pleasant." With a snap of the wrist, he tossed a notepad to the brooding lieutenant. "Now, what were you about to say, Barnes?"

"Criminals using drones are sure to remove all markings."

"But we don't know for sure they did so in this case. Not only that, our forensics team is pretty damn good. Sam Block has a way of seeing things that aren't there. We can't let this opportunity escape us. Another thing. If the drone itself gives us nothing, what about the claw hanging beneath it? That could lead to a tool shop or even a toy store."

"I can climb that there locust tree and take hold of that there drone without disturbing the baby eagles," Tony offered.

"I doubt that," Jimmy said. "You're a great climber, Tony. I've seen you practice, and you're amazing. But you can't guarantee a branch won't break. Have you ever looked into a bald eagle's yellow eyes? Those sharp eyes see great distances and through all kinds of tangled growth. Do you want to be attacked by mama or papa bird? You saw what happened to that drone. I doubt you realize the strength of an adult eagle."

"What about those grappling hooks you used to get your cam equipment up that neighboring locust tree?" Clarence asked. "Couldn't we grab the drone with one of them, pull it loose from the branches, and drop it into a net?"

"If by grappling hooks you mean those many-pronged devises used to pull dead bodies from the river, they're not what we used," Jimmy explained. "Our smooth, single hooks were attached to the ends of ropes. We shot them up into the tree in hopes of lapping them over branches and dropping them back down to the ground. Then we'd attached a pulley device to a hook and pull it up. It was complicated and difficult. We never got the right limb on the first try, and seldom got it on the first half-dozen tries. It took us days to get our pulleys working. Forget it for this job. No way could you use hooks. No way."

"What the fu ... ?" Goldstein cut himself off. He looked annoyed. "Why not bring in a helicopter, grab the drone and the nest in one swoop, fly off with them both, and have it done with." His words brought glances of distain from the others. "I mean, this is crazy!" he bellowed. "It's like we're trying to chop liver with a toothpick. I'm not saying we should deliberately hurt the babies. We grab 'em, then nurse 'em until they can fly."

"Make sense, Lieutenant," the chief said.

"I think he's being facetious," Clarence said.

"Yeah, that's me." Goldstein looked down at his notes to avoid glaring stares from the others. "Facetious."

"Whatever we do, we have to think of the legality of it all," Charley mentioned. "Remember, the bald eagle is not only a protected species, it's the symbol of the United States. And, frankly, I don't know what all that means when it comes to approaching or protecting such birds. Has anyone here looked up facts about the federal law?"

The six men glanced from one to the other. Jimmy-the-Birdman scratched his head, and Clarence shrugged his shoulders. Tony posed as if in deep thought. No one raised his hand. All looked at the chief of police.

"I guess I should have, guys," the captain said. "I really should have, but the judicial part of eagle life hasn't been on my front burner. I just didn't think about it."

"Fear not," Charley said as he pulled his new iPhone from his pocket. "I'm trying to catch up to the times we live in. Actually, it was Claudia's idea to get this thing after the birth of the bivouac and the flow of communication and information that followed." Tapping with his finger, he Googled "*federal laws on bald eagles*" and immediately received several paragraphs. "I'll quickly give you the highlights." Scanning the material, he said, "Well, it looks like we're ... Let me read this: '... prohibited from take, possession, sale, purchase, barter, offer to sell, purchase or barter, transport, export or import of any bald eagle, alive or dead, including any part, nest, or egg ... Take includes, pursue, shoot, shoot at, poison, wound, kill, capture, trap, collect, molest or disturb ...'"

"That's enough!" the chief exclaimed. "Goddamn!"

"It sounds like you could end up behind bars for frying a bald eagle's egg," Charley said with a glint in his eyes. "Want to hear about the fines and imprisonment?"

The chief scowled. "No!"

Tony raised his hand. "But, like I said, I can carefully and silently seize that there drone without disturbing them eagles. Honest t'God. I can do it with my finesse," Tony said. "You guys don't understand my finesse."

"Your finesse?" Chief Morris questioned.

Suddenly, all eyes were on Tony.

"My artful, careful, delicate, crafty ways of climbing them there trees, maneuvering through them limbs and branches, silently slivering along them limbs like a boa constrictor, carefully touching with my sensitive fingers. I gots the best tools in the world, from ascenders to descenders. I won the blue ribbons and trophies that prove my skill. I've got the pliable body, legs and arms to do the job. Together, I call it my finesse."

No one said anything for a lengthy moment. Then Clarence asked, "How much longer before the young birds fly?"

"Only a few weeks," Jimmy answered. "Maybe twenty days or less. Their wings are now sleek and black. Fuzz has changed to feathers. I think we should just wait."

"I hate to lose the time," the chief muttered.

Charley asked, "May I change the subject?"

"Go ahead," the chief said.

"Don't laugh at me. But have any of you considered that the senator's widow and her lover might have something to do with the flyovers and fire? Maybe this is really far-fetched. But I woke up dreaming about it last night. Lillian Rimespecker has lots of money. She could hire any thug she ..."

Clarence interrupted: "But why would she? Hell, she got rid of the damn Ermengarde Choker. Remember, it was hers, a special gift from her old man. Do you really think she'd want it back? Why, for chrissakes?" He shook his head. "And another thing. You don't know that she's so flush. Access to her assets may be a problem for her."

"Stateside maybe," Charley said. "But not overseas. Anyway, I'm damn sure she'd like to save the choker for her partner. It's worth millions. Ruth Nettlebaum may own it now, technically. But we don't know what will happen after their legal woes carry them to who knows where. Maybe Lillian Rimespecker would like to seize it and hide it away on some secret island, hoping it will bring riches to her sweetheart someday."

"Or, are *you* hoping to inherit it?" Goldstein whispered loud enough for all to hear."

Charley bristled. "Don't you dare go there, Lieutenant."

Goldstein began to speak, but was stopped by the chief who said, "By the way, did you know the widow is out on bail? Got the word this afternoon. From Judge Nutley's court. Heard it just before our meeting.

"We didn't do our job," Goldstein said. "Not enough ev ..."

"Not now, Lieutenant!" Chief Morris had heard enough, and he wasn't happy. He stared into space and kept rubbing his forehead with his right hand. The other men began to feel uncomfortable as time elapsed and the chief remained mum. Finally he said, "You can go.

We're finished." He looked at the lieutenant. "You stay, Marv. I think we'll take a ride to Ruth Nettlebaum's place. We haven't checked it out in quite awhile."

Chapter Eighteen

"Hello?"

"Good morning, Jordy."

"Oh! Hi, Uncle Clarry!"

"How y'doing? And how's George?"

"I'm doing okay. And George is great! He's the most wonderful dog in the whole world. He's curled up right next to me. I'm sitting on the edge of my bed."

"That's where I'm sitting. On my bed. I was anxious to call you early."

"I can picture you in your bedroom. If you're sitting on your bed, you're surrounded by paintings on the walls. I like your room, especially all the colors in your art collection."

"What a strange recollection for a kid your age. I didn't think you knew a still-life from a landscape."

"I'm older than my years. Didn't you know? That's right out of the mouth of Miss Nevious, my art teacher. Right now, I bet you're staring at that painting of the ships."

"Yep. The ships coming into the harbor. It's the first thing I see every morning. The light from the window reflects on it and tells me if the morning is sunny or gray."

"I love that painting. Did you forget that I slept in your bed once upon a time? It was the Fourth of July after the fireworks show at Radcliff Park. When I awoke, I saw the painting light up from the morning sun. The ships were coming right at me."

"Well, then, that painting is yours."

"What do y'mean?"

"I want you to have it."

"No way! It's your favorite."

"I'll bring it with me tomorrow."

"Tomorrow?"

"Yeah. We have things to do. Like seeing your family's attorney, Peter Dexter." Clarence waited for a reaction, but Jordan offered nothing. After a lengthy moment, Clarence said, "So, tell me more about George."

"I love him so much already. He's much too big for a lapdog, but he tries to be one. He'll jump up on me, make an effort to circle around and sit. When that doesn't work, he'll slide to my side and cuddle up. He's smart. Really smart. Somebody taught him lots of things. If I say, 'Sit,' he sits. And I didn't teach him that. Whoever taught him and lost him must be sad. I think about that. I wonder if someone is out there somewhere looking for him. It would hurt me so much to give him back, but I guess I'd have to."

"Please don't fret about that. Laura Barnes said the SPCA did a thorough job of hunting for his owner. They didn't put him up for adoption until they were sure he was homeless. You'll give him a good home, I know that." Clarence yawned. He stretched, stood up, stretched again, and glanced around his bedroom—a room decorated tastefully with framed landscapes and seascapes on all four walls, and furnished with a handsome cherry-wood chest-of-drawers, a matching dresser and a four-poster bed. A framed photograph of 10-year-old Jordy and Uncle Clarry fishing from an old wooden bridge across a tree-shaded creek rested atop the chest. After moving close and examining the painting of the ships Jordan admired, Clarence said, "Hold on, Jordy," and slipped his phone into his pajama pocket and took the white-framed canvas down from the wall and placed it by the door. He grabbed the phone quickly and asked, "You still there, Jordy?"

"Yeah, I'm here."

The labradoodle jumped off the bed, looked up at Jordan and whimpered.

"I think George wants his breakfast," Jordan said as he scratched the dog's head. "We'll get something for you soon, 'cause you're a good boy. Yes, you are. Such a good doggie."

"Do you have enough supplies for him?"

"Oh, yeah. We stopped at a pet store on the way home from the SPCA, and Mrs. Barnes picked out everything—dog food, toys, comb and brush, flea repellent, a really nice doggie bed, leash and collar, ID tags, everything. She was wonderful."

"Yes, she is. She has a great love for animals."

"George went right to his bed last night. I have it here in my room. Near the window. But then I pulled him out of it and up onto my bed. I guess it wasn't the right thing to do, because we kept waking each other all night long. I turned over too many times. But he stayed with me."

"Last night I woke up remembering a time long ago when you lived in that house on Lavendale Street. You were just a little tot and I was your babysitter. The sky had turned strange shades of yellow and gray after a brief shower. We thought the storm was over. You were sitting on a radiator in a bay window looking up at the changing sky. Suddenly, an intense clap of thunder and streak of lightning shook the house and scared the hell out of us. You were hit. Electricity literally raced through your body and the radiator. You screamed and cried. I was scared out of my mind. I grabbed you and ran toward the door. But then, all of a sudden, I knew you were okay. Perfectly okay. Sound. Whole. Unmarred in any physical way. But so damn frightened you were shaking."

"I remember," Jordan said. "I think it's the only thing I remember from age four. You carried me to my room and read stories to me. You sat beside my bed and stayed there until I fell asleep."

"You didn't like all the stories. I had to cut some of them short. You know, like before someone was put in an oven or given a poison apple. Even Miss Muffet had to face a spider. Why is it that so many kid's stories and fairy tales include scary stuff." Clarence howled like a wolf and cackled like a witch.

Jordan laughed.

"As for remembering from age four, I'm sure you recall more than that thunder and lightning strike," Clarence said. "Like maybe those wasps that got up your shirt sleeve when you were playing in the mud. You were screaming and crying and I didn't know why. As hard as you tried, you couldn't explain what was happening."

"Oh, I remember that. But I was older than four. Maybe five or six? They stung me again and again and you couldn't understand what was happening."

"When I figured it out, I grabbed your arm and squeezed and squeezed, hoping to crush, mash, pulverize the damn creatures. When I pulled off your shirt, three dead wasps fell to the ground. I slapped some mud on your arm, hoping it would reduce the sting until we reached the medicine cabinet."

"That's the kind of thing a guy doesn't forget, Uncle Clarry."

"How about Eddy, do you remember him?"

"You mean Eddy the Teddy Bear with the weeping eye?"

"See? You do remember from age four. I couldn't sew on a button worth a damn. But I tried to replace Eddy's missing eye with a big blue button. I'd push in the needle. It would go straight into Eddy's head, and I couldn't turn it back out again through the button hole. I solved the problem by sewing Velcro over the spot of the missing eye and on the back of the button. I stuck 'em together. Voila! It worked!"

"But the eye drooped."

Clarence laughed heartily. "Oh, boy did it droop. It hung like a big bulging eye falling from its socket. But you loved Eddy anyway. You know why you called him Eddy, don't you?"

"Because I had trouble pronouncing the letter T."

"Yeah! Teddy was Eddy the Eddy Bear!"

Jordan giggled.

Neither Uncle Clarry nor Jordy spoke, but they were quietly linked in memories for a lengthy moment. The teenager broke the silence: "I remember the first time you took me to the circus. It was doubly special because I got out of going to Washington. It was one of those Uncle Clarry stayovers. I got excited every time you were asked to stay over. Because we'd do something special together. Even if it was just to go out and buy ice cream cones. If I'd hear Mom say to Dad, 'Let's go to the theater tonight,' I'd wait and listen, knowing she would ask, 'Is Clarence available?' Then I'd be excited all day long, waiting for whatever the night would bring."

Clarence became teary-eyed and muttered, "Enough of the memories. Look, I'll see you in the morning. I figure you haven't been taking care of things at the house. Have you been paying the bills from your trust fund? You're only permitted to draw a limited amount each month from that fund, you know."

"I haven't been paying any bills."

"Ye gads! I should have suspected. Haven't the utilities threatened to turn off everything?"

"I don't know. The mail's piled up in the entrance hall."

"Well, we're going to straighten things out. Remember, I pretty much ran that house for years. I wrote your father's checks, filed your father's receipts, organized his desk and file cabinets. I handled all details for your mother's social engagements. I did everything a good secretary should do. So I know the ropes. We'll put it all together, and then we'll dump it all on Peter Dexter's desk. Let the family lawyer handle the works. And we'll talk plenty about you and your days ahead. Do you plan to stay alone in that house? I mean, for God's sakes, you're a teenager, all alone, living in that big, roomy place. What do you feel as you walk from room to room? Do the good memories outnumber the bad ones, or is it the other way around?"

Jordan didn't respond, and Clarence feared he had tread too far again. Get back to the dog, he told himself. Quickly. "What's George doing?"

"Licking my hand."

"You'd better feed him. And take him for his morning walk. Did he make any mistakes in your room?"

"Do you mean, did he pee or poop? No. Not that I see."

"Well, get going. He needs food and exercise."

* * *

The morning was bright and sunny. Only a few white-and-fluffy clouds floated across a blue sky. Clarence would have been chipper anyway, even if the morning had been gray, but the beautiful day lifted him from high spirits to a feeling of bliss. "God bless George," he whispered to himself as he walked up the pathway to the Rimespeckers' portico, carrying the painting titled, *Into the Harbor*, under his left arm. He could barely believe Laura's success in amalgamating boy and dog, and he gave himself an A grade for dreaming up the canine strategy.

He actually tapped out a tune when knocking on the door. He was surprised not to hear George barking as most dogs do when visitors knock. When the door opened, he was not only stunned, he was held speechless for seconds. Standing there in the doorway, staring directly into his eyes, was Lillian Rimespecker, looking her regal self and smiling slightly.

"Hello, Clarence," Lillian said. "Jordan said you might be stopping by. Please, come in." She stepped back, allowing Clarence to enter. "He said you were worried about the mail. I took care of it. All of it."

Clarence placed the painting on the floor just inside the door, leaning it against the wall.

"What have you there?" Lillian asked.

"An oil painting by a local artist. For Jordy. He admired it."

"Really?"

"Where is he? And the dog?"

"He and I have had words over the dog. I'm not sure this is the right time to bring an animal into this house."

Clarence was so provoked his cheeks quivered. His anger caused his heart to palpitate. A dry mouth hampered his speech as he asked, "Where are they? Jordy and George?"

"In the kitchen. I believe Jordan is feeding the dog his breakfast. You may visit them there, if you so wish. I can see you're upset by my concern about introducing a dog into our family. This is a period of transition. And I don't want to complicate family-building."

"Family-building?"

"My friend Ruth may be brought into the mix. I have to be careful. She loved her cat."

Clarence was aghast by the implication. "Jordy loves his dog beyond belief. You can't separate them! No way!"

Lillian walked toward the library. "Clarence. Now, now. Make sense. The boy has had that dog for all of two or three days. For heaven's sake. Heart strings don't bind that quickly.

Thoughts rampaged through Clarence's head. He knew that Lillian was out on bail awaiting trial. He knew that Ruth Nettlebaum was missing and wanted by the police for questioning. He was certain that Jordan would never accept Lillian's lover as part of his family. And, to him, it made little sense that Lillian had come home and was even considering such a blend, especially with the trial looming.

"You're surprised I'm home, aren't you?" Lillian said as she stopped at the library doors, turned, and faced Clarence. "This is my house, Clarence. A trial date has yet to be set, and I'm free to live my life as I please in the meantime."

"Your actions bring much more instability than a dog would bring."

"How dare you!"

"I'm no longer an employee of this household, Mrs. Rimespecker. Surely you'll permit me to speak my mind. I'd like to stand on an equal plane with you. In fact, perhaps you'll allow me to call you Lillian, something you suggested many years ago when you flirted with me. There was a time when I really felt you cared."

"Flirting with men was part of my defense. It helped hide my true self. I learned to use it abundantly as a young girl in Newport society. It was so much a part of my disguise that it eventually bubbled forth with great ease. Have you any idea what it's like to play a role for most of your life?"

"I'm sure it's very difficult."

"I'm well tested. I wear thick armor. I'm not afraid of a murder trial. Bring it on. No senator's wife, that I know of, has been tried, convicted, and imprisoned for any crime."

"You're extremely cavalier about your plight."

"I have reason to be. And not only because I've retained one of the nation's best attorneys." Lillian held her head high and smiled before looking down on Clarence and saying, "If you're here to see Jordan, please go to the kitchen. And don't build up his hopes about keeping that dog. This is not a time for complicating our lives. I don't what to deal with any new issues."

"I can't believe what I just heard. Who brought complications and issues into your family? You, by the truckload! By the cheating and murdering truck load! And, I must say, your comings-and-goings are disruptive."

"Get out of my house!"

"I think not. I have business with your son."

"Get out!"

"No! But I will raise the white flag. Let's both shut up. I'll go see Jordan and George, then get the hell out of here." Clarence began to walk away, then turned back. "Tell me, Lillian, did you have a pet dog when you were a child?"

"We had dogs. But they were kept outside where they belonged. Foxhounds. I'd hear them howling at night when I lay in bed. My father was active with the premier foxhound club in Rhode Island."

"That's not quite like having a pet."

"I suppose little Suzy Parker was my pet. A sweet little girl who lived by the waterfront. It broke my heart when her family moved away. I'll tell you what. Tell Jordan that if he fences in the backyard and builds a substantial doghouse, perhaps we could accommodate George outdoors for a test-run. If my partner and I find this arrangement works, he can stay outside. At no time, however, would he be allowed in the house."

"George is a house pet. He loves to wrestle on the floor and jump on beds. He loves to sit at his master's feet and feel his hand in his curls. He loves to play games and chase kids around the house." Clarence shook his head. "But I'll pass on your half-hearted proposal to Jordy."

Suddenly a ball came rolling and bouncing down the corridor and into the foyer, followed by George, who pranced about and leaped. Wagging his tail wildly, the dog caught the ball, flopped in front of Clarence and dropped the ball at his feet. Jordan wasn't far behind. He stepped slowly into the foyer, ignored both Clarence and George, and immediately confronted his mother, who stepped back against the library doors as if fearful of the labradoodle.

"He won't hurt you, Mother," Jordan said. "Although I'm sure he knows you don't like him. You keep giving him all the wrong signals."

"Your mother has proposed a trial period," Clarence said, "if you keep George behind a fence in the backyard."

"No way!" the teenager asserted. "George is going nowhere!" Jordan was in turmoil. His feelings and thoughts were fighting each other. The love he wanted to feel for his mother was twisted around loathing for her actions. Such a contradictory mix built a strange interlacing of ideas normally opposed to one another.

"Well, I really didn't want him out there in the backyard, anyway," Lillian said. "And fencing in the yard would have been an ugly move. Clarence, perhaps you'll be kind enough to take him back to the SPCA."

"Mom!" Jordan exclaimed. "Are you listening to me? George is my dog. He's not going anywhere. He's staying with me."

Lillian turned toward Clarence.

"Don't look at me!" Clarence asserted. "I'm not taking that dog anywhere. If you want a cat for your friend, it'll have to learn to live with George."

"Oh, my God! That would be the last situation I'd allow in this house."

"You want me to hate you, don't you, Mother?" Jordan's lips trembled. "Why is that? You hurt me by leaving, and then hurt me by coming back."

"No! My God, no! I love you."

"What the hell kind of love is that? And why would you want a couple felines in your house rather than your son?"

"Stop it! Stop it!" Lillian screamed.

Jordan stepped so close to his mother that his nose was almost touching hers. "It's true, isn't it? You're telling me I can't live here with my dog because you want to live here with your damn concubine and a fucking cat."

"How dare you talk to me like that!" Lillian slapped her son hard across the face. "I'm your mother." She raised her hand as if to strike again, but held back. The teenager's face reddened, leaving an imprint of her stinging fingers.

"I'm sorry," Lillian said. "I didn't mean to do that."

"Are you really and truly my mother? Just because you gave birth to me, doesn't make you so. Mothers don't act like you. They don't have secret hideouts where they keep their lovers hidden from the police. Where is Ruthy-Doofy-puddin'-in pie, anyway? Huh! Where is she? You want this house for yourself and your screw-dee-doo-mate? Okay. Take it! 'Cause I'm leaving."

"And where, pray tell, do you expect to live?"

"I'll make out." The dog leaped joyfully at the boy. "George and I will make out."

Clarence's head was spinning. His inclination was to yell out, *Come with me!* But his thoughts went to Terry, his upcoming marriage, and his elderly mother. Surely he had to lay some groundwork with his "brownstone" family before bringing home a full-grown "son" and his dog. Yet he tossed such thoughts aside for the compelling sentiment that had impelled him for years. "Come with me!" he called out, well aware that no opposition would stop him anyway. Besides, he was confident that his fiancée and his mother knew his deep feelings. How could they not, since such fervor oozed from his very being again and again.

"I didn't think you were going to ask," said Jordan, his body trembling, his cheeks streaked with tears. He rushed toward the door with George at his heels. When he saw the harbor picture near the entranceway, he stopped suddenly, his heels squeaking on the ornate tile floor. He picked up the framed oil painting and held it against his chest as he looked back at Clarence and allowed a softer but plaintive look to erase the more severe lines of anger. Within an instant, he fled out onto the portico.

"Come back here!" his mother screamed. "You're my son!"

"I'll take good care of him," Clarence said softly as Lillian brushed against him as both hurried outside.

"Jordan, please!" Lillian yelled as she watched the boy and his dog scamper down the walkway toward Clarence's car. "Damn you, come back here! I love you! Do you hear me? You're my son, my baby, and I love you!"

Clarence hurried down the steps, and then turned and looked up at Lillian. "He'll be okay. I'll see to it."

Lillian called after Clarence as he turned away and quick-stepped toward Jordan: "You can't take him! You're kidnapping him! I'll have you arrested and jailed for this. He's underage. The law will not permit him to be divorced from his parents at sixteen years of age even if he so wishes. You'll be punished, Clarence. Whatever the penalty, I'll see it comes down hard on you, so help me God!"

Clarence walked on. He had no idea of legalities pertaining to such matters. But it did not figure in his mind that freeing a boy from a scandalous woman, who was charged with a felony, could be judged as a kidnapping, especially in light of that teenager's desire to flee. This was a woman suspected of killing the boy's father, a woman who deserted him for lesbian love, a woman who wished to deprive him of his pet dog.

George leaped for the backseat of Clarence's car as soon as Jordan opened the door and called out, "In, boy! Jump in!" The teenager ruffled the fur on the dog's rump as he leaped. "That's a good boy, George." The dog settled down behind the passenger's seat, slowed his tail-wagging, and watched his young master slide onto the front seat next to the driver. As soon as Jordan was settled, the labradoodle tried to reach him to lick his neck, but fell back as the car jumped forward and stopped. Clarence had started the car, only to brake it suddenly when he saw Lillian running toward them. The distraught woman ran into the street and pounded on the car with her fists.

Clarence rolled down the driver-side window. "Please Lillian. You're going to hurt yourself. Step back and let us go. I promise I'll be in touch."

"Jordan, I love you!" Lillian screamed.

Clarence moved the car ahead slowly until it was totally free of the hysterical woman, then lowered the gas pedal and the car sped forward.

George barked several times. Then whimpered.

Lillian stood in the middle of the street, her eyes following Clarence's car. Her arms hung at her sides as she breathed hard, each gulp of air lifting her shoulders as tears streamed down her face. "I need you, Ruth," she muttered to herself. "Oh, God, I need you, Ruth."

Clarence drove about a half-mile through a well-to-do neighborhood shaded by Norway maple trees before he pulled the car to the curb, took his hands off the steering well, flipped them palms up, and stared at them. "Why are my hands shaking?" he questioned, more of himself than of Jordan. "Because of our explosive departure? Or because of my commitment to you, Jordan? I want to do what's right by you. You know that, don't you?"

"You always said you wanted a son like me."

"And so be it! But that doesn't mean it isn't a life-changing thing that twitches my nerves. Wow! All of a sudden I'm Big Daddy! Don't get me wrong. I'm glad of it. I just have to realize what it is, what it means. I want a complete and proper adoption. You have to finish school. We have to plan for college. Holy, shit!"

"You don't really want ..."

"Yes I do!" Clarence interrupted. "With all my heart and soul! There's nothing I want more."

"Then just let things happen, Uncle Clarry. Stop thinking way ahead. College will take care of itself. First order of business: How do we get my belongings out of that house with Mom there? Everything that's mine is still back there. My clothes, my sports equipment, my books, my nature collections, my computer, my camera. All I have with me are the clothes on my back."

"We'll ask Tony to help get your stuff."

"Tony? You mean Tony Paluto?"

"Yeah, he'll figure out a smooth way of doing it without upsetting your mother. He still has keys to the house and the garage."

"Tony?"

"You'd be surprised the things he can do. He's been the chief go-getter and doer at the bivouac."

"He doesn't know my things."

"You'll make a complete list. I'll help you. We'll describe everything. Give exact locations. We'll work out a complete plan." Clarence sucked in a deep breath of air. "But first off, we'll simply ask your mother. She may allow us to gather up your things without a fight."

"Good luck with that."

With his nose on the window, George barked at a woman walking down the street with her Pekinese. Startled, the woman flinched and then glared angrily into the car.

"We'd better get going," Jordan said. "Neighbors will wonder what we're doing here."

"You're right." Clarence started the car with calmer hands and drove away under the shade of the maples.

"Y'know, I still have my keys to your mother's house, too. And I betcha Hilda does, also. None of us were really properly fired. None of us got pink slips. Your father was shot and your mother was in limbo, and we just assumed we were dismissed."

"Tony got fired."

"You mean he got screamed at by the senator. I don't know if a verbal attack counts. Yeah, he got tossed out that night, but without proper notice and not in writing. The truth is, neither Hilda, Tony, nor I were properly dismissed. We could have a case against the Rimespecker Estate or your mother. I may know why none of us has taken action."

"Why?"

"I recently woke up to the fact that paychecks have continued to be deposited directly into my account. Rightfully so, perhaps. Do you think that Tony and Hilda may be aware of that, too." Clarence grinned. "That will end, possibly now, if your mother is truly trying to reorganize the household."

Chapter Nineteen

Clarence tapped the horn lightly and then sent Jordan from the car to Terry's brownstone. He called out the driver-side window, "Ring the bell. She'll hear it way back in the sunroom." The teenager bounced sprightly up the walkway and steps. Clarence told himself that this bright morning of sunshine presented a good day for this new venture in living.

The boy's presence would not be a surprise to Terry, because Clarence had filled her in by phone the night before. His step-by-step method of bringing them together was deliberately planned. He wanted no sudden plunge for her, and he wanted time for her to think and digest between his interweaving efforts. Terry's gracious acceptance of his relationship with Jordan had surfaced long ago, and her few get-togethers with him had been positive, but Clarence knew enough about people to realize that a view expressed at one time about a situation doesn't always hold together when that situation finally occurs.

"Welcome to our Brownstone Colony," Terry said as she stepped down toward the sidewalk and pointed with a sweeping motion to the solid row of three-story dwellings that made up an entire city block. "Hope you'll be happy on this side of the city line." She greeted the boy warmly, squeezed his arm, pecked a kiss on his forehead and followed him to the car. So far, so good, thought Clarence, who carefully eyed his fiancée and Jordan for any nuances that might reveal any inclinations.

First sign of anything negative came from Jordan. After opening the front passenger-seat door for Terry, he just stood there, not making any effort to get into the car. He had a certain glint in his eyes that made Clarence suspect his train of thought.

"What is it, Jordy?" Clarence asked.

"Why can't George come with us?"

"Like I said, the bivouac's a busy place. He could get in trouble."

"Please?"

"And we're having a deeply serious meeting of three wise men, including you—three conspirators plotting an escapade."

"George is a brilliant dog who can sit in on our meeting," Jordan expressed playfully. "He won't give away any secrets. I promise. Besides, Miss Terry, here, hasn't met him yet."

"I thought George would be good company for my mother while we're gone," Clarence said with a not too convincing smirk on his face. A moment's thought caused him to add: "Change is good for both of you. Detachment will shake up George's instincts, and he'll be so happy to see you when we get home. You'll see."

"Really?" Jordan grinned. "I think you're dreaming up reasons or excuses. In truth, you're really trying to test George's and my separation anxiety?"

"Hey! Don't be a wisecracker, now. Where did you pick that up?"

"It's a big subject on TV's Animal Planet. Some dogs chew pillows, eat the furniture and wreck the house when they're left alone."

"Separation anxiety?"

"Right on."

Clarence knew he would give in, seconds before he said, "If we bring him with us, you'll have to keep a close watch on him."

Terry glanced from Jordan's eyes to Clarence's and smiled. "Jordan's gonna win this battle. And I suspect he'll win lots of other battles, too." She looked at the teenager and winked. "Go get your dog. I wanna meet him."

"I'll back up the car. Hold tight." Clarence put the car in reverse and slowly slid it back along the curb.

Jordan had the door open before the car came to a full stop, and he left it hanging as he raced toward the house.

"So, how's it working out?" Terry asked, pleased to get a moment alone with Clarence. She was anxious to show her fiancé that she could accept the teenager and make him part of their life together, even though she felt a mixture of concerns and emotions that stirred her guts.

"Good. Really good, considering."

"Considering?"

"Well, it happened suddenly. No time to prepare or think things out. He slept in my room last night, and I took the guestroom. But we're figuring on making the third floor into his pad. It's unfinished, and it'll take work, but it's an entire floor, four large rooms. And the idea thrilled him. He said, 'It'll be like my own apartment.'"

"Your third floor is just like mine, I'm sure. You could open up between them."

"I don't think he needs eight rooms," said Clarence, who was moved by her offer and pecked a kiss on her forehead. "Lots of folks don't realize how big these city brownstones are. Of course, nothing's going to compare with what he had."

"In terms of space or love? Only he knows what he truly had."

"Anyway, it'll be good for him and for me to have a major project, like the third-floor refurbishing—something to work on together. There's nothing better than an undertaking like that to help build a binding relationship. Especially when y'have a definite goal."

"You'll learn a great deal about each other," Terry said softly as she gently squeezed his shoulder. "I bet there will be testy trials along with satisfying moments. It'll teach you a lot about one another that you never suspected."

Clarence could tell that Terry was trying hard to be the best third-person she could. "Just like you and me," he said, "Jordy and I have had our ups and downs throughout the years. But this will be intense, I'll grant you that. No matter what we do, there will always be an undercurrent."

"Undercurrent?"

"An underlying resolve that we're trying to build a new life together."

"There's no man better fit to pulling it off than you."

"You're too kind."

"No. I know you. You're a perfect fit for him. But then you know that."

Clarence simply stared into Terry's eyes thoughtfully.

"What is it?"

He tossed her a kiss.

She smiled and wrinkled her nose.

"I talked to his mother this morning," Clarence said, his tone turning deep and serious. "I haven't told him yet. He was in the shower, and I thought I'd get it over with while he was busy. She was not out of control like yesterday. I could tell she was trying hard to be civil. That is, until I broached the subject of picking up his belongings. I could almost feel her back stiffen over the telephone. With hard-ass conviction she insisted she would not relinquish her only bargaining chips."

"Will you try again?"

"There's no use. She was stubborn and vehement. That's why I'm pulling together this strategy meeting."

"Three guys? Why am I here?"

"You're just along for the ride. For the most part, that is. I will need you for one little thing. Lillian knows my voice. She won't know yours over the telephone. So, you'll play the role of the package-delivery lady."

"What?"

"Shush. Enough. Here come Jordan and George."

George raced Jordan to the car as Clarence's mother stood in the doorway waving. The dog leaped onto the backseat, but retreated slightly when he saw Terry up front. Jordan nudged him and slid in beside him.

"Miss Terry, this is George," the teenager said.

The reluctant dog pulled back as Terry reached for him from the front passenger seat. She managed to pat him on the head.

"He'll warm up to you in no time," Clarence explained. "We suspect he was kicked, hurt or frightened by a stranger. But just wait until he gets to know you. He's quite affectionate, really, a testament to his original owners, we think. They trained him well in proper doggie conduct and even taught him some tricks."

Jordan's mind was elsewhere, as revealed by his question: "Uncle Clarry, do you think we could install a bathroom on the third floor?"

"Ah, still dreaming about your third-floor penthouse, are you? " He glanced at the boy. "I suppose we can ask a plumber."

"Look at this!" Terry interjected. "Look!" George was stretching his neck and leaning his head on her shoulder. He was licking her left ear.

"That was quick!" Clarence expressed in delight. "Maybe it's your perfume. You do smell good this morning."

"Did you ever have a dog, Miss Terry?"

"Why don't you call me *Aunt Terry*?" She turned and winked at the teenager. "I mean what the heck, if this guy at the wheel gets *Uncle Clarry*, why shouldn't his fiancée get *Aunt Terry*? Can you buy that, Jordan? Or is it *Jordy*?"

"Yeah!" Jordan bounced in his seat causing George to get playful and paw at him. "I like what you're selling, Aunt Terry. It's a deal. Call me Jordy." He leaned forward and tapped her on the shoulder. "Now, please level with me. When are you two lovebirds getting hitched?"

"You just caused your uncle to shiver," Terry said.

"No way!" insisted Clarence, who was warmed by Terry's words and the interplay between her and Jordan. "It's approaching fast."

"It is?" Terry asked in wonder.

"I figure we'll tie it to the flight of the young bald eagles. Think about that. Wouldn't that make it special?"

"You're joking! Now you're going to the other extreme—too soon. Fledging time for the eagles is only weeks away."

"Fledging?" Jordan asked.

"That's when they're ready to fly from the nest," Clarence explained. "July is fading away, and August is approaching. Jimmy has the approximate date pinned down. How's this for an idea? We clean out the bivouac and borrow the land from Charley and Claudia for our outdoor wedding. They'd be thrilled. We set up the altar in front of the woods, just where the first of the trees burst forth. And to the right or left we'd erect a computerized big-screen TV that would show the eagles leaving the nest in real time and flying skyward over the Bitterlick Creek just as you and I, Terry, say 'I do'."

"Fanciful!" Terry proclaimed. "Dramatiic! But impossible."

"You're right, of course. The big moment couldn't be timed with nature's calling. But allow me to dream a little, and I'll come up with a variation that works. And each of you should keep spinning your thinking caps. You hear that, Jordy? The best man can play a big role in putting it together and pulling it off."

Terry turned and smiled at Jordan. "You know what he's doing, don't you, Jordy? He's so concerned that your arrival will scare me into thinking our wedding plans will be derailed, altered or postponed for some reason that he's trumpeting an impending, creative and imaginative ceremony. Here it comes! Soon! And with trees and outdoor beauty and flying eagles."

"That's unfair!" Clarence asserted.

"No it's not!" Jordan barked. "I'll keep lighting the fire under him, Aunt Terry. For every inch we proceed with my inclusion, I promise you two inches toward the wedding."

"You're a sweetheart, Jordy," Terry said.

George began to whimper. His tail was down, his ears back. He looked out the window as his whimpers turned into squeals.

"Uh-oh," Jordan said. "George has to pee or poop. You'd better pull over."

"Snap on his leash," Clarence suggested as he turned the car into a cluster of sumac and giant mulleins. "We don't want to lose him in this wooded area."

"It's on." The teenager pushed and kicked the door open.

Jordan and George scampered into a thick growth of sassafras and sycamore trees, while Clarence wasted no time pulling his phone from his pocket.

"Who are you calling now?" Terry asked.

"I want to add some tidbits to what I told Claudia this morning. I don't know why, but my mind is popping with ideas today."

* * *

Claudia placed a coffee pot and a plate of jelly doughnuts on the dining room table and made an effort to chase her husband from the room. But Charley stayed in his chair and was quick to reach for a doughnut.

"No, Charley! They're bringing the young Rimespecker kid with them. I'll betcha he'll down more than a few of these."

"Well, I'll deprive him of no more than one. Okay?" Charley bit into a doughnut that oozed jelly, dribbling it onto his chin.

"Watch it! Here!" Claudia came to the rescue with a napkin.

"Only three guys?" He wiped his lips and chin. "Why are they meeting here?"

"Tony doesn't want to break his promise to the Boy Scouts. The troop picked out two trees for him to climb. He's gonna demonstrate the use of micro-pulleys and climbing spikes, among other things. But I think a bigger reason for coming here lies with Clarence. He wants to introduce the entire bivouac operation to the murdered senator's son. Apparently he's on a crusade to involve the boy in activities that'll help him erase a lot of ugliness."

"He told you that?"

"Pretty much so." Claudia's thoughts produced a grin. "And there may be something else."

"Oh?"

"He asked me if we'd be open to leasing our unused grassland for his upcoming wedding to Terry—post-bivouac, of course."

"You're kidding? Holy smokes, you're full of news."

"That's because I beat you to the phone for a change. Twice! I held him on for you the second time, waiting to hear you flush the toilet. You were obviously stuck on the pot."

"I'm guessing you mean they want an outdoor wedding in the rear. Right?"

"Yepper. But I told him our land wasn't for rent." Claudia giggled. "After some kidding around, I said we'd be delighted to see them married—for free, of course—in our backyard, if we were invited to partake."

"You invited us to their wedding? Since when do we invite ourselves to other peoples' weddings?"

"He said our participation was part of the plan. Our gang of a half-dozen or more bivouac organizers will be featured, along with the eagles' flight and choker rescue."

"You gotta be kidding! What's he been smoking? Does Terry approve?"

"He didn't say." Claudia slid behind her husband and began massaging his shoulders, only to stop suddenly and step away. "Y'know, Charley. In some respects I'll be sorry to see the encampment leave. It's taught me a great deal about our life together."

"What do you mean?"

"I think our lives had become too insular. It was just us. Oh, we had our friends, and we'd eat out now and again with Jimmy and Laura. We'd go shopping. And we'd visit Cousin Ruth once a year. But really, we had become our own little island. I'm not saying we didn't enjoy each other. And, in a lot of ways, we had a perfect marriage. But this bivouac has opened the world. People, ideas, woodland animals, birds, cookouts, Boy Scouts, plant-life, singing songs, late-night conversations, hiking and a definite goal at the end of the resplendent tunnel. We couldn't live with all of it all of the time, of course. But we gotta grab onto something more when the bird-watchers, scouts and others vacate."

"And I bet you have an idea on how to begin this new life."

"Clarence and Terry have given the Rimespecker boy permission to bring his pet dog here today."

"He has a pet dog?"

"Thanks to Laura."

"Uh-oh. I think I see where this is going."

"I know years have passed. But I still get teary eyed over Bingo."

"Need I remind you again that I've always been open to ..."

"I know," Claudia interrupted. "I know. I know. Forget all that. I've made up my mind. First step post-bivouac? We get ourselves a rescued greyhound. In fact, maybe we'll get a pair of them. After the tents go, it'll be a perfect time to remodel the acres of land we have out back. We need more around here than a couple boxes of bees, for godsake. We'll build doggie runs and comfortable canine housing."

"You're thinking outdoor living?"

"No, no, no. I want them to have the run of our house. We'll get big cushions and doggie beds for them to lie on and lots of toys to play with. We'll install flipping doors and outdoor fencing that will permit them to come and go, allowing them to run in and out as they so please." Claudia walked around the table, stopped behind her husband, and kneaded his shoulders. "Do you know how many greyhounds are killed each year from track injuries or because they're no longer fast enough to bring in big bucks for their keepers?" She tapped him on the head. "More than three thousand!"

"What have you been doing? Researching?"

"Yes, as a matter of fact." She began pacing around the table again.

"You really are serious about adopting, aren't you? My God, Claudia, how long have you been mulling this over?"

"For too many years. But it was the bivouac that switched on my motor. And when Clarence told me this morning that a labradoodle named George absolutely turned the Rimespecker boy from morose to a good-natured kid in a matter of days, well, I knew that now was the time to dump it all on you. And I must say, you're taking it well."

"Like I said, it was always you that brought it up, then backed away. And I know why. The hurt was deep and tore you apart."

"Stop! What did I say? No more of that. In fact, we might even build our haven for two greyhounds into a sizable rescue operation. How does that sound?"

"Like you've walked miles in your own dog-depleted desert and finally found an oasis where the water turns to wine. And if we inherit millions from Ruth, we can build a Disney-like castle for the pleasure of many greyhounds."

"Damn you, Charley! Why did you have to spoil things? Don't you dare suggest anything like that again! You know how I feel! Let Ruth live on some deserted island somewhere with that choker around her scrawny neck. Sick introverts persist in living long to torture others. Her persistence won't allow her to die until she lets go at a decrepit age. Mark my word! When she dies a wrinkled-up old lady they can bury the blasted Ermengarde with her."

"You've obviously been suffering through repulsive nightmares about Ruth."

Claudia did not respond in words. She took a seat as far from Charley as possible, folded her arms on the table, and lay her head in the fold.

"I'm glad level-headed Clarence is arriving. After their meeting, maybe you can have a session with him."

Claudia raised her head. "I don't need counseling. I confess I got carried away." She forced a smile. "I'm sorry, Charley." She gazed into his eyes. "But you're right about Clarence. He has a way with him that calms the spirit and fixes knotty problems. You've become close friends in a short time."

"Strange about friends and acquaintances. You can know some for years and never get really close. Others, like Jimmy, you've known since ever and the bond will always be there. Then again there are the new friends that become so close because of a certain affinity that's hard to define. Common interests have something to do with it, I'm sure. But it's much more than that. Magnetism is too strong a word, perhaps. But there is a certain pull. Affinity is the only word that fits. Clarence has it. At first I saw him as this staid, proper, serious, efficient, senatorial secretary. He was skillful at playing a roll. When he escaped from the restraints he became the warm and fuzzy guy that Terry and the Rimespecker boy knew all along. Do I make any sense?"

"You're a warm and fuzzy guy, too, Charley. I guess his fuzz and yours stick together like Velcro."

"I think I hear them. Yeah, they're coming up the walkway. Get Tony t'come in from the woods. If he's high up and occupied, call him on the scoutmaster's cellphone."

Chapter Twenty

Clarence sat on one side of the Silvesters' dining table in a room nearly vacant of other furniture. By design, Tony, Jordan and Terry sat on the other side, directly across from him. It was as if he were directing a small choir of three. He wanted full-face and frontal eye contact of each member of his ad hoc committee.

George the Labradoodle was stretched out on the floor, tethered to Clarence's chair by his leash, the end of which was looped around a mahogany leg.

"Do you want me to stay?" Terry asked.

"For a brief moment while I explain your role. Then you can leave and join the bivouac if you so choose. Jimmy can fill you in on the latest details about the young eagles. Or you can have a chat with Claudia and Charley. I'm sure they would like to hear more about our wedding plans. But you're welcome to stay if you'd rather. I suppose it really depends on how much you want to know about our covert mission."

"Is it safe for me to know the secret details?" she asked, a teasing smile turning her lips slightly as she adjusted herself in her seat for a longer wait.

"Terry! I don't think you'd dare spring a leak, would you?"

"I don't know. If you're too naughty I might open the flood gates. I don't want to visit any of you in jail."

"Let's get serious." Clarence assumed a sober visage. "Our mission is to secure Jordan's belongings, against his mother's will, load them on a truck, and transport them to my house. Since Madam Rimespecker is vehemently opposed to the transfer and will fight us every inch of the way, I see no other way to proceed except through clandestine means." Clarence stared at the threesome for a long moment, then said, "Interrupt me at any time. Shoot me down if you think I'm wrong. Please. I intend this to be an open bull session, not a monologue by me."

"You're thinking burglary?" asked Tony.

"Yes, but not necessarily illegal burglary." Clarence smiled. "I know what you're thinking. Is there any other kind?" He grinned. "Listen carefully now. Hear me out. And if I'm way off base, tell me so." He looked directly at the former chauffeur. "Tell me, Tony, did you get a paycheck from the House of Rimespecker last month?"

Tony blinked and looked sheepish.

"You don't have to tell us if you cashed it. I got one, too." Clarence pulled a check from his pocket and waved it in the air.

Tony nodded.

"Did you ever receive an official notice of dismissal?"

"No."

"Then, technically, you were never fired. Right?"

"The senator shouted at me. Remember? He yelled 'Get out of here! You're fired!'" Tony's impersonation of the senator was so loud that George awoke with a start, growled, barked and sprang to his feet.

"Easy does it, boy," Clarence said softly. He rubbed the dog's head and scratched his back. The bewildered animal glanced about, yawned and lay back down.

"Yes, Tony, I remember that day very well," Clarence said. "The senator yelled at you in anger, in the heat of the moment." Clarence kept his eyes on Tony. "It meant nothing. You never got a pink slip. You never got an official letter ending your employment. What about proper notice? Never got that did you? You were due at least a month's notice, I'm sure. And what about severance pay? I know I didn't get any."

Jordan nudged Tony, grinned and said, "I guess you were never fired, my friend. Maybe you belong to me. I here and now claim you as my property." He motioned to Clarence. "Toss me the dog's chain and collar, Uncle Clarry."

"Zip your teenage lip, Rimes!" Tony laughed as he kicked Jordan's ankle.

"Ouch!"

"Let's face it," Clarence said, "neither Hilda, nor I, nor you, Tony, were actually or properly fired. We just assumed we were because the senator was dead and his wife was missing. So, we were out of work. Right? Not exactly. Not while the estate still stood, I suspect. Not while living pieces of the family existed, as did its lawyers and financial holdings. None of us followed through with anything, did we? Did you,

Tony, call the law firm of Dewitt, Boyton and Dexter? I didn't. I doubt
that Hilda did. Of course if we had, we might have prompted a hard slap-
down and official firing from the family attorney or the in-again, out-
again lady of the house."

"And then there's me," Jordan said.

"Right! The son. The heir apparent." Clarence stiffened and saluted.
"You, Jordy, were to be my next discussion point. Now that you injected
yourself into the mix, you're definitely next on the agenda." He looked
the teenager up and down. "That's the same shirt you had on yesterday.
Friends, the boy, here, needs a clean shirt. Believe it or not, he's wearing
my underwear—spanking clean underwear, of course, directly out of my
top dresser drawer. We can buy him a new toothbrush, but not his
grandfather's baseball bat signed way back in the nineteen-forties by
Ted Williams. A bunch of vitally important stuff belongs to this young
man, and he wants to move it from one house to another. Simple enough,
isn't it? All we're doing is helping the rightful owner move his
belongings. So, let me summarize: Employed servants of the estate, with
keys to the property, are helping a Rimespecker heir to relocate."

"Sounds like a solid argument to me," Tony said, "but I ain't no
lawyer." He lifted his arm, squeezed his fist, and showed off his biceps
muscle. "But I can lift and carry pretty much anything yous guys want
me to lift."

"If we're stopped by the cops, I think they'd buy that argument,"
Clarence said. "And Chief Morris knows us. He'd reason right along
with us rather than accept anything the widow Rimespecker had to offer.
He has contempt for her."

"That's the truth," Tony said as he flexed his muscles again. "She's
gotta be on the bottom of his shit-list."

"You do still have your keys, don't you, Tony?" Clarence asked. "I
have mine."

"Yeah."

"To the pickup truck?"

"Yeah. To that, too."

Clarence looked at his fiancée and shook his head. "I didn't mean to
keep you here so long, Terry. I got ahead of myself."

"No problem. I found your rationale intriguing."

"Intriguing?"

"I'd have to study it carefully before declaring it free of holes."

"You're wondering about your contribution, right? It's simple. Open the doors! Clear the way! Lift the gates!"

"What?"

"We have to be certain that Lillian Rimespecker is not home on the day or night—preferably night—that we pull our raid. This is a woman who likes to move about, enjoys shopping sprees in elegant stores, welcomes long sessions with her hair stylist, enjoys the theater, engages in private gambling sessions in wealthy homes, dines often at the finest restaurants, visits nail salons and has a monthly date with her personal pedicurist. Your job, Terry, is to find out when and for how long she'll be out of the house on a given day or two. It has to be a sure thing, or as close to a sure thing as possible. We can't have her showing up as one of us is carrying Jordan's model of the Neanderthal man out of the house, or loading his antique German toy-chest on the pickup truck."

"Exactly how am I going to do that, Clarence?" Terry asked.

"I've come up with a plan. But perhaps you folks will have better ideas. Let's do a little brainstorming. I'll lay out my scheme first, and you guys can pick it apart." Clarence cleared his throat twice. "Terry, you'll pretend to be a package-delivery rep. You'll call up Mrs. Rimespecker and say, 'We have a large package here to be delivered to Senator Rimespecker's residence. It must be signed for, so we need a guarantee that someone will be home at the time of delivery. Perhaps you can tell us when not to deliver.'"

"And if she won't cooperate?" Terry asked.

"She will if you do a good job." Clarence gave her a hard and steady stare. "And I'm confident that you will."

"I'm glad you have such confidence, because I sure don't. What if she wants to know the contents of the package?"

"Tell her its computer parts. She won't know what her husband ordered before his unfortunate demise. Be creative. We'll come up with every possible scenario, and we'll practice aplenty before you call."

"What if she doesn't know what time she'll return from the doctor's office, or from a DAR meeting, or from lunch with a friend?"

"Or from a little snooky with Ruthie?" Tony added.

Everyone but George was quiet after Tony's remark. They stared down at the table. Only the dog whimpered.

"Push her to another time or day," Clarence finally said. "Tell her we don't deliver on the west side on Thursdays or whatever. You're clever. You'll figure it out. I've heard how professional you speak over the phone when it's official business."

"Kind words won't get you everything you want, Clarence, dear. But for Jordy's sake, I'll play the role this time." Terry rose from the table. "Am I excused, now? I'd like to go visit with Charley and Claudia."

"Yeah, go ahead." Clarence said. "I'll fill you in later, if necessary. And we'll practice, practice, practice. Won't we?"

Terry ignored him.

"Together! We'll practice together."

She continued to ignore Clarence, and looked at Jordan. "Is it okay if I take George with me? Look at him. He's not enjoying this. He looks bored."

"Yeah, I guess so." Jordan tapped the table to get the dog's attention. "You be a good boy, now." He looked at Terry. "He probably has to take a leak, anyway. Keep him close to you. Don't let him wander off."

"Don't worry. I'll keep him tethered."

Terry wasted no time in chasing Clarence from his seat so she could seize the dog's leash. She and George departed quickly. As soon as the door slammed, Jordan was on his feet and proclaiming, "The things belong to me, so I should be able to take them when I move from one house to another. Aren't we making too big a deal out of this?"

"Maybe so, Jordy," Clarence said. "Then give me another scenario. I'm just trying to avoid a lot of screaming and yelling. Your mother has power. She can cause a lot of trouble. She'll definitely cause a lot of delays, starting with the first nine-one-one call. It doesn't matter if her arguments are sound, you won't get your belongings before the first snow storm, if then. She powwows with Judge Elizabeth Bentley and knows a little too much about Judge Horace Green's flirtations. Remember what happened to Florence Gibbons when she tried to keep your mother off the Flower Club Executive Committee? Don't get me wrong, I always admired your mother in many ways. You know that. At one time I felt that the three of us were a compatible force against the senator's heavy hand. But believe me, it's not wise to get her back up. Our best moves must be aimed at keeping the Lady Wolf from the door until her trial begins. And that shouldn't be too long."

"But your plan will definitely anger her," Tony said.

"You're right, of course. But she's peaking with anger right now because of Jordan's flight. If we do this quickly—boom, boom, in and out, done—it'll be part of the same explosion of fury. I don't know another way. Come on, now. Let's talk it out."

Jordan and Clarence sank slowly into their seats.

"Tony, at one time I thought of dumping this entire activity in your lap."

"I could do it!" Tony's head sprang up like a Jack-in-the-Box. He grinned. "Y'want me t'do it? Hell, I'll take it on."

"I knew you'd say that."

"Really. I could put it together and carry it out. Bing! Bang! Boohey!"

"No, no, no. That would be unfair, especially since we have a young man here who knows what he wants and where it is. You'd have to take a list. And you wouldn't know the locations of many items. Jordy's got to be on the team. And if he and you are game, so am I. So be it! We're the three musketeers."

"One for all, and all for one!" Tony proclaimed.

"I assume the pickup truck is still in the garage directly below your former quarters, eh, Tony?" Clarence questioned. "Right under your old bedroom?"

"Well, I didn't take it with me. So, I guess it's there. I can sneak by and check it out."

"No need," Jordan said. "It's there. Who would've taken it?"

"And that particular garage door opens directly opposite the kitchen delivery door," Clarence said. "Am I right?"

"We call it the cellar door," Jordan said. "It leads to stairs that go up to the kitchen and down to the basement. Hilda always referred to the landing between the flights as 'The cellarway.' She stored canned good on shelves there, and mason jars filled with things she preserved, like tomatoes and peaches and stuff."

"But, as I picture the layout, it is the shortest route for carrying things out from the West Wing, right?"

"From my room," Jordan explained, "you'd have to go down the main stairs, then switch over to the back stairs. They're narrow and curved. But it's the shortest way, and definitely the only way for us to pull off this venture."

"That's right." Clarence said. "We're not going to be loading-up out front. The long driveway to the cellar door becomes pretty-much hidden toward the rear. If we pull off this caper after dark, we'll be even more secluded. Do the cops patrol the neighborhood at night?"

"I've often seen squad cars circle around the area," Jordan said. "But I can't pinpoint the times."

"They come through just after dark," Tony said with assurance. "I know this, 'cause they'd shine their goddamn lights up the driveway and right through my freakin' windows. Of course, since the murder, they might have changed their routine. The house looks empty so much of the time."

"If we can avoid the police, good," Clarence said. "If we can't, we'll be ready for them with an innocent explanation about moving the Rimespecker heir, who, we'll point out, happens to be right here with us."

"The stuff we're moving, is it all in your room?" Tony asked Jordan.

"Most of it. Some clothes are in a hallway closet. And there's a bunch of mementoes and souvenirs in a trunk under a window-seat in the lavender guestroom. Both are just down the hall from my room. I'm not sure if there's anything of mine in the attic. If so, I guess I don't need it if I haven't seen it or thought about it for years. Besides, I think Dad cleared the attic out a year or so ago. But, I have been wondering about furniture."

"What about it?"

"I've got a lot of space to fill atop the brownstone, and I figure we'll buy some new furniture. But there are a few pieces I'd sure like to keep if possible. Some good stuff. Not only that, it seems mighty foolish to take time to empty and sort through the contents of drawers, when we could just snatch an entire chest-of-drawers. What do y'think?"

Clarence bit his lip and failed to respond.

"I'll tell y'what, Rimes," Tony said. "You point to furniture yous really want, and if I can carry it on my back, we'll take it."

"Careful what you promise, Tony," Clarence said. "We're gonna make one trip and one trip only."

* * *

While Clarence, Tony and Jordan talked on about their covert plans, Terry sat on a bench outside with Charley and Claudia and discussed wedding plans. The bench was located near a fire pit about a quarter of the way back from the wooded boundary. It presented a striking view of the lower end of the Silvesters' property, despite the clutter of tents and roving volunteers. George, the dog, lay at their feet, having just had a brisk walk around the property and the privilege of sniffing lots of tents, supplies and enthusiastic dog-lovers.

"It's all Clarence's idea," Terry said.

"But what about you?" Claudia asked. "How do you feel about it?"

"Oh, if it's not an imposition, I think this would be a beautiful location for an outdoor wedding. If I sound hesitant at all, it's for two reasons: First off, I don't entirely trust Clarence's enthusiasm. Secondly,

I fear we're pushing ourselves on you."

"You're not pushing anything on us," Claudia said. "You'd be giving us something. We'd be delighted to see you wed here. Wouldn't we, Charley?"

"Absolutely! We'd be honored. This very spot would be perfect. Look up at the background of trees, and just think of the backdrop that display of greens and autumn colors would make for a wedding once these tents are gone. Those maples and pines would frame you guys and the minister." A quizzical expression spread upon Charley's face. "But what's this about trusting Clarence's enthusiasm?"

"Well, he had better be all for it, like he says, and not just laying it on because he wants a perfect fusion with Jordan."

George edged his way from Terry to Claudia, who had been quietly luring him to her end of the bench. "What a wonderful doggie you are," Claudia said as she petted him. "Yes, you are." She bent down and nuzzled with the dog, then lifted his front paws onto her lap. George looked longingly into her eyes as if he knew she was an ardent friend.

Terry glanced from George to Claudia. "Wow! I detect a sudden attachment."

"He's a beauty!" Claudia said as she nuzzled with George again.

"You obviously should have a dog of your own," Terry remarked.

"Thank you for saying that, Terry." Claudia grinned at her husband. "After bivouac, these acres may become greyhound land."

"You're kidding?"

"We're thinking about it."

Terry glanced at Charley expecting a comment, but he sat mum. She looked skyward and changed the subject. "That's a heavenly blue sky today, but what if it rains on our wedding day?"

"A lot of people have outdoor weddings," Claudia said. "I guess they have alternative locations, or rain dates."

"Clarence wants to complicate the ceremony even more by timing it with the eagles' flight, surely a time when the whole world will be watching. The interest in those birds is extreme. Can you imagine the flood of media descending on this place?"

"There's no way he can time that," Charley said. "But maybe he can film the flight or something and make it part of the wedding."

"I hope he realizes that the young eagles will be leaving their nest within weeks," Claudia said. "You might not have much time to plan. And what about the choker? How does it play into this?"

Chapter Twenty-One

Dressed in a pink silk negligee with soft flowing lines, Lillian opened the closet in the West Wing's Green Room and gazed at herself in the mirror attached to the inside of the door. She pranced around and circled about, making efforts to view herself from as many angles as possible. She backed up, halfway across the room, then stepped forward quickly, allowing the soft, flowing material to flare outward, exposing her naked legs.

The silk-and-organdy-trimmed room was a perfect setting for her current guise and behavior. She danced from the closet to the slipper chair where she sat upon its green satin slipcover. Within seconds, she stretched out her legs, allowing the negligee to split and slide from her supple, creamy-white flesh.

Minutes later, Lillian became fidgety, sped across the room and lay upon the queen-sized, four-poster bed. She gazed up at the canopy of ruffles and tassels that partially blocked her view of the prints of Edgar Degas' oil paintings—pictures on the walls that complimented the bedroom's French provincial décor of ornate cream and gold furniture. She slid down from the headboard until her view of the walls widened and her legs dangled over the foot of the bed. The footboard rose no higher than the bulky mattress and heavy comforter that depicted green leaves and white rosebuds.

Now her eyes rested on *After the Bath IV*, a gold-framed print of a Degas work that featured the backside of a naked woman standing on one leg as she dried herself with a towel while projecting her posterior. *The Bath II*, hanging to the left, also featured the buttocks of a naked female— a woman positioned awkwardly on her side with her elbow and leg held high. *After the Bath, Woman with a Towel*, hung to the right of the others. It depicted a woman pulling a towel across her waggling derriere.

Again and again, Lillian's imagination placed Ruth in the Degas paintings. Ruth became the petite dancing girl pirouetting magically upon her toes and seemingly floating on air as she stirred Lillian's heart. She became the dancing girl, curtseying and holding a bouquet of flowers. She became one of the blue dancers tangled together in a painting from 1899—a work that brought tears to Lillian's eyes.

Later, Lillian's lustful desire pushed her toward the head of the bed where she grabbed a pillow and held it tightly against her bosom and whisper, "Ruth, oh, Ruth," as she squeezed.

Solidly held by her libidinous daydream, Lillian was startled when the French telephone on the ornate night table rang. Attempting to gather her wits, she sucked in air twice and then reached for the phone.

"Hello?"

"Hello, Lillian. It's me. Ruth."

"Oh, hi. I've been thinking about you. In fact, I'm squeezing a pillow right now and pretending it's you."

"I need more than a pillow. Pretense no longer works. I need you."

"I know."

"Please, Lillian. Please come and get me."

"I wish I could. But I can't keep you here. Not right now. Like I said, the time will come."

"You can hide me. No one will know I'm there."

"You don't understand. I can't take a chance while I'm out on bail. Just think of what would happen if somebody saw you. They'd strip me of bail. Both of us could end up behind bars. Conspiracy charge. That's what they'd like."

"Not if we're careful."

"Ruth! The cops want to know where you are. Don't you think they're watching me?"

"You're belittling our cleverness. Don't discount our resourcefulness."

"I'm trying to tie a bunch of loose ends together—matters that bring people to the house. For example, Peter Dexter, our attorney, is meeting with me in Joe's office tomorrow for an afternoon of resolving legal problems. We haven't even set a date for probate yet. On top of that, we need to untangle a bunch of other legal conundrums. Yesterday, I finally found a glazier to fix the cracked kitchen window near the breakfast nook. Prudential sent a nincompoop on Tuesday who couldn't understand the changes we want in homeowner insurance. Oh, and by the way, after a good bit of misunderstanding, the Post Office agreed to deliver your mail here. I can't begin to list all the things that have to be done. I've got to get a guy to cut the grass before the neighborhood association blacklists us. Jordan tended to nothing out front or in the backyard. The Blackwater Oil Company sent a notice saying we're overdue for our annual checkup and cleaning of the furnace. Oh, and I'm flooded with Senatorial publications and other Washington stuff I don't want. So much has to be cancelled."

"You can keep me hidden."

"No way! I'd be a nervous wreck all the time. If the mailman knocked, my heartbeat would race. I jump now when the paperboy tosses the newspaper on the porch. How do you think I'd feel if you were hiding in here while someone rang the bell or peeked through a window? Which reminds me, a woman from UPS phoned today to clear the way for delivery of some computer parts. I have no way of knowing what things Joe set up before his death."

Lillian shifted position, put the pillow behind her and sat up against the head board.

"Hello! Are you there?"

"I'm here. Just getting comfortable."

"Hide me in the attic."

"Now you're being silly."

"I've never been more serious. Don't you want me?"

"Of course I want you! I want you more than anything in the world. But I wouldn't hide someone as precious as you in an attic. You deserve the diamonds, rubies and emeralds of the Ermengarde Choker and so much more. I want to give you a paradise of glittering surroundings that match the choker. An attic! Dear God!"

"You don't understand. I'd rather be a prisoner in a dirty old dungeon and have you, than a princess in a palace without you."

"Please. Be patient."

"I could stay in the attic until nighttime, then come down and appear at your bedroom door at the stroke of midnight like a winged fairy descending from heaven and yearning to be engulfed in your arms."

"Oh, God don't do this to me. You're not helping me fight off my yearnings and temptations."

"You need me, don't you? Just as much as I need you? Please. Let's take a chance. We can figure out a way. All I'd need in the attic is a cot, a chair, a potty-chair, bottled water, and some candles."

"You're insane!"

"No, I'm not. I'd much rather be in an attic prison with little to sustain me than in this fancy room with all these goodies surrounding me. I appreciate what you've done. But I need you, not all this stuff. The only room service I want is a tray from you on the attic steps when it's time to dine."

"Oh, Ruth."

"And you never visit me here."

"You know I can't. Don't you think they'd follow me? They'd be stupid cops if they didn't. Anyway, I deliberately put you faraway to keep me away."

"Maybe you're a bit paranoid?"

"No. But ..."

Ruth interrupted: "Please. Pretty please. I want to suck on your toes."

"Oh, Ruth, I do need you. Let me think about it. Maybe you could divide your time between the Lavender Room and the attic. It's a beautiful bedroom, and it's right next to the attic door. Maybe you could scoot up and down as necessary." Lillian grabbed the pillow from behind her and tossed it to the end of the bed. "No. Maybe not. It's dangerous. And how would I get you here? It would have to be after dark. Way after dark."

"I'll find a way. Is there a midnight express?"

* * *

Three days later, as dusk turned to dark and a clear night splattered the sky with stars, Ruth Nettlebaum was busy wrapping bedsheets around the canvas of a cot in the Rimespecker attic—a large one-room space that engulfed the entire upper floor of the house. Covered in old, soiled, rosebud paper, the walls of the attic slanted in four directions and were cut by alcoves leading to pairs of dormer windows—one pair facing in each direction.

Ruth fluffed her pillow carefully, fearful of disrupting items she had stored inside the pillowcase, under the pillow so as not to hurt her head too much at bedtime. She moved a bottle of water close to the cot, adjusted the placement of her potty-chair, and pushed her wicker chair further out from the cot. Spreading the strands of wicker, she was able to implant candles in the arms of the chair, for use later if necessary. She reminded herself to ask Lillian for candleholders. At present, the attic was lighted only by one naked lightbulb hanging from the center point of the ceiling. And she was in a panic to turn that light off because darkness had fallen over the community.

Finished with her attic preparations, Ruth gave one last glance at the arrangement and seemed satisfied. Then she began to descend the creaky attic steps, tiptoeing even though there was no one in the house to disturb. Lillian had left late and would get home even later, probably in the early hours of the morning. This was her rare night of private-house gambling at Riverview Manor, the home of Kenneth K. Wentworth, wealthy Wall Street financier, whose Colonial mansion rested on a triangle of rich loam at the junction of the Babette and Grandpike Rivers. Betty and Ken Wentworth occasionally set up a table of seven for blackjack in their recreation room—a plush room replete with red-leather chairs, potted palms and a mahogany bar. Lillian not only looked forward to the intense gaming; she craved Betty's stuffed mushrooms and smoked sausages. And it was always a night for playing man-hungry by flirting with the dealer, handsome Jack Nuttly, a Wentworth friend and product of Atlantic City. This night, however, could send her home earlier than usual because of her libidinous need for Ruth.

Feeling her way from the attic to the Lavender Room door, Ruth reached inside the room for the tiny flashlight she had positioned on a small table near the door—a flashlight she then used to reach a small bedside lamp that gave her just the amount of glow needed to maneuver around the room.

The Lavender Room was the West Wing's duplicate of the East Wing's Green Room, except for color, some knickknacks, and the display of artwork. Lavender replaced green on the slipper chair, canopy, comforter and all other trimmings, frills and trappings. Prints of Van Gogh's paintings, framed in dark purple with lavender matting, lined all four walls, starting with *Starry Night* on one side of the door and ending with *The Potato Eaters* on the other, with plenty of sunflowers and self-portraits in between.

Ruth readied herself for bed, rolled down the comforter, turned off the bedside lamp and lay upon the sheets and pillows that Lillian had sprinkled with lavender water.

Time crawled slowly for Ruth and was made painful by her knowledge that Lillian would arrive home extremely late. She turned, twisted and shifted often as she kicked at the comforter bunched at the foot of the bed.

Eventually, she began to doze, but was suddenly alerted by the sound of a car in the driveway. She sprang up in bed and froze. For a lengthy moment, she just sat there petrified, knowing full well that Lillian would not be arriving home so soon after her departure less than an hour ago. With trepidation, she reached for the flashlight and used it to help reach the door and move into the hallway. She felt her way to the attic door and, as planned in case of an intrusion, tiptoed up the dark stairs using the tiny flashlight to help guide her.

Ruth turned off the pocket-sized light and, in complete darkness, worked her way to the pair of dormer windows that overlooked the driveway and garages. Electricity lifted her hair. Her heartbeat raced as she looked down and saw activity below. A car was parked on the grass at the end of the driveway and someone in black was speaking softly to another person in dark clothes who was lifting the door of the last garage, the one at the end of the row, just opposite the cellar door to the house. She watched that figure enter the garage as a third male, youthful in his gait, hurried from the car toward the cellar door. She stayed frozen until the pickup truck was backed out of the garage, then hurried, as best she could in the dark, to the cot where she pulled a gun out from inside the pillowcase. Reaching under the cot, she seized her shoulder bag, opened it, placed the gun inside, and hung the bag around her neck.

Outside, Jordan unlocked the cellar door and led the way into the house. Clarence and Tony followed, in that order, each carrying boxes to be used for packing books, clothes and sundry items. All three wore large, industrial, high-beam flashlights hanging from their necks and positioned at mid-chest. They waited until they were inside the house before turning on the flashlights, but did so before they reached the kitchen and back steps.

They had planned well and knew exactly where they were going. After reaching the third floor, Jordan opened the door to his bedroom and they dimmed their lights as they entered. Each knew his assignment and went to work: Tony pulling schoolbooks from a bookshelf and arranging them in a pasteboard box, Jordan collecting and boxing his valuable items and gifts that bestowed strong memories, Clarence lifting clothes from hangers in the closet and folding and boxing them.

All three were careful, and while hasty, did not over-rush, knowing the late hour that Jordan's mother was expected to return. Clarence kept warning the others to be cautious on the stairs while carrying boxes and bulky items.

Ruth sat on the top step of the attic stairs, nearly petrified and staring down at the door while clutching her gun with both hands. She heard the intruders moving furniture and other items, but couldn't fully fathom what was happening.

Tony carried the computer and Jordan followed with the printer. The heaviest item was the chest-of-drawers, which they had decided to take after much debate. It was difficult for two men to carry it down the stairs, despite removing a couple drawers, but Clarence and Tony accomplished the task by moving slowly step-by-step and resting now and then.

Ruth remained sitting at the top of the attic stairs, becoming more terrified as the noises continued. She was unable to stabilize her gun, for her entire body trembled. Her sweaty hands squeezed the weapon, but could not steady it even when she pressed her elbows into her belly to support her arms. When the sounds of moving objects and tramping feet ceased, she listened intently and could hear conversation in the hallway below, but could not understand a word.

"We still have to empty a closet just a few yards down the hallway," Jordan told the others. "It's mostly winter clothes. And then there's the window-seat in the Lavender Room right next to us. It holds a collection of memorabilia. Stuff I've collected over the years. A lot of it has deep meaning for me."

"Why don't you and Tony tackle the window-seat," Clarence suggested. "I'll toss your winter clothes into a box."

Immediately on entering the Lavender Room, Tony said to Jordan, "Someone's been in here recently. I can smell it."

"Yeah, a woman," Jordan said. "It's perfume or something. And look at the bed. It's all messed up." He leaned down and picked up something from the floor. "Look at this."

"What is it?"

"I think it's a lady's locket on a chain."

"Open it."

Jordan opened the locket, stared at it, but said nothing.

"What is it?"

"A picture."

"Well, I figured that. What's wrong?" Tony stared at Jordan. "You look upset." He frowned in puzzlement. "You ain't gonna tell me, are yis? He paused and bit his lip. "Hey, Rimes, that's okay."

"I'll tell you." Jordan clenched his teeth. His face reddened and his eyes watered. "Yeah, damn it. I'll tell you. What the hell. It contains a picture of my mother with her breasts showing above a low-cut blouse. There. Y'got it?" He slipped the locket into his pocket.

"Oh. Sorry, Rimes." Tony stepped toward the windows. "Is this the seat."

"Yeah. Open it up." Jordan hurried to Tony's aid. "Here. Let me help you."

While Tony and Jordan struggled to lift a chest out of the window seat, Clarence toiled in the hallway folding heavy jackets, suits, overcoats and other cold-weather clothes. He placed the items in a large pasteboard box.

As Tony and Jordan carried the chest down the stairs, Clarence followed with the box of winter clothes.

"We think Ruth Nettlebaum has been in the house," Jordan told Clarence.

"You're kidding?" Clarence responded.

"Someone was sleeping in the Lavender Room recently," Jordan said. "Pretty sure it was a woman. Crazy thing, though. If she was visiting Mom, why would she be over here on this side of the house?"

"Why did you say 'recently?'" Clarence asked.

"It smelled like a fox had been there not long ago," Tony said.

"Fox?"

"He means a foxy woman," Jordan explained. "A hot number. Get with it, Uncle Clarry."

"Holy shit!" Clarence exclaimed. "Y'think she could still be in the house?"

"If so, she'd hide and run away," Jordan said. "I wouldn't expect a confrontation. And by the way, I wouldn't call her foxy. Although I've never seen her, except for that mug shot they keep using in the newspaper."

"I heard she was a mousy, undernourished recluse," Clarence said.

As the three "burglars" continued to load the pickup truck, Clarence questioned Jordan as to whether anything remained in the house that he wanted. "Did you want to check the attic? You said there might be some things up there."

"I'll run up for a quick look," Jordan responded. "You guys stay here."

"No we'll follow you, just in case."

Jordan hurried and reached the third floor while Clarence and Tony were still on the second flight of stairs. He pulled open the attic door and shined his flashlight up the stairs where the strong beam set Ruth aglow. She stood at the top of the steps radiating in brilliant yellow as her negligee glistened.

Ruth could see little but the bright light and the vague image of a person. She pulled the trigger and the gun went off with a flash and a bang. The bullet struck Jordan in the chest and he fell backwards, tumbling hard on the hallway floor as his scream turned into a groan and then silence. Ruth scampered down the attic steps and ran down the hallway as Clarence and Tony raced up the remaining steps to the third floor. They saw her take flight in the darkness, but could make out little. Her fleeing image was indistinct.

Neither man took off after her, for they were too intent on reaching Jordan. Clarence switched on the hallway lights, and both fell to the floor on their knees where the teenager lay still. Tony ripped off his shirt and used it to suck up blood as he put pressure on Jordan's wound. Clarence seized his cell and punched numbers.

"Nine-one-one emergency. Your location, please."

"Help! Jordan Rimespecker, son of the late senator, has been shot." Clarence's voice quaked. "We're on the third floor of the senator's house. Hurry! He's badly wounded."

"Your location, please?" The female emergency operator's voice was intense. "Please sir! Your location."

"One-fifty Dorian Boulevard, in the Oxhaven section of East Bitterlick. It's the big house sitting alone on the triangle hill. The police know the senator's house, damn it! Come quickly! The kid's bleeding profusely."

"Please stay on the line, sir. Police and medics are on the way."

"Tony, get some material for a big bandage," Clarence urged. "I'll take over here." He squeezed his cellphone into his shirt pocket, applied his hands to Tony's blood-soaked shirt, and put pressure on the boy's wound.

As quickly as he could, Tony entered the Lavender Room, glanced about, raced to the bed and pulled a sheet from under the bunched comforter. He was back at Clarence's side within seconds. Together they tore the sheet into usable sizes, stripped Jordan's torso while disturbing him as little as possible, and tightly bandaged his chest by wrapping bedlinen around his upper body, just below his shoulders.

"Use some of the rest for padding," Tony suggested. "Push it under the bandage. It'll tighten the whole thing."

As Clarence folded and shoved, they could hear sirens. At first, far off. Then, growing near.

"You go with them to the hospital." Clarence said. "If they won't let you in the ambulance, take my car and follow them. I'll drive the pickup home, grab Terry's car, and meet you back at the hospital. Keep in touch by phone."

"I have keys to all the Rimespecker vehicles. I'm most comfortable with the Bentley. I'll drive it. Unless Lady Rimespecker drove it to Wentworth's. Which I doubt. She likes a driver. Probably took a taxi."

"Drive whatever. Just follow them, and get there. They'll take him to the closest hospital. That means into the city."

"Cloverton Memorial."

"Right."

"The cops won't let us leave until after a lot of questioning."

"We're lucky we're in the township and not across the city line. Chief Morris knows us. He knows our connection to the Rimespeckers. And he'll understand why we're moving the kid."

"You hope." Tony studied Jordan's face. "Do you think he's in a coma?"

"No. After he was shot, he fell hard and hit his head. My guess is, the bullet and the fall knocked him out. Look! Look at his eyes. His eyelids are twitching." Kneeling close to the teenager, Clarence pronounced each word clearly: "Jordy, can you hear me? Jordy?"

"He seems to be breathing okay."

"Oh, God, I love this kid so much." Clarence's eyes continued to moisten.

* * *

Bald and lanky Jamison Ambroise, a genteel butler dressed in his navy blue blazer and red bowtie, had a dead serious expression on his face when he stepped back into the recreation room at the Wentworth mansion where five men, two women and the dealer sat at the blackjack table intently engaged in the game. He proceeded directly to Lillian, stood behind her briefly, then leaned over her shoulder and whispered, "Mrs. Rimespecker, there's been an unfortunate incident at your home."

Startled, Lillian turned and looked up at Ambroise. "What is it, Jamison?" She immediately thought of Ruth.

"There's been a shooting, Ma'am."

Lillian pushed back her chair and stood as her body quaked. Others around the table looked alarmed. Ken Wentworth, the handsome 62-year-old host, rose and immediately walked around the table toward Lillian. A physically well-developed gentleman, Wentworth owned dark piercing eyes, a small mustache and thick salt-and-pepper hair, almost white at the temples. "What is it, Ambroise?" he asked.

The butler looked directly at Lillian and quietly said, "It's your son,

Ma'am. He's been taken to Cloverton Memorial Hospital."

"Oh, dear God! How can that be? It must be a mistake! Jordan hasn't been at the house in days. Where did you hear this?"

"On the radio in the kitchen, Ma'am. Police report. WNNT twenty-four hour news."

"I'll take you to the hospital, Lillian," Ken Wentworth insisted as he approached her. "Ambroise, tell Carlton to bring the limo to the front."

"No!" Lillian exclaimed, thinking of Ruth. "Not to the hospital. Take me home first."

* * *

Lilian was an emotional wreck by the time the Wentworth limousine reached her house, where she saw three patrol cars—two parked in the driveway, one on the street. Also in view were several policemen milling around, and a couple in their cruisers writing reports. She demanded that Wentworth and his driver remain in the limo. "I have personal reasons I'll explain later," she asserted. "Please stay here. Or, better yet, why don't you leave? Thanks for your help. I'll be in touch." Unaccustomed to running, she twisted her ankle in her rush to the front door, but kept moving anyway as quickly as she could.

Wentworth was well aware of some of Lillian's problems, so he held himself back from doing or saying anything. Minutes later he ordered his chauffeur to drive him back to Riverview Manor.

"Are you sure, sir?"

"Yes. We have guests waiting back there. She'll be all right. I see plenty of cops."

Lillian ripped through yellow police tape strung from column to column on the portico and entered the house to immediately face a uniformed officer.

"Hey!" the policeman yelled. "What are you doing? Who are you?"

"I'm Mrs. Joseph J. Rimespecker, the late senator's widow," Lillian answered. "This is my house. Please tell me who shot whom and why."

"Oh, Mrs. Rimespecker. I'm sorry to say your son was shot and has been taken to Cloverton Memorial Hospital. We have a suspect, but she's not been apprehended. Your secretary and chauffeur were here at the time of the shooting. They witnessed the suspect's getaway, and they aided our police unit and the paramedics."

"Then you know who did this. Is that what you're saying?"

"Let's just say we have a suspect. But she's not in custody."

"You needn't hold back. I know who the hell you're talking about. And you damn well know I know it. Where did the shooting occur?"

"West side. Up three. It's taped off. I wouldn't go up there."

Lillian rushed by the officer. Limping slightly, she held the railing while pulling herself up the central stairs. When she reached the West Wing hallway where her son had lain wounded, she encountered police investigators, including forensic personnel and cameramen taking pictures. She pushed by everyone, despite warning yells from the officers, and entered the Lavender Room. After glancing about, she hurried quickly to the bed, fell to her knees and pounded the mattress with her fists. "Goddamnit, Ruth, how could you shoot my son?" she screamed. Seconds later, she picked up a pillow and smelled it. Then, in a fit of rage, she threw the pillow across the room. She whimpered, then bellowed as tears streamed down her cheeks.

After pushing herself up from the side of the bed, she reached high, grabbed the frilly canopy material and yanked in fury, ripping a section, tossing it angrily to the floor and stomping on it. She headed for the door, stopped, looked at Van Gogh's *Potato Eaters*, pulled the framed picture from the wall, gritted her teeth and used all her strength to throw it into the chest-of-drawers in which she had carefully laid out clothes for Ruth. The frame broke into sections as glass splattered into countless pieces. Next, she pulled down *Starry Night*, and slammed it into the chest. The crash brought Lieutenant Goldstein into the room.

"What's going on?" the lieutenant asked.

Lillian grabbed a self-portrait of Van Gogh, screamed, and slammed it down on Goldstein's head, causing the lieutenant to stagger. He caught himself by grabbing the doorframe as glass and sections of the frame flew in all directions.

Chapter Twenty-Two

Jordan Rimespecker was treated in the Emergency Room at Cloverton Memorial Hospital, where he gained consciousness, but was kept sedated. A bullet was removed from his chest. It had lodged between two ribs, about six inches from his right shoulder, just below his collarbone. He was later moved to the Intensive Care Unit where his condition was declared critical.

Tony, who had scrubbed himself clean of Jordan's blood, was wearing one of the teenager's golf shirts and looked presentable as he argued with a nurse in the hallway just outside the ICU. His pleas for entry were denied, action typical of protocol at such units, particularly aimed at non-family members. Minutes later he called Clarence from within the Bentley, which he had parked earlier in the hospital's underground garage.

"No sense coming here," he told Clarence. "They won't let me in. So they ain't gonna let you in."

Jordan was not moved from the ICU until four days had passed and his condition had been upgraded from critical to serious. He was glad that Bed #1 of Room 212 on the second floor had been recently vacated, eliminating a roommate. Bed #2 was now his without a double flow of visitors. It also pleased him that Bed #2 was on the window side, overlooking Cloverton City Park and its tennis courts.

The teenager was now off a liquid diet and on soft food. And after his initial semi-satisfying lunch, he received his first visitor. As the nurse left with his tray, Tony Paluto marched into the teenager's room carrying a potted Norfolk Island Pine and wearing Jordan's red-and-white-striped golf shirt. He stared through the pine branches and saw Jordan sitting up in bed and hooked up to an array of wires and tubes.

Seeing Tony with the evergreen branches in his face caused Jordan to laugh, and subsequently groan in pain. "Yowl! Damn it!" Laughter, unfortunately, caused a sharp pang in his chest and shoulder. "Damn, I can't laugh without getting a nasty jab," he muttered, "even though they got me loaded up on pain killers."

Tony leaned over the bed and accidentally tickled the teenager's nose with the prickly evergreen needles.

"Don't! I might sneeze, and that'll hurt." Jordan gently pushed Tony with his left hand.

"So, tell me, how y'doin', Rimes?" Tony took a close look at Jordan's bandage, a large binding compress across his chest and around his right shoulder.

"Hanging in there. Living on other dudes' blood. They pumped in more than a score of transfusions. Thanks for the bush, man."

Tony placed the short-needled pine on the window sill. "These things grow indoors in pots," he explained. "Thought you'd like one for your new attic apartment."

"Thanks. I'll make it a focal point. It'll be perfect for the front dormer windows." Jordan looked Tony up and down. "I see something familiar. Where'd y'get that shirt?"

"It's yours. Wondered if you'd notice. After I soaked my shirt in your freakin' blood and cleaned myself up, I stole one of your golf tops from a box in the pickup truck. I didn't want to look like a shirtless bum at the hospital. They wouldn't let me see you anyway. Wore the shirt today t'get yis t'open up in case you was floatin' in funnyland or something."

"Thanks for saving my life, man."

"Anytime, Rimes. Anytime yis need a muscle and a rescuer's lasso."

"You can keep that shirt in memory of one hell of a night."

"Thanks, buddy."

Jordan tried to throw up a high-five with his left hand, but misfired.

Tony grabbed his arm and rendered a tender squeeze of comfort. "Take it easy, man."

"So, fill me in. I've picked up some tidbits from the hospital grapevine. I'm told it was Ruth Netttlebaum who shot me."

"She's the number-one suspect. Exton and I saw a woman flee, and we're pretty damn sure it was her. Who else wouldv'e been hiding in that house?" Tony lowered his voice. "Your mother's behind bars. They revoked her bail."

"For hiding Ruth?"

"No. For attacking the police."

"What? You're kidding."

"After Exton and I left the house, she caused quite a rumpus while the cops were trying to do their forensic stuff."

Jordan looked away from Tony as a creepy feeling made him shiver. It was a feeling he hated, but couldn't shake off—a feeling tied to love-hate ambivalence. He stared out the window while tightening his jaw and gritting his teeth. But within minutes, he forced a smile, gazed on his visitor and suggested, "Sit down, man. Tell me some good news."

"We've stripped your wallpaper." Tony sat in a chair at the foot of the bed. "Them dirty rosebuds are history."

"You're kidding?"

"It was Terry's idea and Exton liked it. They wanted to give you a head start on fixing up your new living quarters. And I jumped right in. The old wallpaper cracked and crumbled as we scraped and stripped. What a freakin' mess, but we cleaned it all up. Did all four rooms. When Terry sees you, she'll load you up with wallpaper samples she picked up at the mall."

"Geez, man. That's a hell of a move by you guys. Thanks. I can't wait to fix up that attic. What about the stuff we loaded in the pickup?"

"It's all safe. Still in the truck. Parked behind the brownstones."

"I wonder how long I'll be here. The doctor won't even give me his guess. I'm gonna be antsy as a trapped rat before I escape the chains."

"The wedding's off until you're better. Your Uncle Clarry said there's no way they'll set a date until you can take part. He says you're gonna be his best man even if they gotta push yis wounded body in a wheelchair. Eagles or no eagles."

"Speaking of eagles, anything new on that front?" Jordan grimaced as he tried to adjust his body to gain a bit more comfort.

"Jimmy made it clear again to everyone that them there birds won't fly from the nest until ten to twelve weeks from hatchin' time. Believe it or not, that time expires within a week or two. He calls the eleventh week the hot zone. He's been handing out written hot-zone instructions to everyone, including the press. And them media guys are staking out territory. They're not all from the good ol' USA either. The BBC pulled in a truck right next to a couple unhappy German dudes from *der Spiegel*. And they weren't the only European reporters I saw. Some guys from *Die Zeit* were pushing through a crowd working its way up the creek. And yesterday, a Reuters reporter and a persistent Frenchman were in the dining room trying to pin down Jimmy to an exact date. Face it, the media interest is generated by the choker, not the birds. And disappointment swells when Jimmy tells 'em he still can't see the choker in or near the nest. He's decided to set up monitors here and there around the bivouac so the volunteers and the media can see the nest. And he's handing out iPhones to some of the captains that don't have them. So, now, birdwatchers and choker freaks ain't gotta smother him no more with questions."

"That's a change. What about guarding against the thieves and wackos?"

"The monitors are not outside the campgrounds. Besides, he feels that we got things under control, and time is short. Frankly, he didn't have much choice. The situation and pressure is getting pretty crazy as time closes in, and there ain't any choker in sight."

"Damn, I wish I could get out of here. I'm gonna miss it all."

"The dates are converging, and that's not so good. Your mother's trial date is in the middle of the eagles' hot zone, about the same time Exton wanted his wedding. Can you believe that?"

Jordan's body twitched, causing pain in the chest and shoulder. He said nothing for a moment as he tried to calm himself and slowly and steadily suck in air. Finally, he muttered, "Trial date? You didn't tell me."

"Oh God, I thought I had. I meant to, back when I mentioned her bail being revoked. You looked dismayed and I held back. Sorry." Tony pulled a piece of paper from his pocket and studied it. "Judge LeRoy P. Cattwell has set August 26 as the date for opening arguments. I never heard of him, so I wrote down his name. Three judges recused themselves because of some association or contact with your mother. They must have fished Judge Cattwell out of an obscure swamp or something. No one I talked to seems to know a damn thing about him."

Jordan sought a change of subject, and his dog came easily to mind just as a heavy-set, brunette nurse entered the room.

"Have you heard anything about George?"

"Not really," Tony said. "Your Uncle Clarry did mention that Terry likes to walk him. I'm guessing they're getting on fine."

"Excuse me," the nurse said. She nodded to Tony and then focused on Jordan. "It's time to take your blood pressure and check your temperature."

While the nurse tended to Jordan, Tony fidgeted, pushed himself up from the chair, stepped to the windows and gazed down on activity in the park. When he heard her leave the room, he turned toward Jordan and said, "Well, I should be shovin' off. I'm headin' for the bivouac. I wanna pin things down with Jimmy. He's been getting some high-powered requests that I gotta torpedo."

"I'll vote for you, Tony. Don't fret. You'll be first up the tree."

Tony took the boy's left hand and squeezed. "I'm gonna ask Exton if I can push your wheelchair at his wedding. If necessary, that is."

Jordan grinned. "Get out of here!"

Tony walked to the door, turned, looked back and winked. "See y'soon, Rimes." After he punched the air with his fist, he started to tread down the corridor.

"Wait, Tony! Come back here!"

"What is it?" Tony stepped back into the room.

"I want to tell you something that's difficult to talk about, especially for guys." Jordan paused in thought for a lengthy moment. "I've known you for many years, but I really never *knew* you until recently. It's hard to explain. But you were that chauffeur who slept above the garage. I'd see you come and go. You'd say 'Have a good day, Rimes,' when you'd see me heading off to school in the morning. And you'd say, 'Hi, Rimes,' if we passed each other later in the day. Now you're much more than the guy who brought me that little tree. What did you call it?"

"Norfolk Island Pine."

"Yeah. Norfolk Island Pine. And you're much more than the guy who helped save my life. You're pretty damn special in the way you've become part of the team. You're a good friend." Jordan looked down as he struggled for words. "It's like we have a buddy-buddy relationship. You're there for me. And I want to be there for you. Damn it. I'm not doing a good job of explaining my feelings."

"Stop with the damn mushy talk, Rimes. I can't take it."

"I want you to understand."

"Look, kid, I understand. You said it better than the average thirty-year-old. In fact, I must say that you think and talk like yous is twice your age. You ain't no empty-headed teenager. How come? Does your Uncle Clarry have something to do with that? Don't answer. Just think about it."

Jordan was tongue-tied.

"I ain't perfect, Rimes." Tony laughed. "I'm conceited as hell when it comes to climbing trees." He flexed his muscles. "I don't care what they think. I can climb that freakin' locust tree better than anyone." He shook his head and chuckled, then hurried off.

Jordan closed his eyes and rested until he heard chatter outside his door. Clarence peaked in, then walked in, carrying a cactus in a Mexican pot and several magazines. Right behind him was Terry with rather large books of sample wallpaper.

"Hello! Hello! Hello!" Clarence put abundant enthusiasm into his greeting. "How the hell are you doing?"

"Hi, Uncle Clarry! I'm doing okay if I don't move too much." Jordan turned his eyes on Terry. "Looks like you have a heavy load, Aunt Terry. Wallpaper samples, I've been told. Why don't you dump them on the other bed? The nurse can give them to me one by one. Can't believe you guys have been scraping off that old wallpaper."

Terry unloaded on Bed #1, then stepped to the side of Bed # 2, leaned over and kissed the teenager on his forehead. "How did you know?"

"About the wallpaper? Guess. Tony was here. In fact, he left only about twenty minutes ago."

"Now, help me," Clarence said, "before I get stabbed again by this mean little fellow. He's pricked me twice already."

"Thanks, Uncle Clarry. Cacti turn me on. And that's a beauty." The barrel-shaped cactus was fat and bulging from its colorful pot. "Put it on the windowsill next to the Norfolk Island Pine." Jordan took a deep breath. "Now. Sit down, both of you. Thanks for coming."

"I brought you some magazines, including *Sports Illustrated* and a couple comic books."

"Thanks. But before you say another word, please tell me about George. It's been a killer, not knowing how he's doing."

"Great dog, with lots of get-up-and-go," Clarence said. "He's always sniffing for something that's missing. And I figure that's you. He grabbed your pillow the other day and was carrying it around the house."

"He has endless energy," Terry added. "I enjoy giving him his morning walk. And it's good for me. I'd still like to shed a few pounds before the wedding. And George is helping."

"I wish the hospital would permit dogs to visit. I'd like to give him a big hug."

"He'll be waiting anxiously to see you," Clarence said.

Jordan changed the subject abruptly: "About the wedding. Don't wait for me. The very fact that you want me as your best man ... Well, that's enough. Y'know?"

"The wedding can wait, damn it," Clarence said. "We want to see you walk or be pushed down the ... I can't say aisle, can I? Down a strip of carpet on Charley's grass, or whatever we put together."

"How do you feel about it, Aunt Terry?"

"I'm with Clarence all the way."

"Uncle Clarry, do you remember that old man who grew vegetables and went door to door giving them away? In our old neighborhood, years ago? Remember?"

"Mr. Higgins at the end of the street."

"Yeah. He handed me this big green squash I could hardly carry. As he left, I looked up at you and whispered something about him being a nice old man. You told me to tell him how I felt. I wouldn't. I couldn't. But you pushed me and I ran to him and timidly said, 'Mr. Higgins, you're a nice old man for giving away your vegetables.' He laughed and said. 'And you're a nice young man for saying so.'"

"And that put a big smile on your face. You were so pleased. Why bring that up now?"

"It was something Tony said. He made me realize that you not only attended to my growth and taught me a lot of basics. You also gave me the ability to read people, understand relationships, and have the guts to express sensitive feelings. If it hadn't been for Mr. Higgins and that big green squash and other things you pushed me into, maybe I wouldn't have had the backbone to tell Tony what I thought of him."

"And what's that?"

"No, man. That's between Tony and me."

"Fair enough. I see him as a strange mix. He murders the English language, trumpets his own skills, but has a sensitive nature and a desire to help with whatever. He'll never turn you down, and you can't help but like him."

Jordan looked at Terry and said. "You're marrying the man who made me what I am. There! I had the guts to say it."

Clarence grinned broadly and said, "And you're a nice young man for saying so."

Terry laughed.

Jordan looked about. He wanted to throw something at Uncle Clarry, but couldn't find or reach a thing. He twisted his torso and yelled, "Ouch!"

Just then, the brunette nurse stepped into the room and asked, "Is everything all right in here?

"Everything's fine," Jordan said.

"You have four more visitors waiting downstairs at the main desk," the nurse said. "The receptionist was reluctant to send them up. You've had a busy day, and visiting hours are almost up. You've got about an hour more."

"Who's down there waiting?" Jordan asked.

The nurse picked up the phone, punched numbers, and asked for the names. "Thank you." She looked at Jordan and said, "There's a Mr. and Mrs. Silvester and a Mr. and Mrs. Barnes waiting in the lobby."

"Wow! The whole gang in one day."

"Are you up to it?" Terry asked.

"Sure."

"We'll take off," Clarence said. "They won't allow you six visitors at one time. Not in this wing, anyway."

Terry tossed a kiss. "Take care. And let us know about the wallpaper. I've marked a few designs that seem fit for a tough guy like you. Check out the one with the canine paw prints. And the one with the nautical flags."

About 15 minutes after Clarence and Terry left, the Barneses and Silvesters came smiling into the room. Laura, as usual, was the most bubbly, shaking flowers in the air as she tapped her feet and hummed a tune. She put the vase of red carnations on the windowsill between the cactus and the Norfolk Island Pine.

Claudia placed a box of chocolates on a stand next to Jordan's bed. "Not for now. For later. When you're allowed."

After Jordan's appreciative words of thanks and the visitors' warm greetings, the foursome pulled chairs around the foot of the teenager's bed, sat, and offered a bit of chitchat, until the patient said, "Please! I want to know about the bivouac. What's happening?"

"The entire camp seems restless as hell!" Jimmy pronounced loudly. "Everyone seems on edge."

"Tony was here," Jordan said. "He's eager to climb."

"Well, I don't know about that yet. I got this pack of credentials from a guy in Switzerland who's had vast experience. I've gotta check him out. Plenty of slimy worms have been working me over. I have to be careful. This Swiss cat sounds almost too perfect. That makes me suspicious that he might be a thief. Then again ..."

Jordan's mouth hung open and his eyes bulged. "But Mr. Barnes, Tony's a super dude, and he's ready to go."

"Calm down, Jordan," Jimmy said. "Nothing's decided."

"Don't let my old man get your ire up, Jordan," Laura said. "He's already got me fuming over the cost of monitors and iPhones for the bivouac gang. Our money! He's spending more of our money. We'll have to take out a loan. And I wanted desperately to help out our local

SPCA and, in particular, the Nagelstone Center for Large Animals. Seriously, the large animal clinic is considering closing down. And that would be a sin. They're really hurting. And the SPCA is so underfunded that the County Commissioners are talking about merging it with the Ulmer County unit.

"Maybe we can help a little," Claudia said. She looked at her husband.

Charley said nothing. His mind was on Ruth and the choker. Within a moment, his cellphone rang and he unconsciously pulled it from his pocket. He became well focused, however, when he heard the voice of Randy Houck, scoutmaster of Troop 24.

"Hey, Charley, we got a near riot goin' on here at the bivouac. One of the young eagles flew from the nest, and everyone went wild."

Within seconds, Jimmy's cellphone vibrated and he yanked it from his belt. "Hello?"

"Mr. Barnes, it's Tony. I just arrived at the camp a few minutes ago. One of the baby bald eagles took flight. It circled around overhead a few times and then disappeared in the distance. The entire bivouac crowd seemed to go crazy. Most of 'em was trying to take pictures with their cellphones. Everybody seems to be rushing up the road or through the woods and upstream toward the locust tree. They think the other two birds are about to take flight."

As Tony excitedly poured out his words to Jimmy, Randy Houck was shouting into Charley's ear: "I have no control over the scouts! The boys are running off and disappearing! They want to be part of the action. And the newspaper reporters ask questions I can't answer. The television people are the worst. They don't care where they push their cameras and equipment as they elbow their way."

Tony kept describing the scene to Jimmy: "The media guys are in a frenzy 'cause they think we're gonna bring down the Ermengarde Choker. They're pushing people out of the way in an effort to get upstream. Oh, boy, here come the press helicopters. I can hear them overhead. Now I see them. Two of 'em."

"That bird fledged early." Jimmy said. "He or she is at least a week ahead of schedule. I'm partly at fault for the chaos. I didn't prepare people. The purpose of our bivouac was to protect the birds and rescue the choker. And, damn it all, we did one hell of a job of saving those young eagles from death at the hands of jewel thieves. We should be happy that an eagle flew from the nest. Everyone should have looked skyward and cheered for a job well done."

"What now?" Tony asked.

"You'd better get to the locust tree and prepare yourself to climb, just in case the other two birds fledge. My guess is, they won't leave this soon. Charley and I and the gals will get there as soon as we can. You hold the fort until. Okay?"

"I'll do my best."

Charley was still listening to Scoutmaster Houck: "I'm responsible for these boys, and, frankly, I'm scared. If one of them drowns or cracks his head on a rock, I've had it. Their parents come down on me for the damnedest reasons, like a bloody nose, a cracked lip, or poison ivy on their dickydoodles."

"Grab a bullhorn from Tent Number Five," Charley suggested. "It'll help you round them up. We'll get there as soon as we can."

"Please, tell us, did the eagles fly away?" Jordan asked after Charley and Jimmy tucked away their phones.

"One did," Jimmy said. "We gotta shove. Sorry Jordo."

"I told you, all four of us should not have come here at the same time," Laura said. She continued to chastise her husband and Charley as only she could, jumping about and tossing her fists in the air.

"Down Laura, down!" Claudia cried out in the tone one speaks to a dog.

Chapter Twenty-Three

S he wore a floppy black hat and a veil over her face, this woman in a trench coat who mounted the many broad steps of the courthouse in Cloverton City, the county seat. Over her shoulder, hung an extremely large, summertime, straw bag that bulged with heavy items. Obviously in a hurry, she quick-stepped her way up to the massive bronze doors of the county courthouse and leaned against the wall momentarily to catch her breath before surreptitiously glancing about and slipping into the stately building. She pulled the bag from her arm and rubbed her shoulder for a few seconds before returning it and adjusting her hat.

She attempted to straighten up, despite the pull of the heavy bag, as she walked through the lobby to Courtroom A. After opening the door to the dimly lit chamber, she slowly worked her way up to the gallery, the raised balcony-like area running along the inner-rear wall and partway around the sides—an area that often accommodates an overflow of spectators at a popular trial. She ran her hand along the heavy oak railing that fronted the gallery, leaned over and stared down at the rows of seats below. Before leaving, she took her time scanning the judges' bench, witness stand and jury box, then hurried to the gallery exit.

Back in the lobby, the woman looked about before stepping into a small alcove that held a black-marble drinking fountain. She was not thirsty, but wet her lips and pretended to sip water while several people walked by. She adjusted her hat and veil, listened intently, saw no one, and stepped from the alcove.

Minutes later the veiled woman stepped into Courtroom B, where a trial was in session. She was stopped by a courthouse official. "May I help you?"

"Sir, I'm a friend of the defendant," she whispered, not knowing that *two* defendants were actually on trial in this case—brothers suspected of raping their neighbors' babysitter. "I'd like a seat in the gallery, please."

The court officer allowed her to proceed despite her mistake, and she took a seat in the front row where she dropped her shoulder bag to the floor, grasped the heavy oak railing, lifted herself slightly and scanned the spectators below. She did a quick count, and judged the number of people at about 25. Pleased that she was the only person in the gallery, she sat back and relaxed briefly, then picked up her bag and quickly left. The distribution of spectators pleased her—heavy below and none above—although, she would have preferred an even bigger audience on the main floor for greater impact.

The veiled woman showed indecision again as she stood in the spacious lobby before the row of courtroom doors. She glanced to the left, then to the right, and finally shook off her ambivalence and hurried to Courtroom C. She was able to proceed far enough into the chamber to see a portion of the gallery before being approached by a court officer. Immediately, she began to back out of the courtroom on seeing a row of heads above the railing in the gallery. "Sorry, wrong place," she mouthed silently to the officer before turning and hastening to the door. Her heartbeat quickened. She tugged on her veil, fearing that someone or another might see through it. A second visit to the water fountain gave her time to think.

The woman was somewhat disappointed that the galleries did not have easy and immediate access to restrooms. Such facilities were available from the lobby only and, therefore, could not serve her purpose. After considerable thought, she decided that such a layout would impose only minor difficulties as long as her trench coat slipped off easily and nobody occupied seats in the gallery of the Rimespecker murder trial.

A slight smile touched her lips briefly, but faded quickly as she pushed the massive doors and stepped out into the sunlight. She switched her heavy bag from one shoulder to the other and bowed her head while tugging on her veil again.

"Just hope and pray," she muttered to herself as she left the courthouse, holding onto her hat as she scurried down the broad steps of the imposing building. "God, please give me no one in Lillian's gallery."

* * *

The veiled woman did not return to the courthouse until the second day of Lillian Rimespecker's first-degree murder trial for the premeditated killing of her husband, the late Senator Joseph J. Rimespecker. Her decision to skip the first day grew from her fear of too many gallery spectators. The media had predicted an overflow crowd.

Reluctantly, Tony Paluto was on the witness stand when the veiled woman mounted the steps to the galley of Courtroom A on the second day of the trial. The prosecutor, a heavy-set gentleman with slick black hair and a neatly trimmed beard, was pacing before the witness stand as he asked, "Mr. Paluto, please tell the court what you saw that day as you drove up the driveway of the Rimespecker's home in that pickup truck."

"I seen Mrs. Rimespecker and ..."

Larry Hawkins, the prosecutor, interrupted: "That's Mrs. Lillian Rimespecker, I presume? Be as specific as you can, Mr. Paluto."

"Yeah. Mrs. Lillian Rimespecker. I seen her and another lady headin' up the path to the front door." Tony was tense, and his eyes seemed to bulge in that jockey-like, heavily-lined face as he told himself he'd rather be climbing a tree.

The veiled woman was disappointed to find an elderly couple, probably man and wife, sitting in the front row along the railing of the gallery. She decided to remain in the courtroom anyway, in hopes that the couple might leave. After biting her lip, she sat in the same row, five seats away from the white-haired pair. She placed her heavy bag on the floor. Leaning over the railing, she judged the number of spectators in the chamber bellow to be about 35.

"Are you certain it was Lillian Rimespecker?" the prosecutor asked Tony.

"Yeah! Absolutely. I would've known her anywhere. I worked for them Rimespeckers for more years then I can count." Tony glanced toward Lillian, who sat next to her attorney at the defense table. Almost demure in her demeanor, Lillian was obviously playing a new role, one far from her usual guise. She wore a gray suit and tightly buttoned blouse of white cotton. Tony could not see her face, but assumed it was grim.

"And the other woman. Did you recognize her?"

"No, Sir. Didn't know her from nothing."

"What did you do next?"

"I parked the pickup truck in the garage, washed up a bit at my place above the garages, and then went to the house."

"Why?"

"Why what?" Tony shifted in his seat.

"Why did you go to the house?"

"I was told to report to the boss as soon as I returned from an assignment. Mr. Exton, the senator's number-one man back then, said it was important."

"How many minutes passed between the time you saw Lillian Rimespecker enter the house and the murder of the senator?"

"I don't know."

"In your judgement."

"Honest t'God, Mr. Prosecutor, I don't know."

"Your honor." Hawkins addressed Judge LeRoy P. Cattwell, a small, bald man with prominent ears, wearing dark-rimmed glasses low on his nose. "Your honor," he repeated after a deliberate but unnecessary sigh of frustration. "Please direct the witness to answer the question."

"Your honor," interrupted Manuel Dewitt, the defense attorney, who rose to his feet. "The witness answered the question. He clearly said he does not know how much time elapsed." A tall, lanky, freckled redhead, Dewitt was a trial lawyer from the law firm of Dewitt, Boyton & Dexter, long engaged by the Rimespeckers. Until this trial, however, he had not been well acquainted with Lillian. Peter Dexter, Lillian's usual attorney for non-trial activity, did not, to her dismay, handle criminal cases. He had directed her to Dewitt. But she was not comfortable with him, despite Dexter's assurances.

"Move on, Mr. Hawkins," the Judge instructed.

"Let me put it this way, Mr. Paluto. In the time between your entry into the house and the murder of Senator Rimespecker, could anyone other than the accused have sufficient knowledge of the house and enough time to find a bedsheet in a linen closet on the third floor, cut holes in it for eyes and prepare it as a disguise for murder? The only other person on the third floor of the East Wing was a woman who had never been in that house before and didn't know the door of the linen closet from that of a garbage dump."

"Your honor," Dewitt called out. "Mr. Hawkins is testifying, not asking a question."

"Ask a simple question, Mr. Hawkins," the judge said. "Or yield to the defense."

"I'm finished with this witness, your honor. But I reserve the right to recall him." Hawkins turned abruptly and returned to his seat.

Still in the gallery, the veiled woman reached into her straw bag and toyed with a roll of duct-tape, nervously trying again and again to sink her fingernails into it. She then fingered the roll in a frustrating attempt to find the beginning of the tape, not because she wanted to unroll it, but simply out of nervousness.

"Your witness, Mr. Dewitt," the judge said.

Dewitt ambled slowly toward Tony. "Let's see now, Mr. Paluto. You testified that you did not know the woman who accompanied Lillian Rimespecker into the house on the day in question. Is that correct?"

"Yeah. That's right."

"If she and the defendant stayed together in the house, whether in the East Wing, third floor, or elsewhere, it would have taken little extra time, indeed, for Mrs. Rimespecker to introduce her to a linen closet. Would you agree?"

"Yeah, I guess."

"Your honor!" Hawkins leaped to his feet and lifted his right hand. "The defense attorney is leading the witness."

"WIthdrawn!" Dewitt called out. "I withdraw the question." He paced the floor, stopped, looked into the witness's face and said, "Tell me what activities you engaged in within the house before the senator was shot?"

"Oh, hell. A lot of ugliness. I got fired."

"Fired?"

"Yeah. I got into a nasty argument with my boss, the senator. It was ugly. So, he screams at me, fires me, and orders me to get out!"

"I'm sorry to hear that, Mr. Paluto. I assume this argument and firing took time."

"Sure did, but the yak-yakking that led up to the blow-up took even more time. I was trying to tell the senator I didn't like my assignment as Vinny Esposito, the jockey, and I wasn't going to lie to them nice bird people anymore."

Dewitt's demeanor, including his smile and bright eyes, indicated pure pleasure. "And during all this time, any newcomer in the house could have learned the whereabouts of many things, including a linen clos ..."

"Objection, your honor!" Hawkins protested. "The defense attorney is testifying."

Judge Cattwell hammered three times with his gavel, then said, "Objection sustained. The jury will disregard the defense attorney's last pronouncement."

Dewitt was pleased that he had made his point, despite the objection. "I'm finished with this witness, your honor."

"You may step down, Mr. Paluto," the judge said.

"I'd like to call Clarence Exton to the stand, your honor," Hawkins said.

"Clarence Exton," the clerk repeated.

As Clarence made his way to the witness stand, the veiled woman in the gallery was beside herself having prayed over and over again for the elderly couple to vacate the area. Lack of success, despite her intense concentration, angered her to the point of damning God and then praying to Him for forgiveness. Frustration came in waves as she sought means to force the elderly pair to leave the gallery. At one point, she considered leaving, finding a deli, and returning with odorous Limburger cheese, squeezing it and allowing the soft and juicy cheese to run down the backs of the couple's seats, surely causing them to flee from the stink. Her fear of being caught and of becoming strongly offensive herself squelched the idea. Restlessness forced her to get up and walk to the lobby without her shoulder bag, only to return within minutes and sit in the same seat.

After being sworn in, Clarence sat upright and attentive in the witness stand as Hawkins approached him. Offering a weak smile and nod, the prosecutor began by asking the witness to describe his relationship with the Rimespecker family. That proved an easy task for Clarence, who for years had often explained his position as the late senator's private secretary to curious friends and acquaintances. He immediately figured that Hawkins would use him for background information and an overall look at the relationship between the senator and his wife.

"So, when did you see a change in that relationship?" Hawkins asked. "In other words, when did they grow distant?"

"That's hard to explain," Clarence answered, "because the Rimespeckers were extremely busy people, each going his or her own way. I will say, however, that an increase in separation grew in recent years."

Lillian lifted her head and stared at Clarence from the defense table. Until this moment, she had deliberately stared into her lap like a dispirited woman in meditation.

Clarence took no notice of Lillian and kept his eyes on the prosecutor who moved closer and closer to the witness stand as if preparing to lunge.

"Did this disengagement reach an explosive point?" Hawkins asked.

"I'm not quite sure what you mean."

"Did they fight?"

"To tell you the truth, the senator never seemed to notice that Mrs. Rimespecker's outside activities kept increasing. He was preoccupied with his duties in Washington and spent much of his home-time working in his office. It was not so much Mrs. Rimespacker's absence that brought things to a head. It was the Ermengarde Choker. When he discovered it missing, he went berserk. He screamed and slammed its container onto his desk."

"Was he aware of who took the choker?"

"At first?" Clarence paused in thought. "I don't know. He didn't let on. But later, when he realized that his wife had given it to her lady-friend, things got really strange. That's when he sent Tony Paluto to the Birdman."

"Because of the vast media coverage, it's unlikely that anyone in this courtroom lacks knowledge of the Ermengarde Choker and the eagles' nest, but we cannot make that assumption. Please detail, for any jurors that may be uninformed, events related to the choker and their relationship to the defendant and her husband."

Clarence sighed. After a quick glance toward Lillian, he began slowly to tell the tale of the choker and what he knew of the defendant's relationship with Ruth Nettlebaum and its effect on the late senator and the entire Rimespecker household. He showed himself to be an excellent, truthful and detailed storyteller.

* * *

Tony Paluto was so glad to get out of the courthouse that he leaped and jumped about like that tree-climbing monkey he was often labeled. Down the courthouse steps he flew, and up the street he soared, escaping quickly to his car. He was anxious to return to his practice tree—the black locust twin near the nesting tree where the two eaglets still awaited their fledging. So as not to confuse anyone, he was eager to inform newcomers in the growing crowd upstream that the departed eagle was still returning now and again to the nest and surrounding trees and would continue to do so for several more weeks. Now a student of the birds, Tony had learned that "to fledge" was not a single act, but took practice.

Tony had moved his total encampment from bivouac headquarters to the flat area under the eagles' tree—the large patio-like stretch built by the volunteers who diverted the rapids and secured a sturdy work platform. All of his tools, gadgets and gears were laid out in orderly fashion on a large strip of canvas that also folded atop them for protection from inclement weather. No one could say he wasn't ready to climb to the eagle's nest.

Driving well above the speed limit, Tony lowered his right foot and sped to the encampment, thankful of not being recalled to the witness stand, but concerned that he might be required to return to the courthouse on another day.

Late afternoon found him back along Bitterlick Creek and comfortable. He stood firmly grounded under his practice tree and surrounded by a group of curious Boy Scouts, birdwatchers and other volunteers.

"This is a black locust tree like the one holding the eagles' nest," he pointed out to the gathering. "Locust trees differ from most other trees because they're legumes. Does anyone here know what a legume is?"

"Peas and beans!" someone yelled out.

"Who said that?" Tony asked.

An Eagle Scout eagerly raised his hand. A tall, slender youth, he was decorated with an array of merit badges.

"You're right," Tony said. "Can you elaborate?"

The uniformed, sandy-haired scout answered: "A legume is a plant that returns needed nitrogen to the soil and helps other plants grow."

"Very good!" Tony said with enthusiasm. "It's freakin' hard to believe that a big tree is a member of the pea family, but it is. Peas, lentils and all them different kinds of beans we eat are legumes. Look up into this tree and you'll see pods hanging like they hang on bean plants and other legumes. Another fact, the tree's springtime blossoms are abundant honey-makers. Bees crave them flowers that give 'em locust nectar. Each spring, Charley Silvester's honeybees swarm all over this tree and, of course, our bald eagles' tree right over there."

Tony spun around and grabbed the tree-trunk as if beginning to climb, then let go and turned back to the crowd.

"Something else," he said. "Unlike its cousin, the honey locust, the black locust has only small thorns at the base of its leaves. I seen honey locust trees with batches of long, pointed thorns on their branches, some really big clusters popping out right on their trunks. Y'gotta know your trees if yous gonna climb 'em." I ain't plannin' t'get jabbed in the groin by them thorns."

Tony winced when he saw Jimmy cutting through the crowd. He stopped talking and stared at the Birdman.

"Tony!" Jimmy exclaimed. "Hi! I see you're a teacher as well as a climber."

"How y'doin', Mr. Barnes. Just explaining about locust trees."

"Well you're gonna be doing a lot more than that very soon. Within days, I'd say. I want you to be my initial climber, the first one up that nesting tree. I'm tired of weeding out the scumbags and liars when I already have a good climber. Okay, my man?"

Tony danced a little jig. "Hallelujah! Thank you, sir! You sure got my blood churnin'. I'm rarin' to go!"

Someone in the crowd clapped, and then the entire gathering joined in. As the clapping waned, one man yelled out, "Go Tony!"

Jimmy punched the air with his fist. He waved and walked off through the gathering, looking back with a smile now and again.

Focusing on the scouts and other volunteers, Tony said, "Y'ain't heard it all yet. Another interesting locust oddity. These here trees reproduce by sending stems underground and shooting up baby trees all over the damn place. Sometimes a homeowner will plant one in his backyard, only to wake up one morning to find its offspring growing fast on the other side of his property. Look around here. You can see them all over the place."

Many in the crowd turned their heads.

The sun was setting, and the countless little locust trees were casting elongated shadows on the rounded boulders and ragged rocks of the intricate terrain. Their silhouettes formed a vast assortment of odd shapes that mixed with other curious shadows from nature's intricate formations. Also casting shadows in and about the spectacular valley and uplands of the creek were the vast number of newcomers who had ventured up the Bitterlick Creek from the main bivouac area and elsewhere after the one eaglet flew from its nest. Many slept in blanket rolls at night. Others pitched tents where possible. No orderly rows existed, for the terrain would not allow it. But the scattering of human intrusion did not destroy the spectacular beauty, especially when the sun was low in the sky and the shadows long.

Among those intruding on nature were members of the media, a group growing day by day. Newspaper and wire-service reporters often stood alone, rolling in blankets at night. Television crews, however, needed more space, and some of them were forced to camp farther from the Bitterlick water-gap than they had intended. A few were in fields of high grass and weeds a quarter or half a mile away from the cliff and the rocky and wet terrain.

Police Chief Morris had finally assigned two officers to patrol the area near the nesting tree. The growing crowd had alarmed him because the Ermengarde Choker was, hopefully, still in the tree or nearby. The uniformed officers walked back and forth under the tree, now and again stopping to rest, usually sitting on large rocks or squatting on a sheet of canvas.

Tony began to climb his practice tree. He was equipped with all sorts of tree-climbing paraphernalia, from climbing spikes and straps to friction savers and saddle bags. He was partway up the tree when a branch creaked, cracked and gave way under his weight. He looked down on the crowd and called out, "Black locusts often have brittle limbs, but if you're properly equipped, you won't fall. That's why y'gotta know your trees and their idiosyncrasies. Right now the trunk and I are affixed like Velcro buddies."

Minutes later, Tony was about a quarter of the way up the tree when he turned and glanced down and around. Amidst the many, he saw the patrolling officers grinning and staring up at him from under the eagle's tree. He waved, and they saluted.

Chapter Twenty-Four

Claudia Silvester was summoned to testify for the prosecution at the murder trial of Lillian Rimespecker. The subpoena was a complete surprise to her and to her husband and most others familiar with the case.

"You don't know anything about the murder, for chrissake!" Charley barked on the day the writ was delivered. He and Claudia were busy redecorating and moving furniture back into their dining room. "What the hell? I don't get it!" Charley came down hard on the floor with a chair he was moving.

"Hey, watch it! That's an expensive Queen Ann's chair." Claudia stopped pushing a server, put her hands on her hips, and stared at Charley. "I think they summoned me because of my relationship with Cousin Ruth. They think I know more than I do."

The subpoena had arrived several days after the start of the trial and following a meeting of both attorneys with Judge Cattwell in his richly furnished chambers of dark wood, green velvet draperies and black leather armchairs. An ornate gold-framed portrait of Justice William O. Douglas hung on the wall behind the judge's desk.

"He wants to add a name to the witness list, your honor," Dewitt said that afternoon.

The judge turned one way, then the other in his richly appointed mahogany and black leather swivel chair that occupied space behind his highly polished desk. Hawkins and Dewitt remained standing, for Cattwell offered no seat to either the prosecutor or the defense attorney.

"And you wish to object, Mr. Dewitt?" Judge Cattwell asked, his eyes showing a touch of annoyance.

"No. Not necessarily."

"Then why are we here in my chambers?"

"Lack of discovery regarding Claudia Silvester, your honor. My esteemed colleague has given me nothing to review in the way of discovery."

"Is this true, Mr. Hawkins?'

"That's because there is nothing of substance to submit to the defense attorney, your honor. We're talking about Claudia Silvester, the only living relative of Ruth Nettlebaum. Blood relative, that is. At the start of discovery, I saw no reason to include Mrs. Silvester. But when I found an almost complete absence of material related to Ruth Nettlebaum, I thought maybe I should take a look at her only living relative. Claudia Silvester must know something about her cousin. They did see each other and communicate. It's just possible she harbors clues to why Lillian Rimespecker had reasons to kill her husband—reasons related to her cousin's entanglement or liaison with the senator's wife. Did Nettlebaum in any way influence her lover's need to kill? What might Silvester know about the Ermengarde Choker's role in the murder, if any?"

"Larry, my friend, you're indicating right now that there's some discovery."

"No way, Manny! My tidbits of speculation indicate nothing. When you come up blank with someone like Nettlebaum, you've got to go fishing. And I confess that fishing is exactly what I'm doing. I'm not even going to prep Silvester, so don't let that bug you. Believe me, I'm not planning any big surprises. I'm simply hoping her presence on the stand will provoke something." Hawkins turned toward the judge. "Your honor, please allow me my little fishing expedition."

The judge aimed a steady stare at the defense attorney. "If you have no objection, Mr. Dewitt, I say we allow the prosecutor to include this woman on his witness list, devoid of discovery. Who knows? She might help your case."

"Thank you, your honor," Hawkins said.

Dewitt nodded his head reluctantly.

"Come on, Manny," Hawkins said. "I'll buy you a drink."

* * *

Days later, as time approached for Claudia to appear in court, Charley agreed reluctantly to accompany her to the County Courthouse, despite his desire to stay home because of Jimmy's predictions. In fact, he hated the idea of going to court with impelling possibilities looming overhead. No way did he want to leave the Bitterlick Creek Valley, because tomorrow was the first of three days that the Birdman foresaw as prime fledging periods for the two remaining eaglets. And he was well aware that Tony's ascent would follow sometime thereafter, on a signal from Jimmy, possibly bringing to a head the mystery of the Ermengarde Choker.

"You're annoyed," Charley said at the dining room table. The room was back in order, fully furnished, and a far cry from its summertime use as bivouac headquarters. The Silvesters were eating grilled cheese and tomato sandwiches for lunch as the encampment on their property continued to thin out. The campers had been trudging upstream for days, causing an explosion of people near the eagles' black locust tree.

"Annoyed? No, not at all. I know how much you want to be here. Believe me, I'd rather be upstream with you tomorrow than in court testifying." Claudia bit into her sandwich and chewed. "I just don't want to go to court alone. And I'd rather someone else drive."

"They're not going to bully or torment you." Charley sighed and sucked in air. He looked into his wife's beseeching eyes, hesitated, then said. "Okay, I'll go."

"Hold tight. First, let me talk to Laura."

* * *

The County Courthouse steps were bathed in morning sunlight as Laura and Claudia climbed toward the big bronze doors. Laura's cellphone jingled a tune when they reached the midpoint. She seized it from her purse.

"Hello?"

"It's me, Honey! You won't believe it!" Jimmy's voice was highly animated. "The birds have taken wing!"

"You're kidding!" Laura turned to Claudia. "The eagles are fledging!"

"Oh, my God! Jimmy was right on the mark."

"You called it, Jimmy," Laura said as she and Claudia stopped climbing and stood halfway up the massive flight of steps.

"Pure luck," he said. "I missed by a mile on the first bird. This time, eagle number two was immediately followed by eagle number three."

"Can you see them now?"

"They're circling overhead. What a beautiful sight on a perfect morning!"

"Are you sending Tony up the tree?"

"Not right away. The young birds may come back to the nest. They're not sure of themselves yet. We'll keep watching. When they're off in the distance and adequate time has passed ... In other words, when there's a long enough break I'll send him up. The monitors show no signs of the choker. And the media guys are in a panic. We need more cops to control the crowd."

Claudia tugged on Laura's arm. "Tell me! Tell me!"

Laura turned to Claudia and explained, "They're flying in circles overhead. No sign of the choker."

"I've gotta get into the courtroom, Laura. Stay here and get the scoop. Fill me in later with every detail." Claudia hurried up the remaining steps. Her phone beeped as she pushed opened the heavy doors and stepped into the lobby. A glance at the phone's ID message told her Charley was calling. She caught her breath, then answered, "Hi, love. I know all about it, Charley. Jimmy's on the phone with Laura."

"I know, but I thought I'd join in," Charley said. "One bird flew into the distance. I can just about see it. The other one is sitting in Tony's practice tree, looking toward the nest and the sky. It can't make up its mind."

"I can't talk, Charley. I'm heading for the courtroom right now. I'll call you when I can. Probably not until after I testify."

Police Chief Morris was stepping down from the witness stand as Claudia entered the courtroom, and his forensic chief was being called to testify.

"Samuel Block to the stand, please," Hawkins said.

"Samuel Block!" the clerk echoed.

The chubby, middle-aged forensic expert waddled his way toward the witness stand. He wore a blue-and-white striped shirt and a red bowtie fastened loosely around his thick neck. A few strands of hair were combed over his bald crown. Breathing deeply, he placed his hand on the Bible, was sworn in, said "I do," and climbed awkwardly into the witness stand.

Hawkins stepped close to the witness and said, "Mr. Block, please tell the court what you do as East Bitterlick's chief of forensics."

"Well, I study crime scenes for evidence and analyze findings in the laboratory, often unearthing minute details that prove guilt or innocence. That might include examining a dead body, gathering dust particles, scrutinizing bullet casings, collecting DNA and blood samples and endless other perusals and probes."

"What did you find at the scene of Senator Rimespecker's murder?"

"The most damning things we found were cartridges or cylinders from a twenty-two caliber automatic pistol. The late senator owned four such guns. All identical. We recovered three of them, all properly registered under his name. It's likely that the missing gun is the murder weapon—a pistol used, of course, by someone with access to it."

"Someone with access," the prosecutor repeated. "You mean, someone like his wife, Lillian Rimespecker?"

"Objection!" Dewitt leaped to his feet. "The witness—and Mr. Hawkins, to his shame—are making two assumptions. First, that a particular, family-owned, twenty-two automatic killed the senator. Secondly, that that particular gun fell into the hands of Lillian Rimespecker. How many twenty-twos are out there, all over the county, the state, the nation? Thousands? Millions?"

"Objection sustained," the judge ruled. "The jury will disregard the witness's entire testimony about the weapon used in the murder, as well as the defense attorney's editorial enhancement. Watch it, Mr. Hawkins. You know better."

Judge Cattwell reached for his glass of water, sipped three times, and wiped his lips. "You may proceed," Mr. Hawkins.

"I have nothing more for this witness at this time, your honor." As he stepped back toward his seat Hawkins added, "But I may wish to recall him."

"So be it," the judge said. "Mr. Dewitt, your witness."

The defense attorney rose, but remained at his table. "Mr. Block, in your extensive examination of the murder scene, what did you find that directly linked Lillian Rimespecker to the murder of her husband? For example, did you find her fingerprints anywhere at or near the scene?"

Block hesitated, then said, "No. No recent fingerprints."

"Thank you. That's all, your honor."

Blocked turned toward the judge. "But ..."

"I'm finished with this witness, your honor," Dewitt said with a tone of impatience.

"You may step down, Mr. Block," Judge Cattwell said.

The prosecutor rose again. "I call Claudia Silvester. Hopefully, she's in the courtroom. Claudia Silvester?"

The clerk repeated: "Claudia Silvester."

As Claudia walked up the center aisle from the rear of the courtroom, the veiled woman, again sitting alone in the gallery, placed her arms on the front-row railing, leaned forward and watched the witness's every step. Her eyes stayed focused on Claudia as she was sworn in and took the witness stand. She whispered to herself, "Sorry, Cousin Claudia. But you never understood."

Hawkins was slow to ask his first question, as if searching for something appropriate. He paced in front of Claudia, squeezed his bottom lip with his thumb and forefinger, then finally looked at her and said, "Mrs. Silvester, please explain your relationship to the mysterious Ruth Nettlebaum, the alleged associate of the accused, Lillian Rimespecker."

Claudia cleared her throat, wet her lips, and said, "Ruth is my cousin."

"First cousin?"

"Yes."

"Then surely you can tell us much about this enigmatic woman who, I'm sure, no one in this courtroom has ever met, let alone seen."

"Your honor," interrupted Dewitt. "What in God's name is the prosecutor attempting to do with this preamble to his questions? Is he beginning the foreword to a novel or something?"

Judge Cattwell waved his gavel. "Get to the point, Mr. Hawkins. Ask a question."

Claudia spoke before the prosecutor had a chance to rephrase: "Ruth and I were not close. My husband and I saw her, perhaps, once a year. She was not an easy person to get to know. She lived a quiet life alone, until recently."

"Tell us what you can about her relationship with Lillian Rimespecker. And, in particular, about how that relationship may have had a link to the murder of Joseph Rimespecker."

"There's nothing I can tell you. Ruth never mentioned the senator's wife. We never knew she had a relationship of any sort with Mrs. Rimespecker until we saw the portrait."

"Portrait? What portrait?"

"On the last visit that Charley—that's my husband—and I made to Ruth's house, we found her missing. We also found her beloved cat Pinwheel dead, and a beautiful oil painting of a woman on her living room wall. We realized later that it was a portrait of Lillian Rimespecker."

"What was your reaction?"

"We found it strange."

"Irrelevant, your honor," Dewitt called out. "This whole line of questioning is irrelevant. Mr. Hawkins is wasting the court's time. I suggest you strike it all. It has no connection to the murder."

Judge Cattwell stared at prosecutor. "I'll give you a smidgen of leeway, Mr. Hawkins, subject to connection."

"I'll connect, your honor." Hawkins turned toward Claudia. "What did you notice about the portrait, Mrs. Silvester?"

"What do you mean?" Claudia shifted nervously.

"Oh, you know. What was she pictured wearing, for example?" Hawkins knew exactly where he was leading the witness, for he had seen and examined the portrait himself.

"She was dressed beautifully in the very stately manner of a queen. A bit haughty, perhaps." Suddenly Claudia's eyes widened and her brows arched, "Oh, she had that choker around her neck. You know, the one in the news. The Ermengarde Choker that everbody's talking about. It was spotted in that bald eagles' nest."

"Did you ever see that choker? I don't mean in oil colors or on a computer screen. I mean the very choker itself."

"Yes, Charley and I saw Ruth wearing it two or three times over recent years."

"Did Miss Nettlebaum tell you how she came to possess it?"

Sitting nervously in the gallery, the veiled woman was scraping the finish off the railing with her fingernails. She chewed on her bottom lip until it bled.

"From a special friend," Claudia testified. "That's what she said. Someone very special had given it to her. I don't recall her exact words. But she liked to show it off. She pranced about and danced with it."

The veiled woman made a tight fist, brought it toward her lips, and bit down hard on the knuckle of her index finger. Seconds later she muttered to herself: "It looked so pretty and bright on Pinwheel."

Laura entered the courtroom quietly and slipped into a seat toward the rear, just under the gallery rail.

Hawkins offered Claudia a warm smile and asked, "Did your cousin allude to any protectiveness offered by a woman of Lillian Rimespecker's stature?"

"No. As I said, she never mentioned the senator's wife."

Hawkins lifted his chin and looked upward in thought, turned suddenly, glared at Claudia and said, "Gorgeous piece of jewelry, that choker. In a tug of war, precious enough to kill for, wouldn't you say?"

"Objection!" Dewitt shouted as he leaped to his feet.

"Withdrawn, your honor. I rest my case." Hawkins hurried back to the prosecution table, deliberately avoiding the judge's venomous stare.

A rumble of chatter rolled across the courtroom. Judge Cattwell hammered three times with his gavel. "Order in the court," he called out. After pausing a moment, he hammered three times again. "Is the defense ready to proceed?"

"We are, your honor," Dewitt said. "The defense calls Lillian Rimespecker."

A bit of a rumble started again, for many were surprised that Dewitt would call the defendant as his first witness. The judge used his gavel again, tapping lightly twice. "Order, please. May we have order."

"Lillian Rimespecker," the clerk called out.

The defendant held herself erect and strode confidently toward the witness stand. Again dressed modestly, she wore a navy-blue suit and a pale blue blouse buttoned tightly around her neck. A single strand of pearls was her only adornment. When swearing in, she spoke softly in response to the oath. Then, without hesitance, she climbed directly into the witness stand and smiled ever so slightly at the defense attorney.

Dewitt hesitated for affect. Then, in a dramatic and piercing tone, asked, "Did you kill your husband?"

"No, sir," Lillian answered firmly. "I did not. I've never killed anyone, let alone my husband. And I have no intention of ever killing anyone."

"She didn't kill him, I did!" shouted Ruth Nettlebawm from the galley. Ruth had tossed off her hat and veil, unbuttoned and thrown aside her trench-coat, and stood behind the gallery rail half-naked. Her only clothing was a bright pink ballerina tutu, selected to please the woman she loved. She jumped over the railing and fell from the gallery until the rope around her neck tightened and she bounced to a sudden thud that echoed in the courtroom. That rope, tied to the railing by a double square knot, also held a brown envelope attached by duct-tape just under Ruth's chin and the noose's slipknot. The defendant and the judge were the only persons facing the galley and, therefore, the first to see her jump. Others turned immediately and within seconds the entire courtroom was in an uproar. Gasps, shouts, cries and shrieks resounded throughout the cavernous space.

Lillian shouted, "Ruth! Oh, no, Ruthy! My God, Ruthy! My Ruthy!" She collapsed and several court attendants and spectators raced to her aid.

Claudia turned and nearly fainted when she saw her cousin dangling and spinning, the pink tutu flaring outward. She screamed, but her wail came to a choking halt. Unable to bring up a sound from her larynx, she put her trembling hand over her mouth and tried to stand, but her knees buckled and she slid back into her chair.

Ruth's body dangled near Laura. In fact, if Laura had seated herself four chairs to her left, Ruth's feet and rose-colored toenails would have hovered directly over her head. Though she had never met Ruth, Laura immediately figured out her identity when she heard Lillian cry out her name. The still-twitching woman had plunged so close to her, startling her to the extreme, that she couldn't control her shaking body as she searched for Claudia in the milling crowd. The judge pounded and shouted for order. He dialed 911, as did many others throughout the courtroom.

* * *

Later that day, Chief Morris sat at his desk reading Ruth Nettlebaum's suicide note—a lengthy epistle taken from the envelope she had secured with duct-tape on the hanging rope. He stretched it out on his blotter and adjusted his eyeglasses. Ruth had handwritten her note in perfect cursive.

The chief read: *This is my suicide note and my confession of murder. I'm writing it in an effort to be understood, as well as to free the woman I love from any guilt and bring an end to her murder trial.*

On the day that Senator Joseph Rimespecker was killed, I accompanied his wife Lillian to their home. We arrived when their chauffeur was driving the family pickup truck up the driveway toward the garages. We assumed that he saw us, and that altered our plans to stay overnight.

Inside the house, Lillian pointed out the library on the first floor, and showed me the senator's office door on the second floor, explaining that it was often closed when the senator was at work at his desk. On the third floor in the West Wing, she explained where each door led and how to use each facility, then led me into the Green Room.

Lillian's anxiety over not having seen her son was extreme and she pled with me to stay in the Green Room and allow her to visit him. She left me alone and I disobeyed, because from the moment I saw that closed office door I could think about little but killing the senator, freeing Lillian from hell, and having her for myself. Within seconds I found what I needed for a disguise in a hallway closet.

The gun I used to shoot the senator had been given to me by Lillian at the same time she gave me the Ermengarde Choker. It was to be used for my protection and to safeguard the choker. You'll find it submerged behind my mother's gravestone in the small cemetery of Calvary Methodist Church. It's in a buried flowerpot that holds a red-blooming geranium above ground level.

While Lillian was with her son, Jordan, I used a bedsheet to play ghost, and hurried to the second floor in my stocking feet. I knocked on the senator's office door, he answered and I shot him through the sheet again and again and again in the head, chest and belly.

I'm sure the so-called "smoking gun" is sufficient evidence of my guilt, but if more is needed, I'm certain that forensic experts can find my lipstick residue on the bedsheet, despite it being washed. I held a corner of the sheet in my mouth as I pinned it around my body. A bite mark and pin holes might also be detected by skilled forensic scientists.

I used the same gun to shoot Jordan Rimespecker. That shooting was a mistake, for when I gazed down on him from the Rimespecker attic I saw only a bright light shining into my eyes and I panicked. I know I hurt Lillian beyond belief that night, begetting another reason for my demise.

The death of the senator was a gift I was giving to a woman who gave me the happiest days of my life. Before I met Lillian, no way could I have imagined the bliss I felt in her arms. Each day became more beautiful as my thoughts never left her even when we were apart. There is no possible way that I could live without her. She enabled me to go out in the world and see things I never before dreamed I would encounter. Before Lillian, I pretended to expose myself to others, to sing on stage, to prance about in fancy clothes, to strum an instrument, to recite Shakespeare, read poems by John Keats. Mirrors became my necessity. Through a mirror I could sing Madame Butterfly to myself and pretend I was the audience. The craving to unveil myself made my fears of leaving the house intolerable. Lillian cured me.

Goodbye,
Ruth Nettlebaum

Chief Morris folded the suicide note, pushed it aside, leaned back in his chair and shook his head. For moment after moment he simply stared at one wall, then another. Finally, he sat up straight, blew his nose, gathered himself together and reached for the intercom button. Lieutenant Benjamin Goldstein was quick to answer.

"Whatcha got goin', Benny?"

"Finishing up paperwork on the fish-market break-in. Why? What's up?"

"When you file that away, will you take a little ride over to Calvary Methodist cemetery and dig up the Rimespecker murder weapon for me?"

"The what?"

"You heard me."

"Holy smackeroons! That suicide note must've taught you plenty."

"You wouldn't believe. I'll let you read it. But only if you want looney-toon nightmares. I thought I had heard everything, until this morbid affliction floated into our bailiwick."

"Hold on, chief. I got news at this end. Tony Paluto's headin' up that black locust in the morning. And the Birdman's cryin' for more cops."

"God help us if they can't find that choker. Or maybe it's the other way around."

"There's no answer to that puzzle. What happens happens."

"I've changed my mind. I'll go with you."

"What?

"I'll go with you to the cemetery. Hop over here, and I'll fill you in. And we can talk about tomorrow on the way to Calvary." Chief Morris glanced at the picture of his family—wife, two daughters, a son and himself—that stood next to his green-shade lamp on his desk. "How's your family, Benny?"

"My family? They're okay. Amy ran into the schoolyard flagpole a couple days back, got a big egg on her forehead. Other than that, we're okeydokey."

"And the wife?"

"Marge is Marge. You know Marge. She's doing okay. Misses her mother since the funeral. But she's hanging in there."

"We're lucky, y'know. There're a lot of wackos out there. Crazy people. Really crazy people. Y'know?"

"Chief, what's with you? Y'need some mood pills or something? The suicide note must've done you in."

"Get over here. And bring a shovel with you. Grab a small one or a trowel from the janitor's closet."

The chief clicked off the intercom. He picked up the framed picture of his family, gazed at it briefly, kissed it, and gently returned it to its spot under the lamplight.

Chapter Twenty-Five

The hour was late when Charley came in through the back door with more papers tucked under his arm. Claudia was tidying up in the kitchen and greeted him with the words, "The newspaper and TV reporters pestered me all day long. The phones kept ringing until I turned everything off and refused to answer the knocking at the front door. They just don't understand why I don't want to be a millionaire. It's not the money. Nothing's wrong with money. It's what comes with it."

"Bare with the badgering." Charley said. "Things are coming to a head fast."

"Some reporters are okay. In fact, some don't know that we're Ruth's benefactors, but the word is getting around among the seasoned newsmen, especially those from this side of the Atlantic. I suspect Chief Morris or some of his men have loose lips."

"Or it's the lawyers Morris shared the document with."

"Carney Cox of the *Beacon* comes across as well-polished and is always pleasant with me, yet he knows more about us than I appreciate."

"But he gets his facts straight. He's a good reporter."

Charley stepped into the dining room and tossed his papers on a pile of documents growing bigger by the hour on the table. He glanced from the pile toward the kitchen and Claudia. A peculiar expression altered his face, suggesting a struggle within his psyche. He questioned whether he should allow a widening gap to grow. "I'm going to hit the sack early," he called out as he headed for the stairs.

After Charley got ready for bed, instead of crawling under the covers, he put on his bathrobe and went back downstairs to face Claudia in the dining room. He had a fuzzy idea it was important to descend into whatever. She had just finished replacing candle stubs with new tapers in the candelabra on the breakfront.

"We had this room back in shape," she said, eying the huge pile of papers on the table, many of them spilling over here and there. "I was hoping it would stay that way." She turned her eyes on Charley. "Hungry? Is that why you came down? There's some leftover cream cheese in the refrigerator. You could finish it up. Your favorite crackers are in the cookie jar."

"I'm not hungry. I just wanna look over some papers."

"What is all that stuff anyway?" Claudia walked to the pile and pulled a blueprint from the middle of the stack. "A log cabin in the pine-barrens? My, my. Are you planning your final days on earth—alone."

"That thought never crossed my mind."

"And look at this. Hmm. What did you order from Macro Systems, L.L.C.?"

"Ahhh! You caught me. Survey equipment. We've had no way of surveying our land or surrounding acres. Thought it would be helpful."

"Why?"

"Can't I have my own little secrets?"

"I suspect this one's not so little." She flipped over some of the papers. "You've been playing hide-and-seek with your covert exploits for quite some time. I could tell something was afoot. My God, look at this stuff. When did you start collecting?"

"When I realized what might happen to us."

"That sounds ominous. You're scaring me." She tightened her lips and stared at him. "Please, Charley. What is all this?"

"This? You mean this pile?"

Claudia grimaced. "No, I mean the dots in the wallpaper."

"It's a pile of information that'll tickle my brain. Maps, deeds, survey results, realtor reports and some of my own sketches."

"For what purpose? Whatever you're up to, it sounds bigtime."

"Bigtime? If we don't plan ahead, we can trip and fall bigtime. Originally, it was to be a surprise."

"I confess I was snooping in your pile."

"Maybe that's why I unconsciously left it out on the dining-room table."

"How unconscious were you?"

"I'm not sure."

"Maybe you really wanted me to see it. You can keep a secret just so long. And I think this one's been nagging at you for quite some time." Claudia backed up against the breakfront, grabbed the rococo trim behind her with both hands, and struck a resolute pose. "I saw some papers about the electric company's land near the Nagelstone center where Laura hangs out with the animals. What the devil are you up to, Charley? Come on. Level with me."

"You're the one who wants to build and operate a greyhound rescue outfit or something like it on our property. Ever think that my cache of records, deeds and maps might have something to do with that?"

"A greyhound retreat in our backyard is one thing. But one on electric company land miles from here? You're not fooling me, Charley. This has something to do with us becoming millionaires. And you're scaring the guts out of me."

Charley studied Claudia's countenance for several seconds, then aimed his remarks at what he thought lay under and barely oozed through her façade. "She's dead, Claudia. Dead, dead, dead. Cousin Ruth is dead. What do you think is going to happen to the choker? Eh? What? You don't want to talk about it. And that's being foolish. It's going to happen, and you can't stop it. There's nothing wrong with dreaming, planning, thinking ahead."

"Going to happen! Wake up, Charley. What exactly do you think is going to happen? Nothing may happen, 'cause the choker's missing. Gone with the wind!" Claudia threw up her hands and spun around as she repeated, "With the wind."

"It's there somewhere. I have no doubt whatsoever about that. Our bivouac was perfect. No way did anyone snatch that choker. No possible way. We had everything covered. That nest was never disturbed. If the choker isn't under debris in the nest, it's down below among the rocks, or stuck in one of the crevices in the precipice."

Claudia stared at her husband for an uncomfortable moment. "I didn't know I married a man who wanted to be wealthy."

"I don't! Never said I did! We're gonna give it all away. Millions here! Millions there! It's all part of a plan that'll please you. In fact, you might say that you inspired it. I'll name it the Claudia Giveaway Plan if you like."

"I don't want to be associated with millions. The thieves and beggars will come by the score. The media and social networks will spread our names everywhere." Claudia extended her arms wide and shook her head. "Our pictures will be plastered on front pages. We'll have to move and change our name. Our entire lives will be turned upside down."

"Not if we act fast and handle things right. I know what I'm doing." Charley crossed his heart and tapped the table three times. "It's been churning in my head for weeks."

"Churning for weeks? Now, that I believe."

Charley stepped near to his wife, put his arms around her waist, pulled her close and kissed her on the nose. "Okay. I'll stop being so secretive and lay it all out for you." He took her hand. "The way things are piling up, I really have no choice. Come on. Over here. Sit next to me." He pulled her toward the table and the overflowing heap of papers. They sat shoulder to shoulder. Digging into the pile, he pulled out a Manila folder and opened it, spreading its contents before his wife. "Take a look at this." He pointed to a parcel of land on a map that depicted broad acreage from the coastline inland. "See the section I outlined with a black felt-marker?"

"That's near Tomcrest, where we used to run the dunes and splash in the water."

"Right! I'll be damned. You know your coastline."

"You used to dig up those little sand-crabs and press them in my hand and I'd scream and you'd laugh. Ick! I can feel them wiggle now."

"This patch of land is Tomcrest's feeble answer to a bird refuge. The gulls and sandpipers like it. But the town really doesn't maintain it. The dunes and the clumps of tall grasses capture debris that doesn't get cleaned up until some irate residents man the shovels and buckets. Tomcrest's mayor tells me they'd gladly unload it for the right price. And we can pay that price—and much more. Now forget that for a moment, and look at the inland parcel I've marked in red."

"Scrub pine," Claudia said.

"Holy hell! You've got a good memory."

"I remember the butterflies."

"The ground's still sandy, but fertile enough for scrub pine, gnarled junipers and tall weeds like mullein, burdock and thistle. It's a tasty stretch for certain birds that like seeds. The only thing it's lacking is milkweed for the disappearing red knots, a very fixable problem."

"Now I presume we move to the strip of land you've marked in blue."

"Right on! This band of land is heavily forested with tall pines and fir trees. Walk upon the quiet bed of needles at night and you're sure to hear the hoot of an owl and the cries of other night creatures." Charley moved his finger farther west on the map to the fourth band of land, this one outlined in green. "Here we have the deciduous trees, the leaf bearers. Maples, oaks, poplars and plenty of hardwood trees. A lot of common nesting birds flourish here—the kind we find prevalent in our backyards."

"Thanks for the lesson, Charley. Now get to the point."

"If we put these four bands together it gives us a multicolored belt from east to west—a four-way diversified cocktail of bird life, including a heap of migrating birds as well as predators like hawks and eagles. And we shouldn't forget the woodpeckers. If we were to make this whole diversified tract into a bird sanctuary, it could become one of the biggest and best on the East Coast. Wouldn't it make a beautiful gift for a friend we love, a guy with a nickname that fits? And we can do it. Like they say, money talks. With our gift from Ruth we can absolutely do it and so much more."

"My God, Charley, what are you thinking?"

"Stay with me, now. Y'gotta get the whole picture."

"By the way, the lost choker is no *gift* from Ruth. Scrap that word gift, please. She was forced to list a benefactor. Whose name could she put on the dotted line? Who did she know? Strange she didn't list Pinwheel-the-cat."

"Please, pay attention. The areas marked in blue and green belong to Harold Shellcroft, the developer. He scrapped his planned development there for the open land near Penrose Creek, where he's building condos now. He'll unload this land for less than its worth. And we can afford to pay top dollar. Now, the red band between the black and the blue is Upland Township wasteland. I haven't talked to anyone in Upland yet, but their cash-strapped schools need funds. They couldn't turn us down. If they did, the townsfolk would burn down school headquarters."

"You're crazy, Charley. You're making deals with people, aren't you? We don't know the future. You're gonna come crashing down off your inflated image of your status and wealth. We're just average folks right now, with no fortune in sight. The Bitterlick Creek probably dumped the damn choker in a pisshole."

"What's a pisshole?"

"I don't know. But it doesn't sound good."

"Let me finish. Please."

"We should be in bed. Tony's starting his climb up that locust tree early in the morning. You don't wanna miss that."

"I wanna give Jimmy a complete gift, all wrapped up in a handsome briefcase. Not just prospects and possibilities, but completed paperwork, deeds in our name for his signature and quick transfer. I wanna include all the trimmings that go with the deeds, things needed for building and operating one of the finest bird sanctuaries ever. The final package should contain paid up receipts for needed equipment, for stabilizing the land, for building structures, for erecting lookouts, and for everything else a sanctuary should have."

"Oh, God help us." Claudia started to rise from her chair. "I'm going to bed."

"No don't!" Charley grabbed her arm and pulled her down into her chair. "Don't! Please. Y'gotta let me tell it all. Now that I've started, I've gotta finish." He searched and found papers marked PMC-Electro, Inc. You mentioned the electric company's stretch of land from the Nagelstone Vet Center to the peach groves near Francony Mills."

"They were gonna build a power plant there."

"No longer."

"People picketed.

"They scrapped the idea when they combined with Cloverton and hooked up with the atomic power plant at Sunfish Creek. That land's up for grabs. Put it together with Laura's beloved Nagelstone clinic and include the local SPCA over here on the eastern edge, and what do you have? Not only the makings of a tremendous animal-care facility, but something that'll make Laura shed tears of joy. The open land and the wooded acres can be used for the expansion of both facilities, with miles of countryside to spare. No one will lose their jobs from the impending shutdowns. We can hire indoor and outdoor staff. And veterinarians in the area will eagerly become affiliates."

Claudia sat there stone-faced. Finally, she whimpered, "All built on a dream."

Charley went on: "And all of this will be finalized, put in Laura's name, and stuffed into her beautiful leather briefcase. We gotta have as many documents signed, sealed and delivered as possible before the presentation."

Claudia began to push herself up from the table again, only to be held by her husband, who said, "That's two briefcases, each to be wrapped in a big red ribbon. They will blow Laura's and Jimmy's minds! Wow! Can't you just see it? Damn, I get all wiggly inside thinking about it." Charley paused to catch his breath. He leaned back and sucked in air. Softly, he spoke in a direct, serious, thinking-man's manner: "I'm figuring on putting together five briefcases before we turn from immediate friends and start giving to any do-good organizations."

"Stop it!" she yelled. "Let me go! I'm just going to the kitchen for a drink of water. My mouth is dry from grief." She hurried away, only to return in short order and sit across from Charley where he couldn't grab her arm.

Charley began to explain the intended contents of the third briefcase, the one proposed for Clarence and Terry. He said it would differ from Jimmy's and Laura's because of dissimilar needs. With excitement and animation, he described a beautiful house resting among flowers in a fertile valley. "From us to them, with love." The plans, the architect's drawings, maps, the builder's specs, the subcontractor's invoices, the landscapers' scope of duties, the receipts of everything paid in full and all details would be contained in the briefcase, Charley explained. With continued enthusiasm, he detailed: The house would include an addition on one side for Clarence's elderly mother, with separate entrance and abundant medical needs. A wing would also extend from the other side of the house, with separate entrances, for Jordan and his dog, George. The young man's quarters and a doggie-door would exit onto a ballfield, swimming pool, and outdoor canine facilities, including runs, pathways, playthings, and a doghouse designed by the same architect who drafted the house.

"And Terry would be able to grow all the flowers she loves—hollyhocks, zinnias, marigolds, morning glories, petunias, you name it," Charley explained. "And deeper from the house, Clarence would have his vegetable garden, beautifully fenced in, and always stocked with perennials like rhubarb, horseradish and asparagus. Annual plants and seeds, by contract, would be shipped in yearly by the Burpee seed company."

With restraint, Claudia made an effort to speak calmly: "Charley, I've been long aware that something's been brewing in that crazy head of yours. But to this extent? My God! When did you find time to ..."

"With the help of this," Charley interrupted as he pulled forth and held high his iPhone. "In the woods nearly every day with a tree-stump as my desk. We're living in a new world, Claud. It's all at our fingertips." He ran his figures through his hair and smirked. "Of course, a few trips here and there were necessary, when you weren't looking."

"I confess I allowed you to slide a bit. I said nothing when you turned down pizza with the Barnes on a Friday night, yet got home later than I did."

Charley's mind was elsewhere: "Oh, and I forgot. Full college tuition for Jordan goes into the Exton briefcase with the flower seeds and the doggie-door."

"Heaven help us." Claudia grimaced. "I'm going up to bed." She started to leave. "You can sneak into the woods in your pajamas, sit on your stump, and secretly call in your order of milkweed seeds."

"Not very funny." Charley chased after her, grabbed her arm and said, "Wait! I haven't mentioned Tony."

"What about Tony? Does he get a briefcase?"

"Of course. But it's empty right now. I called a logging company, but nothing came of it. I talked to a guy at a tree farm, but they don't use climbers. I'd like to buy him property in which his talents are needed. The truth is, I wish he'd work for us. We need a hard-worker like Tony to put together all the items laid out in your briefcase."

"My briefcase?"

"That's where it all started. And it's one essential reason for all the secrecy and the survey equipment. Thinking back to our beloved dog Bingo, you first mentioned getting another greyhound as a pet. Remember? Then you doubled it, because number-one would need company. That got me reflecting, and then to heavy thinking that led me to investigating. I hate to repeat myself, but you do know that thousands of greyhounds are killed every year because of racing injuries or because they've become too slow to please their owners and bring in the cash?"

"Yes. About three thousand annually."

"Right."

"You've mentioned it often. You needn't repeat the facts and figures. And I'm thrilled about the idea of helping greyhounds. You know I'm all for it." Raising her voice to its highest volume without screaming, but cutting the air sharply, she continued, "When and if we know it's possible!"

"With help from national greyhound organizations, we can build a state-of-the-art rescue facility. We'll buy more land on each side of our property. Why? Because we can. People don't turn down millions."

"Stop! You just shot another bullet into my heart. And it's painful. Don't you understand? I don't want to crawl out on that artificial limb you're building. Believe me, when it's cut off, it's gonna hurt like hell. Now, I'm going to bed. And don't you dare try to stop me."

"Go on. What the hell? The big surprise is spoiled anyway."

"Get your mind on something else, Charley." Claudia turned and looked back at her husband. "Like your ... your ... your honeybees, for example. I haven't heard you mentioned your bees in God knows how long. There was a time you fussed over them day after day."

"Didn't I tell you? I'm bringing in more hives tomorrow. At least five more boxes. I want to build up our apiary to the point where it's a large operation worth moving to new property. I was thinking we'd buy the clover fields over by Maywood Junction."

Claudia was speechless. She stared bug-eyed at Charley briefly, with her mouth open, then turned and hurried off.

Charley returned to the table and began to look through some of his papers. Within minutes, however, he was yawning. He folded his arms on the table and cradled his head in them. His frustrating words with Claudia were not enough to keep him awake. He fell asleep while attempting to count the number of fence posts on the north side of his property. Fifty minutes later, when the brass-and-glass German Clock on the breakfront chimed midnight, his head popped up so fast that it strained his neck. He shook his head carefully, rubbed his eyes, and slowly pushed his way up on his feet. Tiptoeing, he made his way up the stairs.

"I'm still awake," Claudia said as she heard Charley sneak quietly into the bedroom. "You can turn on the light if you have to."

"No, I can feel my way in the dark."

"You know, Charley, what you're trying to do for our friends is the most selfless, kind, generous thing I've ever heard of. I think I could travel the world and not find another human being that has toiled as hard as you have for a group of buddies. It's beautiful. You're a very good man. A very special person. And you're my husband. I want so very much to tell myself how lucky I am to be married and loved by such a bighearted guy. But you're not supposed to count your eggs before the chickens lay them."

Charley slipped into bed and lay still. In time he said, "By the way, I've already contacted Christie's."

"Who?'

"Not who. Christie's. The big auction house in New York City. The one that handles famous paintings, like Van Gogh's *Irises*. And boy, were they accommodating. They'd love to handle the Ermengarde Choker for us."

"The anxiety I feel is raging," Claudia said. "Damn you. What am I going to do about you?" She kicked him, gently. "I can't help but love you despite my anger."

"Sorry I've screwed up your psyche or essence or whatever."

"Come here," Claudia said. She rolled over toward him, seized him tightly in her arms and held him close. "I'm not going to ask you how much you've already invested," she whispered into his ear. "I don't want to know."

Chapter Tenty-Six

The newspaper readers of the region awoke the next morning to find the Cloverton City *Beacon* heavy with local news and pictures on the front page. The right-side top, typically used for the lead article, displayed the following three-column headline:

Rimespecker Murder Trial Ends with Charges Dismissed, Widow Absolved of Killing

On the upper left side, a detailed follow-up story about the suicide of Ruth Nettlebaum and the unearthing of the murder weapon in the Calvary Methodist Church cemetery was topped with the following two-column headline:

**Forensic Analysis of Weapon
Affirms Guilt of Widow's Lover**

A picture of Police Chief Morris holding the gun's flower-pot crypt in his right hand and leaning on the tombstone with his left hand shared space between the two lead articles with a youthful photo of Ruth Nettlebaum that Carney Cox had finagled from the captain's cache of evidence from the Nettlebaum house.

Below the newspaper's fold, next to a picture of Tony Paluto dressed in his climbing gear, was a three-column headline that read:

*Former Rimespecker Chauffeur
Set to Climb Locust Tree in Hunt
For Lost Jewel-studded Choker*

A small one-column story in the bottom-left corner, the kind journalists tag "a stick of type"—meaning two inches deep—rounded out the local news on the front page. Its tiny headline read:

**Cloverton Hospital Upgrades
Condition of Late Senator's son**

Tony was quick to read the story about himself before he passed it around to others crowding into the valley of the Bitterlick. Despite the roughness, wetness and jaggedness of the terrain, people were pouring into the area. Many were newcomers attracted by the inordinate amount of publicity through newspaper articles, the broadcast media and the Internet, finally prompting Chief Morris to send more men. In fact, he requested help from the State Police, who accommodated him with a unit of troopers. Unexpectedly, sightseers were tramping in from miles far south of the valley, where the land was flat and the fields high with a full-summer's growth of grasses and weeds—dry growth that crunched under the feet of the tramping trekkers. Pollen poured into the air as fields of goldenrod were agitated.

Bitterlick Creek was alive with color and movement near the black locust tree where Tony readied himself. The morning sun had already moved from east to southeast, bringing its beams of light to the valley, brilliantly brightening the rapids with yellow-orange light that flashed and flickered on the rushing deluge. The slower waters, whose trickling rivulets flowed between and amidst rocks, picked up brilliant sparkles from the sunlight as it erased the shadow of the cliff. The dark blue-green of the deep pools, caused by whirling eddies that abutted large rocks, contrasted with the flickering and shimmering luminosity.

As in the evening, morning shadows were long, but stretched into the opposite direction. The early sunlight spread a vast assortment of silhouettes and reflections throughout the valley, making it a fairyland of shapes among the sparkles.

The most spectacular display of color came from the strata that built the cliff—a precipice formed by ancient upheaval of the earth. The layers of rock began at ground level and continued to the very top of the cliff—broad belts caused by the shifting of the earth during early formation years. They presented a display of color, now gradually being brightened by the spreading sunlight. Deep crevices between the strata created spectacular dark and light contrasts among the colorful bands as the sunlight made its turn around the cliff. Deep-red rock stretched across a layer of yellowish sienna, which rested upon a slate-blue strip of rigid stone. A dusty-purple swath lay upon a ribbon of ivory-colored rock, and a wide burnt-orange belt stretched across a streak of greenish gray. Extending outward from the others, a creamy mocha ridge appeared to be flowing and dripping, though it was as hard as granite. It shaded and darkened a violet-gray stratum beneath it. As morning advanced, the strata picked up the intricate shadow of the black locust tree that Tony was preparing to climb. The tree stood so close to the "layer cake" of rock that Tony knew he could work from either locust limbs or stone footing. "I can easily jump back and forth," he told Jimmy.

Downstream at the Silvesters' house, sightseers parked their cars wherever they could squeeze into a spot. The road in front of their house was lined with vehicles on both sides. At odd angles here and there, some early-birds had parked in the surrounding fields, now blocked in by the curb-huggers. A few presumptuous folks had even parked cars and motorcycles on the Silvesters' front lawn.

Many parents pulled strings of youngsters behind them as they hurried through Charley's and Claudia's property and the woods to the stream. Many were unprepared for the wet, rocky and muddy creek bed and banks. Few brought boots. Late summer and autumn flowers—the water-lovers who sucked moisture up through the mud and between the rocks—were heavily tread upon along the banks of the creek where vegetation had thickened as fall approached. Bur-marigolds, robin's plantains, boneset, joe-pye weeds and arrowheads were smashed by trudging and trampling feet to the dismay of the nature-loving bivouac crowd.

Fear of trouble and injury engulfed many throughout the valley when the crowd grew larger than expected and children ran about, splashed in the water and slipped on the rocks. Jimmy used his megaphone again and again to alert parents and warn youngsters. Township police lined the eastern side of the creek, that closest to Tony and his tree. Across the stream, State Police Troopers stood on guard, the distance giving them better overall perspective. In some regard, their view of Tony as he climbed would be better than those looking up from under the tree.

Tony and Jimmy were in deep conversation directly under the tree when Laura, Claudia and Charley approached, but kept their distance. All five stood on the broad, flat work-area created at the very start of Operation Bivouac. Police Chief Morris was there, too, kneeling and examining some of Tony's tools.

"On my first climb," Tony told the Birdman, "I'd rather not carry the heavy industrial flashlight. I'll save it for later, in case I have to climb again to search the deep crevices between the strata of rock." He adjusted his dark glasses, which were attached to his chinstrap and helmet. "If we're lucky, that won't be necessary. Same goes for the long-handled gripper. I'll need it when and if I have to go deep. Otherwise, I want my limbs to be as free as possible for easy maneuvering. I'll be handling a shitload of gadgets as it is." His shirt and pants were woven from a soft mesh-like, flexible material and contained no buttons or anything else that might be an impediment to smooth movement. Heavy rope girdled his waist and was already looped around a tree limb well above his head.

"Can your gripper pick up small things?" Jimmy asked.

"It's a bit longer and heavier than the kind your 90-year-old neighbor might use to grab a can of beans from the top shelf in her kitchen. But it ain't too heavy for me. It's similar to what you find in hospitals and nursing homes. Don't worry. It'll pick up the choker if we can reach it."

Laura sighted Clarence and Terry approaching from downstream, wearing high boots and splashing their way against the current. She waved and shouted "Over here!"

"We see you!" Clarence yelled in return.

Laura stepped to the edge of the flat work-area, toward the newcomers and away from the Silvesters, giving Charley a chance to talk to Claudia about something on his mind. "Has Clarence said anything to you recently about his wedding plans?" he whispered.

"No. Not really."

"Do you think, by any chance, we could get them to delay their wedding?"

"Well, they haven't set a date because of the Rimespecker kid. So what do you mean? Delay it from when?"

"I mean, put it off until maybe the middle of October. What do y'think?"

"Why?"

"I'd like their briefcase to be their wedding gift. It would be fabulous! Absolutely the most fantastic wedding gift anyone could ever receive. But I'm afraid I can't have it ready before mid-October."

"It may never be! Period!"

"Come on, now. Help me. Please. I was thinking that we could use that occasion to present all the briefcases. At the reception. Long after the actual wedding ceremony."

"Charley!"

"Our whole gang will be there, but not a big mess of other people. Remember, this is a small backyard wedding with a reception in our house."

"You don't take away from someone's special occasion in that way. It would be most inappropriate to give gifts to others. The day belongs to the bride and groom, not to Laura or Tony or the Rimespecker kid, for God's sake."

"We can do it if we handle it right. Blow the trumpets and make the big presentation to the bride and groom. Then blow the trumpets again and announce that Clarence and Terry want to share their special day with their friends. Make all the briefcases a part of their beautiful, happy day. Besides, this is a special group. They all love each other and would be thrilled for each other. It would be an explosion of joy!"

"You're forgetting the hen who failed to lay her eggs."

Charley ignored the remark. He said, "We could tell Clarence that the colorful red and yellow leaves on the trees in mid-October would make a much more beautiful setting for their wedding. The sugar maples peak about then. Brilliant orange-red."

"Or you could send Jordan Rimespecker on another risky mission sure to injure him again. That'll delay things."

"Now you're getting nasty."

"Shush! They're coming. This is no place to talk about your damn briefcases."

As Claudia and Charley greeted Clarence and Terry, Laura was pointing toward Tony, who was pulling himself up to the first set of limbs on the black locust. Many in the crowd clapped, and a fair-haired youth yelled, "There goes Spiderman!" Tony turned and waved to the growing throng after securing his feet in solid crotches among the next cluster of limbs.

"I won't be greetin' y'all again until I come down," Tony called out to the crowd as three TV crews aimed their cameras at him and countless others snapped photos. "From this point up, it's all business," he added. Turning toward the tree trunk, he then tested his cellphone and radio-backup device by calling Jimmy on both. He took a firm hold onto his rope as the Birdman gave a final wave from the ground. Tony didn't look back. His well-developed biceps gave his arms the strength to pull his weight up to the next set of limbs. A creak and a crack didn't trouble him; he simply shifted weight in accordance to messages from his well-trained ears and feet. Through years of climbing, he had trained his body parts to react to cues from the trees. He recalled his youthful years when he did fall and break bones.

He gave only a cursory look at the stratified vertical mass to his side as he concentrated on the tree, knowing that a scrutiny of the layered rock would come later, if necessary. At one point, however, he was jolted by sparkles and turned quickly to find the glitter was only mica within an outcropping of schist.

In time, his careful and deliberate climbing carried him to the point where he could see above the heap of boulders on the other side of the creek—the lower embankment in West Bitterlick Township. A vast view of treetops suddenly sprang into his vision. The western horizon became a giant brush of feathery green with occasional taller trees poking the sky here and there.

To the north lay Cloverton City, its tall buildings blurred by a morning haze. And to the south, fields of newly plowed earth were ready for the sowing of winter wheat. They joined patches of alfalfa, stubble from harvested corn, and the remains of soybeans to create a patchwork that reminded Tony of his grandmother's quilts. The squares of tan, dark green, yellow and deep brown rolled over hills and flowed into valleys as if a giant quilt were being waved in air.

Tony's communication devices hung on braided string that allowed them to be slipped in and out of pockets with ease. When he sighted the crashed drone hanging in the tree a few feet above his head, he stopped climbing and pulled forth his cellphone.

"Mr. Birdman, that snooping drone that crashed into this tree is right above my head. Do you want me to lower it on a wire, drop it into a net, or bring it down with me?"

"What's easiest for you?"

"Even though it's small, I'd rather not be burdened with it if I'm scanning crevices on the way down. There's plenty of netting down there not far from your feet. But if I simply drop it into a net, it's gonna get banged up again and again as it bounces off limbs and branches long before you catch it. I'll tell yous what, I'll give the drone a good onceover on this trip, but use my spool of wire later, maybe on the trek down. That way I can lower it gently."

"Okay. That'll work."

Tony tossed his rope over a limb high above his head and pulled himself up to another crotch. He repeated that and lifted his body just above the drone, close enough for easy examination. He phoned Jimmy.

"What's up?"

"The drone's a typical four-legged, spider-like creature with initials carved into its square, deep-blue belly."

"Initials?"

"Yeah. H. M. M."

"Hah! It figures. Hans Mahler Melhausen. That Swiss bastard. I figured he was too slick to be an honest climber. What about the claw?"

"That's exactly what it is—a mean-lookin' claw with six digits that have sharply pointed tips. A grabbing device. Looks like it's separately powered by a battery. Probably dead now. Yous can play around with it after I lower it. I'm sure it was built to pluck the choker out of the nest."

"Now, go find the elusive Ermengarde Choker."

"That's my mission, sir," Tony said sharply, as if addressing a military commander. "To the top of the tree, I go!"

The tree was steady for many more minutes, but began to sway as Tony reached the upper quarter. Swaying gradually increased as he climbed higher and higher. He was well aware that the upper branches of black locust trees grew narrow, that at the very top they became switches that flip and flap in the breeze. Tony knew what lay ahead.

Across the creek, the state troopers who stood among the onlookers could see Tony easily, high among the feathery branches. The Silvesters, the Barnes and others, who looked up from under the tree, got only glances of him now and again as he pulled his way up.

Suddenly the eagles' nest was in his sightline. He leaned toward it, only to be flung back by a gust of wind. He settled down and waited. When all was calm, he again bent and stretched his body toward the large nest, not expecting to see the choker, for he was well aware that if that band of glittering gems was in the nest it was well hidden. He had viewed the Internet and the bivouac monitors too many times. Fighting off a touch of unease, he told himself to take his time. He waited until the rows of pinnate leafs lay perfectly still, then leaned into the nest and fingered its makeup of twigs, leaves, pods, grasses and husk. His eyes worked as hard perusing as his glove-covered fingers did searching. A large piece of cornhusk grabbed his attention, but no choker lay beneath it. His search was thorough and ended when he seized his phone and called Jimmy.

"What's up, Tony?"

"I ain't found nothin'. It's not in the nest. I didn't expect it would be. I'll scan the rocks on the way down, but I'm pretty sure I'll need to hike up again with bigger and better tools."

"You were hoping for an easy go-of-it."

"Of course. But hidden behind that hope was realistic doubt. You, Mr. Birdman, might as well prepare people. The fewer dejected faces I'll have to confront the better."

"There's a growing bunch of gloomy faces staring at me right now, our close friends among them. I guess my expression tells the tale. The guys behind the television cameras look devastated. Oops! Claudia just stuck her tongue out at Charley. Apparently, I communicate well without words."

"I want my long-handled grabber and heavy flashlight. Ready them for me. Hand them right to me, so I can do a quick turnaround and leap toward the heavens. By the way, it's a beautiful sight up there." Tony glanced up. "Oops! I forget the fuc ... freakin' drone. Hurried right past it."

"Forget it. It can rot up there for all I care. We have to concentrate on one thing."

"I'll get it later. Right now I need two things."

"Grabber and flashlight. Right?"

Tony didn't follow his own script. When he reached the ground and eyed so many questioning faces, he smiled, waved and called out, "It ain't over yet, my friends. Hold tight! We'll find it."

Jimmy hung the square, boxy, power-laden light around Tony's neck where it lay against his well-developed chest. Police Chief Morris thrust the grabber into Tony's hand, stopping the climber's leap briefly while he fastened it to his waistband.

"Up and away!" Tony yelled as he secured his feet on the tree trunk, yanked his rope and flew upward like a bantam-weight Tarzan. He climbed but a short distance before switching on the light and aiming its high beam into a crevice that offered glimpses of bird dirt, cobwebs and a small snake skeleton. Tony judged the stratum's overhang to be too narrow to hold him, so he pushed and pulled himself up the tree, skipping small fractures and stopping at a solid limb that beckoned him, for it leaned right into a wide cleft. He pulled himself belly-down like a lizard out on the limb until it creaked and bowed slightly. Using his forearms, he pushed his torso high enough to free the flashlight from between his chest and the tree limb. A little skillful wiggling and lifting allowed him to support his body while he secured the flashlight and turned it on. He saw bats hanging upside down inside the chasm, moved the light-beam to and fro below them, saw nothing sparkling, and quickly backed off, scooting backward on the limb.

Tony rested briefly, leaning back against the trunk and stretching his legs out on a fat limb. But his anxiety pumped his adrenalin and started him climbing a bit too soon, according to rules once set by his favorite instructor of long ago. Next stop was a thin stratum of greenish-gray rock that arched slightly as it spread across a narrow opening. Tony thought it was worth probing because a dip in the band opened a basin capable to catching falling objects. He readied himself to jump, but stopped abruptly and swung back on his rope when he spotted a hornets' nest hanging below the basin—a nest with hornets flying all about it. "Son of a bitch!" he barked to himself.

Up he climbed, maneuvering to another locust branch that neared a parallel layer of rock—this dark-reddish layer projecting from the precipice far enough to catch falling objects and giving Tony hope. It was also sturdy enough to hold a crawling man the size of Tony, and the crevice above the slab was wide enough to allow mobility for working arms. Tony found that, with care, he could even project his head part-way into the fissure. He was certain that no other crevice in the entire precipice was open wide enough to allow even partial entry of his helmet.

Tony did a lot of squirming on the rocky surface, but finally lay in a workable but awkward position—workable enough to operate his grabber in several directions. He poked and prodded in wet and sticky wads of rotted leaves and other debris that the wind had obviously blown into the fracture over time. The only evidence of human-made items was a red-but-filthy, deflated balloon twisted in the tail of a smashed kite. Tony jabbed and poked at the shattered remains until he could see beyond the splintered pieces. His searching eyes and the strong beam of light were not enough to carry his view deep into that direction because of a gradual dip. Such a slope downward could carry an object into oblivion.

Still hoping, Tony squiggled and squirmed into a new prone position where the stratum he lay upon extended much farther into the chasm before the escarpment slowly descended. As he moved his flashlight, he suddenly caught sight of brilliant sparkles of white, red and green in the beam of light. He was so shaken that he actually thought his heart had stopped beating. He made an effort to breathe hard as tingling raced through his body. He also made a strong effort to calm himself, deliberately closing his eyes and counting slowly to 10. When he lifted his eyelids, the brilliant sparkles were still there, so dazzling in their glitter as to be unmistakable. Tony knew he had found the Ermengarde Choker; it's deep location, he surmised, the result of heavy rain and wind, possibly violent storms. His greatest fear? That he could nudge the choker, causing it to slip away and slide down the slope, never to be seen again. The dripping wetness of everything within the crevice troubled him. He kissed the gripping device and prayed for just the right touch when it and the choker made contact—not too hard, gentle at first, and secure in its grasp. After a deep sigh, he examined the device carefully, pulled its trigger again and again, slid his fingers along the rod, and moved the grasping clasp back and forth.

Tony's first attempt went awry. The rod was long enough to reach the choker, but as the clasp began to pinch on the slippery silver metal between the gems, the choker popped out, springing up like a greased marble between a person's fingers.

Frustrated to the nth degree, Tony lay quietly for minute after minute, attempting to think peaceful thoughts of mallard ducks floating among lily pads in a park pond. Forcing such thoughts, however, didn't calm his tight muscles. He switched to sheep in a pasture, but a slight spasm bounced his left knee, which he grabbed and held tightly. In time, he regained his confidence and began to toy with his grasping device.

Finally certain of his readiness, Tony made a painful effort to stretch his body, particularly his arms, hoping to add another inch or two to his reach. Little by little he inched the long, narrow tool toward the choker. Just as it touched the jewelry, a muscle spasm attacked his right arm, jerking the clasp and sending the choker slightly farther down the slope. Tony cried.

Meanwhile, down in the valley, a monstrous crowd had gathered around Jimmy and the locust tree where reporters pumped the Birdman and others with questions. Police on both sides of the creek were struggling to keep order. Charley, Claudia, Laura, Clarence and Terry stayed as close to Jimmy as possible, realizing he needed their support. At times, however, Claudia drifted into the crowd for fear a reporter might have recognized her and would ask questions she had no desire to answer. But she always worked her way back, feeling for Jimmy, who was being pummeled with queries.

Although television and the Internet kept Jordan informed to a degree, Uncle Clarry used an iPhone to relay personal pictures and details to him at the hospital. The boy's favorite nurse had supplied pillows to prop up an iPad on his bed.

Carney Cox of the Cloverton City *Beacon* had pushed his way into the front line of reporters and called out loudly to Jimmy: "You haven't heard from Paluto in a helluva long time. Are you worried?"

"Concerned, of course," Jimmy answered. "But when Tony's working hard, he gets mighty intense and concentrates on the task, forgetting secondary needs."

"Have you tried to reach him?"

"Oh, yes. Again and again, but he's not answering. I'm guessing his hands are full."

"John Pawling of the BBC," called out another newsman, identifying himself. "I haven't had luck pinning down the exact worth of the Ermengarde. I wonder if you might enlighten me, Mr. Barnes."

"I wish I could, but we've had the same difficultly. It hasn't been appraised in years."

"I spoke with Karl Ludwig in Geneva, who brokered the deal for Rimespecker. He said his last recorded figure was much too old and worthless. In line with today's money, he guessed that its worth had quadrupled, at least, since the early days when it passed through his hands."

"My colleague, Charles Silvester, mentioned that Christie's, the auction house in New York, is doing some preliminary studies."

"Preliminary to what?" Pawling asked.

Jimmy glanced about and looked confused. "Frankly, I don't know. I can't answer you." He could not find Charley anywhere.

"About the eagles!" shouted a thin, youthful reporter, who was squeezed among bulkier newsmen. "Lester Parker from *Bird Life* magazine," he called out. "Could you tell me if you think your bald eagles will return?"

"Ah!" exclaimed Jimmy. "A question about birds! I do much better with birds than with gems. I suspect they might return, unless we've traumatized them. But you probably know that."

"Yes, but I needed a quote from you, Mr. Birdman." Parker grinned.

A broad-shouldered, bull-faced reporter from the *Washington Post* was the next person to identify himself, giving his name as Harry Marintini. "The choker's been exposed to the elements for considerable time," he commented. "Are you worried about it being tarnished, scratched or broken?"

"Not at all," Jimmy replied. "Those gems are harder than anything they touch. A diamond will cut just about any surface. As for the silver setting, yeah, it'll tarnish, but polish right up. Even a scratch can be buffed away."

"Vicky Flood from *Philly Dot Com*," called out a stocky woman with a mop of curly amber hair atop her head. She pushed herself forward. "If Mr. Paluto finds the choker, what happens to it next?"

"That's up to the estate of Ruth Nettlebaum."

"Her estate?"

"I can refer you to her attorney. He's the Rimespecker family lawyer, provided by her friend."

"What exactly does her estate contain?"

"Her house and little else. I understand she left no will. That may mean her few holdings will go to the state. You should really talk to Peter Dexter of Dewill, Boyton and Dexter. The choker has its own documentation. Just like on your insurance papers, a beneficiary is listed on the dotted line."

Vicky Flood stepped closer to Jimmy and squawked, "And whose name is on that dotted line?"

"Why not get that information first hand from Mr. Dexter?"

Still squawking, Flood, asked, "Is it her cousin, Claudia Silvester?"

"I've been told so, but that's third-hand information." Jimmy suddenly jumped. "We've got a call!" he yelled. Nervously, he grabbed his select cell as it vibrated. "Yes, Tony?"

"The tip end is in my sight," Tony reported. "I think I can grab it, but I'll need some things. I don't wanna come down 'cause I'm in a difficult prone position. Frankly, I don't wanna shift any major part of my body. Send Musky up to the third level. It's marked in red on the large scroll. He's the best y'got down there. Have him bring cable and bracing hardware, pole extension parts, rigging hardware, and number three size saws with scabbards."

"You need a saw?"

"I'm gonna use tree wood to build a brace for my elbow and forearm. Something I can fasten down to rock and lean on firmly. I'll tell Musky how to cut the pieces. I need a steady aim if I'm gonna grab this thing by its tail. I can't allow the slightest twitch. Aiming becomes more difficult as I extend the distance. And I have no choice but to lengthen the gripping pole."

"I don't like the odds."

"Oh, hell, I'll get the damn thing. I ain't gonna fail. No way! Fear not, Mr. Birdman! Fear not!"

* * *

More than an hour later, Tony followed Musky, a musclebound dwarf shaped like a shrunken mesomorph, down to ground level and the cheering crowd. Each carried a sack of tools and a few lengthy poles and extension pieces that they dropped quickly.

"I have it!" yelled Tony. When his feet felt securely affixed to the earth, he pulled the Ermengarde Choker from his pocket and waved it in the air to the shouts and cries of the swarming mob. A group of boy scouts pushed their way toward him, surrounded him, lifted him in the air, and carried him through the horde to the shouts of "Bravo!" and "Yay Tony!"

Tears flowed from Charley's eyes. Caught in a swirling mob, he stretched his neck and looked for Claudia, but couldn't find her.

Chapter Twenty-Seven

Another transformation of the Silvesters' backyard reached its apex on the Saturday of Clarence's and Terry's wedding. Not only were all signs of the bivouac gone, but new thick-and-healthy sod had been laid, turning the acres into rich green grass from the house all the way to the vivid colors of the woods. An altar, constructed of rosewood and oak, reached up from a slight mound of freshly dug and smoothly packed earth circled by a thick rim of white and yellow pansies.

The far background, that at the very end of the Silvesters' property, was nature's pure, untouched contribution to the wedding scene. It was composed of the reds, yellows, oranges and russets of the deciduous or leaf-baring trees of mid-October at their peak of autumn brilliance.

Warm fall weather delighted the wedding party and its close associates—a small group of eight who had become a circle of intimate soulmates during an unbelievably active summer they now called the bivouac season.

A white-carpet runner split the verdant grass and extended from the back of the house to the altar. Tested again and again, because of Charley's insistence, the runner tripped none of several installers forced to practice the hesitation steps used by most brides and bridesmaids. The entire strip of carpeting was edged on both sides by pots of gardenias in full bloom, the strong fragrance of their pure white flowers enveloping the entire acreage and surely exciting the bees in the expanded apiary. Plant nurserymen had created an entire garden of late summer and autumn flowers between the woods and the altar, stretching the width of the property. Tree ferns and other tropical plants, in ornate terra-cotta pots, were arranged in groupings to the north and south of the altar.

An arching trellis of latticework intertwined with climbing vines and flowers had been constructed about a dozen yards in front of the altar, just high enough to force the bride to duck slightly as she passed through and under. Charley had asked for heavenly-blue morning glories, knowing Terry's fondness for them, but was reminded that they would not bloom for an afternoon wedding. Moonflowers had been vetoed too, for they unfold in the darkness of night. The nursery went to extremes to locate enough late-blooming clematis and Australian bower vine to entwine on the trellis with other autumn flowers.

Charley spared nothing for this so-called simple wedding. Not pleased with any local musical talent, he hired a combo from New York City, agreeing to up the ante if they'd play certain traditional selections on his list. He even tossed in extra for transportation and sleep-over costs, not realizing—or not caring—that the band had already included those costs in its billing.

Several days before the plant nurserymen were invited to dramatically transform the back acreage into a Garden of Eden, Charley had hired the Universal Fence Company, Inc., to install new fencing around the entire grounds. He did this despite his plans, sharply implanted in his brain, to soon expand his holdings to the north and south of his present property lines. The stark-white plank fencing stood out for its newness and fresh paint, its installation being another salute to the Exton-Smythe wedding. Yet to Charley it was also another glance into future decision-making. He was pleased, but still unsure about the types of fencing or enclosures he wanted for the eventual Claudia Greyhound Retreat, his working title for the adoption and care facility he envisioned for retired racing dogs and others greyhounds in need.

Since the wedding rehearsal had been held at the church, neither the bride nor the groom had seen the finished outdoor site until now. They had studied Charley's sketches, but now, each took a separate tour of the transformed yard and garden, and each was overwhelmed by the beauty. Charley and Claudia received heart-felt thanks again and again.

Keeping true to their pledge, Terry and Clarence had invited only 24 people, figuring about a dozen individuals would sit in chairs arranged in rows on each side of the white carpet. A few early guests arrived at 1:30 p.m. for the 2 o'clock wedding and were immediately seated on the bride's side of the white carpet by an extremely attentive usher or groomsman named Tony Paluto, who was well-fitted in proper afternoon wedding attire—including cutaway coat, crimson double-breasted vest, silver-gray ascot tie and pinstriped trousers. Minutes later, two old high-school chums of Clarence were seated by Tony on the other side.

More guests began to arrive as Laura Barnes, the maid of honor and only female attendant in the bridal party, kept fussing with her blue-taffeta dress upstairs in the master bedroom—a room of Oriental décor, featuring a Chinese motif on the furniture, ebony carvings, Ming vases and Tibetan tapestries. Although she knew Laura for a relatively short time, Terry had chosen her over old school chums because of her "blithe spirit and sparkle." Affinity had brought the two women especially close as the bivouac grew to its climax. Laura's buoyancy fed Terry's need to cavort. Now, in this Oriental bedroom, Laura turned away from the full-length mirror and gazed at Terry when the bride sought approval. "One more overall look, please," urged Terry, who wore a full-length silk gown featuring a fitted bodice with a V-neckline and low torso trimmed with French illusion, hand-detailed rose petals and tiny flower pearls. A crown of pearls held her fingertip four-tiered veil.

"You look beautiful!" Laura said enthusiastically. "Absolutely beautiful!"

"My tears are ruining my makeup," Terry said as she wiped her cheek. She put her hands on her waist. "I've lost several pounds. Can you tell?"

"Believe me, Terry, you're the perfect bride in all respects."

"You might think I was a kid, the way I'm blubbering." She blew her nose. "My God, I'm a middle-age woman getting hitched to a guy I've known for years."

"It's still your first marriage. And it means a lot to you."

Terry looked at Laura and gradually began to smile. "Yes, you're right. It's my first. And I've long wanted it. I guess I have a right to cry a little."

The groom and his best man arrived already dressed in their wedding outfits. Young Jordan looked particularly handsome in his cutaway coat and ascot necktie. His entire trappings had been cut to fit his slender body. The teenager's unruly blond hair was neatly trimmed and severely combed 1920s-style, turning him into a figure from an F. Scott Fitzgerald novel. Clarence looked his best, but was troubled by the slight curvature of his spine. How badly he wanted to stand perfectly erect for his bride. His mood was a peculiar mix—happy for the occasion but disconcerted that the entire wedding, down to the smallest detail, was being paid for by Charley and Claudia. He kept telling himself to be grateful. After all, Terry had no family to provide a suitable, let alone lavish, wedding. And these nuptials comprised a meager event for a millionaire.

Clarence and Jordan walked into a house that was nearly gutted of its regular furniture. The living and dining rooms were readied for the 4 p.m. wedding reception. Silver and white were the featured colors—a theme that lightened and brightened the rooms. The caterer and wedding planner had shared ideas so that the serving utensils, dishes, flat-wear, candlesticks and all other table pieces went well with the overall décor of the rooms, including the silver streamers with white ball-fringe that flowed from mid-ceiling of both rooms to the windowsills and cornices.

"Don't be upset if I mess up the toast," Jordan whispered. "I never gave one before."

"Don't sweat it, kid," Clarence said. He grinned and placed his hand on the teenager's shoulder. "You could mumble, misquote and go blank and I'd still appreciate it."

Hoping to disappear until called to the alter, the groom and best man aimed for the stairs, but were suddenly stopped when a guest came in from the backyard complaining about the bees buzzing about her head.

"Y'know, y'gotta lotta bees flying around out there," said the guest, Thelma Harper, a chubby, gray-haired woman and friend of the bride. She and Terry had been coffee-house buddies when they both worked for The Java Hut many years ago. "I'm not up t'getting stung. But even if they play nice, nobody likes 'em buzzing about their ears."

Clarence immediately headed for the backdoor, but was stopped by Charley in the kitchen. "I'll take care of it," Charley insisted. "You're the groom. Get out of here! Go upstairs, but stay away from the bride." He grabbed Jordan by his shoulder and whispered into the boy's ear. "Take care of him. That's what best men are supposed to do. Tie him to a bedpost if you have to." After a moment's reflection on flowers and honeybees, Charley called out to those gathered in the house. "Stay indoors, everybody. Don't let anyone out the backdoor until I say so."

Outside, Charley was devastated when he saw other guests moving because of bees. One elderly gentleman, who remained seated, was using his bare hand to swat at a pestering bee. "Don't do that, sir," Charley said as he approached the guest. "That'll anger the bee, and she might sting you. She won't hurt you if you leave her alone."

Hurrying down the white carpet, Charley came to a quick stop at the arched trellis when he heard it humming with bees. "Oh, my God," he mumbled to himself. He glanced about, looking for Tony. "What the hell are we gonna do?" He pictured the bride getting her veil caught in a tangle of vines and bees as she passed under the arch.

Suddenly honeybees seemed to be buzzing about everywhere, and Charley blamed himself. Not only had he greatly increased the bee population, but he had ordered the creation of a lavish garden of beauty and fragrance. "You idiot, you! What were you thinking?"

"Yo! Boss!" Tony came rushing from the woods. "We got a big problem. Wait 'til y'see what I just seen."

"Tell me about it," Charley said cynically. "I'm well aware of the bees. They're chasing the guests into the house."

As Tony approached, he said, "I suspect it's a bigger problem then you realize." He stood still and breathed hard, attempting to catch his breath. "They're doing that dividing thing they do when it's time to multiply."

"It's called swarming."

"Yeah! Well, them buggers are swarming."

"Y'gotta be kidding!"

"No I ain't! There's a big mess of them hanging on that bright red tree." Tony pointed directly toward a tall sugar maple growing at the edge of the woods. "Right straight ahead. Down from that there altar. But that's not all, there's a smaller mess of 'em on the back of the altar." He pointed again. "The preacher's not gonna like that."

"Holy shit!" Charley began to walk toward the altar. "Well, we got two things going on at once here. Swarming bees aren't going for the flowers. The flowers must be attracting bees from the remainder of the colony."

"I'm thinking you shouldn't have gotten all them new bees. And then them flowers."

"Stupidity on my part. My dichotomy."

"Your what?"

"Split thinking. It's a problem I have. A dichotomy. I'm totally wrapped up with my honeybees and the future colony I plan to build, and thinking of nothing else. Then again, another time, I'm planning this beautiful setting for Clarence's wedding, and thinking of nothing else. I get transfixed on one thing and forget the other exists."

Reaching the altar, Charley grunted swear words as he viewed the swarm.

"The other swarm's much bigger," Tony said.

"I don't have time to even try to move the swarms back to the hives. That's a big operation, and I might need help. The wedding starts in a matter of minutes. Besides, there are all these other bees flying around sucking nectar and gathering pollen from the flowers. The only thing we can do is move the wedding indoors. God, help me! Claudia's gonna kill me. And the bride? Oh my God! She must be in tears."

Charley took a hasty look at the swarm on the sugar maple. It hung on a lower limb like a giant, oval balloon with thousands of small moving parts.

"Ye gads!" Charley exclaimed. "Come on! Let's get back to the house. We have to set things up for an indoor wedding." Perspiration was making him uncomfortable, especially because he was dressed in a suit, tie and stiff-collared shirt. Bubbles of sweat appeared on his forehead. He pulled the fancy, decorative handkerchief from his suitcoat pocket and wiped his face. Salty moisture between his collar and his reddening neck irritated his skin. "Crisakes, I'm sweating in October!" He ran toward the backdoor, and Tony followed.

Inside the house, a small crowd gathered around Charley, who was red-faced and panting. Jimmy, the Birdman, looked him up and down, then asked, "Are you okay? You don't look it. What can I do?"

"He's got a case of dichotomy," Tony said.

Jimmy glanced from Tony to Charley. "He what?"

"I've gotta figure things out," Charley said. He talked to the crowd: "Will you give me space? Please. Clear away from me." He walked into the dining room, stopped and stared from one end of the long dining table to the other. It stretched from where he stood all the way through both rooms, stopping at the front wall of the living room. It was beautifully set with white linen tablecloths and napkins, white china edged in silver, crystal goblets that sparkled, and slender white candles in ornate silver holders.

"It might not be orthodox, but it's beautiful enough for the actual wedding ceremony," Charley whispered to Tony.

"A sit-down wedding?" Tony questioned.

"People sit at a church wedding, don't they?"

"I think they stand when the bride enters. But not at a table set for a feast."

"Everyone can push his chair back and stand at the proper moments—if necessary. We can explain it to the minister, and he can direct them. What else can we do? We don't have a choice. If we're late with the ceremony, we'll push the reception dinner off to later."

"Where y'gonna put the band?" Tony asked.

"It's a small combo. We can squeeze 'em into that corner, over there." Charley pointed to the north corner of the living room. "I gotta go upstairs and see the bride," he said as guests began to crowd around and ask questions. "You stay here, Tony, and start to seat people." He raised his voice: "Listen, everybody! We have to move the wedding indoors. Please have patience. Mr. Paluto, here, will take care of you."

As he started to climb the stairs, Charley looked back and saw the minister, the Reverend Nathan K. Inglesby, enter through the front doorway. A stocky, round-faced man with a horseshoe-shaped rim of hair around his bald crown, the Reverend Mr. Inglesby looked confused by the milling crowd until Tony took his hand and started talking. Charley hurried up the steps, assured that Tony would explain the situation to the pastor. Upstairs, he knocked on the door to the master bedroom.

Claudia answered, opening the door slowly, and giving her husband a look of despair. "Oh, it's you."

"Let me in," he said as he pushed the door.

Charley found Laura sitting in the corner on a chest adorned by Chinese figures. Holding her head in her hands, she stared at the floor and looked disheartened. Claudia sat on the corner of the bed, attempting to comfort and placate a wounded and irate bride who was stretched out on the comforter and heaving as she cried hysterically.

"Oh, Terry," Claudia said. "You're ruining your beautiful gown. You shouldn't be lying on it. And the train is hanging onto the floor all twisted up. Come on, now, get yourself up."

"Everything's ruined!" Terry bellowed.

"No way!" Charley barked. "The wedding's about to begin! We're holding it inside in the beautifully decorated white-and-silver rooms downstairs. Come on! Hurry up! The minister's waiting! We're all set to go!"

Terry managed to lift her head, then her torso. She looked bewildered.

Laura digested every word from Charley's mouth and was immediately on her feet, bouncing about in her usual frisky but assertive way and pressing Terry to shape up and prepare to march down the steps.

* * *

Terry's ninth grade history teacher, Fanny Minkwater, a silver-haired, buxom woman of 68 years, had just finished singing *Because*, a song not usually in the combo's repertoire, when Laura appeared at the top of the stairs. The combo, known as the Bronx Boomers, quickly switched to music with a definite cadence as Laura made her first move downward.

Eliminating the hesitation step, the maid of honor took each step carefully, holding her gown up slightly and gripping her nosegay of violets with her left hand only. She was relieved to reach the bottom step and the security of the ground floor. As she made her way to her seat at the table, the Bronx Boomers prepared to switch to Richard Wagner's *Bridal Chorus* from the opera *Lohengrin*, more commonly known as *Here Comes the Bride* by church-wedding-goers in the western world.

The bride appeared at the top of the steps a moment before a member of the Bronx combo trumpeted the fanfare from *Lohengrin*. She carried a cascade bouquet of white carnations and a white orchid. Everyone seemed to hold his or her breath as Terry took her time, tried to stand up straight, grabbed the railing only twice and reached the newel post without dropping her flowers. Clarence's elderly mother, seated near the front door in her wheelchair, shook but managed to rise to her feet and clap while smiling broadly. Everyone followed. Tony left his assigned place and lifted the train of the bridal gown as Terry made her way to the groom and his best man. Clarence and Jordan stood across the table from the Reverend Inglesby, who wore his clerical gown and collar for the ceremony.

"Please, dear friends," the minister said. "You may be seated."

Surprisingly, everyone remained standing as if in tribute to an agonized bride and her groom. The honeybees had destroyed the outdoor observance, but they had built a plaintive warmness among the guests, each of whom was touched in a heartfelt way by the circumstances.

Terry's feelings of turmoil were somewhat placated by the dazzling surroundings and smiling guests. Her stomach was still tight, her nerves on edge, and her chattering teeth held firm by a locked jaw. But the glamour and warmth of the occasion were slowly dissolving her anguish.

The Reverend Inglesby's place at the table was between the living and dining rooms. He spoke in deep tones that carried well in both rooms: "Dearly beloved, we are gathered together here in the sight of God and in the presence of these witnesses, to join this man and this woman in holy matrimony, which is ..."

Charley's mind was elsewhere. His thoughts crowded out the minister's words. Visions of the contents of each briefcase invaded his brain again and again. He couldn't escape them. In fact, he couldn't slow down or speed up the images, even when he tried to tie words and phrases to them—tributes he planned for his presentation.

The minister continued: "Clarence, wilt thou have this woman to be thy wedded wife, to love together in ..."

Jordan was mentally rehearsing his toast to the newlyweds, something he had been doing for days. So, he gave little attention to Mr. Inglesby's liturgical pronouncements until he felt a sudden twitch in his right arm as the time for ring presentation neared.

Clarence repeated the minister's words: "I, Clarence, take thee, Terry, to be my wedded wife, to have and to hold, from this day forward ..."

Jordan pulled the ring out of his pocket with sudden gusto and carefully passed it to Clarence as he concentrated on the moment. His serious expression finally dissolved when he saw a broad smile on the groom's face, for Uncle Clarry's happiness was also his happiness. He smiled, too, as he intently listened while the minister proclaimed the couple man and wife. And he felt a surge of warmth as the bride and groom kissed with fervor. Terry's sublime expression revealed a radical change in her mood.

* * *

The wedding-planners had suggested not using the kitchen for food preparation because of expected high movement of traffic in and out of the house through the backdoor. This turned out to serve the situation well. The caterers pulled their truck onto the front lawn at 4:30, having been warned of a possible delay in the wedding ceremony.

The Bronx combo had been instructed to play Felix Mendelssohn's *Wedding March* as the guests left the ceremony and proceeded up the aisle, or in this case, the white carpet. No one had instructed them otherwise, although they realized that no place for a recessional existed in the crowded house. Guessing, that for some reason, Mendelssohn was not to be left out of the occasion, they burst forth with the *Wedding March* as the waiters paraded into the house. Many of the guests were amused. Some giggled.

A team of five waiters, each wearing a black blazer with red bowtie, carried serving trays and large covered dishes through narrow space down both sides of the long table. Immediately, escarole and cucumber salads, dotted with tiny black olives and cherry tomatoes, were positioned at each place-setting while the entrée and its side dishes were grouped in serving platters placed here and there along the lengthy table. Claudia and Laura had helped Terry select food they believed would appeal to all the guests: roasted boneless chicken with mushroom sauce, carrots candied in pineapple marmalade, scalloped potatoes and green-bean casserole. Laura's suggestion of fried okra had been vetoed.

After a brief blessing by the minister, champagne was poured at each sitting. Just about everyone stared at Jordan as they seized their Waterford Elegance glasses. The 16-year-old best man was well aware that it was his time to toast the bride and groom.

Jordan stood, lifted his wine glass, cleared his throat and began: "Let us all stand and raise our glasses to the bride and groom." He held his glass high as the chairs scraped the floor as everyone rose. "We salute two beautiful people; may they be endlessly happy together. Their marriage is built on fond memories of each other, giving them a head start and an opportunity for building beautiful days together for years to come. Let this toast remind them that ..."

The teenager suddenly went blank. Everyone at the reception felt uncomfortable and mentally urged his recovery. As they pulled for him, he perspired slightly at the temples.

"I don't know if it's proper," Jordan finally said, "but I can't give this toast without making it personal. Please forgive me if I'm out of line." He cleared his throat again. "The groom is my Uncle Clarry, who practically raised me from childhood. He's not a blood relative, but just a kind soul who gave much of his life to helping a struggling kid in a dysfunctional family. I doubt that I would be here today if not for him."

Jordan choked up. His eyes moistened.

"My Uncle Clarry helped me with my homework," Jordan began again. "He gave me my first baseball, took me to the zoo, showed me how to grow a lima bean in wet cotton, patched up my cuts and bruises, packed lunches for after soccer games, gave me books to read, taught me the names of all the different trees, and kept my secrets. He's now married to a warm and wonderful woman who has reached out to me. I know that the bride is usually given away by her father. But in a strange sort of way, I feel that I'm giving away my Uncle Clarry to the bride. Yet I know it isn't so. In truth, I'm gaining an Aunt Terry. She's welcomed me as a part of her new family." Jordan raised his glass. "To the bride! We salute you! May the bride and groom have endless days of happiness, yet have patience with each other during inevitable dips. Here! Here! To the bride and groom!"

Jordan sipped his champagne, and all others joined in. He could feel his racing heart as he slid into his seat. Those around him tried to hearten him with smiles, raised fingers, nods and high fives. Terry threw him a kiss, and Clarence punched the air with his fist, smiled broadly and winked at him.

Chapter Twenty-Eight

Charley had planned to ask the newly married couple and a small group of bivouac buddies to remain after the wedding reception for a special presentation. But he kept changing his mind on how and when to distribute his gift briefcases. Surely he should present the newlyweds with their gift first. Right? After all, this was their special day, their celebration. Then again, why not build up to their surprise by giving to the others first? Wouldn't holding theirs to last make for a resounding climax? The debate in his head went on and on.

After the six tables that had comprised the one long table were cleared away, dancing and partying continued for hours and Charley became more and more reluctant to ask anyone to leave. As he leaned against the newel post and watched young and old couples dance, he realized that unless he became a bouncer, some guests, other than the bivouac group, would still be present until the end. "So what!" he muttered to himself as he glanced across the room at Clarence's mother who nodded her head and fell asleep every time the combo stopped playing. Just wing it with the briefcases, he told himself, whenever it feels right. And hope for the best.

"Where are the newlyweds?" Charley asked Claudia after thanking her again for partaking in the near-chaotic occasion and for putting up with him. He kissed her on the cheek as he led her off the dance floor.

"Out front," she replied. "The photographer's taking more pictures of them under the willow tree."

Charley pecked a kiss on her cheek. "I'll be back for another dance," he said as he hurried off. He looked for Tony and found him drinking beer at the kitchen table with Jordan, who was eating his third piece of wedding cake.

"Did you tell each one?" Charley asked Tony.

"Yeah," Tony replied. "The deed is done. None of our gang will leave. Not even this dude." He held up his Pilsner glass and saluted Jordan.

The teenager looked up at Charley with questioning eyes. "What are you up to?" he asked in a soft whisper.

Tony smirked. "He ain't gonna tell you, Rimes. I think he wants to make the final speech of the night."

"I have something for the newlyweds, and I want our special group to be present. All eight of us. Okay? Okay?"

"Okay, man!" Tony echoed loudly.

"Why the hell am I waiting?" Charley grabbed Tony's beer and gulped down the remainder. He looked at Jordan and said, "Wipe the icing off your lip, my boy. I'm putting you to work. I'd like the two of you to do me a big favor. Move this table into the dining room. Then help me bring down a half-dozen heavy briefcases from the closet in my workroom upstairs. Do you mind?'

"Hell, no!" Tony replied.

Jordan was already on his feet and grabbing the end of the table with both hands.

Charley went looking for his wife as the two ex-patriates of the late Senator Joseph Rimespecker's household moved the table, and then ambled into the living room and waited at the foot of the stairs. He found Claudia talking about music with the Bronx Boomers' head-honcho, Hank Hannibal, during a dance break—probably the last break of the night, for only two couples had cleared the dancefloor after the last go-round.

Leading the way up the stairs, Charley directed Jordan and Tony to his workroom at the end of the hallway. The room was cluttered with books, tools, a drawing board, computer, printer, a slide projector and screen, a small TV, and a desk loaded with paperwork. "Over here," Charley said as he opened a closet door where half a dozen heavy briefcases were lined up on the floor. "If we each take two, we can do it in one trip."

And so it was that the briefcases were carried downstairs and to the far end of the dining room and lined up on the relocated kitchen table. Some of the chairs that rimmed the dancefloor were moved and semi-circled around one side of the table while Charley took a position on the other side, deciding to stand after a moment of indecision.

Tony and Jordan rounded up all the guests and participants remaining at the reception and invited them to sit facing the desk and Charley. The bride and groom were seated at center-left. They whispered to each other excitedly, their expressions revealing anxious anticipation.

"Thank you, thank you, everybody!" Charley called out as he counted a dozen people, including Clarence's frail mother, who sat in her wheelchair to the right, against the wall and somewhat away from the others. He took an official-looking envelope from the inside breast pocket of his suitcoat and waved it in the air. "Most of you—probably all of you—know the story of the Ermengarde choker, and I don't intend to repeat it. And I needn't tell you the contents of this envelope from the legal offices of Dewitt, Boyton and Dexter, except to say that it affirms what Claudia and I understood to be the results of our benefactor's death. Claudia and I have no desire for riches, and like most people who win the lottery, we want very much to share our largess with friends and needy organizations and will be doing so for some time to come. First order of sharing, however, involves an unusual and exceptional group of friends who bonded this summer during what we now refer to as the bivouac season. This group is *unique*. And I use the word *unique* correctly, meaning *the one and only of its kind*." Charley glanced among those present. "At this time I'd like to thank the bride and groom for allowing me to intrude like this during their wedding reception."

Clarence called out: "Hey, we welcome this! We thank you, Charley. After all, Terry and I are hard-core members of the bivouac corps."

"And now," Charley said, "I'd like to ask my wife to join me." He eyed her in the back row. "Please, Claudia, come on up here."

"No, Charley, I'm going to stay right where I am. But I have a few words to say, just in case you're a bit too modest." She glanced about. "I want you all to know that my husband doesn't take the easy path when giving special gifts. He puts in endless hours working, traveling, calling, negotiating, pursuing, maneuvering, writing, sketching, photographing, surveying, wrangling, outbidding ..."

"Stop it!" Charley yelled. "Stop it! Stop it! How many words do you have written on that notepad, my dear? And I suspect the last words are 'and making hell on earth for me.'"

"I was trying to be funny or outrageous or something, Charley dear, and at the same time tell our friends that you did toil as hard as any man alive putting together one wedding gift and five other gift briefcases for extraordinary soulmates. Believe me, my husband's total devotion to the task was incredible. Perhaps a wife shouldn't be so openly boastful about her husband. But I'm the only one who knows the facts and, therefore, the only one who can tell the true story. Let me illustrate his modus operandi: Little Chuck wins a dollar shooting marbles. His girlfriend could use that dollar to buy an apple. But Chuck finds handing out cash unbecoming. So, he travels the world looking for just the right apple tree, collects its seeds, and produces, through great effort, just the right apple for his girlfriend."

"I must say, Claudia, you worked mighty hard putting that together. But it's a lousy metaphor." He winked and tossed her a kiss.

"It gets the point across," Claudia said.

"If I may proceed. I'm separating one briefcase from the others." He pulled the wedding couples' gift from among the group and set it aside. "We'll open Clarence's and Terry's gift last. Okay, now, let's see. Jordan, would you come forward and be so kind as to turn each remaining briefcase over so that the flap and clasp are down and the names are hidden. Then shuffle them while I look away."

The teenager eagerly complied, making a full production of the effort. He slapped each briefcase flat on its clasping side so that its owner's name or names, so neatly engraved in gold on the deep red-brown leather, were hidden against the table top. He then swirled the five cases around and between each other and left them disbursed at odd angles.

"Thank-you, Jordan." Charley placed his right hand on a briefcase, walked his fingers slowly to the edge and grabbed the handle. He lifted the case to its upright position and read the engraved name aloud: "Dr. James T. Barnes. Oh, we got the Birdman first! Come on up here, Jimmy!"

Jimmy rose from his chair next to his wife in the second row, tapped her gently on the shoulder and uttered, "Oh, God, here goes," in his deep, resonant voice. Laura responded with a nervous giggle. Within seconds pint-sized Jimmy faced his old friend Charley across the table and seized his briefcase. "This better not be some big, fat joke! Should I open it here?"

"Nah. Take it back to your seat."

Jimmy moved fast, knowing the hour was late and five presentations followed his. Back in his seat, he whispered to Laura: "I'm not good at receiving gifts, especially opening them in front of a lot of people." The clasp went snap-pop when he pushed it. The first thing he took from the briefcase was the map of the extensive properties that Charley had purchased for him. He looked confused at first. But then his eyes lighted. "Ah, hah! I see the Atlantic coast at Tomcrest. I think that's the spot where the turtles come ashore and lay their eggs. And what's this? There are a number of parcels of land marked on this map."

"And they all belong to you," Charley called out. "Together they'll make the biggest and best bird sanctuary on the East Coast. All you have to do is sign some papers in that briefcase to transfer the land from me to you."

"My God, this includes the scrub-pine and weed belt where the song birds feast. I know this land. And here's the forested range where rich soil underlays thick beds of pine needles. Bobby, the Chesapeake Hawk, was spotted on a Shortleaf Pine near this creek over here. First time its leg was banded. You've marked the hard-woods in green. These parcels bring together every type of land and growth needed for a completely diversified bird sanctuary. Y'know why? Because the combined tract starts at the shore, but runs deep inland to very different terrain."

"Like I said, it's yours."

"I won't take it! It's too much!"

"Yes you will! Look at the rest of the stuff? Dig into the briefcase."

"Here's a deed."

"There's one for each parcel. Keep looking."

"Architect sketches? Holy hell!"

"And the builders' contracts. Lots of them. All paid for in advance. For feeding stations, bird-watch towers, ornithological laboratories, avian rest-stops for migratory birds and so much more."

"You're kidding? And what's this? A letter from a guy named Herman Simpkins?"

"He's a farmer not far from the tract who's gonna produce, in his greenhouses, thousands of milkweed plants for you and the red knots. He thinks it's kinda funny, because he's known milkweed since he was a kid playing ball in the open fields. He's already growing some in a greenhouse that gets early morning sun because of a low horizon. He wants the plants off his farm before they produce all those seeds that fly around on little, white, fuzzy parachutes. He said his grandmother used to treat and heal warts with the milky juice from the stems."

"You're having pipe dreams, pal. This can't be. I won't accept it."

"Would you rather have the money? No! I don't think you would. That's not fun! A gift has to be seen, touched, felt, maybe even walked on. Here is my entire gift to you all wrapped up in one. This is my and Claudia's gift to a very special friend. And it doesn't even have to be shared with your wife. How about that? Laura gets her own briefcase."

"Seriously, Charley, I would just feel so uncomfortable accepting so much from you, my dear friend."

"If you won the lottery, Jimmy, what would you do with the money?"

"I don't know."

"Think about it."

"I suppose I'd give a lot of it away."

"To whom?."

"Friends, first of all."

"And that's what I'm doing. But, like Claudia said, I don't want to give away that dollar bill I won playing marbles. I want to travel wherever necessary, find the right seeds and put together the best and shiniest golden apple. You have to accept my apple, Jimmy." Charley put his hand over his heart. "I'd be extremely hurt if you didn't." He stared directly into Jimmy's eyes, finally forcing his friend to look down. "Didn't your mother teach you that it's just as important to be a good receiver as it is to be a good giver?"

Jimmy handed the briefcase to Laura, sped back to the table, hurried behind it, embraced Charley, and didn't let go for an extended moment. "I don't want to face people with red eyes," he whispered. Charley at once realized that his buddy was weeping. He had never before seen the little man with the deep baritone voice shed tears. Jimmy had always seemed so stoic.

Within seconds, however, Jimmy forced himself to turn, face the audience, and say, "This is the most wonderful and beautiful gift ..." He choked up, and then started again: "Try to imagine what it's like for a retired orn ... ornithologist to be given an entire bird sanc ... sanctuary and all its parts and pieces. This is beyond belief."

Everyone felt the emotion and most of the guests were now on edge, wondering about what lay ahead, whose briefcase was next to be opened, and what impassioned feelings might pour forth.

Laura wiped away her tears and squeezed her husband's hand as he sank into the chair next to her. She kissed him on the cheek.

Charley took a moment to remind everyone that it was Jimmy, the Birdman, who had discovered the Bitterlick Creek bald eagles and introduced them and the Ermengarde choker to the world of Internet viewers. He also reminded them that it had been Jimmy who laid the groundwork for the bivouac, called to arms throngs of birdwatchers, enrolled Boy Scout Troop 24, saved young avian lives by monitoring the fledglings, came close to predicting their flights, and sent Tony up the locust tree on choker-discovery day.

Jimmy raised his hand.

"Yeah, Jimmy? What is it?"

"Is there a need to wait? Or can I get right to work on my tract of land?"

"It's yours. Go right at it."

"But Christie's hasn't auctioned off ..."

"Ah, I get it!" Charley interrupted. "Fear not. Everything's paid for. A guarantee of millions of bucks brings with it a massive flow of advances. No loan or courtesy is turned down. All you need do, Jimmy, is sign some papers. The rest is on me."

Charley then reached for another briefcase, hesitated briefly, smiled at his audience, allowed his hand to land and played spider with his fingers as he walked them to the handle. He pulled the case upright and read the engraved name: "Anthony J. Paluto." He grinned. "Yo, Tony! It's your turn. Come on up!"

Tony had never been shy. But he was somewhat apprehensive, wondering what the briefcase might reveal. Reaching the table, he grabbed his gift and showed off by lifting the heavy leather case above his shoulder with his musclebound right arm. Reaching his seat in the third row, he was still a bit playful and fiddled with the clasp for a lengthy moment, deliberately building suspense before he said, "Well, here goes!"

Charley knew that a thick folder of job opportunities in the areas of tree climbing, logging, forest management and conservation was the first item Tony would encounter and pull from the briefcase. He knew that the jobs listed ranged from entry-level tree work to advanced opportunities in training and educating. Thorough in his search, he had conducted numerous interviews with employers and reached the conclusion that Tony had the knowledge and drive for an upper-echelon position, but lacked the polish and language skills. So, he decided to take a gamble, hoping and praying that he would not hurt his friend.

Tony explained the folder's contents to the small gathering and took his time judging the job opportunities. "A lot of the good jobs are in the Northwest," he commented. "Washington, Oregon, Montana. I know that country."

The truth was: Charley wanted Tony to remain in the East and work for him and Claudia. He saw the former chauffeur as his foreman or overseer of the Claudia Greyhound Retreat. But he had pledged to himself to lay everything out equally. So, he had packed the briefcase with a wide assortment of jobs. The choice was to be Tony's and Tony's alone. And Charley knew a decision was near at hand, for Tony had let it be known that he had depleted his savings during the summer bivouac and had no stomach for sponging off his mother beyond this fall.

The next item that Tony pulled from his briefcase jolted him briefly. It was a brochure, taped to a disc of the movie *My Fair Lady*. It depicted a curvaceous woman holding a whip. A fancy-lettered italic caption atop the pamphlet read "*America's Henry Higgins*." Inside, on page 2, in Roman type, a short paragraph read: "Debby Dawn will turn an uncourtly man into a suave gentleman within six months."

Charley had experienced misgivings about tackling the question of Tony's English, and was extremely unsure of himself when he decided to include the brochure. Now, seeing Tony's stern and serious expression shook Charley to the point where he deeply regretted including it. No way did he want to hurt this man for whom he had tremendous fondness. He wondered if his attempt at cleverness had even made the situation worse. After all, Tony may never have seen *My Fair Lady*, a film produced in 1964.

"Hey, Tony, I'm sorry if I slapped you where it hurt," Charley said. "You mean the world to me, and in no way would I want to ..."

Tony interrupted boldly: "You didn't hurt me! This stuff doesn't hurt me! It would take a lot more than blasting my freaking tongue to hurt me. I know I mess up the language. Bad habits are hard to break. And believe me, I've tried again and again to fix my English. Even tried studying the dictionary. But that's a no go. Learned some big words, though."

"You see, this guy Henry Higgins," Charley attempted to explain, "took this gal from the streets of London and ..."

Again in loud cutting tones, Tony interrupted: "I know all about Henry Higgins. He took Eliza Doolittle, this Cockney flower gal off the London streets and pounded proper English into her head in an effort to make her a lady. I seen *My Fair Lady* three times on late night TV. I can even tell you something else: That there movie was adopted from a play called *Pygmalion* by George Bernard Shaw. Bet you didn't think I knew that. Right?"

"I'm sorry, Tony," Charley uttered softly.

"Don't be. You did right. Hell, if you're gonna pay the way, I'll go see this ..." Tony glanced at the brochure. "I'll go see this Debby Dawn, America's Henry Higgins. Ha! Does she just take in men? She's a good-looking broad."

"I meant well, Tony," Charley said. "You have what it takes to ..."

"Let's move on," Tony interrupted. He pulled forth a pack of drawings, blueprints, survey results, contracts, letters and written descriptions—all having to do with the creation of the Claudia Greyhound Retreat—except for two anomalies: pictures of a massive cherry picker and a stump grinder.

"Let me explain," Charley said. "My wife's briefcase contains the exact same material, except for a couple pictures of tree removal equipment. It all has to do with the establishment, right here on these grounds, of a facility for greyhounds, many of whom have been misused by the racing industry. I need a manager, an outside man, a foreman to help organize and run things."

"I want it! I'll take it!"

"Now wait! I haven't begun to explain."

"Hey, Charley! Listen closely! If you want me for that job, you got me."

"I'll pay extremely well."

"Did I ask? I want to help you and Mrs. Silvester build and run the retreat. I've heard the both of you talk about it. And I know how much y'wanna do this. And I ain't kidding! I mean I isn't ... I aren't ... I mean I am not kidding!"

"You're pulling my leg."

"Yeah." Tony laughed. "And I'll check out Debby Dawn. Gotta talk proper English with them there dogs."

"We're going to rebuild this house, enlarge it greatly and tie it to elaborate canine facilities with kennels, playrooms, outdoor runs, waiting rooms, veterinary medical labs, adoption viewing areas and everything else we and the dogs need. The grounds will be expanded greatly to the north and south. And set far back from the road near the southern boundary will be a garage for the equipment pictured in those two photographs. The cherry picker will take you high, and the stump grinder will take you low. Adding those machines to your present tools, talent and equipment will give you the nucleus for your own private tree removal company. If that's not enough, you can learn to help out at C. and C. Honey Hives, our expanded apiary three miles down the highway."

"I don't know about them there bees."

"Get t'know them and their ways, and they won't hurt you."

"I think you've spoiled your wife's briefcase presentation by packing her greyhound stuff into my case."

"Oh, she pretty much knows all about the greyhound retreat. She snoops. Hell, if I didn't do a good job with that, you think I'd be putting together these other packages? She'd be chasing me down the highway."

"Charley!" Claudia called out. "You sure know how to bend and twist stories. But I will say this to you, Tony, Charley has hoped and prayed all along that you'd join us. I'm sure he's got a big, fat contract in that briefcase for you to sign. The rest of your package was simply to balance things out. Gotta balance things out, he kept saying."

"I think it's time to stand and stretch," Charley said. "If you gotta use the john, please do so now. And Jordan and Tony, please check and see who needs a drink. It's late, so keep it non-alcoholic. Claudia, why don't you heat up the coffee pot."

Laura, being the wiggly type, suffered through each minute of suspense. She had no idea what her briefcase held, but hoped the contents had something to do with animals. By clenching her teeth, she had forced herself to stop picking on her fingernails, but began again when Claudia's name was called instead of hers.

"Do you mind if we skip you, Claud, since it's getting late and your greyhound retreat was pretty much covered during Tony's turn?" Charley asked.

"Praise the Lord!" Claudia exclaimed. "I'm delighted to escape. If there's anything I don't know about the greyhound plans, I'm sure you'll fill me in." She walked to the table and reached out for her briefcase. "But I'll take my gift now." Seizing it, she said, "It's heavy. And that's a good sign."

Laura was up next. She tripped as she hurried from her seat and caught her dress on the last chair in the row, falling forward into the arms of young Jordan, whose quickness saved her from a nasty plunge to the floor. Jordan didn't hide his pride. Anything he could do for Laura enthralled him. He was extremely fond of her, ever since she introduced him to his dog, George.

The small crowd was unsettled by Laura's near fall, and person after person consoled her with kind words.

Slightly embarrassed, Laura was quick to toss off any chagrin, right herself, grab her gift and parade happily back to her seat, swinging her briefcase freely. Seated, she opened her case and examined the first few documents quietly before she exploded.

"Oh, my God, I can't believe this!" she yelled. "Holy macaroni! The Nagelstone Center! I'm the proprietor of Nagelstone! Those horses, oh my God! All those horses. Those colts. The newborn, who needs care." She couldn't hold back tears and within seconds was crying openly. "And this sheet lists new appointments," she blubbered. "We're not only saving jobs, we're adding jobs! I can't believe it. And all these new buildings."

"And the local SPCA," Charley added.

"I see that! I see that. Do Fanny Mason, Patty Parnell and Zane Cooper know they won't lose their jobs?"

"No, not yet. We want you to tell them."

"Oh, wow! That's fantastic! And look! On this map, the SPCA gets a big addition on its east side. And look at all the land between here and Nagelstone. That's thousands of acres."

"Open land and heavily forested land," Charley added.

"How did you ever bring it all together?"

"Like they say, money talks. We even grabbed up some high-priced personnel, including a couple topnotch vets from the city. And Dr. Nancy Bullock from Greenmont University wants to be a consultant. We've lined up several affiliates."

"I've heard of Bullock. Oh, Charley, I can't believe this. It's beyond my greatest dreams." Laura pushed her briefcase aside, ran to Charley without tripping and leaped into his arms as more tears trickled down her cheeks. Jimmy approached her, and as she broke from Charley, her husband wrapped his arms around her, whispered into her ear, and kissed her.

Several people clapped and chit-chat spread around the gathering as Jimmy led his wife back to her seat. Within seconds she was flipping through more documents.

"And what's this yellow square on the blown-up, sectional map?"

"We need more advice on that. Tentatively, that's a wild-animal clinic bordering on the wooded reserve. Nagelstone doesn't take foxes or bobcats does it? Maybe deer? I talked to Dr. Peter Levinsky at the Cloverton City Zoo, and he said he'd split his time if we had the need and the facilities. What about the need?"

"That's a lot of wooded territory. I think it would be great to have a separate wild-animal clinic. Not only for big animals, but for the raccoons, opossums, skunks and all the little critters." Laura shuffled more papers. "And what's this? A contract with Tony Paluto?"

"He doesn't know about that yet," Charley explained as Tony's head popped up. "You've got a lot of land to manage and he's gonna have a start-up company in tree management. I figure members of the bivouac team should work together. Why not? I'm gonna suggest it to Jimmy, too. His birds need a healthy arboriculture."

Laura's emotions had stirred fervor in the dining room, generating a social buzz as Tony served coffee to the takers. Charley took time out, chewed on a doughnut with his coffee, and asked Jordan to fetch a slide projector from his workroom. "It's right under the window sill. You can't miss it."

"Okay, chief!" Jordan saluted in a comical way.

About 15 minutes later, Charley and Jordan had set up the projector in the living room. The chairs were reassembled and a large oil painting of Bingo the greyhound was removed from the wall—an off-white wall easily substituted for a motion-picture or slide screen.

Charley took Jordan aside and asked if he would mind if they combined discussion of the teenager's briefcase with that of the newlyweds. "After all, you live together. You're one family."

"Whatever you say, chief! But don't forget George. We're a family of four."

Charley's introduction was brief, but clearly explained that the slide he was about to show supplemented material in the newlywed's briefcase and depicted their not-yet fully completed honeymoon house. "Maybe they can take a second trip and get back late," he joked. "That is, if they want this wedding gift. They don't have to take it. They can stay in their city brownstones."

No one knew whether Charley was being sarcastic, or trying to be funny. He knew he was dead serious, for he was well aware that he'd rather waste millions than give the wrong gift.

After the audience was fully settled, the lights were turned off and a brilliant architect's drawing of a field-stone and clapboard house was projected on the wall. The handsome house was surrounded by exquisite landscaping and attractive outdoor additions for human and canine tastes. From swimming pool to doghouse, details were portrayed much more sharply than on an average architect's sketch. Lines were sharp and colors vivid. Directed by Charley in an effort to charm Terry, the architect had depicted flowers on all sides of the house and beyond. Pink, yellow and white hollyhocks reached up the walls on the east side while deep blue, purple and baby-blue delphinium stood erect against the west wall. Such tall plants were fronted by yellow calendulas, marigolds and white petunias. Clusters of impatiens lined the walkways and trellises on the north and south were entwined with morning glories, trumpet vines, clematis and wisteria.

"It looks like I'm hitting you with a lot of gardening, Terry. But you'll be getting the best advice from the topnotch nurserymen in the region. When you're tired of feeling the rich earth and humus in your hands, all you'll need to do is point and say to a gardener, 'Plant it here.' I told the architect to be sure to show, on this portrayal, what flowers will do to your honeymoon house come summertime."

"My juices are flowing," Terry said. "I can't wait until spring."

"It's too much," Clarence said.

A broken voice from the sidelines cut the air: "Take it," Clarence's feeble mother called out. "You hear me, son! Accept it, and be gracious about it."

"Oh, my God," Clarence muttered. "It's overwhelming."

"Now, don't you start, Clarence," Charley said. "Listen to your mother. Keep telling yourself that Claudia's money—and it is hers, remember—is bivouac money for all. She wants you to have it as much as I do. Maybe even more, because it frightens her."

Claudia stood and raised her hand. "Please listen. Let me remind you that there's something else to recall—something that might sober you a little. There are ghosts hovering over us—ghosts that should pick and peck at our brains now and then. If Senator Joseph Rimespecker had not brought the Ermengarde Choker to the United States, and if he hadn't given it to his wife, Lillian, and if she hadn't passed it on to my Cousin Ruth, and if my cousin hadn't signed a document bequeathing it to me ..." Claudia took a moment to catch her breath. "... there would be no millions; there would be no briefcases, and there would be no bird sanctuary, animal clinics, greyhound retreat, tree service, honeymoon house or college resources born of those briefcases."

"And if not for your husband we would not be here relishing in our windfall," Jimmy called out.

"You're all getting too serious," Charley said. "And, for God's sake, this is not a night to talk about the dead."

"Lillian Rimespecker is not dead," Claudia said. "She's out there somewhere, perhaps floating from place to place around the earth."

"Enough, Claudia!" Charley rebuked. "This is a night for celebration. Please let me continue with my slide presentation. That attractive fenced-in area on the right contains Clarence's vegetable garden," Charley explained. "And that enclosed southwest section is devoted to doggie runs, play areas, toy bins, housing and other facilities for George the labradoodle."

Next, Charley focused on the side additions—the one for Clarence's mother and the other for Jordan and George—each with separate entrances as well as interconnections with the central living space.

"When you open your briefcases, you'll find lists, pictures and drawings of the therapeutic equipment and restorative devices built into the elder Mrs. Exton's complex. Everything a teenager desires is being installed in young Jordan quarters. And you'll see that George isn't left out."

"Your separate briefcase, Jordan, contains a far different mix of things," Charley explained. "Go ahead. Open it."

Jordan complied. "Oh, wow! Look at all this stuff!" The first thing he pulled out was an old pledge manual from Sigma Pi Fraternity."

"I put that in there for fun," Charley explained. "I'm not asking you to pledge my fraternity." He forced a laugh. "Dig in there, Jordan, and you'll find everything you need for college no matter where you go. A document signed by me will give you tuition remission. Scholarship possibilities are included in a loose-leaf notebook. Room-and-board, activity fees, book charges and a host of other financial considerations are clearly indicated on cashiers' checks. A leather backpack is flattened and squeezed among various types of notebooks. Electronic equipment, a calculator, recording devices, pens, pencils and other small items are boxed in one corner along with gift certificates at men-and-boy's clothing stores."

"This is much too much!" Jordan exclaimed, believing he should show some reluctance to accept as others did. He laughed as he pulled out a pair of green and white basketball shorts. "Cool, man! But these might not be the school colors."

Throughout Charley's presentation, the newlyweds whispered to each other, but never spoke aloud. Excitement would show again and again on their faces, but was always quickly concealed. When the slideshow was over and Charley turned on the lights, Terry and Clarence burst out with hysterical elation, laughter, giggles and joyful yelps. Giddy to the nth degree, they spoke so fast they were barely understood, the loud chatter of one crowding out the ecstatic cries of the other. They constantly interrupted each other and were unable to get a clear point across amid their plentiful thank-yous. It was Jordan who finally yelled "Shut up! Both of you! Shut up!"

Clarence seemed to awake from an ecstatic nightmare and was suddenly embarrassed. Glancing about, he put his hand over his mouth and briefly closed his eyes. He had generally been a man of full control for most of his life. Now, he seemed in anguish as he tried to gain command of himself, catch his breath and temper his words and actions. Terry found herself red-faced, shaking and shedding hysterical tears.

"The newlyweds have been drinking too much of that so-called pink punch," Laura said with a twinkle in her eyes.

"I'm so sorry," Clarence said. "I don't know what happened to me." He looked at Terry. "You okay?"

Terry shook her head and wiped her eyes.

"We're so grateful for everything," Clarence said. "It's like a dream that got out of hand and went berserk. It's too much to handle. Please forgive our bizarre reactions. Terry and I are so thankful for such a magnificent house in such a beautiful setting that we're handicapped and crippled by the lack of words to fit the deed. We will recover, and we will try to express our feelings when we can find the language that fits. The fact that you've surrounded our house in flowers is like wrapping my bride in a beautiful bouquet or floral tribute. It fits her, and the morning glory and evening primrose that she has become to me. Oh, Charley and Claudia, how can we ever express our feelings fully?"

Laura shook her finger at the teenage best man. "You can stop building your third-floor, brownstone apartment, Jordon."

"I've enjoyed that," Jordan responded. "But I'll be glad to put down the hammer." He barked, snarled and panted. "That doesn't exactly sound like George, but I'm saying thanks for him. He's gonna be pleased to have some of the same advantages as Queen Elizabeth's Corgis. I can picture him playing roughhouse with me in his special play-yard. He'll be living high on the hog, as they say. And that makes me happy." Jordan glanced at Laura and mouthed the words, "I love George. Thanks so much."

Laura tossed a kiss to Jordan.

"Tell y'what, let's huddle," Jordan said, a smile playing around his lips. "Like they do on the football field. Just the eight of us—the bivouac eight."

"Why?" Jimmy asked.

"Comradeship." Jordan answered. "A great way to end an unbelievable day."

"The kid knows what he's talking about," Laura said. "I'm all for it!" She high-stepped and skipped onto open floor-space and spun around twice. "Come on! Put your arms around your sidekicks' shoulders and form a tight circle."

Charley and Claudia chuckled and quickly joined Laura and Jordan. Tony glanced about, watched what the others were doing, shrugged his shoulders and pursued the bride and groom onto the open floor. Jimmy shook his head and followed. They formed a huddle of eight, arms wrapped around each other, shoulders and heads bowed toward the center of the tight circle.

The huddle turned and swayed to the right, then the left, and Jordan was the first to speak: "The Three Musketeers have a battle cry. They proclaim 'One for all, and all for one.' Let's adapt it to 'One for eight, and eight for one.' Come on, let's shout it out! And then raise our hands toward the sky."

They mumbled and stumbled at first.

Then Clarence yelled, "We can do better, damn it!"

Jordan counted: "One, two, three, go!"

The huddle burst into a roar as they proclaimed:

"One for eight, and eight for one!"

Epilogue
Three Years Later

Jimmy Barnes—His bird sanctuary had grown to one of the finest establishments of its kind on the East Coast. Birdwatchers flocked to the retreat, particularly during the migrating seasons of spring and fall. Barnes' staff established a reporting system that now lists hundreds of bird species seeking shelter and migrating, not to mention scores of species in permanent residence.

Since the construction of conference and dining halls, lookout towers, nature trails and picnic pavilions, the State Ornithological Society has met at the Barnes Bird Sanctuary every spring and fall to enjoy birding and fellowship. Last season, Jimmy's research team won the coveted Coastal Habitat Award for balancing hatching and bird-eating of turtle eggs. A milkweed field has already shown an influx of red knots. And Jimmy shares all tales with Laura—from the struggles of a gull with a broken-wing to the baby Baltimore orioles' survival when their nest fell during a storm.

Laura Barnes—Sections of her animal refuge complex have progressed at different rates. It became apparent to Laura and her newly established Board of Directors that, regardless of its financial assets, the Nagelstone Center for Large Animals needed to affiliate with a university veterinarian hospital if it were to gain prestige and compete with entrenched institutions in the field. Laura and her board had approached Bridgeberry University's Board of Trustees during the first year, and after considerable anguish and debate finally received an affirmative vote before the end of the second year.

Laura was hailed by *Peterson's Large Animal Magazine* as the "little kitten turned big cat" in an editorial of praise. She was also honored by the U.S. Animal Protection Society, receiving its Healing Horseshoe Award.

Laura breathed more easily during the third year and was able to turn her attention to mortar and brick. Additions to the SPCA and near completion of the new wild-animal clinic lifted her bubbling nature above her usual electric spirit.

Claudia Silvester—Though it got off to a slow start, Claudia's Greyhound Sanctuary grew into a spacious and comfortable accommodation for 18 dogs by the middle of the second year. The goal was to accommodate at least 25. While the bulk of the dogs arrived from race-track trainers, others came from the police, private owners, the SPCA and welfare groups. Cruelty cases have included dogs with emotional and physical impairments, starvation and neglect being all too common.

A tender-hearted woman, Claudia has reached out in an effort to treat all the dogs as pet-like as possible. Each one has its own warm kennel and run. Two huge exercise paddocks were recently carved out of land purchased as part of Charley's expansion plan. And the final touches on the Silvesters' new house, which adjoins the sanctuary, were underway—a house to become home to selected pups.

Claudia has been persistent in her guidance of Tony Paluto, general manager of the enterprise, who supervises two kennel assistants, Stanley Graham and Debby Paul.

A woman of deep feelings, Claudia has found her very nature as a human being molded by her relationship with the greyhounds. The dogs' growing love for her, and her responding affection for them, has had a profound effect on the animals and her. Warmth, joy and compassion have abounded.

Tony Paluto—His job as general manager of Claudia's Greyhound Sanctuary had grown considerably as the retreat expanded. To better his management skills, the Silvesters arranged for him to spend three months of study, observation and work at the National Greyhound Adoption Program in Philadelphia, where he concentrated on the three major goals of rescue, rehabilitation and re-homing of abused and abandoned dogs. His biggest surprise was the gentle nature of the breed.

As the staff of Claudia's sanctuary grew, Tony began to split his Greyhound time with his expanding tree-management business, headquartered next-door to the canine retreat. By the start of the third year, he had opened satellite offices for forest management in the deep woods of the Barnes Bird Sanctuary and the dense woodlands of Laura's animal rescue complex.

Tony still found time to visit Debby Dawn, "America's Henry Higgins," three nights a week for six months. A year later, he and Debby were married by a justice of the peace in East Bitterlick Township's municipal building. Clarence Exton sold Tony and Debby his and his mother's three-story brownstone for one dollar at the urging of Charley Silvester, a strong believer in "paying it forward." The newlyweds moved into the Cloverton City brownstone shortly after their honeymoon in Atlantic City. After carrying Debby across the threshold, Tony recited, in perfect English, words of Madam de Girardin, 19th Century French author: "To love one who loves you, to admire one who admires you, in a word, to be the idol of one's idol, is exceeding the limit of human joy; it is stealing fire from heaven."

Jordan Rimespecker—His dormitory room was on the 24th floor of 27-story Morgan Hall at Temple University, Philadelphia. He could look out his window on the whole of Center City, at night seeing the metro lights, at daytime seeing the sun send its rays between and among the skyscrapers. Now a sophomore, he had chosen Temple partly because he wanted a city environment rather than college in the boondocks. Tentatively, he selected journalism as his major, with a concentration or minor in sociology. His academic adviser had made it clear that he could switch majors easily during his first two years.

Charley's gift briefcase had paid off well, because Jordan's trust fund and other Rimespecker legacies were tied up in court, partly because of his missing mother.

He played the part of Joe College well, wearing cherry-and-white T.U. jackets and sweaters and attending football and basketball games. He even tried out for the varsity fencing team.

Since late in his freshmen year, he has been dating Sally Buttons, a cute, playfully impish brunette he met in Sociology 101. Sally earned spending money working for the Admissions Office as a university tour guide, and Jordan often trailed her as she led prospective students and their parents around the campus. He would edge close to her as she pointed to the Performing Arts Center and explained that it was once a church called the Baptist Temple, from which the University got its name. He would even help her step down into the Founder's Garden where the "great teachers" names were chiseled into the walls, and he'd sit directly behind her on the base of the Bell Tower where she would speak her final words of Temple pride.

Jordan often traveled home on weekends where his adoptive parents, Uncle Clarry and Aunt Terry, maintained their resplendent honeymoon house. It was George who tempted Jordan most strongly to make the visits. The sophomore knew that his dog always waited by the door for him on Friday nights during the school semesters. Summers were free times for Jordan to romp, play ball, swim and take long walks through the countryside with George. They were also times when Jordan helped Terry weed, water and generally maintain her abundant flower gardens. Clarence's vegetable garden was not overlooked, either, by the grateful student, who worshipped the time he spent with Uncle Clarry cultivating and harvesting the crops.

The major negatives in Jordan's life were the flashbacks, dreams and even nightmares that harshly reflected on times past at Rimespecker House. They weakened as the years passed, and the young man's counselor assured him that they would soften even more in time and perhaps, one day, melt away entirely.

Clarence and Terry Exton—Shortly after his marriage to Terry, Clarence knew it was time to play husband and seek employment. Although a man of many talents, he soon learned that his resume restricted him, because most of his working days had been spent as Senator Rimespecker's personal secretary. He interviewed well, however, because he was composed and likeable. In little time, he secured the position of manager of the country estate of Henry Deven Cadwallader III, Wall Street financier and West Bitterlick Township politician.

Clarence's mother died of pneumococcal pneumonia two months into the second year of her stay in her private quarters of the new house—a stay she called joyful. She was eulogized by her son during funeral services at Trinity Episcopal Church in downtown Cloverton City and interred in that church's cemetery. The bivouac eight were among those attending the services.

Three years after her wedding, Terry still found her belated honeymoon house an enchanted, fanciful, enigmatic, fairy-tale-like place to live. She worked hard to keep it well polished and cared for, fearing it might rebel otherwise. As for outside work, springtime gardening started earlier than ever for Terry, who felt obligated to meet the standards so colorfully drawn by the architect and displayed at the wedding reception. This year, as in the last two, new perennials were in the ground before Jordan arrived home from school in mid-May, just in time to help plant the annuals. And he dug right in, knowing full well that toiling with Terry served more than one purpose.

Spring was also a time when Jordan could start to relax and build his long-standing relationship with Uncle Clarry, turn up his rollicking lovefest with George, and find more ways than gardening to edge his way into Terry's heart. A family had formed, but was still growing as it worked to tie knot after knot.

Clarence also kept close ties with his bivouac buddies, sometimes chatting on the phone and sending text messages to them late into the night. After harvests in his garden, he would often dispatch Jordan to their homes with baskets of vegetables.

Charley Silvester—A year ago, when he pulled Claudia out through the backdoor and into the belly of the greyhound retreat, he was aware of a slight untruth when he declared the sanctuary finished. He knew it would be adjusted and tuned-up until it was no longer needed. And he knew he would toil there with Claudia and Tony as long as necessary, or as long as he desired. But the briefcases had pushed him deeply into the lives of all bivouac buddies and he couldn't pull away. He continued to spread himself around, helping here and there, suggesting this and that, and injecting Claudia's money into his friends' establishments.

His was a busy life, and he liked it that way. But the only enterprise that appeared solely his was the greatly expanded apiary and honey production endeavor, now situated three miles away on land Charley purchased from the Galvaneer Oil and Pipeline Company, Inc. Good weather, mild winters and abundant nectar and pollen in the wild-flower fields in recent years had brought about prolific growth in the hives. Charley's tedious efforts at bottling honey were, perhaps, about to end, for he had just contracted with a firm that touted its ability to mechanize part of the operation.

Although adding anything else to his docket seemed impossible, Charley found time to make adjustments to his and Claudia new house—a large ranch-style dwelling that incorporated elements not seen in other homes. Number one among those elements were automatic canine doors that opened and closed allowing three well-trained greyhounds—the household pets—to enter and exit the spacious house.

Although he seldom talked about it, Charley was well aware of his and Claudia's finances—money-matters that he had turned over to a first-rate financial adviser. He knew their fortune still provided them with abundant riches to give away. Christie's auction had produced a high bid of $110 million for the Ermengarde Choker from Mohammed Ammar Bashshar of Saudi Arabia. The choker was now in the Middle East.

Lillian Rimespecker—The late senator's wife had sailed for Belize shortly after the suicide of Ruth Nettlebaum, according to U.S. authorities, and was believed to reside there now among the Mayan population of the far south.